Betsey

MARCIA CLAYTON

ISBN-13:978-1-8383259-6-1

Published by Sunhillow Publishing

In memory of my parents, Arthur William and Josephine Jane Squire and, of course, my dear son, Paul.

Also by Marcia Clayton

Acknowledgement

Thank you to my husband, Bryan, for his patience and encouragement, and also to my sons Stuart and David for their help along the way.

To Bryan, my sister, Gill, my niece, Sharon, and my good friend, Sylvia, for being the first people to read my book and provide constructive criticism and support.

Special thanks to my talented daughter-in-law, Laura, for producing a fantastic cover for the book.

I would also like to thank the many other authors who have befriended me on social media, providing help, advice, and much-needed moral support.

Last, but not least, the biggest thank you goes to my readers. I have received some wonderful feedback from readers who have told me how much they have enjoyed my books. Their reviews and messages encourage me to continue writing. A simple message, particularly from a stranger, saying they loved my story helps to dispel my doubts over my ability as an author. I can't tell you how much those lovely messages mean to me. Thank you.

CHAPTER 1

It was warm in the kitchen and perspiration glistened on Ellen's brow, as she wrung the water from the clothes she had just washed. She smiled at the small child beside her. "There, Betsey, that's the last sheet, thank goodness. Now, we can hang it all out to dry."

"Mum, can I go out to play when we've finished?"

"Yes, you can later. Just help me to put the washing out, and then we'll have a bit of dinner. It won't be much but we need something; we've had a busy morning."

Ellen hoisted the heavy wicker basket of wet washing onto her hip, leaving her six-year-old daughter to bring the smaller one and the clothes pegs. She set the basket down on the long garden path and lowered the clothes prop to bring the line within reach.

"Right, now you go that end, Betsey, and peg out the smaller stuff, and I'll get these sheets sorted. It's a warm day so they should dry in no time and be ready for Kezia tomorrow. "How are you boys getting on?"

Farther down the garden, two boys were working hard clearing weeds from the vegetable patch. Norman, aged three, came running towards his mother, glad of the interruption.

"Mum, I'm hungry. When will it be dinner time?"

"Not long now, Norman. Just help Barney to pull a few more weeds and when I've put this washing out, I'll find us something to eat."

"Aw, do I have to, Mum? I'm tired, and my hands are sore, look." The little boy held out his hands to show the start of some painful blisters.

"Oh dear, those poor little hands haven't known much hard work yet, have they? I'll tell you what then, you hand me the pegs for the washing; that will help and it will save me bending so much."

Ellen stood upright, placed her hands on the small of her back, and stretched. "Oh dear, my back does ache. Thank goodness the washing's finished, and I can have a sit down after dinner."

Ellen was seven months pregnant with her tenth child, and not in the best of health. She fervently hoped this child would be born alive and thrive, for over the years she had lost no less than six children. Two had been stillborn, and the others had not survived infancy. She still remembered and mourned each tiny child, and was overprotective of the three that had so far survived. When the washing was blowing gently on the line, she wandered down the garden to see how her eldest son was getting on.

"My goodness, Barney, you're doing a fine job; that looks so much better."

"Thanks, Mum. I've weeded all the parsnips and turnips now, and I'm about halfway through the swedes. I like gardening, and at least we'll have something to eat through the winter."

"Yes, and I'm sure we'll be glad of it. Could you dig a couple of potato plants before you come in, please? I'm hoping your dad will bring some meat home from the butcher's when he leaves work; I can make a stew for tea, then. Right, come on, let's go inside and have some dinner."

As they trooped back up the long garden path, a woman called to them over the fence.

"Hello, Ellen, how are you, today?"

"Not too bad thanks, Kezzie. My back aches, but I've finished all the washing, and it will dry nicely today. I should be able to let you have yours back tomorrow."

"Well, that would be helpful, thanks, Ellen. We're busy at the inn at the moment, and I'm struggling to cope with it all. I'm pleased with the extra business now we're taking in travellers on their way to Exeter and London, but it's a lot to see to. I'd never have time to do the washing as well, so I'm grateful for your help."

"Well, it works both ways, Kezzie. I could never feed us on what little Adam lets me have, so the money you pay me makes such a difference. If I could just keep him out of The Red Lion, and sober, our lives would be so much better."

"I know, Ellen, and I feel guilty about it because he's one of our best customers. I told him off last night because he spent a lot of money over the counter. Of course, we're glad of the business, but I hate to see him drink all his wages away when you and the children are struggling to find something to eat. Malachi was angry with me for saying anything. He says it's not my place to lecture Adam on his ways, because if we won't serve him, he'll just drink at The Three Pigeons instead."

"That's true, Kezzie, and I don't blame you. You have a living to make, but I wish he'd stop drinking so much. He was late to work this morning because he had such a dreadful hangover, and Mrs Chown's already warned him he'll lose his job if he lets her down again. He's always worked as a butcher, so I don't know what we'll do if she carries out her threat, and gets rid of him. Apart from his wages, we'd miss the bones and scraps of meat he brings home; they flavour a stew and give it a bit of taste. Anyway, I need to feed these hungry children, so I'll see you later."

Once inside the house, Ellen insisted the children scrub their hands.

"But Mum, mine aren't even dirty," exclaimed Betsey. "They've been in the water for most of the morning; look they even have nigglies."

Ellen laughed as Betsey displayed her fingers, which were wrinkled from being in the water for some time. "I don't know where you got the name nigglies from Betsey. Surely they're wrinkles?"

"No, I think they're called nigglies."

"Well, all right, if you say so. Give your hands a quick wash, anyway, and then sit up at the table."

As the children obediently climbed onto the ancient settle which ran alongside the wall, Ellen cut thick slices of bread from a loaf and spread them with dripping. She passed each child a plate and they sprinkled their meal with salt. It took no time for the food to disappear.

"Mum, is there anything else to eat? I'm still hungry."

"Well, there are a few apples left from the ones Kezzie gave us the other day, so you can have one of those each if you like. Now, I'm going to sit down for a little while, so you can go out to play, but one of you must take Norman with you.

"Oh, not me, Mum."

Ellen gazed fondly at her eldest son. Barney was ten years old, with dark hair and brown eyes, and fortunately, they seemed to be the only traits he had inherited from his father.

"Why not you then, Barney? What have you got lined up to do this afternoon?"

"I said I'd call for Ned and we're going fishing in Shebworthy Pond. I don't mind taking Norman, but he makes too much noise and scares the fish. We didn't catch anything last time I took him, and I'm always afraid he'll fall in. Betsey, can you look after Norman this afternoon? With a bit of luck, I'll catch some fish for us all to eat then."

"Oh, I want to come fishing, Barney. I promise I'll be quiet."

"Yeah, well you said that last time, but you weren't."

"Betsey what are you doing this afternoon? Can you take Norman with you?"

The little girl nodded. "Yes, I don't mind. Come with me, Norman, and we'll have a paddle in the stream; it's so hot today. I want to go and see Gypsy Freda because last time she promised I could watch her make some medicine. She's ever so clever, Mum. She collects herbs and roots and berries and mashes them all up together in a little bowl, and then she makes medicines for fevers and all sorts of aches and pains. I'd love to be able to do that."

"She must like you, Betsey because normally the gypsies won't share their cures with anyone. I know most people don't have a kind word to say about the gypsies, but I've known Freda all my life and she's a good sort. She even delivered you, when you came unexpectedly early, in fact, if it wasn't for her, I don't think you'd be here at all. Perhaps that's why she likes you."

"Shall I ask her for some more heartburn medicine for you, Mum?"

"No, don't ask, because I've no money. I'm all right."

"I'm sure she wouldn't mind, but perhaps she'll show me how to make it. Do you want to come with me to see the gypsies, Norman? Mum can put her feet up and have a little nap then."

Ellen smiled at her daughter, thinking how wise she was for her tender years.

"Yes, I'd like to paddle in the stream, and Barney will never let me go in Shebworthy Pond."

"Well, no, of course, I won't. It's deep, and you can't swim."

"Barney's right, Norman, you must never go into Shebworthy Pond, it's dangerous. The water is always cold even on a hot day, and it's so deep we might never see you again. Anyway, it sounds as if you'll have a pleasant afternoon, and if you could catch some fish, Barney, we could have them for our tea, and save the stew for tomorrow. Betsey, perhaps you and Norman could pick some blackberries? I could put them with some of these apples and make a crumble."

CHAPTER 2

Glad to have been relieved of the responsibility of looking after his little brother, Barney went through a gap in the fence that separated the cottage garden from that of the inn next door. The path was well trodden, for Barney and Ned had been friends all their lives, and spent a lot of time together. Their mothers too were regular visitors to each other's houses.

Barney knocked on the kitchen door of the inn and Ned opened it.

"Hello, Barney, I'm glad to see you haven't got Norman with you; we might catch some fish, today."

"Yes, I know. I persuaded Betsey to take him to the stream for a paddle. I think she's keen for me to catch some fish for tea, so she could see the sense of what I said."

Barney's eyes drifted to the large wooden kitchen table which was laden with food. Kezia had been busy all morning, baking food to be sold at the inn. There were six fresh loaves of bread, a couple of dozen large pasties, and a whole ham from which the steam was still rising.

"My goodness, those pasties smell nice."

"Are you hungry?"

"I'm always hungry, aren't you?"

"No, not usually, and I've just had my dinner."

"Well, so have I, but it was only a slice of bread and dripping and an apple. I could probably have eaten about four slices after all the gardening I've done this morning. What did you have?"

"I had a big bowl of stew and a couple of thick slices of bread and butter. Shall I ask Mum if we can take a couple of pasties with us?"

"Ooh yes, please, I'd love that."

Kezia knew the children from next door seldom had enough to eat, so she readily wrapped the pasties in a piece of cloth and handed them to the two boys. "Now, make sure you bring that cloth back and be careful at Shebworthy Pond. Don't go in the water; I mean it, mind. If I find out you've been in, I'll see to it that you both get a good hiding; it's too dangerous."

"We know, Mum. You tell us every single time we go." Behind his mother's back, Ned rolled his eyes at his friend, then quickly changed his expression, as his mother turned to face him.

"Well, I can't say it often enough. Anyway, I hope you catch lots of fish. You can put them in this basket, look."

The two boys went around the side path of the inn to the front lane where Betsey and Norman were just setting off to the stream.

"I'd like to come fishing with you and Barney, Ned, but Barney says I can't."

"Well, you know you get bored after sitting there a while, don't you? You'll have much more fun with Betsey, paddling in the stream, and I've heard Gypsy Freda's dog had puppies a few weeks ago, so I expect you'll be able to play with them."

"Oh, that's good, I knew her dog was having puppies, but I didn't know they'd been born. Come on, Norman, we need to go this way through the woods. See you later, boys."

Barney and Ned strolled along the track that led to Shebworthy Pond. It had once been a quarry, which had unexpectedly flooded overnight, making further excavation impossible. That had all happened many years before, but a few of the elderly folk in the village still remembered it with sadness, for four ponies had died, tethered in the stable before anyone knew what was happening. It was thought that blasting from the previous day had released an underground stream with catastrophic results.

There were a few other folk fishing at the pond, and the two boys strolled on until they found a quiet spot which suited them. Their rods were simply hazel sticks with a hook at the end of a piece of string. However, the pond was teeming with fish, and their equipment, though modest, usually brought results. They made themselves comfortable in the long grass that surrounded the pond, and Barney reached into his pocket and withdrew a piece of damp sacking. He unfolded it, revealing several squirming worms that he had collected earlier from the garden. The two boys carefully slipped their hooks through the fat bodies of the worms and tossed them into the water. They settled back to enjoy their pasties and await their first bite, and chatted in whispers so as not to scare the fish.

On the way to the stream, Betsey and Norman gathered some of the juicy blackberries which were abundant on the bramble bushes.

"Ow, these are so prickly. And why do all the best ones grow just where I can't reach them?" grumbled Norman.

"I think people have already picked the ones lower down, but there are lots, so it doesn't matter."

"Have we picked enough now; do you think?"

"Let's get a few more, then I can give some to Gypsy Freda for a present; I think she'd like that."

After another half an hour or so of busy picking, Betsey and Norman arrived at the stream. It was a pleasant spot, favoured by the village children, and several were already paddling. There had been a lot of rain over the last couple of weeks and so the stream was quite deep, though sometimes in a dry spell there would be barely a trickle of water flowing. Norman was pleased to see that Silas Carter, Ned's younger brother was there, and also Ben Rudd, whose parents owned the local smithy. They were a bit older than Norman but made the little boy welcome.

Seeing Norman playing happily with the two lads, Betsey joined her friends, Gertie and Maud Hammett. Gertie, aged six, and Maud, aged five, both went to school with Betsey, and the three girls sat on the bank and dangled their legs in the cool water.

"We wondered if you would come today, Betsey. What have you been doing this morning?"

"I've been helping Mum to do the washing. I have to because she gets tired now she's having another baby. It took ages too because she does all the washing for Aunty Kezzie at The Red Lion; I thought we'd never finish. How about you two; what did you do this morning?"

"Nothing much. Oh, we went to the Manor House to see the horses, because Isaac said we could see the new foal. He's so cute; he's only a few days old."

"Oh, you are lucky to have a brother working there; do you think I could see the foal?"

"I don't know; we could ask him. We were only allowed to go today because the farm manager had travelled into Barnstaple. Isaac has to be careful not to get into trouble."

"Oi, stop all that splashing, Tommy Billery. Just because your father's the teacher, it doesn't mean you can do what you like." Betsey glared crossly at the eleven-year-old boy in front of her, but he just laughed.

"An' what you goin' to do about it then, Betsey Lovering? You're only half my size. Anyway, aren't you hot? The water's warm; come in for a paddle." With a wicked grin on his face, the boy skimmed his hand across the surface of the water, splashing it over the three girls.

Within seconds, the three girls had joined the others in the stream, and it wasn't long before they were all screaming with laughter, as they splashed each other and were soon wet through.

"Come on, Norman, we'd better go now and give ourselves time to dry out before we go home, or Mum will be cross. See you at school on Monday, Gertie, and you, Maud."

Picking up their basket of blackberries, Betsey led Norman away from the stream. She purposely hadn't mentioned the fact they were going to the gypsy camp, because she didn't want any of her friends tagging along. The gypsies didn't welcome strangers, but Gypsy Freda had taken to Betsey and encouraged her to visit. Betsey just hoped the old lady wouldn't mind that she had Norman with her today.

The two children retraced their steps for a quarter of a mile and then turned down an even narrower track through the woods. After half a mile or so, they arrived at a clearing, where a dozen or more gypsy wagons were arranged in a circle. The wagons were brightly painted, some in better repair than others. A few of the gypsies glanced up from what they were doing when they heard someone approaching but seeing it was only Betsey, they largely ignored the little girl and her brother, as they made their way to the largest wagon, which was painted bright yellow with red flowers.

Outside the wagon, a young teenage girl with long, curly, auburn hair and walnut-brown eyes was cooking something over a campfire. Norman decided that whatever was in the pot, smelt delicious and made his mouth water. Scampering around the girl's feet were five puppies; their mother relaxing in the shade.

"Hello, Betsey; we haven't seen you for a few weeks. Granny will be pleased; she likes you. And who is this young man you've brought with you?"

"Hello, Jane, this is my little brother, Norman. I hope it's all right, but I had to bring him with me today because my mum needed to rest."

"Well, we don't encourage visitors as you know, but I'm sure we're glad to see you and Norman. Do you want to go in and see Granny?"

"Yes, please, if that's all right? I've brought her some blackberries."

"She'll like that. Now, Norman, I can see you're eyeing up my stew; would you like some?"

"It smells so good, yes, I'd love some, please."

"Hmm, you have some manners too; that's nice to hear, Norman. You sit down there then, and see if you can eat all that up," the girl handed him a bowl and a crust of bread, "how about you, Betsey, would you like some?"

"Oh, yes please, Jane; you are kind."

"Go on then, you go in and see Granny, and I'll bring some in for you. Norman can stay here with me and play with the puppies when he's finished eating."

Seeing that Norman was content with his new friend, Betsey climbed the three wooden steps that led into the wagon. It was dark inside, and it took a moment or two for her eyes to adjust to the dim light. The old woman was sitting in a rocking chair, her old face deeply lined with wrinkles, and her long grey hair tied neatly into two plaits. She rocked the chair slowly back and forth and removed a clay pipe from her mouth to smile widely at her visitor, revealing numerous gaps in her teeth. Every inch of space in the tiny wagon was utilised. Along one side were two foldaway beds for Freda and Jane, used as seats during the day. Along the other side were small, roughly-made cupboards, and a row of hooks from which all sorts of implements were hanging. At the far end, near the back of the wagon, and in the warmest spot, was Freda's rocking chair.

"Hello, Betsey; what a pleasant surprise. I'm so pleased to see you, my dear. What do you have in your basket?"

"Some blackberries. I picked some for Mum, and I thought you might like a few as well."

"That's so kind of you, my dear. Did I hear someone with you, today?"

"Yes, it's my little brother, Norman. I had to bring him because Mum needed to rest this afternoon. He's only three, and I have to look after him. Sometimes, my brother, Barney, takes him out with him, but he's gone fishing today, and Norman makes too much noise and scares the fish, and Barney needs to catch some for our tea."

"Oh, that's all right, Betsey. How is your mum? I think you said she was having another baby?"

"Yes, she is, and she gets tired because she has to take in lots of washing to earn some money. I've been helping her this morning. She's got awful heartburn, and she needs some more of your medicine, but she didn't have any money so she said not to tell you." The little girl looked at the old woman shyly. "I wondered if the blackberries might do instead?"

"Well, you're not backward in coming forward are you, young lady? Seeing as it's you who's asking though, I think I might be able to find some."

Just then, Jane appeared at the door holding a bowl of rabbit stew and some bread.

"Here you are, Betsey. I expect you can do with this, and we have plenty at the moment. There are more rabbits than we can catch. The snares are full of them."

"Ooh, thanks ever so much, Jane; I love your stew."

"Right, sit down there with the bowl on your knee and eat it up while it's hot. Don't worry about Norman; he's having a great time playing with the puppies. I think he might want to take one home."

"Oh no, we can't take one home. There's not enough for us to eat, let alone a puppy, but thank you, anyway."

Jane left the wagon and the old woman watched as the child ate the stew hungrily.

"When you've eaten your stew, do you want to help me make some medicines, Betsey? I have all the ingredients to make one or two, but they need chopping and mashing up in my mortar and pestle. I've been saving them for when you next came to see me," the old woman studied her thoughtfully, "do you know, I never thought you'd survive when you were born. You were the tiniest baby I've ever seen, but I could see you were determined to live. Quite a little fighter, and that's good. You need to be these days. The only thing is, if I tell you my recipes, you must keep them to yourself until you're an old lady like me, and then you can tell just one person to make sure the secret goes on. I don't mind you selling the medicines to others to relieve their pain, though. That would be a wonderful thing to do, especially when we take to the road again. One day, folk will come to depend on you, my dear, just as they do me now, and it will mean you'll always have a way to earn a few pennies."

Half an hour later, Betsey was hard at work chopping up foliage, berries and roots to make medicines for a fever. Freda also showed her how to make a poultice to draw out infection from a wound and reduce inflammation.

"There, do you think you'll remember all that?"

"Yes, I think I will, but could we do it all again one day?"

"Yes, I usually make up a batch of my more popular remedies every week, so if you come regularly on Saturday afternoons you can have more lessons. I'd like Jane to learn all this, but she has no interest in it whatsoever. Luckily, these days, folk aren't hanged as witches for making cures. Not like they were in the olden days. I heard that many years ago three women were hanged in Bideford for being accused of witchcraft; God rest their poor souls. Anyway, now we've finished, let's sit in the sun and see what your little brother is up to."

It was a pleasant afternoon and Betsey joined Norman in playing with the puppies. They were black and white, and so cute Betsey fervently wished they could take one home. Her face clouded as she imagined what her father's reaction would be, and she knew the puppies were better off where they were. Suddenly, they heard a horse approaching, and at once the gypsies were alert.

A young gentleman on a handsome chestnut stallion trotted into the clearing. He looked surprised to see so many gypsies, and then slightly concerned, as several gypsy men approached him.

"Help you, mister?"

"Sorry, I didn't mean to intrude. I'm Thomas Fellwood from Hartford Manor and I haven't come this way before. I thought I was still on our land."

"No, mister, this is common land. Always has been and I hope it always will be. Is there a problem?"

"No, of course not. If it's common land, you've every right to be here."

Freda noticed that Thomas was no longer concentrating on the men around him. His attention had strayed to Jane, and he watched her closely. She wore a bright red skirt and a white blouse, and her long auburn curls cascaded down her back, almost to her waist. Her gold looped earrings glinted in the late afternoon sun and she moved so gracefully it was as if she was floating. Thomas didn't think he had ever seen a more beautiful woman. The men were not best pleased to note his interest.

"Well, if there's nothing else, sir; you need to take that track. It will take you back through the woods, and into the village."

Realising he was staring; Thomas blushed and tore his eyes away from the young woman. He raised his hat.

"Thank you, kindly. I've ridden the countryside so many times I'm not sure how I've missed this clearing. It is indeed a secluded spot. Anyway, I'll bid you all a good day."

A little later, Betsey and Norman also said goodbye to Freda and Jane and made their way home, Norman carrying the basket of blackberries, and Betsey happily clutching an earthenware bottle of heartburn mixture for her mother. The old woman impressed upon her the need for the bottle to be returned, and the little girl promised to do so. On their way back they met up with Barney, Silas, and Ned, who were all walking home together. Both of the elder boys were delighted with their afternoon's fishing, for in their basket lay ten fish. Seven of them were greenish brown with red eyes, and about nine inches long. The other three were bronze in colour and slightly smaller. Betsey and Norman admired their catch.

"Oh good, you caught some fish then. What sort are they?"

Barney pointed to the greenish-brown ones. "These are tench, and we always seem to catch a lot of them, and I think the other three are bream. I think Mum prefers them to eat, but any of them will taste delicious fried in a bit of dripping."

"You have the three bream then, Barney if your mum likes them, and three of the tench. I'll take home the other four tench for us; that will be enough for one each for me and Silas, and Mum and Dad."

"No, it's all right, Ned; we should split our catch in half and share the bream."

"It's generous of you, Barney, but I'm lucky because I never go hungry, and I know you do, so no, please take the fish home. I've enjoyed our afternoon; let's do it again soon."

CHAPTER 3

The next morning, Ellen was even more glad that the washing had dried the day before, as it was wet outside. As she folded the dry sheets, she hoped Adam would stay in bed all morning. The night before he had once again, frequented The Red Lion, and she knew he would have another hangover. At least it was a Sunday and she didn't need to wake him to go to work. That was a godsend, for with his vicious temper these days, she dared not provoke him. It was still early, and she decided to have a quiet cup of tea before the children got up. As she sat at the kitchen table she tried to remember when things had changed. She and Adam had been married for over twenty years, and the first few of those years had been happy, but as one child, after another died, and there was just never enough money to go around, he had gradually turned to alcohol, and now he could not do without it. She suspected his awful temper was because he was ashamed his drinking was out of control. When sober, he had always been kind and considerate, but that was seldom the case these days when almost every penny he earned was spent at the inn.

She knew that just like her, Kezia would be up with the lark, and she decided to take the dry washing around to the inn before the children were up. Putting a thin grey shawl around her shoulders, she picked up the heavy basket of washing and surveyed the scene from the back door. It was raining heavily, and she knew she would get soaked. Putting an old piece of canvas across the washing, she set off, and within minutes, her feet were sodden as the water poured through the holes in her ancient shoes. Although it was mid-September, it was a chilly morning, and she shivered as she hurried along the path, grateful that someone had laid cobbles at least some of the way to save trudging through the ever-deepening mud. At the inn door, she knocked with difficulty, and Kezia opened it.

"Oh, my goodness, Ellen, you should have left the washing until later. Isn't the weather awful this morning? You'd never think it was so warm and sunny yesterday."

"Well, I knew you'd be up, and I wanted to bring the washing back before Adam gets up; I don't like leaving the children alone with him these days, it takes so little to upset him."

"Will you stay for a cup of tea? We were just having our breakfast, but you're welcome to join us."

"No, it's all right, thanks, Ellen, I'll not intrude."

"Well, let me just find some money to pay you before you go."

"No, can you hang on to it until Adam's gone to work tomorrow, please? If he finds it, you'll have it all back before the day's out, and I must buy food and candles. I'll call in tomorrow on my way to the shop if you don't mind."

"No, I don't mind, but what a sad state of affairs it is. That man needs a hard kick up the backside, and I know a few who'd like to oblige."

Ellen grinned ruefully. "It would make no difference, Kezzie. I think he's ashamed of himself as it is, but he can't live without the drink; he's had a hard life."

"Well, who hasn't these days, but yes, of course, if that suits you, I'll pay you tomorrow."

As she saw her neighbour out, Kezia sighed, and returned to the breakfast table where her husband, Malachi, and sons, Edward and Silas, were tucking into bacon and eggs; a Sunday treat and a change from their normal bowl of porridge.

"Poor Ellen, do you know she wouldn't even take her money, in case Adam finds it and spends it in here later? It's so sad; that man needs a damned good hiding. I wouldn't put up with it if he was my husband."

"I don't think she has much choice, love. I don't believe she walks into quite as many doors as she would have us believe. I think our Adam is a bit handy with his fists where Ellen is concerned."

"Yes, I think you're right, and that's why she brought the washing back now; she didn't want to leave him with the children. What are your plans today, Mal?"

"I'm going up into the loft to examine the roof. I see there are damp patches on three of the bedroom ceilings, and that must mean the roof's leaking. I'm half afraid to look to tell you the truth, but today's an ideal day to do it because with this heavy rain I shall soon see what's what."

"Can me and Ned come up into the loft with you, Dad? I've never been up there, and I'd like to see."

"No, Silas, it's no place for you and Ned. It will be dirty, with lots of spiders, and probably rats and mice, so it's not a nice place to go."

"I don't mind. I'm not scared of rats and mice, or spiders." Silas, aged eight was indignant.

"No, I don't suppose you are, lad. Nevertheless, I don't want either of you following me up there. The loft isn't boarded out, and the inn's so old that if you put one foot in the wrong place, you'll soon put your leg through a bedroom ceiling and I don't want even more expense. No, if I'm in the loft this morning, you'll both have to help your mother."

The Red Lion Inn was an ancient building, and according to a date carved on the fireplace, was built in 1278, around the same time as the church. It was rumoured that the inn had once been three small cottages before they were all knocked into one. The thatched roof and the tall cob chimney could be seen for miles around, a welcome sight for many a traveller en route to Exeter or London. The thick cob walls and small windows made it rather dark inside, but cosy on a winter's day when a roaring fire would be burning brightly in the huge inglenook fireplace. The floor of the main room downstairs was paved with rough flagstones, and the walls were limewashed, the old oak beams blackened with age. The room was warm and welcoming, with a pleasant smell of burning logs and home-cooked food.

The inn had been in the Carter family for many generations, Malachi having inherited it from his parents a few years earlier. His father, Ernie, and his mother, Maria, had done little upkeep on the building for the fifty or more years they had owned it, and it was now in a sorry state of repair. Their large family had meant there was little money to spare, and they had made do as best they could. Malachi knew this state of affairs could not continue forever.

Mal fetched a ladder from the shed and manoeuvred it up the narrow stairs and onto the landing. He pushed open the loft trapdoor with the ladder, and it fell back with a bang. As he cautiously climbed the ladder, with a lantern in one hand, he noticed that the trapdoor had come off its hinges, and he sighed deeply at yet another job to do. At the top of the ladder, he swung the lantern around and peered into the darkness. He could hear scuttling noises from the far corners, and decided they sounded more like rats, than mice; something he was not pleased about. Carefully, he picked his way across the rafters, knowing that if he put a foot between them, it would go straight through the lath and plaster of the ceiling below. He soon discovered he did not need the lantern to tell him the roof was badly in need of attention, as to his dismay, in several places he could see daylight.

The trapdoor was in the centre of the building and he forced himself to examine the roof in both directions to the outer walls. It was an unpleasant and difficult task for he could not stand upright, and the farther he went, the more despondent he became. He realised this was the first time he had set foot in the loft for many years, and he suspected his father had seldom inspected it either. The old beams above his head were damp with water, and in places, he could feel the rain upon his face. The entire space was empty, but in one corner he spotted a large tin trunk. Intrigued, he pulled it towards him with difficulty and tried to prise it open. However, it was stuck tightly shut and he decided to investigate later.

He returned to the landing, just as Kezia came to see how he was getting on.

"How was the roof?"

"You don't want to know. I could see daylight in several places, and the rain was hitting me in the face. The old beams are soaking wet, and it won't be long before we have a couple of ceilings down. We'll have to do something about it, and soon, but I don't know what; it's going to cost an awful lot of money."

"Oh, why didn't your parents keep it in good repair? They must have known it needed doing."

"Well, I know they had it patched up a few times over the years, but they had the same problem that we have; not enough money. You have to remember they had fourteen children to feed, so there was never a penny to spare. At least we only have the two lads to worry about."

"What will we do?"

"I'll have to go into Barnstaple tomorrow and visit the bank to see if they'll lend us some money. We own the inn, and the building must be worth something even in the state it is, so hopefully, I can get a loan if I use it as security. No doubt it will be a burden making the repayments, but we don't have much choice, and at least we have plenty of custom. Doing nothing is no longer an option. I think I'll take up a couple of buckets to catch the worst of the rainwater, and I'll mend the hatch cover while I have the ladder here. I think I'll ask Gordon Parker to come and tell me how much the repairs are going to cost. I've known him all my life so I know he'll give me as fair a price as anyone. What time are you getting dinner for, and what are we having?"

"Well, as it's a Sunday, I normally like to do a roast, but we need to eat up the fish Ned caught yesterday. He's so proud of them and they're a good size. Seeing as we had a cooked breakfast, I thought I might cook our meal at tea-time and we could make do with bread and cheese for dinner. What do you think?"

"Yes, do that, then it won't matter what time I have mine. I hope Gordon will survey the roof today, despite it being a Sunday."

"I'm sure he will; if you wait an hour or so, I expect he'll be in for his normal tipple."

"Yes, that's true. I'll get on and mend the hatch cover then, and you can tell me when he comes in."

An hour or so later, Gordon arrived for his customary pint of ale. He lived a short distance away in the village, and although not a heavy drinker, he enjoyed a tankard of beer on a Sunday lunchtime. He willingly accompanied Mal into the loft to survey the situation.

"Well, I'm afraid there's no doubt you need a new roof, Mal. I reckon this thatch has been here for donkey's years, patched up time after time, but you're not going to get away with that this time. I suspect the rafters and beams must be a hundred years old or more. I wouldn't be surprised if we have to replace the whole lot."

Ned paled. "Oh, my goodness, Gordon, that's going to cost an enormous amount of money, isn't it?"

"I won't lie to you, Mal; it's a big job, and it's not going to come cheap."

"Can you give me an estimate for just replacing the thatch and I'll see what the bank manager says about a loan?"

"I'll give it some thought, and let you have a price before the day's out, but like I say, I think you'd be better advised to have a whole new roof."

CHAPTER 4

That evening, Ellen discovered Adam looking in her housekeeping tin. She had inherited the old tin recently, following her mother's demise, and she treasured it. Cream in colour, and decorated with bright blue forget-me-nots, red poppies, and yellow buttercups, it was the one thing in the house with any colour, and she often held it in her hands, enjoying its beauty. She had no idea how her mother had come by it, but it had been around for as long as she could remember, and she treasured it.

"Where's all your housekeeping money?"

"Adam, you hardly gave me any, if you remember, and what you did give me is gone. I'm sorry, but I don't have any." She crossed the room and put her arms around his neck. "Why don't you stay at home, tonight? It would be nice to spend the evening together. We used to enjoy each other's company; can't we get back to how it used to be? We were so happy once."

For a moment, she thought she had reached him, for he regarded her with something like affection in his eyes; but then he laughed harshly, and pulled away from her embrace.

"Well, it used to be fun spending time with you, but now I only have to look at you and there's another baby on the way. You're either carrying a child, or recovering from having one, and then most of them die. What's the point?"

"Oh, Adam, you do have a hand in it too, you know. You can hardly blame me, alone."

"That's right; of course, it's my fault as usual. Everything is my fault, isn't it? And while we're on the subject of money, where are your wages from next door?"

"I haven't had them yet, and when I do, I must buy food and candles; we have virtually nothing here to eat, and we're down to our last candle. The children have gone to bed hungry. How do you expect me to put food on the table with the little you give me?"

"It's high time we found Barney a job; he's ten years old for goodness sake. I know you want him to stay at school, but I'd been working for at least three years by the time I was his age. I've heard the miller's looking for a boy. I'll enquire this week; it would be a good place for him to go, though Jasper is a bit odd. Even if the lad doesn't earn much it will be one less mouth for us to feed, and what use will education be to him, anyway? If it wasn't for that Mr Billery moving into the village with his do-gooder ways, there wouldn't be a school for him to go to. We don't need one. I never went to school, and neither did you, and we still can't write our names."

Ellen knew it was pointless arguing with him, and he went out slamming the door behind him. If he had no money, she wondered where he was going. However, when he arrived home later that night, he had found money from somewhere, or borrowed some, because he was even more drunk than usual, and she pretended to be asleep. To her relief, he left her alone for once, and she heaved a sigh of relief as his customary loud snores reverberated around the shabby bedroom. Some women may have complained about the disturbing noise, but for Ellen, it was little enough to put up with for some peace.

The next morning, the children were awake early, and once she had fed them some thin gruel and got them ready for school, Ellen knew she would have to wake Adam up for work. She had left it as long as possible.

"Barney, chop a few logs for the fire, please, and while you're out there, feed the chickens, and see if there are any eggs."

"Oh Mum, can't Betsey feed the chickens and collect the eggs; why do I have to do everything?"

"No, you do them this morning. It's still raining, and there's no need for both of you to get wet. Betsey can do them this evening. Put your coat on."

Leaving Betsey and Norman singing nursery rhymes together, she mounted the stairs and gently shook Adam by the shoulder.

"Come on, love; it's time you got up for work, or you'll be late again. I've made you some porridge and the kettle's boiling."

Adam groaned and opened one bloodshot eye. His breath stank, and his appearance was rough and unkempt. He glared at his wife. "What time is it?"

"I've just heard the church clock strike eight o'clock, so you need to get up if you're to be at work for half past. You'll need to hurry as it is."

Grumbling loudly, Adam swung his feet over the bed, stood up and stretched. He reached for his clothes from where he had dropped them the night before and pulled them on, glancing out of the window at the pouring rain. He stumbled down the stairs and sat at the table. Ellen swiftly put a large bowl of porridge in front of him with a tin mug of tea. He lifted one spoonful of the thin watery gruel and let it run back into the bowl. He glared at his wife.

"This is nothing more than water; how do you expect a man to work all day on this muck?"

"It's more than I've had, Adam, there is none for me, and I have a child growing inside me. If you want to eat better food, you need to give me more money."

As soon as she spoke the words, Ellen knew she had gone too far. The man rose threateningly from the table and swept the bowl and all its contents onto the floor. Not satisfied with that, he threw his cup of tea across the room, and the liquid trickled down the wall.

"Aw, stop your grumbling, woman. How dare you criticise me when all you do is sit here on your backside all day. You've no idea what a hard day's work is like."

Ellen kept her head down and dared not raise her eyes, but suddenly he crossed the room and yanked her to her feet by the hair. "I'm talking to you, woman. Don't you dare ignore me."

He swung her around by her hair, and she stumbled heavily against the table. Not satisfied with that, he slapped her hard across the face, and she fell to the ground.

"Dad, Dad, stop it! Leave Mum alone! Please leave her alone."

Betsey pushed Norman under the table and grabbed her father's sleeve, trying to pull him away from her mother, where he had his hands around her throat and was beginning to throttle her.

The little girl screamed at him. "Dad, don't, please don't. You'll kill her! Dad, stop it!"

Adam swung around angrily at his young daughter and dealt her a blow that sent her spinning across the room. Ellen was coughing and spluttering as she tried to force air into her lungs, and Norman was crying loudly when Barney returned from chopping the wood. His arms full of logs, the boy quickly guessed what had happened and glared at his father, not daring to speak; for he knew the result would be a beating for him, too. Adam snatched his coat from a hook by the door and stormed outside, leaving it open. Setting down the logs, Barney glanced at his mother. Seeing she was sitting up; he went first to Betsey, who was lying stunned on the floor.

"Come on, Betsey; are you all right? Let's get you up and see."

Gently, he helped his little sister to her feet, and she gave an anguished wail as she tried to put her weight on her left foot.

"Ow, my foot. I think I've broken my foot."

Barney helped her to sit on the settle, noting a large bruise already darkening around one eye.

"Just sit there a minute, Betsey while I help Mum up. Norman, fetch Betsey a cup of water."

The little boy, sobbing loudly, came out from under the kitchen table and went to fetch the water. Barney turned his attention to his mother, who was still sitting dazed on the floor.

"Mum, are you all right? Can you stand?"

"Aye, I'm all right, lad. Just give me a hand to get up, will you?"

Ellen struggled onto her knees and put her arm around Barney's thin shoulders. With difficulty, he managed to get her to her feet, and she sank into a chair, tears running down her face.

"Come here, Norman. It's all right. Dad was just angry; he didn't mean it."

The child ran to his mother and she pulled him onto her knee, wiped his nose, and dried his tears. His small body convulsed with sobs as she tried to comfort him. "Betsey, you come here, too. I have two knees you know."

Betsey hopped across the room to her mother and sat on the other knee. "Oh, Mum, I thought he was going to kill you. I did. You've got red marks all around your throat. Are you sure you're all right?"

"Yes, but let's take a look at you. You've got a nasty bruise coming, and I think you're going to have a black eye. Barney, can you wring out the dishcloth in clean water and let me have it, please?"

Gently, Ellen held the cloth over Betsey's eye and then encouraged her to stand up. "Just see if you can walk a bit, love. I'd like you to go to school if you can."

Gingerly, Betsey hobbled around the room. "That's it, I think you just twisted your ankle; it's not broken. Do you think you could go to school? I want you to learn all you can; you don't want to end up like me."

"I swear when I'm a bit bigger, I'll give him a hiding he'll never forget, Mum. He shouldn't be allowed to treat you like he does, and all for no reason. You'd done nothing wrong. It's not fair."

"No, Barney, lad; it's not fair, but you'll soon find out that life isn't fair. We just have to accept our lot and get on with it. Now, it's time you and Betsey left for school, or you'll be late."

"Shall I stay at home to help you today, Mum? It won't matter if I miss one day."

"No, Barney you get yourself off with Betsey, and call for Ned and Silas like you usually do. Oh, and don't mention any of this to anyone. No good will come of it. Betsey, if anyone asks, you tripped and fell down the stairs. It's important. Do you understand?"

"Aye, Mum. That's what I always say, but no one believes me."

CHAPTER 5

In an unusual show of affection, Barney took Betsey by the hand as they left the house. "Are you all right, Betsey? Does it hurt much?"

"My head's aching and my foot hurts when I put my weight on it, Barney." At her brother's kind words, Betsey began to cry.

"Aw, come on, Betsey, don't cry. I wish I was big enough to protect you, but I will be one day, and then he's got it coming. Look, Ned and Silas are waiting for us by the gate. I think Uncle Mal's there too, with his horse and cart."

They greeted their friends, and Mal studied Betsey anxiously. "Oh no, not again, Betsey. Did your father beat you?"

"No, Uncle Mal, I tripped and fell down the stairs."

Mal snorted in disbelief. "Well, we all know that's not true, don't we? Are your mother, and Norman, all right?"

"Norman's fine, but Mum isn't too good."

"I shall tell Mr Billery when we get to the school, and perhaps he'll get the constable to arrest your dad."

"No, we've been told to say nothing, Uncle Mal, and we mustn't. If Dad goes to jail, we'll end up begging on the streets, and Mum says that will be even worse."

"Are you limping?"

Betsey nodded. "Yes, I twisted my ankle when I fell and now it hurts."

"Well, luckily, I can give you all a lift to school this morning on the cart. I'm going into Barnstaple on some business."

The three boys climbed onto the cart and Mal picked Betsey up and sat her beside them. Ned was thin-lipped as he put his arm around Betsey. She was such a kind little girl, and so small for her age that Ned always felt the need to protect her. As a toddler, he had first seen Betsey when she was a tiny, wrinkled baby with an angry red face. She had been screaming her head off, and he had a soft spot for her, though he would never admit it. His parents, having married late in life, only had him and Silas, an unusually small family for the times. Ned thought he would like to have a sister, although his friends told him sisters were nothing but trouble, and he was better off without any. He decided Betsey was as good as.

When they arrived at the school, Barney and Ned went to a large classroom where the older pupils were accommodated and taught by Miss Elworthy, an old maid who had lived in the village all her life. Betsey and Silas joined the younger children in Mr Billery's class. Silas greeted his best friend, Richard Martin, the son of the local cordwainer. He was one of the few children in the village, well-shod with shoes that did not leak. Betsey, limping badly, went and sat next to her friends, Gertie and Maud Hammett, who had paddled with her in the stream only a couple of days earlier. Before Gertie could enquire what had happened to Betsey's eye, Mr Billery arrived and told the class to stand up.

The schoolteacher wished them all good morning and proceeded to take the register. As he called each child's name, they replied with "Yes, sir", and sat down; Betsey with some relief, so she could take the weight off her foot. The master then told the children to take their slates from their desks and began to chalk letters on the blackboard, telling the younger children to write a row of the letter 'A', and the older children to write a sentence containing the word 'apple'.

As the children became engrossed in their writing, Mr Billery strolled around the room, looking at their work. He stopped beside Betsey, noticing the red mark across her face, and her rapidly closing eye.

"Why, Betsey; what's happened to you, this morning?"

"I tripped and fell down the stairs, sir."

"Are you sure that's what happened, Betsey? It's the second time this month you've come to school with bruises. I can't believe you're that clumsy. Are you hurt anywhere else?"

"Yes, sir, I know I must be more careful. My ankle hurts, sir, but Mum thinks I've just twisted it."

"May I see, Betsey?"

The child nodded and held out her leg, exposing a swollen and bruised ankle. "Oh dear, that is quite nasty. Children, get on with your work whilst I find a bandage for Betsey's foot. No talking while I'm out of the room. I shall be listening, so if you want to go out to play later, you'd better behave."

Until five years before there had been no school in Hartford village, and none of the working-class folk could read, or even write their names. However, when Amos Billery, a learned man from Exeter, moved to the village, he decided to offer an education to the local children. From a wealthy family, Amos was mourning his wife, when he returned to the village where his great-grandparents had once lived, and where he had spent happy times as a child. Needing something to take his mind off his loss, he bought a large house and used two of the reception rooms as classrooms. At first, people were reluctant to send their children to school, for many of them earned an important few pennies working on the local farms at busy times. From the age of eight, many of them were fully employed, their wages essential to their families. However, once folk learned the education was free, the numbers gradually increased, with most parents willing to forego their offspring's earnings in the hope of a better future for them.

To begin with, Mr Billery taught all the children in one room, as regardless of their age, none could read or write. However, as the numbers grew, he realised he needed at least two classes, and put his mind to finding a second teacher. Miss Elworthy's family had lived in the village for generations, and whilst her family had never been wealthy, they were considered well-to-do. She was over sixty when Mr Billery approached her to ask if she would be interested in teaching at the school with him. He advised he could only offer a meagre wage, as he did not charge the children for their education. He waited for her answer anxiously, fully expecting her to decline. However, she surprised him with a wide smile and the two had never looked back.

Teaching at the school changed Miss Elworthy's life. A spinster, with no living relatives, she was a lonely woman, but now her days were full, and though Mr Billery did not know it, she would gladly have taught the children for nothing. Over the years, since the school opened, the curriculum had slowly widened, and now, in addition to learning their three 'R's of reading, writing and arithmetic, the children were taught geography using a large map on the wall, and a few important dates in history.

Most of the academic learning took place in the mornings, with attention to more practical tasks in the afternoons. Having discovered that Miss Elworthy was an excellent pianist with a tuneful voice, Mr Billery had recently invested in a second-hand piano, and the children now enjoyed learning songs and carols. He was thinking of staging a nativity play at Christmas. Mr Billery knew that most of the children he taught would end up working in service, or on the land, and with this in mind, he tried to provide them with relevant and useful knowledge. On Wednesday afternoons, he instructed the boys in woodwork, whilst Miss Elworthy taught the girls knitting and needlework.

At the back of Mr Billery's house was a large garden. When he bought the house he was pleased to find it had so much land. However, it was overgrown, having been neglected for many years. One day, he came up with a plan to let the children each cultivate a plot so they could learn all about gardening. Most of the parents approved of this, and so when the schoolteacher asked for help in clearing the land, many came forward. Mr Chugg, from Hollyford Farm, was keen for his eldest son, Alfred, aged five, to benefit from an education. One morning, Mr Chugg arrived with several of his farm workers and with axes they cleared the undergrowth. When ploughed, the garden was larger than it first appeared, and was divided into small plots, each shared by two children. Here they grew crops such as potatoes, peas, beans, carrots, parsnips and turnips, and learned how to plant the seeds, weed and thin the plants, and eventually harvest them. The seeds were carefully gathered in the autumn for use the following year, and the produce from the garden helped many families to survive the winter.

Mr Billery returned from his kitchen clutching a bandage, and he instructed Betsey to hold out her foot. Sitting opposite her on a stool, the teacher wound the damp bandage firmly around her ankle.

"There, I know it feels wet, Betsey, but that should help with the swelling. I've bandaged it tightly to give you some support but let me know if it's uncomfortable. Now, are you sure there's nothing else you'd like to tell me about how you came to fall?"

"No, Mr Billery, thank you. I tripped and fell down the stairs; you can ask Barney."

"I'll do that. Now, carry on with your writing, please. I think I can hear the milk cart outside. Children, behave yourselves whilst I'm gone, or you will not get your milk this morning."

When the teacher left the room, the silence continued. None would risk forfeiting their morning mug of milk, for many the first nourishment to pass their lips that day. Ephraim Fellwood was a generous man, and he was aware of the harsh living conditions endured by his workers, and sympathised with them, helping where he could. A year or so before, following a conversation with Mr Billery, he had asked how he could best help, and together they had come up with the idea of a daily ration of milk for all the children. Many of the local gentry thought Lord Fellwood had gone soft in the head, supplying free milk for the children. Fortunately, the local squire had a strong social conscience and cared little for what people thought of him. It was notable that the number of cases of rickets, in particular, had dropped considerably since his intervention.

Betsey normally liked school, but on this particular day, she was relieved when it was time to go home, for her ankle ached. As usual, Barney and Ned came looking for her and Silas, and Barney was dismayed to see that his little sister's eye was now fully shut and she was still limping, despite the teacher's attention to her ankle. He studied her tired white face.

"Come on, Betsey. Do you think you'll be able to walk home?"

"Well, I don't have much choice, do I, Barney? You can hardly carry me."

"No, none of us can on our own, but if we make a seat with our hands, Ned, I reckon we could carry her between us. Shall we try?"

Betsey smiled at him gratefully, for she was dreading the walk home. The two boys clasped each other's hands and bent their knees for Betsey to climb on, and then started to walk. With a few stops now and then for a rest, they managed quite easily, for Betsey was as light as a feather. As they grew more confident, they even made her laugh when they tried to run a few steps. When they arrived at the

Loverings' cottage, they carried Betsey inside and found Kezia talking to Ellen.

"Oh, my goodness, another casualty. How are you, Betsey, my love?"

"I'm all right, thank you, Aunty Kezzie. The boys have carried me home because my ankle hurts."

"You've got a right shiner, too. Look at the state of you. I was going to give you a penny to go to Gypsy Freda to ask for some herbs to ease the pain, but I can see, there's no way you can walk there. Do you think Gypsy Freda would sell what we need to Barney and Norman?"

"Yes, I think she would if they explain. Norman went there with me the other day, so they know who he is."

"Here you're then, Barney. Go with Norman to the old woman, and ask for some ointment for your mother and your sister for their injuries, and something for a headache." Kezia handed the boy two pennies.

"Kezzie, don't waste your money on us, because I can't pay you back. I haven't even been able to get to the shop today, or cook anything, so I don't know what we're all going to eat. There are only a few stale crusts in the house."

"Don't worry about that now, I'll let you have a pasty each a bit later on. I'm not supplying one for Adam though; that man doesn't deserve to eat."

Gypsy Freda was angry to hear that, according to Barney, young Betsey and her mother had taken a fall. She didn't believe it for one moment but willingly sold him the ointment and medicine he wanted, and said she hoped they were both better soon. When the boys returned, Kezia treated Ellen and Betsey's wounds with the ointment and left them eating a pasty each with strict instructions to finish the food quickly before their father arrived home. It was unneeded advice, for the food was gone in no time. Ellen sent the children to bed early, wanting to get them settled before Adam put in an appearance. However, she had no need to worry, for her husband did not come home that night, and she lay in bed wondering where he was. It wasn't the first time he hadn't come home, and she suspected he had another woman. As far as she was concerned, his mistress was welcome to him, and she was relieved not to have to face him.

CHAPTER 6

Following the introduction of the Enclosures Act, wealthy landowners such as the Fellwood family had greatly benefitted, and the Hartford Estate now covered over two thousand acres split into four farms. The home farm was the largest, covering some eight hundred acres, and the other farms were slightly smaller and rented out to tenant farmers. The Act allowed the rich and titled to erect fences around common land, previously used by all the members of a village, and claim it as their own. The peasants who had lived off the land for centuries were tenants, not owners, and too often they were evicted as the rich enclosed the land to rear sheep for wool, a valuable commodity. The Fellwood family had a reputation for dealing sympathetically with such issues, but nevertheless, the poor folk of Hartford had suffered, suddenly finding themselves with less land to graze their animals or grow their crops.

Hartford Manor House was a magnificent building which dated back hundreds of years, though it had been virtually rebuilt in the late eighteenth century after it was devastated by fire. The Fellwood family had lived there for generations, and were able to trace their ancestors back to the Domesday Book.

Close to the Manor House was a hamlet where many of the agricultural workers lived in tied cottages. As well as working on the land, many were employed to burn the lime which was quarried locally. The three limekilns were in almost constant use as the stone was processed into quicklime for spreading on the acidic soil to improve fertility.

Ephraim Fellwood, the Lord of the Manor, was happily married to Lady Helena, and Joshua, at eighteen, was their eldest son and would one day inherit the estate. At nearly seventeen, Thomas, the second son, knew the estate would never be his unless some misfortune should befall Joshua; but he was content with the situation. Joshua had always been raised as 'the heir' and Thomas knew his place as 'the spare'. George, the next surviving child, was thirteen, but sadly deformed with a harelip and a little simple-minded. However, he was a contented child with a loving nature and was adored by all the family. Following the birth of George, several babies had been stillborn or died in infancy, and Margery, at six, was the youngest, and would probably be the last child to be born into the family. She was a precocious little girl, with a pleasant disposition, and as the only daughter in the family, was the apple of her father's eye.

Dawn was breaking as Thomas Fellwood was awoken by someone creeping into his bed. He groaned, and hastily pulled down his nightshirt.

"Oh Margery, what time is it? Can't you sleep?"

He raised his arm sleepily, and his little sister climbed in and snuggled up to him, happily.

"I don't know what the time is, Thomas, but it's nearly light and I want a cuddle. Do you mind?"

"No, of course not, but it's a bit early. Shall we see if we can get back to sleep for a little while? I don't want to get up yet."

"Oh, all right, then." The child snuggled up even closer, and he pulled the clothes over her, and they both lay quietly for a few minutes. Thomas began to drift back to sleep, but then she started to fidget.

"Thomas, what are you doing today?"

The young man sighed deeply. "I guess there will be no more sleep with you around, will there? Well, today I'm going for a ride over the moors if the weather holds. How about you?"

"I want to see Mama because I've not seen her for days, and it's not fair."

"I know you do, but Mama is poorly at the moment, and she needs to rest. Will a cuddle from me do instead?"

"Yes, you're nice and warm, Thomas. I like coming into your bed in the mornings; Joshua usually tells me to go away because it's too early. Can you read me a story?"

"Yes, all right. Find a book, and pull the curtains back, and we'll lie here in bed and read. It's still a bit dark, isn't it? Pull the bell, and we'll get a maid to light the lamp, and bring us a drink."

Within a few minutes, there was a knock on the door, and a maid appeared and bobbed a curtsey. "Good morning, sir, good morning, miss, what can I get for you?"

"Good morning, Thompson. Light a lamp, please, and then fetch me a cup of tea, and Lady Margery a glass of milk."

"Yes, sir, of course."

An hour or so later, having read several stories to his younger sister, Thomas told her it was time to return to her room and get dressed for breakfast.

"Could we have just one more story first, Thomas?" Margery looked at her brother pleadingly with large blue eyes.

"It's no good batting those long eyelashes at me, young lady; I've read loads of stories to you already, and I'm hungry. You get dressed, and when we've had breakfast, I'll take you riding; how does that sound? You don't have lessons today, do you?"

"Ooh, yes, please, Thomas. No, I don't have lessons today because it's Saturday, so I can do what I like."

She ran off happily.

Lady Margery arrived at the breakfast table just before Thomas. Her brothers, Joshua and George, and her father, Ephraim, were already seated.

"Papa, can I see Mama, today, please?"

"No, I'm sorry, Margery, but I'm afraid Mama is still poorly. Perhaps in a few days."

The little girl sighed, but then brightened. "Thomas is taking me riding, today, Papa. Do you want to come, Joshua?"

"No, thank you, Margery but that is kind of Thomas. I think it will be a pleasant day, too. Not a cloud in the sky and the sun is shining. I'd like to, but Papa and I are planning a trip to London soon, and we need to discuss that after breakfast, so perhaps next time."

"Can I come riding too, Thomas?"

"No, not today, George but I'll take you another day when you can ride a bit better. I don't think I can keep an eye on you and Margery at the same time."

George was close to tears, and Thomas quickly continued. "I'll tell you what, later on, I'll take you to the stables and let you ride around the paddock; would you like that?"

The boy nodded happily, as his nursemaid carefully wiped the food from his chin, and tidied him up.

"Goodness, you've got far more patience than me, Thomas. If I go for a ride I like to gallop off on my own."

"Ah, you should try it sometime, Joshua, both George and Margery are excellent company. There's more to life than making money and running the estate. Why don't you take the day off, and come with us?"

"No, not today, thanks, but you're right, and I will one day."

Lord Fellwood got to his feet. "If you have finished eating, Joshua, I suggest we retire to my study to discuss our visit to London. Thank you for looking after Margery and George, Thomas; it's a big help, whilst their Mama is so ill."

Joshua patted his mouth with his napkin and left the table, following his father down the carpeted corridor. Paintings of ancestors adorned the oak-panelled walls, and some of the alcoves contained suits of armour and old weapons. Ephraim seated himself in his comfortable leather armchair and indicated for his son to sit in another chair close to him.

"Now, all being well, and provided your mother is better, I think we should leave for London in about a week. We can stay for a month or so, and that will give me a chance to introduce you to several of my business partners who live in the city. It's such a difficult time at the moment, and I fear there may yet be more unrest. The Corn Laws are serving us well because they protect us from cheap imports of grain from abroad, and let us keep the prices high but, of course, the poor are finding it difficult to find the money, and they're going hungry. Did you hear what happened in Barnstaple, last week?"

His son shook his head.

"Well, it was last Friday, when I was in the town myself, and I must have just missed all the upheaval. My friend, Cecil, witnessed it all, and he was telling me about it yesterday. Old man Sinclair had a large cargo of turnips delivered to his warehouse along the quay, and word spread like wildfire. Before long, around five hundred women, all desperate to feed their families, were clamouring to buy some, but he refused to sell the turnips locally, as he could make more money by exporting them. As you can imagine, this did not go down well, and before long the crowd had swelled to more than a thousand, threatening to dismantle the warehouse brick by brick. Luckily, the local magistrate, William Potter, heard about it, and incredibly, he bought the lot. He stopped a riot by telling the women he would sell the turnips at cost price the next day. I have it on good account that around five hundred of the women camped outside the warehouse all night long, and followed the carts carrying the turnips to the market to make sure none went astray. It just shows how desperate they were."

"Goodness me, no, I didn't know that, but if their families are starving you can't blame them."

"No, of course, you can't; we're so lucky never to have been in that position. I can't believe how many have left the countryside and gone to the towns in search of work. I fear we may struggle to find employees if this trend continues. Not only that, but many of the commoners are campaigning for the right to vote. Goodness knows, where that will lead. I mean, most of them are uneducated and would have no notion what they were voting for, just see what happened at the Peterloo Massacre, last year. A bloodbath by anyone's reckoning. Fifteen people were killed; I would never have believed that could happen in Manchester."

Joshua nodded. "Yes, I know; it's incredible. I mean, you expect bloodshed when there's a war on, but not in the middle of England. I was hoping that with the mad old king dying earlier in the year things would improve, but from what I've heard, no one has a great deal of confidence in his son. You'd think having been Prince Regent for so long, he'd have more idea of what to do, but all he seems interested in is carrying on with Maria Fitzherbert, and goodness knows how many of his other mistresses. We need a strong leader just now."

"Well, I'm pleased to hear you're so well informed, Joshua; it does you credit, and it's important to be so as a businessman. I think you'll find our visit to London most educational. You will certainly find the costumes interesting. The King's friend, Beau Brummell has become quite the leader of fashion."

"Yes, I had heard he's quite the dandy. Where will we stay in London, Papa?"

"Oh, we'll stay with your Aunt Genevieve, as usual. I'm looking forward to seeing my sister again, and I know she'll make us welcome. She'll certainly see a difference in you, for she hasn't seen you in years. I had thought to take Thomas with us because he's never been to the city, but I think that will have to wait for another time. With your mother so poorly, George and Margery have come to depend on him, and he cares for them so well. How about you? Do you have any plans while we're in London?"

"Well, I've only ever visited the capital once before, so I'd like to see some of the sights. Do you think you might have time to accompany me?"

His father beamed at him. Yes, of course, that would be most enjoyable, and you know the old proverb, 'all work and no play, makes Jack a dull boy.'

"I've never heard that. What does it mean?"

"Oh, I thought you'd know the saying. It comes from an old book of proverbs by a man called James Howell. I think the whole proverb is 'all work and no play, makes Jack a dull boy, all play and no work, make Jack a mere toy.' It means no time off from work makes one boring, but too much play makes one ineffective. Where would you like to go in London?"

"I believe the new king is splashing out on rebuilding Buckingham Palace, so I'd be interested to see how that's going, but it's probably early days, so there may not be much to see yet. I've been reading about the Tower of London, too, and that sounds intriguing, with so much history. I saw it from a distance last time, but I'd like to go inside. Also, perhaps St Paul's Cathedral and Westminster Abbey."

"Yes, they are all places worthy of a visit. Maybe your Aunt Genevieve would like to join us. Now, I'm going to show you some of the accounts of the businesses we have in the big city, and maybe after lunch we could ride around the estate, and see if everything is in order. I know we have a farm manager, but I like to take an interest, and I think the workers appreciate it."

CHAPTER 7

Thomas left the breakfast room, followed by the excited little girl. When they reached the stable, Isaac Hammett had their horses saddled and ready. The young stable lad took real pleasure in looking after the horses, and their coats shone; a testament to his care.

"Good morning, Hammett, thank you. Are the horses well?"

"Aye, sir. They need a little exercise. I wondered, sir, if the young lady would like to see our new foal while she's here?"

"Yes, a wonderful idea, thank you, Hammett. Do you want to see the baby foal, Margery?"

The child nodded, and Thomas lifted her, so she could see over the stable door and gaze at the brown foal feeding eagerly from his mother.

"Aw, he's adorable, isn't he, Thomas? Can I go in and stroke him?"

"No, I think we should leave him to feed, and his mother may not like us going in there. Anyway, we need to go on our ride. Come on, let me help you up."

Thomas lifted the little girl onto her pony and mounted his own horse. He led her pony by a rein, but although she was only six, Margery was a competent rider and showed no nerves.

"You don't need to lead me anymore, Thomas. I can manage on my own."

"Yes, I think you can, but seeing as we're going out over the moors, I think I'll hold on to you for a little while, just until your pony gets rid of some of his energy. He's quite skittish at the moment, and Hammett said they were a bit frisky this morning. I'll let you go later when we've tired him out a bit. Now, hold tight; shall we canter?"

With her long blond hair streaming out behind her, Margery Fellwood was soon laughing loudly as they cantered along the rough tracks towards Exmoor. As they made their way down a hillside and into a sheltered valley, they spotted a child sitting by the side of the lane. The little girl had taken a tumble and was trying hard not to cry as she endeavoured to stop her hands and knees from bleeding, using the hem of her dress.

"Whoa, whoa, lad." Thomas reined in his horse and dismounted. "What's happened here, then? Are you all right, my dear? Why I think I saw you at the gypsy camp the other day, didn't I? Is that where you live?"

"No, sir. I was only visiting. I live in the village, but I'm on my way to see Gypsy Freda; she's teaching me how to make medicines."

"Goodness me. This isn't the first time you've been in the wars recently; that's quite a black eye you have there. Let me see your knees. Oh yes, those are nasty grazes. You've taken a bad tumble. Let's go to the stream and I'll bathe your wounds for you."

"Oh no, sir. I'm fine, really I am, but thank you, kindly."

Lady Margery called to her brother. "Thomas, would you lift me down, please? I've got a handkerchief we can use to clean the wounds."

Although she did not know it, Betsey was as white as a sheet, and her damaged eye was now all the colours of the rainbow. Her sprained ankle was on the mend but had given out as she went down over the steep bank, causing her to stumble. Thomas was saddened to see her bruises, and how thin her limbs were. Her dress, although clean, was patched in many places, and it was not difficult to see she was under-nourished.

Most embarrassed now, Betsey sat on the ground, whilst the young gentleman soaked the fine lawn handkerchief in the stream and gently bathed her knees.

Lady Margery introduced herself, holding out her hand. "Hello, I'm Margery. What's your name?"

"It's Betsey, miss."

"Well, hello, Betsey. I think we must be about the same age. I'm six. How old are you?"

"Yes, miss, I'm six too."

When Thomas had bathed her wounds and wiped her tears, Betsey thanked him and assured him she was fine.

"Would you like a ride to the gypsy camp on my horse?"

"Oh, no, sir, I couldn't trouble you like that. I'll just be on my way now, and thank you for your kindness. The gypsies don't like visitors."

"No, come on; I insist. You've had quite a fright, and we're going that way, anyway. Come on, up you get."

Thomas hoisted the child onto his horse and climbed up behind her, taking the leading reins of Margery's pony once more.

"When I happened upon the gypsy camp the other day, I noticed you were talking to a young girl surrounded by puppies. Do you know what she's called?"

"Aye, sir. That's Jane. She's the granddaughter of the old lady I'm going to see; Gypsy Freda. They won't like you going to their camp again, though. Could you drop me off before we get there, please?"

"No, I'd like to see you there safely. You've had a nasty fall, and once you're there they can take care of you. I don't like to leave you here on the edge of the moors on your own. Have you been on a horse before, Betsey?"

"Yes, I've been on an old carthorse, but not a grand horse, like this, sir. The gypsy camp is just beyond those trees."

When they trotted into the gypsy camp, several men eyed them suspiciously, clearly surprised to see Betsey mounted on a horse with a gentleman. Thomas trotted over to where the young girl he had mentioned to Betsey, was talking to a middle-aged man. He gave her a bright smile.

"Hello, ma'am; I hope you don't mind me calling again, but I found young Betsey here after she'd taken a nasty tumble on the moorland path. I think she's a bit shaken up, and her knees could probably do with some ointment, although she is being incredibly brave." He dismounted and took off his hat. "I'm Thomas Fellwood."

"Aye, sir, I know who you are, and thank you for looking after Betsey. Someone certainly needs to. I'll take care of her, now. My name is Jane, and this is Mr Morris, he's the local miller from Hartford."

The girl raised her warm brown eyes to his, and smiled widely, revealing perfect white teeth. For a few moments Thomas was distracted, thinking how beautiful she was, but finally, he remembered himself.

"I'm pleased to meet you, Jane, and you too, Mr Morris. Are you here on business?"

The miller was not best pleased with the interruption, for he had a soft spot for Jane, and had been looking forward to seeing her. "Aye, sir, I'm just delivering a bag of flour to Gypsy Freda."

All this time, Margery sat quietly on her horse; but when the five puppies suddenly appeared from beneath the gypsy wagon, she called out.

"Oh, Thomas, look, what gorgeous puppies. Can you lift me down, please, so I can play with them?"

"Would that be all right with you, ma'am? I've no wish to intrude. I just wanted to make sure young Betsey was cared for. I think she could do with a substantial meal; would you allow me to pay you to provide one for her?"

"There's no need, sir; I was thinking the same thing myself, and Betsey knows she's always welcome here."

"Nevertheless, I'd like to pay you something for your trouble." He reached into his pocket and pulled out a few coins. "Here we are; a couple of shillings, please take them and give the child some food. Would you mind if my sister plays with the puppies for a few minutes? I'll never hear the end of it if you say no."

"Aye, come on, lass, come down and join Betsey, and play with the puppies. Now, Jasper, I've paid you, haven't I? Thank you so much for dropping off the flour; was there anything else?"

The miller was angry at being dismissed, and his face flushed red as he muttered, "no, I'll be off now, then. See you again next week, Jane. I'll look forward to it."

"Yes, see you next week, Jasper." The gypsy girl grinned at Thomas behind the miller's back, as he turned his cart around and left the clearing. "You came at just the right time, sir; Jasper would like to court me, and he won't take the hint that I'm not interested."

Jane disappeared into the wagon and returned with a bowl of water and a cloth to bathe Betsey's hands and knees properly. That done, she smeared ointment onto the wounds. Whilst she did this, an old woman appeared at the entrance of the wagon, and sat watching the proceedings. She sat there thoughtfully, smoking her pipe, and ignoring the young gentleman when he tried to make polite conversation. Slightly embarrassed at her rudeness, Jane explained.

"Don't mind my granny, sir. She's a little deaf, and doesn't take to strangers."

Having allowed Margery to play with the puppies for a few minutes, Thomas pulled his watch from his pocket and consulted it. Betsey studied the shiny gold watch in fascination, thinking she had never seen anything quite so pretty. Thomas saw her gazing at it and held it out to her.

"Would you like to hold my watch, Betsey? I treasure it because it was given to me by my grandfather. It's real gold, and has his name on it, see."

Betsey took the watch, and turned it over and over in her hands, as the sunshine glinted on it. "What does it say?"

"It says his name here, look, Ambrose Fellwood, and the date 1725; I think that's when he was born. I was only five when he died, but I can remember sitting on his lap and playing with this and so it was given to me. Anyway, come on, Margery; it's time we were going."

However, Margery was enjoying herself, and reluctant to leave the puppies.

"Thomas, could we buy one of these puppies from Jane, and take it home with us? I'd love to have a puppy of my own. I promise I'd care for it."

Thomas was about to say no when he saw the longing in his little sister's eyes. He knew she was missing her mother during her long illness, and wondered if the distraction of a puppy would help.

"Well, we don't know if they're for sale, do we?" He looked questioningly at the gypsy girl.

"Aye, sir, they will be for sale, but they need to stay with their mother for at least another couple of weeks until they're weaned. Some folk would let you take one now but 'tis better to wait a while, and I'll not see animals mistreated."

"In that case, Jane, may I call you Jane?" The girl nodded. "May we call again in a couple of weeks to collect a puppy for my sister?"

"Yes, of course, sir, we'd be pleased to see you." She gave him a wide smile, and his stomach lurched.

Lady Margery, delighted to think she would soon have her own puppy, was grinning from ear to ear. He took the small puppy from her arms and passed it back to the gypsy girl. In doing so, their fingers touched, and he almost jumped, as a spark of electricity passed between them. In an effort not to show how the brief contact had affected him, he quickly lifted his little sister back onto her pony, and, retrieving the watch from Betsey, raised his hat as they left.

"I'll wish you ladies a good day then, and we'll see you in a couple of weeks. Betsey, I hope your hands and knees are better soon."

As they rode off, Gypsy Freda slowly took her clay pipe from her mouth and wagged it at her granddaughter.

"You shouldn't have told him he could call again and buy a pup. I could see the way he was looking at you, but he's a gentleman, and you're a gypsy, and nothing good will ever come of that. If he comes again, give him the dog, and then tell him to clear off. You pay heed to what I'm saying, girl; you know I'm right."

Jasper Morris was not a happy man, as he drove his horse and cart away from the gypsy camp. In his thirties, he had so far, been unlucky in love, and was keen to marry as soon as possible. He was besotted with the young gypsy girl, and, despite his mother's disapproval, continued to carry a torch for her. Each time he visited the camp to deliver a sack of flour, he hoped Jane might begin to look kindly on him.

The mill had been in his family for many years, but his father was now a bedridden invalid, and Jasper desperately needed help to run the business. His mother, Morag, encouraged him to find a wife in the village and start a family. However, despite his excellent prospects, no girls had shown any interest in him. He was a somewhat strange-looking man, with a poor complexion.

Jasper's father, John, had been a hard-working man until a year or so ago, when a stroke had put paid to that, and it now took Morag all her time to nurse her disabled husband. Unusually for the time, John and Morag had only been blessed with two children. Their youngest son, Seth, was married with four children, and lived some ten miles away, working as a farm labourer. Jasper would inherit the mill, and the last thing his parents wanted was for him to waste his time courting a young gypsy girl, who would bring no money to the business, and most likely refuse to leave her travelling way of life.

CHAPTER 8

A week or so later, on a Sunday morning, Adam crawled out of bed earlier than usual and told Barney to get his coat on.

"Why, Dad, where are we going?"

"It's time you went out to work, lad. We need the money, and you've had more than enough schooling. I'm told the miller's looking for a boy, so we'll see if he'll take you on."

"Oh, Adam, could we not leave it just a little longer? Mr Billery says Barney's doing well at school and I'd like him to stay as long as possible. I'm sure it will help him get a better job in the long run. Perhaps I could take in more washing to earn a bit more money."

"No, he's ten years old, and it's high time he earned his keep. Anyway, from what I see of it, you can't cope with the washing you do now, and I never see any money from it. Come on, lad, get a move on, or someone else will get there before us." He fixed his wife with a firm stare and seeing her husband was determined, she dared not say more.

Betsey was dismayed but knew better than to voice her opinions. When her dad was drunk and violent, Barney was often her only protector, and she was distraught to think he would no longer be there.

Saying no more, Barney got his coat on and hugged his mother, Betsey, and Norman. He held on to his little sister the longest.

"If I get the job, I'll come back to see you on my day off, Betsey, but you know where the mill is, don't you, so if you need me, you know where to come." He looked at her knowingly, to see if she understood.

Holding back her tears, she nodded and returned his embrace.

Adam was pleased when he and Barney seemed to have arrived at just the right time at the mill. Jasper was looking hot and bothered, as he loaded the sacks of flour onto the cart, and he stopped and wiped his brow, as he saw the boy and his father approaching. Adam had known the miller all his life.

"Hello, Jasper, I hear you're looking for a lad. Would you consider young Barney, here? He's strong and intelligent; you'd get a decent day's work out of him."

"Aye, I am, Adam, he's a bit skinny, though. I shouldn't think he's got a lot of strength."

"Well, times are hard you know, Jasper, but with a bit more food, he'll soon fill out. He's strong and wiry, and he knows he'll feel the buckle end of my belt if he doesn't come up to scratch.

The miller surveyed the young boy.

"What do you think, lad; do you want to come and work for me?"

"Aye, sir, if my dad says I have to then I promise I'll work hard."

"All right then, see if you can hoist that half sack of flour onto the cart, and then take the horse and cart around the yard."

Ignoring the sack of flour, Barney went first to the horse, stroked the old mare's nose, and spoke kindly to her. He then lifted the sack, and with considerable difficulty, managed to get it onto the cart. Saying nothing, he calmly patted the horse again and climbed onto the cart. He clicked his tongue and told the horse to move on, taking the cart carefully around the yard.

Though Barney did not know it, his father was both surprised and impressed, and stood with a wide smile on his face, admiring his son's actions.

"There, what do you think of that, Jasper? The boy's a natural with the old horse; you can see he'd be an asset to any business."

The miller took off his cap and scratched his slightly balding head. "Aye, I must confess he made a fine job of that. All right then, lad, I'll give you a month's trial. You can sleep in the loft above the barn, and come into the house for your meals. I can't afford to pay him much, mind."

"Aw, come on, man, we all know you're one of the richest men in the village; don't be mean."

However, the miller stood his ground, but eventually, the two men agreed on a wage that Adam insisted would be paid directly to him. He ruffled his son's hair and wished him luck as he walked home whistling, pleased with his morning's work.

As Barney watched his father amble off, he felt sad, not for himself, but for his family, whom he knew would miss him, particularly Betsey. His mother too, would miss his help in chopping firewood, and doing all the jobs around the house that his father should have taken care of, but never did. He was startled out of his thoughts by the miller.

"Come on then, lad, there's work to be done. No use standing there daydreaming. 'Twill be no holiday living here, but if you give me a good day's work, I'll see to it that you have a full belly, and it looks like that doesn't happen often."

"Thanks, Mr Morris; I promise I'll work hard."

By the end of the day, Barney was exhausted and had never worked so hard in his life. However, there had been some compensation. At the end of the morning, Jasper had taken him inside to meet his parents, John and Morag, and told him to sit at the large kitchen table. Morag eyed him suspiciously.

"There's nothing to you, lad, I shouldn't think we'll get a lot of work out of you."

"Well, give the boy a chance, Mother. He's worked hard all morning, and good food will soon put a bit of flesh on his bones. Are you hungry, Barney?"

"Aye sir, I'm always hungry."

"Right then, see if you can get that lot down you, and I'll find you a couple of blankets for the loft. You'll be warm and comfortable in there with the animals, and there's plenty of soft hay you can sleep on."

Barney's eyes widened, as the old woman placed a large plate of bacon and sausages in front of him. There were two golden eggs on a large, thick slice of freshly cooked bread, and he could not get the first forkful to his mouth quickly enough.

Morag watched him enjoy every mouthful, and could not help but smile at him.

"My goodness, lad, when did you last eat? I never thought you'd put all that away, although it was only half as much as Jasper managed."

At last, Barney pushed back his plate and sighed contentedly. "My, that was proper tasty, missus. Thank you, so much. If you feed me like that, I promise you'll never wish for a better worker."

The next day, Betsey walked home from school alone, as Ned and Silas stayed behind to play with some of their friends. As she walked home, slowly dragging her feet, she wondered how Barney was getting on. When she arrived home, she carefully opened the gate, for it was hanging off its hinges. Norman came running to meet her.

"Hello, Betsey, will you play with me in the garden?"

"Yes, in a minute, Norman. Just let me get a drink of water from the pump. It's hot today, and I'm thirsty." She grabbed a tin mug off the shelf and went outside to the pump that they shared with several neighbouring cottages. She raised the stiff handle and pulled it down with all her might, holding the mug under the spout. Norman followed her outside. "Do you want some, Norman?" The little boy nodded, and she shared the icy cold water with him.

When they returned inside, her mother was just coming down the stairs.

"Did you tell Mr Billery that Barney wouldn't be coming to school anymore?"

"Aye, he wasn't best pleased, I don't think, but he didn't say much. Can I play in the garden with Norman, Mum?"

"Yes, but then I want you to meet your father at the butcher's shop when he leaves work, and ask him if there are any scraps or bones today. I've got a few vegetables in the larder, but they'd taste better with a bit of meat. See if you can get him to come home early will you; tell him I'm not feeling well."

After playing hide and seek with Norman for a while, Betsey took her little brother by the hand, and they walked to Mrs Chown's butcher's shop. The owner was behind the counter, and Betsey asked if she might see her father.

"Yes, he's out the back jointing a pig, but don't keep him talking long, mind. I'm not paying him to chat."

The two children found their father, and Betsey told him what her mother had said.

"Here you are then, there are a few bones Mrs Chown won't mind you having. There's a bit of meat left on them."

"Dad, Mum says can you come straight home after work, because she's feeling poorly, and she hasn't got Barney to chop the wood for the fire."

"Aye, you tell her I won't be long. I just have to finish jointing this pig, and then call in at The Red Lion to have a word with Mal about something, and then I'll be home."

Betsey relayed the message to her mother, but after a couple of hours, there was no sign of Adam, and sighing deeply, Ellen threw the last log onto the fire and went outside to chop more wood. She fed the children with the stew and saved back a plateful for Adam. However, when she heard the church clock strike ten o'clock, and her husband had not returned, she decided to go to bed, wondering if he would come home at all.

Close to midnight, Ellen heard the back door squeak and Adam stumble inside. Taking no care to be quiet, he mounted the stairs and slammed the bedroom door shut. Climbing into bed, he cuddled up to her and raised her nightdress. His hand explored her body, and moving over her swollen abdomen, it crept up to her breasts. He caressed them, but she steadfastly ignored him, hoping he would give up and go to sleep, but he was having none of it.

"Come on, Ellen, I haven't bothered you for days, but I'm only human, and a man has his needs."

"Oh, Adam, please don't, not tonight. I feel so ill. I was hoping you'd come home early to help me."

"Aw yes, I meant to, but then I got talking, and well, you know how it is. At least we'll be getting a bit more money now, with Barney working. Anyway, I'm sure I can make you feel better." He pulled her over to face him, and his hand crept down between her legs.

"Adam, no, I don't often refuse you, but I feel awful." She pushed him away.

"No; you should know by now, you don't get to say no to me, my dear. I know my rights. Don't you dare push me away."

He smacked her hard across the face. "Now, do as you're told. And for goodness sake, at least pretend you're enjoying it. It's no wonder I have to look elsewhere for a bit of satisfaction, but you'll do your duty tonight."

In the other bedroom, the raised voices had awakened the children, and Norman was crying. Betsey pulled him towards her, cuddling him, and pulling the thin covers over their heads. With tears running down her cheeks, she began to sing softly to him.

"Ring a ring, a roses,
A pocket full of posies,
Atishoo, atishoo,

They all fell down."

She carried on singing to her little brother, trying to block out her mother's screams and ignore what was happening in the next room.

CHAPTER 9

It took a long time for Betsey to get back to sleep that night, though eventually, she soothed Norman, and he fell asleep in her arms. In the morning, the sun was streaming through the window when she awoke, and she wondered what the time was. Normally, her mother came and woke her in time for some breakfast before she went to school. Having had a disturbed night, Norman was still asleep, and she crawled out of bed trying not to wake him.

She listened intently outside her parent's bedroom but could hear nothing. Puzzled, for it seemed late, she eventually plucked up the courage to peer around the door. Her mother still lay in the bed, and she had been severely beaten. There was no sign of her father, and the little girl presumed he had gone to work. She climbed onto the bed and stroked her mother's hair away from her face. Her face was smeared with blood from a nosebleed, and one eye was swollen.

"Mum, are you all right? Mum, speak to me."

Ellen slowly opened her eyes, a little dazed at first, but then focused on her daughter's concerned face. She groaned as she tried to sit up, and then lay back again, as the room swam before her eyes.

Her voice came out as a croak. "Betsey, fetch Aunty Kezzie, please. Where's Norman?"

"He's still asleep."

"All right, leave him where he is, and fetch Kezzie, please. Then bring me some water."

Betsey did as she was told, and ran to the back door of the inn.

"Why, Betsey, you're still in your nightgown; aren't you going to school?"

"Oh, Aunty Kezzie, can you come and see Mum? She's had another fall, and she's hurt. She asked me to fetch you. I don't think I can go to school today; I'll have to look after Norman." Tears poured down Betsey's face.

"Shh, it's all right, Betsey. Don't worry, I'm coming. Mal, see the boys get off to school, will you?" Her husband nodded.

"Come on, Betsey let's go to your mum."

Kezia gasped, as she took in just how badly beaten her neighbour was. "Ellen, this can't go on. I must fetch the constable. Just look at the state of you; I think you've even lost a tooth."

Ellen grabbed the woman's arm. "No, just bathe my wounds, and help me up, and I'll be …"

She was unable to complete the statement, as a sharp pain encircled her abdomen, and took her breath away.

"Oh no, I think I'm in labour. I kept getting pains, yesterday, but it's not my time; I've two months to go yet." Tears glistened brightly in her eyes. "This will be another stillborn child, no doubt."

Kezia bathed Ellen's wounds, fetched her a cup of tea, and made her as comfortable as she could. Then she took Betsey and Norman by the hand and led them to the inn.

"Mal, I'm going to have to leave these two here with you for the day. Adam has beaten Ellen badly, though she swears she fell, and the baby's on the way. Now, Betsey, I want you to be a big, brave girl and fetch Gypsy Freda. Tell her what's happened, and ask her to come and help your mother. When you've done that, I want you to stay here, and help Uncle Mal for the day; can you do that?"

With wide eyes, Betsey nodded. "Will my mum be all right?"

"Yes, I'm sure she will. Now, hurry along and give these pennies to Gypsy Freda, and ask her to come quickly."

Betsey ran to the common, and when she arrived at the gypsy camp, she was so out of breath she could barely speak.

Jane sat her down gently on the wagon's steps. "Just take a breath, Betsey. That's it. Now, calm down. What's wrong?"

Betsey poured out her sad tale, and without further ado, Jane took her on her lap and wiped her tears.

"Now, it will be all right. You know how clever my granny is, don't you?" Betsey nodded.

"Right, you sit there a minute while she sorts out her medicines and ointments, and then you can take her to your mum. Have you had any breakfast?"

The little girl shook her head. "No, but I don't think I could eat any."

"Well, let's just see, shall we? The campfire's burning well, so how about a fried egg on bread?"

Within minutes, an egg with a soft golden yolk was put in front of her, and once she started eating, she realised how hungry she was. By the time she had finished, the old gypsy was ready, and together they made their way back to the cottage.

Sending Betsey into the inn, the old woman entered the cottage by the back door and called out.

"We're up here, Freda, just come up." Kezia peered down the stairs from around the bedroom door. "She's in a sorry state, and there's no way this was a fall. I think I should fetch the constable."

"Well, I'm no fan of the law, so let me see what's what first."

Freda drew in her breath sharply, as she saw the damage to Ellen's face. "Eh, lass, you've taken a right beating, haven't you? Do you want us to call the constable?"

Ellen was adamant. "No, it looks worse than it is. I'll be fine. I'm just worried about the baby; it's two months early."

"Well, I've known them to survive that early, so don't despair just yet. A seven-month child often fares better than one born at eight months. It doesn't make sense, but I've seen it happen many a time."

Next door at the inn, Betsey and Norman were having a nice time. Mal could see they were traumatised at what they had seen and heard, and he put as much time to them as he could, even though there were a million and one jobs demanding his attention. His first task was to make sure they were fed, and he offered them both a bowl of thick creamy porridge. Norman's eyes lit up, and he nodded his head happily, but Betsey said nothing.

"Don't you want some porridge, Betsey? There's plenty."

"Well, Gypsy Jane cooked me a fried egg on bread, so I shouldn't be greedy. Dad says children don't need to eat much."

"I see, well do you think you could eat a bowl of porridge, or are you full up?"

"No sir, I'm not full, but Norman needs it more than me because he's not had any breakfast."

"That's very noble of you, Betsey, but you've both had a nasty shock, and I think you would benefit from a little more food. Now, see how you get on with that."

Mal placed a big bowl of porridge in front of each child and trickled some runny honey on top. Norman plunged his spoon in eagerly, and soon the plates were clean.

"Well done, now, if you follow me, I'll find some of Silas and Ned's old toys, and you can play in the parlour while I get on with a few jobs. Is that all right with you?"

"Yes, Uncle Mal, we'd like that, thank you."

"Excellent, and if you're good, I'll read you both a story later on."

When Kezia came home at lunchtime, she discovered the two children, content with full bellies, fast asleep on her bed.

"Goodness, I didn't expect them to be asleep, Mal; what have you done to them?"

"No, I didn't expect them to fall asleep either, but they've had plenty to eat, and I sat on the bed reading them a couple of stories, and before I knew it, they were fast asleep. I don't think they got much sleep last night, so it's probably best to let them rest. How are things next door?"

"Not good at all. To be honest, I think the old woman is a bit out of her depth, for all she's an expert at delivering babies. She seems to think the baby's lying around the wrong way. I suppose it wasn't ready to be born yet, and the beating's brought things on. I'll just reheat some of that stew I made yesterday and take them some, but I think we should send for the doctor."

"And who do you think will pay for that, then?"

She sighed. "I know; I'd better see if Adam will put his hand in his pocket."

Kezia took the warm stew to her neighbour's house, and the old woman ate it hungrily, but Ellen refused.

"That was delicious, my dear. I must say you make a tasty stew. Are you sure you won't just try a few mouthfuls, Ellen? It would give you strength, and I think you'll need it. This is not an easy birth."

"Freda, I don't want you to think I'm doubting your skills, but do you think we should fetch the doctor to see Ellen? This has been going on for hours, and with it being her tenth child, I would have expected it to be born by now. Especially as it's so early; it's likely to be small."

The gypsy took her time before answering thoughtfully. "I'm not keen on doctors, myself, but I must admit this is not going well, and I would have expected the child to be born by now. There's no sign of the head, and the poor lass is tiring. If you want to fetch the doctor, I'm not against it."

Ellen grasped her friend's hand. "No, Kezzie, don't, we've no money; I can't pay him."

"I know, but we'll sort something out. I'm going to tell Adam what's happening, and see what he says, but I'm fetching the doctor, anyway."

Ellen would have had more to say on the subject, but a strong contraction took her breath away, as she squeezed the old woman's hand.

Kezzie fetched her coat from next door and told Mal what she was going to do. He told her not to offer to pay the doctor because they could not afford it, but she brushed his objections aside and hurried to the butcher's shop. The shop was empty of customers when she arrived, and as she walked in, she saw Adam standing behind Mrs Chown's daughter, Becky, with his arms around her waist. He was nuzzling her neck and she was not complaining.

"So that's how the land lies, is it, Adam? You truly disgust me. Have you seen the state you left your wife in this morning? Beaten black and blue, she is and probably going to lose the baby, and here you are canoodling with her. You make me sick to my stomach."

"What do you mean? I haven't beaten anyone. You've caught me red-handed here, and I admit Becky and I are a bit more than friends, but I'm only human, and Ellen's not much use to me when she's in the family way. What's wrong with her, anyway?"

"You know full well what's wrong with her. You must think I'm stupid to believe she fell yet again; I don't know why she keeps covering up for you. And you, madam, should be ashamed of yourself. What do you see in him?"

The young woman glared at Kezzie. "Well, all right, you've seen we have feelings for each other, but he gets nothing at home, and we get on well, working together all day. So what, if we give each other a bit of comfort; it's none of your business. Anyway, he couldn't have laid a finger on his wife last night, because he stayed here with me."

"Rubbish, you're one as bad as the other, and I don't believe a word you say; you deserve each other. Anyway, Ellen is having the baby, and it's not going well. I think we should send for the doctor, otherwise, I think we might lose them both."

"She'll be fine; good heavens, she's had enough practice. This will be her tenth child, so if she doesn't know what to do by now, it's a bad job."

"Are you going to pay for a doctor, or not?"

"No, I'm not. You're fussing over nothing. Tell her I'll come straight home after work today to see how she is and see the new baby."

"You may not have a wife by then."

Kezia turned angrily on her heel and stormed out of the shop. She hurried to the other end of the village, where Dr Abernethy resided in a large brick-built house. The doctor was a middle-aged man, who had moved south from Scotland. His wife suffered from asthma and bronchitis, and he thought the warmer climate of Devon might benefit her, and it certainly seemed to have been the case. With the move, he had intended to reduce his workload; but with no other doctor in the village, he was often called upon. He was a kindly man, and though he charged for his services, he was known to treat the poorest for free if he felt it was necessary.

As Kezia raised the shiny brass door knocker, she hoped the doctor would take pity on Ellen, for she knew Mal would be cross with her if she paid him, especially with the amount of money Adam spent at the inn. After a few minutes, she was debating whether to knock again, when she heard someone approaching, and a young maid opened the door. Kezia explained her business and asked if she might have a word with the doctor. The maid went to find out, then bade Kezia come in, and showed her to the drawing room.

The room had a thick red carpet on the floor and was comfortably furnished, with stylish chairs and sofas scattered with cushions. The doctor was sitting at his desk, and he peered over his spectacles and smiled at the woman standing before him.

"Hello, you're Mrs Carter from the inn, I believe? How may I be of assistance?"

Kezia observed the man seated in front of her. Although probably only in his fifties, his abundant hair was snow-white and worn rather longer than one would expect in a man of his age. He had a kindly face with bright blue eyes, and he saw she was nervous. He rose to his feet.

"Please, come and sit down, and tell me what the trouble is. Are you unwell?"

"Oh, no, sir, thank you. I'm not here for myself, it's my neighbour, Mrs Lovering. She's having a baby, although it's not due for another couple of months. She's ... well, she had a bit of a fall yesterday, and I think that's brought her pains on. Anyway, Gypsy Freda is with her, and she's delivered a lot of babies with no trouble, but she's worried about this one. It's Ellen's tenth child you see, and usually, it gets easier, but this time she doesn't seem to be making any progress at all, and she's been in labour for hours."

"I see, and you would like me to come and see the lady? Is she agreeable to that?"

"Yes, I'd be grateful if you could come as soon as possible, sir, but no, to tell you the truth, Ellen did not want me to fetch you, as she has no money. I know you'll need paying, sir, and rightly so, but if you could just come and help her, I'll organise a collection later at the inn. I promise I'll see to it that you get your money, even if I have to pay it myself; I just don't have it now."

"Well, we'll worry about that later. If you just give me a few minutes to collect what I need, I'll accompany you. Where is the lady's husband?"

"He's at work in Mrs Chown's butcher's shop, sir. I've told him the situation, but he thinks I'm making a fuss over nothing." She looked down at her feet, embarrassed. "It's not for me to say, sir, but he's not much of a husband in my opinion."

They hurried back through the village, and when the doctor entered the bedroom, the gypsy eyed him with mistrust but seemed relieved. He nodded to her and asked what she thought was the problem.

"To be honest, I'm not sure, sir; I've delivered a lot of babies, but this lass doesn't seem to be getting anywhere. I'm beginning to wonder if the afterbirth is coming before the baby; there's no sign of the head, anyway, and as you can see for yourself, the poor girl has taken quite a beating, though she insists she fell down the stairs. I wonder if she has internal injuries, that are causing the problems."

The doctor glanced at the gypsy with respect, for he knew the travellers found it difficult to trust anyone in authority.

"Thank you, ma'am. Let me take a look, then."

He leaned over his patient and picked up her clammy hand. "Hello, Mrs Lovering; I hear you're making hard work of this; do you feel the need to push, yet?"

The sweat was running off Ellen's brow, and her face was pale. She spoke wearily.

"No, sir, I don't seem to be getting anywhere, and the last two were born within a couple of hours. I don't know what's wrong, but I don't feel right at all. They shouldn't have fetched you, though. I've no money to pay you."

"Don't worry about that; let's just get this child born, and you feeling better." He felt the woman's weak pulse. "Do you mind if I examine you?" She shook her head.

Gently, he lifted her nightdress, noting that for a seven-month pregnancy, her abdomen was not as large as it should be. When he had finished his examination, he took Gypsy Freda and Kezia to one side.

"I'm afraid it's as you feared, ma'am. I think the afterbirth is stopping the child from being born. This is a serious situation, and we'll be lucky to save either of them. I'm going to give her an internal examination, to see if I can change the position of things, but to be honest, I'm not too hopeful."

When Adam arrived home from work just after six o'clock, the doctor was coming down the stairs. He looked angrily at Kezia and the old gypsy. "I told you not to fetch a doctor; who's going to pay him? What's she had, anyway?"

The doctor gave him an icy look. Your wife had a baby boy, sir, but he was stillborn. Your wife too has succumbed to the injuries, which I understand you inflicted upon her; I'm just on my way to fetch the constable to have you arrested."

"Now, just a minute; this is nothing to do with me. I can't help it if she's clumsy, and is always falling about. You ask the children, and they'll tell you, I never touched her. Anyway, I didn't come home last night. You might not approve, but I spent the night with Becky Chown."

"If that's the case, it's hardly something to be proud of, is it? I don't believe you, anyway. The Parish Constable will be here shortly. Go and admire your handiwork."

The doctor pushed past the man angrily, with Kezia and Freda on his heels. Kezia spat in Adam's face as she passed, and the old gypsy wagged her finger at him.

"You're an evil, wicked man. I know you're responsible for this, and how you mistreat your children, although they will not tell on you. It doesn't matter, because you'll get your comeuppance, mister! I curse you! From this day until your last breath, your life will be ruined; you'll never prosper. I curse your black, evil heart."

Adam pushed her impatiently to one side and ran up the stairs. However, even he was shocked when he entered the bedroom and saw the blood-soaked palliasse, and the large puddle on the floor. His wife's now peaceful face was ashen. Kezia had brushed her hair, and made her tidy, and in her arms lay a small, wrinkled child. A bunch of white heather lay on the pillow beside Ellen's head.

CHAPTER 10

Adam leaned over his late wife and gently pushed a damp curl from her forehead. He planted a kiss on her cold lips, and tears ran down his face.

"I'm so sorry, Ellen; you didn't deserve this. I know I've not done right by you, but I couldn't cope when the children kept dying one after the other. I felt so useless that I couldn't provide enough for them, and I could only forget by getting drunk." He paused and wiped his sleeve across his nose. "I know it was just as awful for you, and I made matters worse. I don't know what I'm going to do without you. It's too late to tell you now, but I did love you."

Tiredly, he pulled the sheet up over her face, and that of the tiny baby, and left the room, shutting the door quietly behind him. He went to the other bedroom and stretched out on the palliasse where Betsey and Norman usually slept, but he lay awake long into the night, knowing he daren't seek a drink, however much he might need one.

The next morning, he went to The Red Lion and found Mal and Kezia in the kitchen. They were busy getting ready for the day ahead and were surprised to see him so early in the day.

"Hello, Adam; I'm so sorry about Ellen and the child." Mal held out his hand, and Adam shook it gratefully.

"Thanks, Mal; I'm not proud of my hand in it; I thought she'd be all right. I'm sorry to intrude, but I wondered if you could keep Betsey and Norman until after the funeral. I don't want them coming back to the cottage while Ellen's body's still there, and I've no one else to ask."

Mal glanced anxiously at his wife, and Kezia glared at the man in front of her. "Well, we will, but I'm not doing it for you, Adam, because you don't deserve our help after the way you treated your wife. I'm doing it for Ellen and the children. Anyway, I think they're awake; so do you want to tell them about their mother? They have to know."

"Yes, I know they do." The man sighed deeply. "I'm not good at these things; would you mind telling them with me, Kezzie? I know it's a lot to ask."

Kezia nodded her head. "Yes, come through to the sitting room and I'll call them."

Betsey and Norman were surprised to see their father and looked at him apprehensively. They were uneasy when he sat them one on each knee.

"I'm sorry to tell you, but your mother died yesterday. She's gone to heaven with your new little brother. It'll be just the three of us from now on, but I'm sure we'll manage somehow."

Norman did not understand, but Betsey was horrified.

"Oh no, not Mum. What will we do without her?" Tears poured down her cheeks, and she sobbed bitterly. Norman, upset by his sister's reaction, joined in.

Kezia took charge. "Now, it will be all right. You and Norman are going to stay here with Uncle Mal and me for a few days, and then your dad will sort something out." This made Betsey cry all the harder.

"Kezzie, could I just have a couple of minutes alone with Betsey and Norman, please?"

"Yes, of course, I'll be in the kitchen."

As soon as Kezia was out of the room, Adam put his children down and knelt before them. "I need you to promise me you will not say anything about the argument I had with your mother a couple of nights ago. Just to be clear, I stayed at the butcher's shop that night, and if you know what's good for you, you'll say I never came home. It's important. Do you understand?"

The children stood there silently, and Adam shook Betsey by the shoulders.

"Do you understand, Betsey? If you say I hit your mother, I'll be sent to jail, and I don't know what will happen to you two. I can tell you now, that if you think life's hard at the moment, then you have a lot to learn. I spent years living on the streets, begging for my next meal, winter and summer alike, and I wouldn't wish it on my worst enemy. You do as I say, and I'll do my best to look after you; it won't be easy, though."

Slowly, the little girl, and then her brother, nodded.

"Right, that's good."

Adam held them to him for a few moments, then got to his feet, and re-joined Mal in the kitchen. Ned and Silas were eating their breakfast, and he gestured with his head for Mal to follow him outside.

"Thank you for taking care of them, Mal. I'm going to tell Mrs Chown what's happened, and then see the vicar about the funeral. I'll have to make a coffin because I've no money to buy one."

"Oh, Adam, you get paid a decent wage at the butcher's shop; do you have nothing put by?"

"No, nothing, I drink it all away as soon as I get it; you know that. This is all my fault, but I can't leave the liquor alone; I wish I could. I'm not proud of myself, Mal. Anyway, I'll go and tell Barney. At least he's in paid work, but I don't know what's going to happen to Betsey and Norman. I have to work, so they'll have to fend for themselves."

"I wish I could offer to take them for you, Adam. I know Kezia wants to, but the trouble is we have money worries of our own. The roof of the inn's in a terrible state of repair, and it has to be replaced. I think the building's over five hundred years old, and I reckon it's still the original roof. It's been repaired many times over the years, but it won't do this time. I've been to the bank and they've agreed to lend me the money because the inn has a decent turnover, but the repayments are going to cripple us for many a year to come, and we'll have to watch every penny. Are there no relatives that could help with Betsey and Norman?"

"No, there's no one, since Ellen's mother died a few months back, and my brother lives miles away. He wouldn't want to know, anyway; he has enough mouths to feed as it is. I ran away when I was seven because it was better than being beaten by my father every day. It's all right, Mal; they're not your worry, but if you can just keep them for a few days, I'll be grateful."

Leaving Mal, Adam hurried to the butcher's shop and told Mrs Chown what had happened. She was, of course, sorry to hear of his loss, and agreed he could take the morning off to make the necessary arrangements. From behind her mother, Becky gave him a wide grin, and it was clear she thought Ellen's demise would leave the way clear for their relationship to progress. However, after giving her the briefest of smiles, and a knowing look, he left the shop without saying another word, and set off to break the news to his eldest son.

Barney stood silently, seemingly unable to take in the news of his mother's death. Jasper shook Adam by the hand, extended his condolences, and agreed that Barney could take a few hours off to attend the funeral. Suddenly, Barney glared at his father, angrily.

"This was all your fault, wasn't it? I'll bet you had a hand in it. Did you beat her, again?"

"Of course not. I've never beaten your mother."

Barney snorted. "Oh, not much. I've lost count of how many hidings you've dished out when you're drunk, which is most of the time."

Adam advanced threateningly, but Jasper laid a hand on his arm and stood between father and son. "Now, that's enough, lad; I know you're upset, but that's no way to talk to your father."

Barney glowered at his father. "I'm not big enough to deal with you yet, but I will be one day, and then you'd better watch out because I'll be coming for you. You'd better not lay a finger on Betsey and Norman."

Looking furious, Adam turned away. "I'm leaving now, Barney, because I know you're upset, but I suggest you have a civil tongue in your head when I next see you."

A couple of days later, Adam received a visit from Andrew Wilson, the Parish Constable. Mr Wilson, a wealthy local landowner, was a stern and taciturn old gentleman, strictly teetotal, and a regular churchgoer. His best friend was the magistrate in Barnstaple; and between them, they were determined to bring law and order to the area. He had disapproved of Adam Lovering for a long time and was delighted to think he might finally be able to bring him to book.

He rapped loudly on the door of the cottage, and Adam swore loudly, having just sat down to eat some bread and cheese. He was not having the best of mornings. With Ellen's untimely death he had missed his nightly tipple, and now, stone-cold sober for the first time in quite a while, he was dismayed to see how badly his hands were shaking, and he felt terrible. He opened the door and was disturbed to see the constable standing there.

"Hello, Mr Wilson; what can I do for you?"

"I need a word please, Mr Lovering."

"Well, it's not convenient just now; surely you must have heard I've lost my wife and baby son."

"Yes sir, I am aware of that, and I'm sorry, but I'm told you may have had a hand in bringing about that sad event."

"You do know she died in childbirth?"

"Yes, sir, but Dr Abernethy believes Mrs Lovering had been beaten, and it was that beating which probably caused internal damage, and no doubt brought on the premature birth, which ended so tragically. Mr Billery, the school teacher, also tells me that young Betsey, too, recently suffered a black eye and a sprained ankle. What do you have to say for yourself?"

"It's true Betsey tripped and fell, a week or two ago, and had the injuries you describe; ask the child yourself. As for my wife, it's no secret I've been spending time with Becky Chown recently, and that's where I spent the night before my wife's death. You can ask Becky; she'll corroborate my story. I never came home that night. Ask the children too, if you don't believe me. It may not be what you want to hear, but it does put me in the clear. As for my wife, she always suffered from dizzy spells when she was heavily pregnant, so I expect she took a tumble, maybe even down the stairs. I don't know; as I say, I wasn't here."

The constable surveyed the man before him in disgust. "I'll do that, sir, and you'd better hope they back up your story, for a story, I fully believe it to be. It seems a strange coincidence, that both your wife and daughter are given to so many accidents. I'll have you know, I intend to do my utmost, to put you behind bars, where you belong."

Adam got to his feet angrily. "Well, you do your damnedest, but you'll find no evidence. Now, push off, and let me eat my dinner in peace."

Ignoring the red-faced, belligerent man, Adam determinedly bit off a piece of cheese and tore his crust into pieces.

CHAPTER 11

It was warm and sunny when Ellen Lovering and her baby son were laid to rest in the Hartford churchyard at eleven o'clock on the twenty-fifth day of September, eighteen hundred and twenty. The date coincided with her thirty-seventh birthday, though few knew of it. There were many mourners at the funeral, for she had been a well-liked woman, always ready with a wide smile and a kind word. The coffin, hastily put together by Adam, with a little help from Mal, was rough and ready but was not an uncommon sight for the times. There being no wake, folk quietly dispersed after the ceremony and made their way home.

Kezia had asked her sister, Mary, to mind Ned and Silas, and Betsey and Norman, so that both she and Mal could attend the funeral. As there were no relatives, other than Adam and Barney, they sat in the front pew and accompanied the Lovering family on their way back to the inn.

"You and Barney are welcome to join us for a bit of dinner, if you like, Adam?"

Adam glanced at his eldest son, who was struggling to hold back his tears. "That's kind of you, thank you, Mal. Barney, I expect you'd like to see Betsey and Norman before you go back to the mill?"

"Aye, I would. Thank you, Uncle Mal."

"Good, that's settled then. Have you sorted out what's going to happen to the little ones when you go to work, tomorrow?"

Kezia looked daggers at her husband, but Mal was determined to make his neighbour take responsibility.

"Well, I can't afford to pay anyone to mind them, so Betsey will have to stop going to school, and stay at home and keep an eye on Norman. She's going on seven, and she's quite capable, so I think it will work out all right. If she has a problem, she can always come and find me in the shop; it's not like I'll be miles away."

"Dad, I could come back home to live, and look after them if you like?"

"No, Barney, you have a well-paid, live-in position, and I don't want you to lose it. We need your wage too, and at least Jasper feeds you well. I can see you're starting to fill out since you've been living there, and I'm glad to see it, though I know we don't always see eye to eye."

Kezia opened her mouth to say something, but seeing Mal frowning at her, decided to keep quiet.

Mr Wilson did his utmost to get the children to tell him what happened on the night before their mother's death, but Betsey stuck steadfastly to her story, and Norman refused to say anything at all. Becky showed no shame in admitting she had allowed Adam to spend the night with her, though her mother was disgusted. Therefore, with no hard evidence, the constable had no choice but to give up on the case, annoyed though he was.

For the first few days following their return home, Adam made a real effort to care for his children. He provided the most basic of food, but they were used to that anyway, and he made sure there was enough firewood to last the day before he left for work.

Although not yet seven, Betsey was a capable child who had worked closely with her mother. She was able to make porridge, cut a slice of bread from a loaf, and fry an egg, and if their diet was much the same every day, at least she and Norman did not starve. She knew how important it was not to let the fire go out, and she insisted Norman help her in fetching logs from the woodshed.

Norman missed his mother, and Betsey took on a maternal role far beyond her years, drying his tears, and cuddling her little brother on her lap, telling him the same stories, that just a short while ago, her mother had told to both of them. She tried hard to think of all the things her mother used to do and keep the house and themselves clean. One day, she heated some water in a pan on the stove, used it to wash Norman and herself, and then cleaned the house. Norman suffered her attention but was not pleased by it, though she threatened him with no dinner if he did not co-operate. Heartened with her morning's work, she heated more water in the afternoon and decided she would wash some of the dirty clothes that were piling up in the corner. However, this time, the pan was a little heavier, and some of the hot water splashed onto her arm, making her scream. The pan of water went all over the floor, and she hastily ran to the jug of cold water on the table and plunged her arm into it. When she eventually withdrew it, she was dismayed to see large blisters, and sat on the floor and cried. This time, it was Norman who comforted his big sister.

Although Mr Billery had heard from others why Betsey was not at school, Adam had not seen fit to tell the schoolmaster himself. At the end of the first week, he went to see Adam in the butcher's shop to find out what was happening. Adam seemed surprised by his visit, and not a little displeased.

"Betsey doesn't need any more schooling, thank you, sir. In any case, she has to stay at home and mind her little brother because you don't take children until they're five, and he's only three."

"Don't you think she's too young to care for another child? She's only six, herself."

"Aye, but she'll soon be seven, and many are down the mines by that age, so she's luckier than some. She's a smart maid and she's coping well. There's nothing I can do about it anyway; if I don't work we'll all starve. You don't need to worry, though, we're managing just fine."

"Well, I'm pleased to hear that, and you're right, I don't usually take children until they are five, but in this case, I think it would be beneficial if both Betsey and Norman came to school together. Would you allow that?"

Adam scratched his head. "Well, I suppose that would be all right. Would you feed them at dinnertime?"

The master sighed. "Well, they'll get a cup of milk mid-morning, and I suppose I could find them a small meal. If I do that, will you let them come?"

"Aye, I can't see why not. All right; they'll be there on Monday."

When Adam went home from work that evening and relayed the news to the children, Betsey was overjoyed.

"Oh, thank you, Dad. I'm so pleased we can go to school; you'll like it, Norman, and we get a mug of creamy milk every morning."

Norman seemed doubtful, but at the mention of the milk, he brightened up.

"You'll still have to do some chores around the house when you get home, mind, and you shouldn't need any more to eat because the teacher is going to feed you at dinner time, so make sure you eat all you can."

"Oh aye, Dad, we'll do that all right."

"Off to bed now then. I've stayed in with you all week, but I need a drink tonight. You go to bed and get to sleep. I'll only be next door with Uncle Mal anyway, so I'm not far away."

When Adam appeared at the inn, Kezia was serving at the counter and she looked at him in surprise.

"Why, Adam what are you doing here? Who's with the children?"

"They're fine, Kezzie. I've put them to bed, and they know where I am. Good heavens, I've not had a drink all week, surely I've earned a little refreshment, now it's Friday."

"You shouldn't leave them at night, Adam; you know you shouldn't. I'll bet they're frightened alone there in the dark."

"Rubbish. Children are spoilt these days. My goodness, I've had to fend for myself since I was seven, and I ran away from home. If my father wasn't beating me, he was interfering with me, so I reckoned it would be better if I left. I've never regretted it, though I spent years begging or stealing enough to keep body and soul together. I've passed many a frosty night sleeping under a hedge, or in a barn. Betsey and Norman are lucky with their lot, compared to my childhood."

"I'm sorry to hear that, Adam. It doesn't make it right, though, does it? What would Ellen think?"

Adam scowled angrily. "Are you going to stop your nagging woman, and serve me, or shall I go to The Three Pigeons? If you don't want my business, you have only to say."

"I'll see to this, Kezzie. You serve John over there, look. What can I get for you, Adam?"

Grinning widely now, Adam reached into his pocket for his wages, "I'll have a pint of your best ale, please Mal, and I'd like to buy you a pint too if you'll join me."

No, thank you all the same, Adam. I'll serve you, but it doesn't mean I approve of you being here."

On Monday morning, Betsey was awake early, because she was excited about returning to school. Her father left for work, telling her to find something for breakfast for Norman and herself, and then get off to school. She woke Norman, and cut them both a slice of bread and dripping; then she fetched some logs from the woodshed, and added them to the range, hoping the fire would not be out by the time she got home. Having fed the chickens, she soaked a cloth under the pump, and to Norman's disgust, insisted he let her wash his face and hands, which were rather grimy.

She glanced down in dismay at her filthy dress and noticed Norman's clothes were no cleaner. They only possessed a couple of changes of clothes each, and none had been washed since her mother passed away. She checked in the cupboard, but there were no clean clothes left. Her arm was still sore with blisters; the result of her last attempt to do some washing, and she couldn't bear to put it into warm water yet. She was distressed at their appearance but knew there was nothing she could do about it. Sighing deeply, she took Norman's hand and led him outside to meet up with Ned and Silas for the journey to school.

On the way, they were joined by several other children, and one or two jeered at Betsey and Norman as they were so grubby. With her head down, she tried to ignore them, as a couple of malicious boys held their noses, and pretended not to know what the awful smell was. Ned was furious, and within minutes, he and Silas were embroiled in a fight as they defended their neighbours. The result of this fracas was that the children were late for school. To Ned's delight, George Martin suffered a heavy nosebleed; the result of a lucky punch.

Mr Billery was most annoyed that so many children were late for school, and having dealt with George's nosebleed, kept his class standing until someone would tell him what had happened. Betsey had warned Norman to say nothing, so having obtained no information from his class, he went next door to Miss Elworthy's class. Receiving a stony silence there, too, the master made them all write lines instead of going out to play mid-morning.

Although he was unaware that the state of Betsey and Norman's clothes was the reason for the trouble, earlier in the day, he was concerned about their appearance, and more particularly, the condition of Betsey's arm. The blisters had burst and appeared to be infected. He asked Miss Elworthy to help him bathe the child's arm, apply a salve, and bandage it up.

"Do you and Norman have any clean clothes for tomorrow, Betsey? These are a little dirty."

"Yes, sir; I know. That's how I burnt my arm. I heated some water on the stove to wash our clothes, but then I spilt it over myself, and now it's too sore to put in the water."

"Not to worry then, Betsey. I think we have a few spare clothes here somewhere. If you and Norman put them on, Miss Elworthy has kindly offered to wash the ones you're wearing."

"Thank you, sir, I know my mother would hate to see us looking so dirty, but my father has to work, so he doesn't have time to do the washing."

"No, I quite understand, Betsey. Not to worry, it's nothing that a little soap and water will not put right."

CHAPTER 12

Doctor Abernethy groaned as the hollow sound of the door knocker reverberated loudly through the house. His wife, Janet, was also awakened by the noise.

"Och, what now, Hamish. You never get any peace."

"I know, love; you go back to sleep; I'll deal with this, whatever it is."

Luckily, dawn was breaking, and there was just enough light to see his way down the stairs without lighting a candle.

"All right, all right, I'm coming. Och, do stop all that noise. There are people trying to sleep."

He opened the door and recognised a man he knew to be a footman from the Manor House.

"Hello, Jim, what's wrong?"

"Hello, doctor, I'm so sorry to wake you at this early hour, but I've been sent by Lord Fellwood to ask you to come urgently to see his wife. Lady Helena is poorly, and he begs you to come straight away."

"Very well, come in and wait while I get dressed." The doctor then hesitated and changed his mind. "Actually, no, you go on ahead, and I'll ride over, then I can get home easily. It won't take me long to harness my horse."

"Begging your pardon, sir, but his Lordship sent me with the pony and trap, so you could come straight away.

The Mistress is in a bad way, and I'll bring you home in due course."

Within ten minutes they were on their way, and Lord Fellwood himself came down the front steps of the grand mansion. He shook the doctor by the hand.

"Thank you for coming so quickly, Hamish; I don't like calling you out at this hour, but to be honest, I fear the worst. As you know, Helena has been ailing for weeks, and she had another funny turn last night."

"Come on then, take me to her, please."

The doctor entered the dimly lit bedroom and could hear his patient gasping for breath. He sat beside her and felt her pulse, checking her forehead for a fever at the same time. He asked the maid to bring the lamp closer so that he could have a better look. He was not surprised to see the poor lady's lips were tinged with blue, and her face, pale and clammy.

"How long has she been like this?"

Lord Fellwood glanced at the nursemaid for an answer. "Speak up, lass, tell the doctor what he wants to know."

"Well, she took a little broth for her tea, sir, and seemed to settle quite well, but then she awoke an hour or two ago feeling breathless. She complained of severe pains in her chest and left arm, and so I roused his Lordship."

"I see, well those are all signs of another heart attack, I'm afraid, and I'm sure that's what we're dealing with. As you know, she's been suffering from heart problems for some time so this is not unexpected. I'm afraid there's little I can do to help, but I'll sit by her, and monitor the situation. I'm afraid you must prepare yourself for the worst, my Lord."

For the next few hours, Ephraim Fellwood sat by his wife's bedside, holding her hand and talking to her, but she never regained consciousness. By breakfast time, Lady Helena had passed away, and Lord Fellwood was grief-stricken. Although their marriage had been arranged, and they had barely met before taking their vows, it had been a happy relationship, and they genuinely loved each other. The doctor put a kindly arm around the man, as tears ran down his cheeks.

"Come on, sir; there's nothing more we can do for the poor lady. Come away, and let the nurse do what needs to be done."

"Thank you so much for coming, doctor; I'm grateful."

"Nonsense; I just wish there was something more I could have done to help."

"Just being here was a help; now, come and have some breakfast, though I don't think I can face any."

"Thank you, sir; but I'll decline your kind offer as I promised to call on another patient in the village at nine o'clock, and it's nearly that now. My wife will be wondering where I've got to. How old was your wife, sir?"

"She was forty-five, and we would have been married twenty-eight years, tomorrow. She was only a young girl of seventeen when we met, and I couldn't have wished for a better wife."

"Oh, dear; my condolences, sir. At least you've had a number of years together. Sadly, many of my patients are not even half the age of your wife, when they pass away."

Lord Fellwood sighed deeply. "No, I know. We're fortunate, and there are a lot worse off than us. It doesn't seem to help at a time like this, though."

When he entered the breakfast room, Lord Fellwood found his family already seated around the table. Joshua and Thomas raised their eyes anxiously, and the newly widowed man gave an almost imperceptible shake of his head. Their heads dropped in dismay. Trying to keep his voice steady, and his emotions under control, Ephraim Fellwood gave his children the sad news. George and Margery immediately began to cry, and Thomas took Margery onto his knee and tried to comfort her. Lord Fellwood went to his youngest son and put his hands on his shoulders.

"Now, George; I know it's difficult, but this is the time to show you're nearly a man. Your mother would not want to see you crying. She had a happy life, and at least she's no longer suffering." Tears were running down his own cheeks. "I want you all to be brave for me and support each other. That's important at a time like this. Now, I have the arrangements to see to, so I'll talk to you all again, later."

As their father strode from the room, Joshua put his arm around George and tried to comfort him, whilst Thomas was busily drying Margery's tears.

"Joshua, I think it would be beneficial to take these two riding this morning; can you spare the time?"

"I'm not sure if that would be seen as appropriate, Thomas. Do you think it would be all right?"

"Well, I can't see any harm in it, and I think it would help to distract them for a couple of hours. I'm sure Mama would agree."

"Yes, all right. I'll just check with father, that he doesn't mind."

Although subdued, the ride in the fresh air did both the younger children a world of good. It was, in fact, the first time all four siblings had ridden together, and although they felt guilty, they all enjoyed it. As they neared the village, Thomas spotted Betsey walking along with her little brother, Norman, and he stopped to speak to her. Telling Joshua, that he would only be a few minutes, he dismounted and waited for the children to reach him.

"Hello, Betsey, how are you? Are your hands and knees better? Oh yes, I see they are, but what's happened to your arm? Why is it bandaged?"

"Oh, I spilt some hot water on it, sir, and I have some big blisters. My teacher, Mr Billery, put a bandage on it to keep it clean."

"My goodness, you're always in the wars, Betsey. Surely, you should not have been handling hot water at your age? What was your mother thinking of?"

Noticing the frown that passed over the child's face, and the tears glistening in her eyes, Thomas realised he had said the wrong thing.

He knelt in front of Betsey and Norman. "I'm sorry, Betsey; what is it?"

"Our mum died, sir. I have to do everything around the house now, and look after Norman."

"Oh, Betsey, I'm so sorry. I know exactly how you feel because our mother died just this morning, and we're out for a ride to help take our minds off it. Mind you, at least we have servants to wait on us, so we are not nearly as badly off as you. Would you like to earn two pennies to buy some sweets from the shop?"

"Yes, sir, I'd love to earn tuppence, but I won't spend it on sweets; I'll buy a pasty each for me and Norman; we're always hungry."

"That sounds like an excellent idea, Betsey. All I want you to do, is tell Gypsy Jane that I'm going for another ride later, and I'll be at the old castle ruins at sunset; can you do that?"

"Aye sir, of course. Gypsy Freda won't like it, though."

"Well, don't tell her then. Can this be our little secret?"

Betsey and Norman nodded, and Thomas handed over three pennies.

"There you are, one extra penny for keeping a secret; don't let me down now."

As Thomas remounted his horse, Joshua gave him a puzzled look.

"What was that all about?"

"Oh, it's just a little girl that I've come to know in the village. She took a nasty fall the other day, and I gave her a ride on my horse to cheer her up. It's so sad; her mother died recently as well, and she has to care for her little brother and do everything in the house. I don't know how old she is, but she's so small and skinny."

At this point, Margery joined in. "She's six like me. We went to the gypsy camp with her, Joshua, and we played with some puppies. I'm going to have one of them when they're big enough to leave their mother. Can we get it soon, Thomas?"

Joshua was a little disapproving, but Thomas reassured him. "It's all right, it was where Betsey was headed that day so I just gave her a ride there. Nothing to worry about, and I thought a puppy would take Margery's mind off Mama's illness. It will be even more timely now, and yes, Margery, I should think we can have the puppy soon."

CHAPTER 13

When they returned to Hartford Manor, Joshua went in search of his father to help with the funeral arrangements, and Thomas escorted Margery and George to the schoolroom. He advised their governess they should not be troubled with lessons on such a sad and difficult day and suggested she find a pastime they would enjoy. Miss White was a kind young lady, and she agreed with him.

Thomas couldn't wait for the time to pass until he could ride to the castle; a favourite spot for many locals. Little was known of its origins, though it was thought to have been built around the time of William the Conqueror. It had fallen into disrepair in the fourteenth century, and now little remained apart from the keep and a few crumbling walls. A romantic spot, situated high up on a hillside, the ruin provided an excellent viewpoint of the stunning countryside, and it was not difficult to understand why the site had been chosen, for any approaching enemies would be seen from miles away.

Thomas was feeling nervous as he set off on his horse, Jupiter, a chestnut stallion. It was a sunny day, and as he rode along the lanes and tracks, he admired the scenery. Some of the leaves on the trees were just beginning to turn red and golden, providing proof that autumn was on the way. He surveyed a couple of fields where the corn had been harvested, and now lay bare with only the stubble remaining. Several ravens were busily collecting the few grains left behind, and not gleaned by the village poor. The butterflies in his stomach increased as he came into sight of the old building. He wondered if Jane would turn up, and if she did, what he would say to her.

It was just before sunset, as he galloped up the hill to the ruins. Seeing no one, he settled down to wait, and after a few minutes, he became aware of someone behind him.

"Oh, Jane, you made me jump. I'm so glad you came; I wondered if you would."

"Well, it wasn't easy, because no one in our camp would approve of me meeting you. I had to wait for an opportunity to sneak off unseen."

"Yes, it was a bit the same for me, but I was able to say I was going for another ride. How are you?"

"I'm fine, thank you. I hear your mother passed away during the night; is that right?"

A sad frown flitted over the young man's handsome face. "Yes, I'm afraid so; she'd been poorly for a long time, and the doctor thinks she had heart trouble. She was only forty-five, so not that old."

"I see, I'm so sorry. I expect your little sister will miss her Mama."

"Yes, my brother, Joshua, and I, took Margery and my other brother, George, riding this morning to take their minds off their loss, and I think it did them good. That was when I saw Betsey and asked her to bring you a message."

"Yes, it was Betsey who told me about your mother."

"Where's that whimpering noise coming from?"

Jane reached behind her and drew forward a sack. Opening it carefully, she lifted out a small black and white puppy.

"These are ready to leave their mother now, and I thought it might take Lady Margery's mind off her loss."

Thomas took the tiny creature in his arms and stroked it.

"Oh, he's lovely, isn't he? Is it a he?"

"Yes, it is a male; they're less trouble. No litters of puppies to worry about then. He doesn't like it in the sack, but I thought it was the easiest way for you to carry him on horseback. Is that all right?"

"Yes, perfect; thank you so much. This is just what Margery needs. She'll be thrilled to bits. Can I put him down, or will he run off?"

"He might run back to his mother, so you'd better hang on to him until you put him in the sack."

"How much do I owe you?"

"Oh, that's all right. It can be my gift to the little girl. Shall we sit down?"

Thomas nodded, and they sat in the shelter of the ruins. He reached into his pocket, withdrew a crown and held it out to her.

"I'd rather pay you, Jane. Is that enough? You must have bred them to sell."

"Well, yes, we did, of course, but I'm happy for Margery to have one of them."

"No, I insist. I can afford it, and I'd like you to have it."

Reluctantly, the girl took the money. "Thank you."

"Are you and the gypsies staying long in this area? I mean, you usually keep on the move, don't you?"

"Yes, we don't like being in one place for too long, and we've been here a few weeks now, but Reuben is talking of us staying until spring."

"Who's Reuben?"

"He's our leader, and he decides when we will move on. His mother's poorly at the moment, though, and the site we're camped on is common land, so no one can make us move. We have a stream nearby for water, and it's a sheltered spot so he thinks it's best to stay here for a few months. His mother's old and frail, and unlikely to survive a winter on the move, despite my grandmother's remedies."

"Well, I'm sorry the old lady is ill, of course, but if it means you'll be around for a while, that pleases me. Could we meet again, Jane?"

She studied him intently with her clear brown eyes. "Why would you want to meet with me, again, sir?" I like you, but there's no point, is there?"

"Don't call me sir, Jane." He took her hand in his and turned it over, stroking the hard callouses on her palm, then he raised her hand to his lips and kissed it gently, brushing a curl back from her forehead. She blushed, as his touch sent a thrill through her body. "You're so beautiful, Jane; do you have a sweetheart?"

"No, though Jasper would badly like to court me. He's made no secret of the fact he's looking for a wife, but I can tell you now, I'll never marry him. Poor man, I know he's wealthy, with his own business, but I could never take to him. He seems kind, but he has little to say, and his breath smells. In any case, I'm a gypsy, and I could never leave my folk and settle in one place, so you see, Thomas, there's no point in my seeing you again, either."

"Don't say that, Jane; I can't stop thinking about you. Ever since I first saw you, that day when I was out riding, I've thought of little else. Can we just be friends, while you're in the area? There's no harm in that, surely?"

"You are a persistent man, but yes, all right, I'll meet you here again tomorrow evening, at the same time. It must remain a secret though, for if my folk find out they will not be best pleased, and I don't want anything to happen to you."

"What do you mean?"

"Well, the gypsies don't take kindly to outsiders, and they would not approve of my seeing you. You might find they give you a hiding one fine night to discourage you, and I wouldn't want that to happen."

"What about the puppy? Won't they miss him?"

"I had to tell my granny I was bringing him to you for your sister. She doesn't approve, but she respects my wishes, and I would never lie to her. She'll be pleased with the crown you gave me. That's far more than I would normally expect to get for a puppy. Sometimes it's hard to give them away. No one else will miss the dog. I'd better be going, though."

Thomas reluctantly released her hand. He wanted to kiss her soft lips but was worried he would scare her off. As she ran down the hillside in the ever-deepening darkness, he smiled to himself, pleased that at least she hadn't given him his marching orders.

He gently put the puppy back in the sack and remounted Jupiter. As he picked his way back along the track in the dim twilight, the dog whimpered in fright. As he rode through the village, he passed the cottage where he knew young Betsey lived and wondered if she was all right. He couldn't help but compare her lot in life with that of his little sister, Margery. Both girls were only six, and both had suddenly lost their mothers, but there the similarities ended. Margery lived a privileged life of ease, whereas Betsey was always hungry, and neglected. Sighing to himself, he continued on his way home, knowing there was nothing he could do about the situation, other than be kind to the poor little girl if their paths should cross.

Clutching the three precious pennies in her hand, Betsey pulled Norman along with the other. "Come on, Norman, let's go and see Aunty Kezzie and ask if she'll sell us a pasty each; are you hungry?"

The little boy wiped his runny nose on his sleeve and nodded, a wide smile on his face at the mention of food.

The two children made their way around to the back door of the inn and found it open. They peered inside and found Kezia making bread.

"Hello, you two. Is everything all right?"

"Yes, thank you, Aunty Kezzie, but I just ran an errand for someone, and they gave me three pennies. I wondered if you would sell us a pasty each? I don't know how much they cost, but we're starving."

The woman was shocked at their bedraggled appearance. They didn't look as if they'd been given a wash or a bath, since their mother passed away, and she was horrified to see that they both had lice; the nits hanging in clusters from their hair. Ellen would have been mortified for her children to be so neglected and unloved.

"Oh yes, I think I can help you there, my lovelies. Three pennies is more than enough for a couple of pasties; they're just out of the oven too, so at their best. Just let me put this dough to prove, and then I could give you both a bath before you have your dinner. Would you like that?"

Betsey would not meet her neighbour's gaze. "I'm sorry we're so dirty, Aunty Kezzie; I know we are, but I can't reach the tin bath, or fill it on my own, and Dad says we're fine as we are. Mr Billery gave us some clean clothes a few days ago, but they need washing again now."

"That's all right, Betsey; it's not your fault, and I expect your dad's finding it difficult looking after you two and working all week. Now, if I get a bath ready for you, would you like one?"

Norman was less keen than his sister, but Betsey fixed him with a stern look, and he nodded his agreement. In no time at all, Kezia had lifted the old tin bath from its nail in the washhouse and filled it with water from the three large kettles already boiling on the range.

Betsey was a little anxious as Kezia told them both to strip off their clothes.

"Will anyone come in, Aunty Kezzie? I don't want Ned or Barney to see me with no clothes on."

"No, it's all right, Betsey. They're spending the day with their cousins a few miles away, so they won't be bothering us, and Uncle Mal won't be in until later. Now, I don't know if you realise, but you both have nits. Are your heads itching?"

Norman nodded. "Yes, my head keeps itching, Aunty Kezzie, and it's driving me mad. Please cut my hair off, and get rid of them."

"What about you, Betsey? I needn't cut your hair too short, but if I take off six inches that will get rid of a lot of them, and make the rest easier to find. Your hair is so long it will probably do it good. It will soon grow again, anyway."

Betsey nodded her agreement, so sitting first Norman, and then Betsey, on a kitchen chair, Kezia cut their fine brown hair and told them to step into the bathtub. Once in there, she soaped them all over, telling Betsey to leave her blistered arm out of the water. She then washed their hair, and painstakingly went through it with a fine-tooth comb.

"There, I think that's got most of the little blighters. Nasty little things they are; I'll check your hair again in a couple of days. Now, shall we blow a few bubbles before you get out?"

Kezia soaped her hands and blew through them, making a large bubble which popped suddenly, making Norman blink and laugh. However, she was horrified when tears began to flow down Betsey's cheeks.

"What's wrong, Betsey? Don't you like playing with the bubbles?"

The little girl nodded sadly. "Yes, of course, Aunty Kezzie, I love it; but it's what Mum used to do when she bathed us, and I miss her."

"Oh dear, yes, of course, you do, but I know she wouldn't want you getting upset. Now, I'll just pop next door to your house to see if I can find you some clean clothes, and then I can wash yours. Do you know where they're kept, Betsey?"

"Mum kept our clothes in our bedroom in a box, but there are no clean ones left. I've been thinking I should try to wash them, but I can't find any soap, and I burnt my arm trying to lift the pan of hot water off the stove."

"Well, I'll just see what I can find."

Thinking she must have a word with Adam, Kezia left the two children playing in the bath, and ventured into her neighbour's house, knowing their father would be at work. She was shocked at how dirty the house had become in just the short time since Ellen's death. Betsey had done her best, and at least kept the dishes washed, but there was a pile of dirty clothes in one corner of the kitchen, and the floors were filthy. It was clear that Adam made no effort to help with the chores, and from the large muddy footprints in all the rooms, did not see fit to take off his dirty boots when it was raining. Making her way to the bedroom, she checked in the box Betsey had mentioned, but it was empty. She went back to the kitchen and sifted through the pile of dirty washing, picking out the children's clothes, determined to wash them. However, she left everything of Adam's, deciding he could fend for himself.

Returning to her own kitchen with a big smile on her face, she fetched towels and briskly dried the two children.

"Now, you were right, Betsey and there are no clean clothes. I can find Norman some of Silas's clothes that are too small, but I don't have any girls' clothes because I never had a daughter. Anyway, this dress was in the washing, and it's cleaner than what you had on, so you can wear this one for now, while I wash the others. There, you both look so much nicer, now. Do you feel better?" Both nodded.

"Can we have a pasty now, Aunty Kezzie?"

"Yes, of course, Norman; sit up on the bench there, next to the table and I'll fetch them for you."

In no time at all the two pasties disappeared, as did the large slice of cake, and a mug of milk.

"Now, three pennies is more than enough for your dinner, so go to the hen house and collect four eggs, Betsey, and then come back, and I'll let you have a loaf of bread. Do you know how to cook eggs?"

Betsey nodded. "Yes, Mum showed me how to fry them, thank you so much, Aunty Kezzie. I'll do them for our tea; I think there's a little bit of butter left to cook them in. Should I do some for my dad, do you think?"

"No, I think you should hide the rest for tomorrow, Betsey. I'm sure your dad won't go hungry; he'll probably have something to eat at the butcher's shop."

Thomas Fellwood did not get much sleep that night, for the puppy was missing his mother, and he whimpered all night long. The young man cradled the dog in his arms, and eventually, they both dropped off to sleep. However, he was rudely awakened just after dawn, when he realised the puppy had saturated his bed with urine. Dismayed, he was trying to rearrange his bedding to find a dry spot, when the door opened, and Margery peered around the door. As soon as she spotted the puppy, a wide grin spread across her face, and if Thomas had been in any doubt about getting her a dog, his concerns evaporated immediately.

"Oh, Thomas, you have my puppy. Why didn't you take me to fetch him?"

"I thought it would be a surprise for you. Are you pleased with him?"

The little girl sat on the floor stroking the dog, and she looked up with shining eyes. "Oh, yes, thank you so much, Thomas. He's so lovely. Is he a boy, or a girl?"

"Jane says he's a boy; so what are you going to call him?"

The little girl's face was a picture of concentration. "I'm not sure; what do you think?"

"Umm, what about Gyp because he came from the gypsies?"

"Oh yes, that's a good idea. Do you think he's hungry?"

"Yes, I expect so. Shall we take him to the kitchen, and see if Mrs Clarke can find him something to eat and drink? I need to explain to one of the maids, why my bed is wet. I don't want her thinking I've had an accident."

CHAPTER 14

It was a chilly Thursday morning in late October when the workmen arrived to put a new roof on The Red Lion. There had been a hard frost overnight, unusually early for the time of year, and the men were blowing onto their hands to warm them. The water butts were frozen over, and the grass along the side of the lane was crisp and white. Mal greeted the workers.

"Good morning, lads; my goodness, it's cold this morning. Winter seems to have come early this year. You'll need to keep moving today to keep warm. Still, some of my regulars know a thing or two about the weather, and they reckon we're in for a long dry spell, so I hope they're right. The last thing we want is rain when we've got the roof off. How are you going about this?"

Gordon Parker was the man in charge, and he took off his cap and scratched his head. "Well, it's a big job, so we need to get rid of all the old thatch first, and then see what the rafters are looking like. I suspect they'll have to be replaced, but we'll see. Has it had a new roof since it was built?"

"No, probably not. It was built over five hundred years ago, so your guess is as good as mine, but I reckon it's just been patched up over the years. My grandparents owned it, before my parents, and as far as I know, they never replaced it, so that's going back a hundred years or more. It needs doing anyway; I could see daylight in several places when I went up into the loft a few weeks ago. We've had buckets in place ever since, catching the rain. I'm hoping you'll only have to replace the thatch, and not the rafters as well, otherwise I shall have to go cap in hand to the bank manager again, and beg more money."

"Well, I think you're being optimistic to hope it will just be the thatch after all those years and to be honest, it would pay you to replace the rafters and beams at the same time anyway; it's best to do a thorough job while we're at it. You don't want to be doing it again in a few years."

"No, I suppose not. I think I can get more money if I have to, it's just that the repayments are so steep, and we'll have to struggle for years to pay it all back."

"Well, I'll be able to tell you by lunchtime; we should know the worst by then."

Kezia appeared with a tray loaded with mugs of tea and some of her best currant buns.

"Here you go, lads; grab a quick cuppa and a bun to keep you warm before you start. I won't have it said you aren't looked after at The Red Lion. No ale, mind; I don't want you falling off the roof."

The men gratefully ate their buns, warmed their cold hands around the mugs of tea, and then set to work.

Long before lunchtime, it was plain that the whole roof would need to be replaced. The area surrounding the old inn was littered with ancient thatch and the bodies of long-dead rodents. A cloud of dust surrounded the men as they worked, no longer feeling the cold. Mal came out mid-morning to see how they were getting on, and Gordon drew his attention to the first rafter they had removed. He grabbed a section of it in his hands, and it disintegrated before their eyes.

"I'm sorry, Mal but you have deathwatch beetle in the rafters, and also dry rot. It's not surprising after so many years, but it will all have to go, I'm afraid. Are you sure you can get more money because you're going to need it? The price I gave you was for rethatching only."

Mal sighed. "Yes, I think it will be all right, but I'll ride into Barnstaple tomorrow to make sure. It will have to be done anyway, now you've got this far."

Returning inside, he was surprised to see Betsey and Norman seated at the kitchen table. He raised his eyes at Kezia.

"I've invited Betsey and Norman in for some dinner today, Mal. They've both got awful colds, and I suggested they stay home from school. It's so cold, and their shoes leak, and it won't help for them to get wet. I'm going to have a word with Adam, later; he needs to get them some proper shoes, and warmer clothing, with the winter coming."

Having greeted the two children warmly, Mal drew Kezia into the sitting room, and out of earshot.

"Kezzie, you have to stop doing this; we can't afford it. The roof's going to cost far more than we thought, and I'll have to go into town tomorrow and beg more money from the bank. I'm pretty sure they'll lend it to us, but the repayments are going to cripple us for a long time to come. The last thing we need is two extra mouths to feed."

Kezia pursed her lips stubbornly. "I understand, Mal, but just see the state of those children. I know Ellen would have done what she could for Ned and Silas if the shoe was on the other foot. I can't see them starve."

He sighed deeply. "No, I know. I'm going to have to speak to their father. It's not good enough; he earns decent money at the butcher's shop, and he needs to start spending a bit more on them, instead of on that trollop, Becky Chown. It's disgusting the way he's carrying on, with Ellen barely cold in her grave; his fancy piece should know better, too."

"If you're going into town tomorrow, can I come with you?"

"Well, I had planned to ride, rather than take the horse and cart, but yes, if you want to. I'd enjoy your company. We'll have to set off right after breakfast, though, or the bank will be closed. What about Ned and Silas? They might be home from school before we get back."

"It's all right, Mary and Jack will be here, serving behind the bar, so they can keep an eye on them until we get home."

The next day, Kezia saw Ned and Silas off to school, and then quickly checked on Betsey and Norman. They were both still poorly, and she took them in a bowl of porridge each and told them to stay at home in the warm and keep the fire burning. She quickly chopped a few logs to keep them going, and then hurried back before Mal missed her.

Gordon Parker's friends were right with their weather forecast, for once again it was a sunny day with barely a cloud in the sky, but it was still bitterly cold. As the old horse and cart trundled along the quiet country lanes, Kezia slipped her arm through Mal's and squeezed it affectionately.

"What's all this about then? What are you after?"

"I'm not after anything, Mal Carter; I was just thinking how nice it is for us to have a few hours away from the inn together; just like the old times before we were wed."

"Aye, it is nice, and you barely look a day older than the day I married you."

"Oh aye, I'm sure. I certainly have several grey hairs I could do without, and more than a pound or two around the middle, but you keep going with the flattery; I don't mind at all."

He took her hand in his, and kissed it fondly, smiling into her bright blue eyes. "Well, that's as maybe, but you'll always be the only woman for me, Kezia Carter."

When they reached Barnstaple, Mal left the horse and cart tied up outside the bank in the High Street and agreed to meet Kezia a couple of hours later.

"Will that be long enough for you?"

"Yes, thanks, it won't take me long to spend the little money I have, but I like to browse, and I may see one or two people I know. I don't get the chance to come to the market often."

"All right then; you enjoy yourself, and if you play your cards right, I might just buy you a pie and a pint in The Three Tuns before we set off for home." Kissing his wife fondly on the lips, he removed his cap and entered the bank. "Wish me luck; I'm probably going to need it."

Kezia decided to meander around the town before she did any shopping, and headed down the High Street towards the river Taw. Although some improvements were being made to the run-down area, she shuddered as she hurried past several beggars sitting outside a row of dilapidated cottages, and walked on past a disused timber yard and a couple of limekilns. Deciding there was little to interest her there, she turned right along the Strand, and past the entrance to the Long Bridge. The substantial stone bridge had been built way back in the 1200s, and today it was busy with horses and carts, and people bustling about on their business. She was taken aback at the number of people in the town; it was never this busy in Hartford.

She continued along the quay, which was crowded with sailors from the many ships anchored there; for it was a busy port. Several of the seamen were the worse for alcohol, despite the early hour, and they staggered from the ale houses and brothels which lined the quay and back up the gangplanks to their ships. They were making the most of their freedom, after a long voyage. Smiling to herself, and skilfully avoiding outstretched hands, and declining invitations to follow them, she continued to Queen Anne's Walk, where merchants had carried out their business, sealing deals on the tome stone since the Middle Ages. She knew Mal would not approve of her walking alone in such a rough area of the town, and she certainly would not have done so at dusk, but now, with the sun shining, and so many folk around, she wasn't worried.

After passing the statue of Queen Anne, she walked up Cross Street, and back into the High Street, where she intended to do some shopping. The street was lined with stalls, the vendors calling out their wares, and she was delighted to see the wide range of goods on offer, from freshly caught fish, meat of every description, bread and cakes, fruit and vegetables. The market day had been held on a Friday in the town for as long as anyone could remember, and it was the place to glean any juicy gossip. Farmers from a wide rural area brought their livestock to town to sell in the cattle market, or to purchase new stock for their farms. The animals were herded into an enclosure, and the farmers gathered around to make their bids, as the auctioneers sang out their prices. Butchers also bid for animals to be slaughtered and offered for sale in their shops.

Still having plenty of time, and not wanting to carry her shopping around with her, she decided to continue down the High Street to the bottom, and then stroll back along the other side. As she neared the North Gate of the town, several young boys dressed in royal blue jumpers and darker trousers came towards her, and she realised they had been dismissed from the Blue Coat School for their lunch break. She had heard about the school and thought they looked smart in their uniforms of Barnstaple Bayes, as the material was known. Wishing Ned and Silas could be similarly clothed, she remembered that somewhere in the town there was also a school for young girls founded by a rich merchant called Thomas Horwood. This was unusual for the times, and she wondered if the girls too, were warmly clad in the blue woollens.

Catching sight of a clock on the side of the old town hall, she realised she had better get on with her shopping. She called into a haberdashery shop and purchased a small piece of red ribbon, which she intended to give to Betsey for her hair. She decided to buy some fish for their tea, and a couple of rabbits for a pie, which she could make the next day. She purchased the fish and the rabbits, and then caught sight of a stall selling toffee apples. She knew Mal would disapprove, but it was seldom she had the opportunity to spend any money, and she quickly purchased four apples before she changed her mind, thinking how pleased Ned, Silas, Betsey, and Norman, would be. She decided to give the two Lovering children theirs on the quiet, not wishing to incur Mal's wrath at her wastefulness.

Finally, she made her way to The Three Tuns, an ancient hostelry, and was pleased to see Mal waiting outside for her. "How did you get on?"

"Well, they didn't say no, so that's something, but it's going to take years to pay it all back. We're going to have to watch every penny from now on."

She smiled at him brightly, acutely aware of the four toffee apples tucked away in her basket, and knowing he would be cross.

"How about you; did you get everything you wanted?"

"Yes, I've bought some trout for our tea, and a couple of rabbits for a stew tomorrow. I was a bit naughty, because I've treated Ned and Silas to a toffee apple each, but they don't get spoilt often."

He opened his mouth to protest, but she put her finger to his lips. "Now, before you grumble, they were only a ha'penny each, and yesterday, a traveller gave me a shiny new thrupenny bit, so they haven't cost you anything."

"Right, if you say so, but as I keep telling you, from now on we need to watch every penny, do you hear me?"

She nodded, thinking she must spirit away the other two apples as soon as possible.

CHAPTER 15

When Mal and Kezia arrived back at the inn, work was proceeding on the roof, and the surrounding land was a shambles with all the debris. Gordon Parker came over to meet Mal by the cart.

"Hello, Mal, how did you get on? Will the bank lend you the money?"

"Aye, you needn't worry; I can pay you."

"Sorry, Mal; I know you're a man of your word, but I'm pleased to hear the bank will help. The roof's off now, and there's no going back."

"No, I know, and it looks like you're getting on well."

"Yes, we are. We should be able to start replacing the rafters and beams tomorrow."

"Do you have enough rafters?"

"Aye, I knew they'd need replacing, so I went to the sawmills last week and ordered enough. I knew we could use them on another job if we didn't need them here, so it wasn't a problem. The last thing we want is to not be able to finish a job when we have a roof off. We have large tarpaulins to cover the roof if the worst comes to the worst, but it's always difficult to keep the rain out. Now, we found an old tin trunk up in the attic, and we've hauled it down. Bloody heavy it was too. Do you know what's in it?"

"Oh, yes, I'd forgotten about that. No, I've no idea what's in it; I found it the other day when I went up to look at the roof. It must have been there for a long time because I never heard my father mention it. I couldn't get it open. Have you managed to open it?"

"No, I didn't try. None of my business. Anyway, I must get on, but it's over there look, outside your back door."

By this time, Kezia had gone on ahead to unpack her shopping and check all was well with Ned and Silas. She put the trout and the rabbits in the larder and then reached into her basket for the toffee apples. She told the boys to hold out their hands and close their eyes, and they were delighted when she folded their fingers around the sticks of the toffee apples.

"Ooh thanks, Mum; can we eat them now?" Silas's eyes gleamed.

"Yes, I think you can. Tea will be a bit late tonight, so you'll be hungry again by the time it's ready. Go on, run off and enjoy them."

Just then, Mal arrived at the back door and beckoned to his two sons.

"Do you two want to come outside and watch me open a treasure chest?"

The two excited boys and their curious mother followed him outside. Mal went to the outhouse, and returned with a hammer and chisel."

"What is it, Dad?"

"It's an old trunk that was in the attic. I saw it the other day when I was up there, but I couldn't get it open and it was too heavy for me to lift down on my own. The workmen found it when they were doing the roof, and thankfully, they've lifted it down. Let's see if we can get it open."

Mal put the chisel under the lip of the lid and took a swipe at it with his hammer, but it took several blows before the lid finally succumbed to his labours. When, at last, it creaked open, the first thing they saw was a name and date, painted roughly on the underside of the lid: Jago Carter 1640.

"My goodness, this trunk's been here a long time. I guess he must have been an ancestor of mine. Let's see what Jago has left for us, then."

Removing a faded red cloak which lay on top, Mal gazed in wonder at the contents of the chest. He felt moved to think these items had been placed there so long ago, by a member of his own family. Tied up with a fragile piece of string, was a large bundle of documents, which he put to one side to examine later. Gently, he removed a pair of pistols and a dagger. A large leather-bound bible, dark green in colour, he handed to Kezia.

"What else is in there, Dad?" Ned, distracted from eating his toffee apple, could scarcely contain his excitement.

"Patience, boy; I don't want to damage anything. This lot must have been up in that loft for more than a hundred years; it's incredible. Now, what do we have here?"

With difficulty, he lifted out a rough wooden box measuring about a foot square. Painted on the lid of the box were the words 'Merchant Royal', and inside, packed in straw, was a salt-glazed stoneware jug. It was heavy; light brown in colour, and stuffed with old paper. The boys were disappointed.

"Aw, it's just an old pot. I wonder why they saved that."

"Hold on, it's heavy, I think there's something in it." Mal removed the paper, carefully laid the jug on its side and raised it. Several coins rolled out, and the boys squealed in excitement.

"It is some treasure, after all, Dad. Are we going to be rich?" Silas jumped up and down, with a wide grin on his face.

"I doubt it; I don't even know what the coins are. They don't look English, but they're so black and dirty, it's hard to tell. I wish they were gold sovereigns, then we would be laughing. We'll clean a few off later, and see if we can tell what they are. There are a lot of them, anyway."

He continued searching the trunk and found another identical wooden box with the same inscription on the lid, and inside a matching stoneware jug. It too was full of the same coins. Kezia got to her feet,

"I'll get the tea on; I don't think there's anything in there that will pay for the new roof, unfortunately. I quite like the jugs, though. I'll wash them later, and you can try to clean the coins, Mal. I reckon they're foreign, so no use to us. It'll be interesting to see if we can read anything on the paperwork, though."

The aroma of freshly cooked trout soon filled the kitchen, and along with fried potatoes and some crusty bread, the family were soon eating their fill. Mal went to relieve Mary in the bar, and to their dismay, Kezia insisted Ned and Silas wash the dishes, whilst she went next door to see how Betsey and Norman were. She went around the back, and after knocking on the door and receiving no answer, she let herself in. As she suspected, there was no sign of Adam, but she was pleased to see the fire in the old range was still burning. The cottage was in darkness, and so, raising the candle she had brought with her, she called out to the children.

"Betsey, Norman; it's me, Aunty Kezzie. Are you all right?"

"Oh, yes, Aunty Kezzie, we're in here. I was afraid to answer the door in the dark."

Kezia moved into the next room, where Betsey and Norman were huddled tightly together in one corner, a thin blanket around their shoulders.

"Why haven't you lit a candle, Betsey? You know how to do it from the fire, don't you?"

"Yes, I do, but we haven't got any. Dad's not come home from work yet, and I don't know if it's bedtime or not."

"Oh dear; this is not good at all, but I do have something to cheer you up, though it must be our little secret. Can you both keep a secret?"

The two children nodded with wide eyes, for the only secrets they usually had to keep, were to lie about something unpleasant.

"Now, here's a slice of bread and dripping each, and when you've eaten that, I have a little treat for you. Do you like toffee apples?"

"We don't know; we've never had one."

"Well, I'm sure you'll like these." Kezia reached into her basket and passed each child a thick slice of bread and dripping, and then showed them the toffee apples.

Norman grinned widely at the sight of food, and Betsey was pleased too. "Oh, thank you so much, Aunty Kezzie, we're so hungry. I was hoping Dad would be home early tonight and bring us something to eat. I kept the fire going all day like you said, and I cooked the eggs you gave us, but that was a long time ago."

"Right, now you eat all that bread up quickly, and then enjoy these apples; they'll do you good. Now, I hope you don't mind, Norman, but I have another little present for Betsey because she's worked so hard looking after you. Betsey, do you like this pretty red ribbon?"

The little girl's eyes shone. "Can I touch it?"

"Yes, of course. I thought it would look nice in your hair, now that it's all clean. Shall I put it in your hair, for you?"

The child nodded, and Kezia swiftly caught up her hair and put it into a ponytail. "There, that's better. The next time you come to my house, I'll check again for nits, and put a brush through it, and do a proper job. Now, I'll leave you my candle so you can see the way to bed when you've finished eating, but do be careful to blow it out before you go to sleep, won't you?"

Betsey nodded. "Yes, I know I must do that; Mum always told me." The mention of her mother brought tears to the little girl's eyes. "Thanks ever so much, Aunty Kezzie, I don't know what me and Norman would do without you."

Kezia hugged both children, trying not to let them see how upset she was, and then returned home. She didn't tell Mal of her visit, for she knew he would not approve, but she couldn't just stand by and see Ellen's children destitute and do nothing about it.

Many hours later, when the inn was closed, and at last, they had some time to themselves, Mal and Kezia pored over the old paperwork they had found in the trunk. There were several documents written in Latin that they were unable to read, and a hand-drawn map. They were puzzled by the map, but then Mal exclaimed.

"Oh, I see, I think it's a map of the village. Look, there's the church and across the road, it says "RL". That must be The Red Lion. I'm no sailor, but the coastline looks about right, I should think. I reckon these dotted lines are the old tunnels, and if they are, there are one or two I didn't know about. I think they were dug many years ago when there were religious troubles, and people used them to escape persecution, but since then, they've been used for smuggling. I know there's one that goes from our cellar to the church, and it seems there are a few others I didn't know of. I must ask your father if he knows of these tunnels when I next see him. I think he's the oldest man in the village, and your family's always been involved in smuggling. Not a word about this to anyone, Kezzie. If this map fell into the wrong hands, there could be a lot of trouble."

"Mal, I'm Raymond Chugg's daughter, and as you say, my family have been smugglers for years; do you seriously think you need to tell me to keep quiet?"

Mal chuckled. "No, I guess you know well enough how to keep your mouth shut. Now, let's have a closer look at that bible; it must have cost a bob or two. I'd be surprised if any of my ancestors could have afforded this. Look, what's that name written inside? John Limbrey? I've never heard that name, have you?"

"No, it's not a local name. I wonder if Jago Carter stole all of this?"

"Oh dear, I hope not; as far as I know the Carter family has always been law-abiding, but I suppose all families have a black sheep somewhere along the line. I think this would make a bit of money but I've no idea where I could sell it, and it would probably cause more trouble than it's worth. Here are a couple of the coins I cleaned off, look; they're not English so they're of no use to us. I might show them to your father; he's a clever man with a long memory, and he's about the only one I'd trust to keep his mouth shut. Now, I've heard the name Jago somewhere before, but I can't think where. Do you know?"

"Yes, and you should remember too. It's written in your family bible, up there on the shelf; shall we have a look?"

"Aye, it's getting late, and we need to get to bed, but I'm curious now."

Reaching up to the shelf at the side of the chimney breast, Mal lifted down the heavy bible.

"I've always wondered about this bible. I mean it's nothing like as grand as the one in the chest, but it's still a fine book. I think my granny, wrote all these names in there."

He opened the Bible and ran his finger down the long list of names.

"There she is look, Katel Trethewey, born in 1699. I remember her; I think I was about ten when she died, so she would have been nearly eighty and that's a good age for a woman, especially when you see how many children she had. Of course, they didn't all survive. I remember my mother, telling me that Katel came from Cornwall from a well-to-do family, and they didn't approve of her marrying my grandfather, Amos. That's how this bible came to have all this information for sure, and why my family has always been able to read and write. My granny passed her knowledge on and saw to that."

"Look, there's Jago Carter; I knew I'd seen his name somewhere. I'm glad you taught me to read and write too, Mal. Look, he was your granny's grandfather, so I think that makes him your Great-Great-Grandfather. My goodness, that's going back a bit, isn't it?"

"It certainly is. I seem to remember Granny saying that some of her ancestors were sailors, so perhaps Jago brought this back from the sea with him. If all this is stolen perhaps that's why the trunk has lain hidden for so many years; they would have been afraid for it to be seen, and then it was probably forgotten. Look, he died in 1656, so that may not have been long after he came home from the sea if he was a sailor. It would explain these odd coins too; they're certainly not English, more's the pity."

Kezia rose and put her arms around her husband's neck. "Come on, then, let's get to bed and worry about it tomorrow; it's been a long day."

CHAPTER 16

It was a bitterly cold day in late December when Lady Helena Fellwood was finally laid to rest. Mal Carter waited quietly on his horse as the cortege passed him by. Lord Fellwood had hired a black carriage specially designed to carry the coffin, and the grand vehicle was pulled by four handsome black horses. Several fine carriages followed, carrying the many mourners to the 12th-century church in the centre of Hartford. Following a lengthy service, the coffin was placed in the family vault, and a fine spread awaited the mourners at Hartford Manor.

As Mal waited at the side of the narrow lane, his breath hung in the frosty air, and the cold penetrated his clothing. He caught sight of little Lady Margery, the youngest child, peering out from the carriage, the tears running unchecked down her cheeks, and he removed his cap and bowed his head, thinking grief had no more respect for the rich than the poor.

Mal was on his way to see his father-in-law, Raymond Chugg, who was now over ninety, his mind still as sharp as a tack. The Chuggs were the tenants of Hollyford Farm, which they rented from the Hartford Manor estate. Mal was relieved when at last the cortege had passed him by, and he dug in his heels, urging his horse forward, keen to get moving and warm up. He cantered down the lane, passing

112

the village pond, which was frozen hard. Once he had left the village behind, he let his horse have its head, and as he galloped across the desolate Exmoor landscape, he laughed with sheer exhilaration.

When he arrived at the farm, he reined in his horse as young Alfred Chugg waved to him from the stable. Alfred, aged five, was the great-grandson of Raymond, and usually at school with Ned, Silas, Betsey, and Norman, but today was a Saturday.

"Hello, Alfred; how are you, today?"

"I'm fine, thank you, Uncle Mal. Have you come to see my dad?"

"No, I'd like a word with your great-grandad if he's around?"

"Yes, he's just gone in for something to eat; he's been out here helping Dad all morning."

Mal accompanied the boy inside, thinking there couldn't be too many people who were still working so hard in their nineties. Alfred led Mal around to the back door and took him into the kitchen where several of the Chugg family were enjoying bacon and eggs.

"Good morning, everyone, I'm sorry to interrupt your meal; I just wanted a quick word with you, Raymond, if that's all right?"

Alfred's mother, Margaret Chugg, smiled at him. "Of course, it is, Mal; you know you're always welcome here. Sit yourself down and I'll get you some breakfast. Would you like some bacon and eggs?"

"Well, Margaret; it's hard to refuse on a cold morning like this. Thank you."

"Good; is everyone well?"

"Yes, all fine, thank you."

In no time at all, he was tucking into sausages, bacon, and two fresh farm eggs dished up onto a slice of freshly baked bread. He made small talk as he ate, but did not mention the purpose of his visit until he was alone with Raymond in the sitting room.

"Now, what brings you here today, Mal? I know you're a busy man and unlikely to pay a social call on a Saturday morning."

Mal surveyed the old man, whose brown face was deeply lined with wrinkles, and there was barely a hair on his head or a tooth in his mouth. However, he was still a powerful-looking man, despite his age, and Mal found it hard to believe he was over ninety.

"You know me too well, Raymond; not a lot gets past you, does it? I wish I knew your secret; I believe you're fitter than me, despite your years."

"Clean living, hard work, and a clear conscience, my boy, that's all it is. Now, come on, tell me why you're here."

Mal relayed the story of the old tin trunk he had found in the attic, and Raymond scratched his bald head.

"Well, that is interesting. I remember your granny, Katel. A pretty woman she was, and from a wealthy Cornish family, I believe. I remember the day she married your grandad, Amos Carter, right here in Hartford church. I stood outside watching, along with most of the village. I was only a little tacker, mind, probably around six or seven. I heard her family was against the marriage, but her father doted on her, and in the end, he saw she was provided for, though I believe he had threatened to cut her off without a penny."

"Our family bible says they were married in 1734, and she was called Katel Trethewey."

"Aye, that's about right then, because I was born in 1728; I'd forgotten her maiden name, but then I probably never knew it at that age. I do remember thinking what a pretty lady she was, though."

"Right, well on the inside of the lid of the trunk it had the name Jago Carter, and the year 1640, though according to our bible he was born in 1615. He would have been the grandfather of Amos Carter who married Katel. I should think he was a seafaring man, and perhaps 1640 was when he set sail. There was also an expensive leather bible in the trunk with the name John Limbrey; did you know him?"

"Nay, lad, I can't say that I did. What else did you find?"

"Well, that's why I'm here, Raymond. Inside the trunk, there were two small wooden boxes, each with a stoneware jug inside, and they were full of these old coins. I've brought a few to show you," Mal reached into his pocket, "here, look. They're not English, unfortunately. If they were, I'd be a rich man. Do you know what they are? Oh, and on the wooden boxes it said 'Merchant Royal'; I'm guessing that must have been the name of a ship."

Raymond turned the coins over and over in his hands. "Well, I can tell you, these are Spanish pieces of eight; you probably have a tidy sum there."

"Oh, is that what they are? I thought they might be Spanish, but I wasn't sure. Well, they're no use to me, are they? I mean, even if I went and asked the bank manager in Barnstaple about them, I'd probably get thrown into jail for stealing them. Who would believe I'd found them in my attic?"

"Well, I expect people would believe you if you showed them the trunk, but I'm not sure they'd give you anything for them. I think I'd just hang on to them if it was me; you never know, they might be worth something one day. What did you say the name of that ship was?"

"The Merchant Royal. Why, do you know something about it?"

"It rings a bell, and I have a feeling I may have heard my grandad speak of it. If it's the same ship that I'm thinking of, it capsized off Lands' End, and several sailors drowned. One of them was local, and my grandad knew him, and that's why he mentioned it one day."

"See, I knew you'd be the man to ask, Raymond. Can you read Latin?"

"Nay, lad, I can only just read a word or two of English, never mind Latin. Why do you ask?"

"Oh, there are several papers with Latin writing on them, but it's not important. Now, I think you'll be able to understand this map, though. What do you think this shows?"

Mal unfolded the ancient map, and carefully smoothing out the creases, laid it on the table. Raymond leaned over it using a magnifying glass, then he straightened up, and stared at his son-in-law curiously.

"Do you know what you have here, Mal? You have a dangerous document in your possession."

"Well, I think it shows the position of the old tunnels around the village; am I right?"

"Aye, without a doubt, and if this fell into the wrong hands, a lot of local men would suffer; many of them in this family. These tunnels have been in existence since the olden days. I've always been told they were originally dug to allow folk to escape when they were being persecuted for their beliefs, but in more recent times they've been used regularly for smuggling, and as you know, Mal, they still are. I'm not familiar with all these tunnels, though, but they could be helpful." The old man gave him a knowing look.

"I know your family's always been heavily involved in smuggling, Raymond, and mine too from time to time, come to that. That's why I've brought it to you; I think you're the best person to have it."

"Now this, you could probably get a tidy sum for, especially if you had a mind to offer it to the gaugers. Might help towards the cost of that new roof I hear you're having done. I bet that's costing you a pretty penny."

"Aye, it certainly is. The rafters and the beams were so rotted, I think they must have been the originals from when the inn was built. I've had to take out a bank loan that's going to keep us poor for many a year to come, but there's no way I'd ever sell this map, Raymond. Why my ancestors would turn in their graves, and you know I'd never betray you."

"I'm pleased to hear that, son, and if you're going to leave this with me, I'll get some of the younger men to check out these other tunnels that are shown. If they still exist, they could be useful in years to come. Too many folk are taking an interest in our clandestine activities of late. One thing I can tell you, though; and that is The Red Lion Inn last had a new roof when your granny, Katel, married Amos Carter. I told you she had money, and the first thing she did was to pay for a new roof; I can even remember it being done, so that's going back over eighty years. No wonder it needs a new one. Anyway, thank you kindly for this map, and the next time we have a successful haul, I won't forget your generosity. I'll see to it that you're rewarded. As far as the bible and the coins are concerned, I think I'd just hold on to them. That's probably why they're still in your attic; no one has thought it safe to sell them, but you may be able to one day."

Leaving Raymond and the Chugg family, Mal rode home and relayed the tale to Kezia. Having assured her the family was in good health, he told her what her father had said, and she smiled as he told her of Raymond's delight at receiving the map. She was disappointed, but not surprised to learn it was best not to sell the other items they had found, and they decided to put the trunk, the coins, and the bible, all back into the attic when the roof was finished, along with the Latin documents. The two stoneware jugs she decided to keep, and stood them in pride of place on the large mantelpiece over the kitchen range.

That evening, Kezia was taking a turn behind the bar, when Adam appeared and ordered a tankard of ale. It was late, and he was already the worse for wear for drink, having been to The Three Pigeons first.

"Ah, Adam; I've been wanting a word with you. I went to see Betsey and Norman a couple of evenings ago, and they were sitting alone in the dark, hungry, and shivering with the cold, waiting for you to come home from work. They had no candles and were so frightened they wouldn't answer the door until I called out to them. I bathed them both the other day because I don't think they've had a wash since their mother died. They were filthy, and they both had nits. Adam, what are you thinking of? Do you not care for them at all? What would Ellen say?"

Adam slammed his fist onto the bar, making all the folk around him jump in surprise. "Aw, shut your mouth, woman. 'Tis none of your business. Can't a man enjoy a quiet drink without your nagging? I'm fed up with hearing it. Goodness knows why I came in here. At least I get a bit of peace at The Three Pigeons."

Mal stopped what he was doing, and grabbed the angry man by the scruff of his neck.

"You'll apologise to my wife for speaking to her like that, Adam Lovering, or you'll find yourself outside on your backside in the snow."

Adam began to struggle and tried to punch the landlord, but he was too drunk and Mal was too strong for him.

"Get your filthy hands off me. Don't you worry, I'm going, and I won't be coming back; you'll miss my money, and I hope your new roof catches fire! And I'll tell you another thing, while I'm at it, my children are none of your business, and you're not welcome in my house anymore, so keep out. If I catch you in there nosing around again, I'll have the law on you for trespass. Now, get your hands off me."

Finding new strength, he threw off Mal's grip and stormed out of the room.

CHAPTER 17

Since their first clandestine meeting at the old castle ruins, Thomas and Jane had met regularly. Every time they saw each other they arranged their next meeting, for the fewer people who knew of their relationship, the better; their families would be equally horrified if they came to know of it. Although both knew no good could come of it, neither was willing to end the romance just yet, and they counted the days until they could next meet.

It was usually easier for Jane to absent herself from the gypsy camp than for Thomas, for if he mentioned going for a ride, both of his younger siblings, George and Margery, begged to go with him. Sometimes he relented and took them, for he enjoyed their company and knew they were missing their mother. However, he knew he could not rely on either of them to keep his meetings with Jane a secret.

On a cold day in December, not long before Christmas, Thomas sneaked out of the house quietly and went to the stables, where young Isaac Hammett hastily saddled his horse for him.

"I would have had your horse ready for you, sir, had I known you were going out."

"Yes, I know you would, Hammett, thank you, but it was a bit of a spur-of-the-moment decision to brave the elements and go for a ride. It's such a chilly morning."

"Aye, 'tis that, sir. The water troughs are iced over, and with the snow we had yesterday frozen solid underfoot, the ground is slippery; you'll have to be careful."

"Yes, I see that, thanks, Hammett. I reckon we might be in for a bit more snow yet; the skies are heavy with it, aren't they?"

"Aye, sir, they are, and my father says there's quite a blizzard coming later. He's usually right, so you might not want to stay out too long. The horse will be glad to get out though; he needs some exercise."

"Right, thanks then, Hammett, I'll be on my way. I probably won't be much more than an hour or so, but a short ride will blow the cobwebs away as they say. I'll see you later."

Thomas took his time riding towards the castle, for he did not want to risk his horse stumbling and throwing him. As he neared the woods, he saw the little girl he had befriended walking along the track. He could see that the thin clothes she wore were inadequate for the freezing temperature, and on her feet were the oldest of shoes, almost falling apart. He called out to her, worried she might be frightened by his approach.

"Hello Betsey, what are you doing out on such a cold morning? You need a thicker coat, this morning. Aren't you cold?"

The child's nose was red and she was shivering violently. "Aye, sir, I am cold, but these are the warmest clothes I have. I'm on my way to see Gypsy Freda; I'm hoping she might spare some food for me and my brother, Norman."

"I see. Well, I'm not going all the way to the gypsy camp, but I can take you part of the way. Would you like to ride up here with me, again? I can wrap my cloak around you, and warm you up a bit."

"That's kind of you, sir. Yes, please."

Thomas dismounted and lifted the child onto the horse, then clambered up behind her. He pulled his cloak open and wrapped it around her, and they set off, Betsey enjoying the warmth of his body and that of the horse below her. A little of the feeling began to return to her icy feet, making them hurt as they thawed, and she hastily brushed a few tears from her face, hoping he hadn't noticed.

"I know your mother died, Betsey, but does your father not provide food for you?"

"No, not much, sir; he's at work most of the time, and he doesn't always come home, so we're on our own a lot. I'm trying to look after my little brother, Norman, as best I can, but it's difficult. Aunty Kezzie, from next door, has been looking after us since Mum died, but Dad had an argument with her last week and said she can't come to our house anymore, so things are worse than ever at the moment. I've had to leave Norman at home on his own this morning because his shoes are even more worn than mine, and he can't come out in this cold weather. It'll be all right, though, I'm sure Gypsy Freda will help; she's always been kind to me."

Thomas could not believe a father could be so neglectful of his children and resolved to have a word with his own father to see if anything could be done. However, while he was perusing the matter, they heard a sharp scream from up ahead.

"Hold on, Betsey, I think we'd better find out what's happening; it sounds like someone's in trouble."

Kicking the horse with his heels, Thomas urged the beast into a canter, and they soon arrived at a clearing in the woods where they saw the miller, Jasper Morris, trying to kiss no other than the gypsy girl, Jane. Infuriated, Thomas leapt from his horse and pulled the man away from the girl.

"Get off her, you ignorant beast; can't you see she doesn't want anything to do with you?"

Jasper angrily shook himself free of the hands that held him and turned on the young man before him.

"Why don't you mind your own business? 'Tis nothing to do with you. I was only kissing her, anyway. I love Jane, and I want to marry her; I was just trying to convince her. I'd be a good catch for her and she'd want for nothing. I'd treat her right. Now, get lost; you might be a gentleman, but this is nothing to do with you."

"I'm going nowhere. Now, be on your way, before I teach you a lesson you won't forget."

Thomas angrily shoved the man in the chest, but the miller, far from leaving, took a swing at the younger man and landed a punch which just brushed his cheek. Infuriated, Thomas retaliated, and within seconds both men were exchanging heavy blows and ignoring the screams of Jane and Betsey to stop. The miller was the larger of the two men, and much the stronger, for a lifetime of hauling sacks of corn and flour had built up his muscles over the years. Thomas had been in few fights in his life, and his only advantage was that he was far nimbler than his opponent and better at ducking the blows which were raining down upon him. It was lucky he was, for any one of them could easily have knocked him out cold. Jasper dodged backwards, trying to get out of range of an uppercut blow from Thomas, and caught his heel on a stone, half hidden by the thin layer of snow that lay on the ground. He stumbled backwards and fell heavily.

Thomas leant forward and gulped in the air, glad of a short respite and a chance to catch his breath. Suddenly they realised that Jasper was not getting up, but lying where he fell. Assuming he was winded, Thomas continued to use the time to recover, but then began to wonder if the miller was feigning injury to lure him nearer before taking another swing at him. He glanced at Jane, and she shrugged her shoulders and went cautiously towards the prone figure lying on the ground.

"Come on, Jasper, get up man; you'll freeze to death lying there on the snow."

She slapped his cheek gently, but there was no response, and at first, she thought he had been knocked out.

She lifted his head and then gasped in horror, as blood covered her hand.

"Oh no, I think he might be dead, Thomas! Look, he's hit his head on a sharp stone; it's half buried by the snow."

"No, he can't be. Let me look."

Thomas, now breathing easier, felt for a pulse on the man's neck. Finding nothing, he was now more concerned and put his head on the miller's chest. Hearing no heartbeat, his face blanched.

"Oh my God, I think you're right; I think he's dead. I never meant to kill him."

"No, of course, you didn't; it was an accident."

"Yes, but will people see it that way?"

"Probably not, and I know who'll be blamed for this; the gypsies, we always are. It was common knowledge he was after me, and he's been warned off more than once by the men in the camp. I bet they'll get the blame."

"No, I won't let that happen; I'll tell the truth and explain that Betsey and I came across you when he was trying to force you; it will be all right."

"Oh, no, don't do that, Thomas, we'll never be able to meet again, if anyone knows you were involved."

They both suddenly remembered that Betsey was present. Throughout the fight she had remained seated on the horse, unable to get down on her own, and was doing her best to keep the frightened animal calm. They looked at her in dismay, and Thomas lifted her down.

"Betsey, you'll have guessed that Jane and I have feelings for each other, and have been meeting secretly because our families would never approve of our relationship."

"Aye, sir. I know you've been meeting for a while, but don't worry, your secret's safe with me. You've both been kind to me, and I'd never tell tales. It was an accident, though, wasn't it? You didn't mean to kill Mr Morris; he was just unlucky he fell and hit his head on a stone."

"Yes, he was, but I'm not sure his family or the law will see it that way."

"Well, why don't we just leave him here and be on our way? No one need know any of us were here."

"She's right, Thomas. No one needs to know; the only thing is, he's too near the gypsy camp. If he's found here, they'll still be blamed. We'll have to move him somewhere else."

Betsey joined in. "Yes, I think Jane's right. If you can put him back on his horse, I could lead it through the woods to Shebworthy Pond; there's a shortcut not many people use, and there's hardly anyone about on a cold morning like this. It will be better if you two go home, so no one knows you were ever here."

"Betsey, we can't ask you to do that; you're only a little girl. In any case, how could you get him off the horse?"

"Well, if you lay him across it on his belly, I reckon if I push his feet he'll just fall off."

"I don't know; what if you meet someone?"

"Well, even if I do, I'll just say that's how I found him. No one will suspect a little girl like me of having hurt him, but I don't think I will see anyone. It's bitter out this morning."

"It could work, and we don't have many choices, do we?"

"What about my face; can you see I've been in a fight?"

"No, not really, Thomas; you were so nimble he didn't land many blows on your face."

Having decided it was worth a try, Thomas and Jane struggled hard to heave the miller back onto his horse. He was a heavy man, and it was extremely difficult, but with Betsey holding the horse steady, they finally managed to lay the body across the saddle. Thomas hid the bloody stone in the undergrowth, whilst Jane picked up some brushwood and obliterated all signs of the fight.

"Betsey, I still think one of us should go with you; it's too much to ask of a little girl," Thomas smiled at her, "you're a true friend, but I don't want you to get into trouble on my account."

"I won't, sir; it will be all right." Betsey determinedly took the reins of the horse and led it off through the woods. She glanced back over her shoulder. "Can I come and see you later, Jane?"

"Yes, of course; come on then, Thomas, we'd better both get home or all Betsey's efforts will be in vain."

Betsey slowly led the horse up the steep hill through the woods. Although she had made light of her task, she was worried the body may fall off the horse too soon and decided if that happened, she would just have to leave it. Her feet were once again frozen and soaking wet, but she was no longer shivering, the exertion making her warm, and bringing roses to her cheeks. Despite her tender years, this was not the first dead body she had seen, and she was not afraid. At least this man had never wanted for anything in his life, nor died of starvation, as had some of the tramps and vagrants she had seen lying by the roadside from time to time.

As she had predicted, she saw no one, and after half an hour or so she was in sight of Shebworthy Pond. This was where she thought she might see someone, for folk liked to fish there and find a free meal. However, on such a cold day, there was no one, and she thankfully heaved a sigh of relief. Not far from the pond was a fallen tree, and she thought this might be a suitable place to push the body from the horse. Thomas had balanced the body over the horse, so that the head and arms, and most of the weight was distributed on that side. He had been worried the body might fall off before Betsey reached her destination, but knew it would make it easier for her to tip it off when the time came.

Betsey grasped the dead man's heels and pushed with all her might. The body shifted slightly, and with one more push, gravity did the rest. She did not look at him but whacked the horse's haunch with a stick Thomas had given her, and the startled beast cantered off. Quickly, she turned tail, and taking a circuitous path, headed back towards the gypsy camp. As it came into sight, Betsey saw Jane looking out from the gypsy wagon and she waved to her.

"Hello Betsey, what brings you here on such a cold morning? You look frozen, my dear; come and sit by the fire."

The little girl gladly warmed herself, her feet once more beginning to hurt. Jane fetched a blanket and wrapped it around the child. She took off her wet shoes and dried her feet, massaging them to get them warm.

"I'm sorry to ask, Jane, but I've no one else to turn to; could you spare a crust of bread for me and Norman, please? We're so hungry. I've had to leave him at home on his own this morning because his shoes leak worse than mine."

"You go in and sit with my granny and get warm, and I'll find you a bowl of stew and some bread. Is everything, all right, Betsey?"

"Yes, everything is fine, thanks, Jane." The little girl grinned at her knowingly

CHAPTER 18

Feeling extremely guilty, Thomas kicked his heels into his horse and urged it toward home. He could understand the logic of the little girl leading the horse off to give him and Jane a chance to return home and establish an alibi, but it did not sit easily with him. He was worried she would be unable to push the body off the horse, or worse, that someone would see her and wonder how a body came to be draped across the beast in the first place. He was sad, too, that a man had died, and although it had been an accident, he felt responsible, and not sure they had taken the right course of action. He wondered at the determination and resilience of such a small child and resolved to reward Betsey in some way as soon as he could.

He cantered into the yard, and Isaac Hammett appeared from the tack room where he had been working, having sought refuge from the cold.

"Hello, sir; you didn't stay out long then. 'Tis bitter this morning, isn't it? I don't blame you."

The boy took the reins and waited for his master to dismount.

"It certainly is, Hammett. I intended to have a much longer ride, but this wind goes through you rather than around you, and my hands are frozen, despite my warm gloves. Still, I enjoyed the fresh air for a little while, and at least Jupiter had some exercise."

Back at the gypsy camp, Betsey was happily tucking into a hearty bowl of rabbit stew. It was too hot to eat, and the little girl could barely wait for it to cool; so hungry was she. In the meantime, she contented herself with dipping the thick crust of bread into the delicious gravy and blowing on it to cool it before she could put it to her lips. Gypsy Freda watched her thoughtfully.

"Is everything all right at home, Betsey? I know you lost your mother, so it can't be easy. Is your father looking after you?"

"Well, I miss my mum, and Dad has to work, so me and Norman are on our own a lot since Barney got a job at the mill. We're both going to school now because Mr Billery said Norman could go, even though he's only three. He gives us milk and some dinner, so that's good. It's just after school, and at the weekends, when we haven't got much to eat."

"Doesn't Mrs Carter from The Red Lion keep an eye on you? I thought she was friendly with your mother?"

"Aunty Kezzie is kind and she would like to look after us, but she fell out with Dad a week or two ago, and he told her she was not to come to our house anymore. I miss her because she used to come in every day and hug us too. Dad never cuddles us anymore. I cuddle Norman to sleep, and I sing to him like Mum did because he likes that."

"Have you finished your stew?"

"Aw, yes, thank you; it was lovely. I've warmed up now, but I must get home to Norman; he doesn't like being on his own and he's hungry too."

"Well, I think Jane's looking for a pot for you to carry some stew home for him, so while she does that, why don't you come over here and sit on my lap and I'll tell you a story? Would you like that?"

Betsey nodded, the unexpected kindness bringing tears to her eyes. She climbed onto the old woman's lap and was soon encircled by a warm embrace and covered with a cosy blanket. She rested her head against the gypsy's bony chest and relaxed, delighted to be treated as a child for once. Ten minutes or so later, Jane reappeared at the entrance of the wagon and smiled when she saw Betsey snuggled up cosily on her granny's lap.

"My goodness, Betsey, you do look comfortable; that used to be my favourite spot when I was little; has she been telling you the story about the barn owls?"

Betsey nodded. "I must get home to Norman, though."

"Yes, of course, you must; now here's some stew for Norman; I've put it into this old jar so you'll have to be careful not to spill it. It's hot so be careful not to burn yourself, but it will soon cool in this weather, and there's some more bread for both of you. Do you think you can carry it all right?"

The little girl nodded. "Thanks ever so much, Jane; the jar will keep my hands warm. I feel much better now, and I loved hearing your story, Gypsy Freda."

"Aye, I thought you would. I'll tell you what, when the weather's a bit better, bring that little brother of yours; I've got two knees, so there's room for one more on the other one, and I know plenty of stories. See you next time."

Betsey hurried home as fast as she could without spilling the precious stew. She let herself in through the back door and called out to her brother. He sat hunched in front of the fire and was delighted to see her.

"Are you all right, Norman?"

The little boy nodded, gazing intently at the container in her hands, as a delicious smell reached his nostrils. "Is that some food for us, Betsey?"

"No, this is all for you, Norman. I wonder if you can eat it all up?"

As it was a Saturday, their father left work a bit earlier than usual, and Betsey was pleased when he came straight home instead of going to the inn.

"Hello, Dad; have you brought us anything to eat?"

"Aye, here are a couple of buns I bought from the bakery. You can have them for your tea."

Norman's face lit up, and Betsey was pleased to find her father in a good mood.

"Aw, thanks, Dad; they're nice. Is there one for you?"

"No, it's all right, I had something at work. Now, I'll go chop some logs for you to keep the fire going, and I've brought home a couple of candles too."

Betsey was surprised. "Oh, that's good, Dad; we've only got a little stump left."

Deciding now was as good a time as any, Betsey broached the subject of shoes.

"Dad, my shoes are falling apart, and Norman's are even worse; do you think we could have some new ones?"

"Why, Betsey, shoes cost an awful lot of money; let me see."

Betsey handed him the two pairs of shoes and he turned them over in his hands. "Yes, they've seen better days, I'll grant you that." He scratched his head. "I can't afford new ones, though, but I think there's an old leather apron of mine out in the shed; I'll cut that up and see if I can mend the soles with it."

"That would be grand, Dad, thank you. Mr Billery says we'll get frostbite if something's not done, and we've both got awful chilblains, look." The child held out her foot, which was covered in red swellings. "They itch something terrible."

"Aye, I know what they're like. I was never without them as a lad. As for Mr Billery; you can tell him your shoes are none of his business."

The next morning, Betsey was awoken by the sound of the church bells ringing, calling the congregation to their

Sunday worship. Their cottage was only just across the road from the church, and so the bells were always loud. Norman was also awake and together they went downstairs where they were pleased to find their father already up and about. He had made repairs to their shoes, and she was surprised to find he had made a fine job of it. She was relieved, for frozen feet were no joke, and at least now, Norman would be able to go out and about again. She had worried they would have to stay home from school if the weather didn't improve, and they would certainly miss the food the teacher provided.

"Thanks for mending our shoes, Dad; that's much better. Come on, Norman put them on, and keep your feet warm."

Adam merely nodded and continued eating a pasty that he had brought home with him from work the day before. Betsey peered into the larder to see if there was anything there for her and Norman to eat. She was pleased to see that the remainder of the bread Jane had given her the day before, was still there, and had not been consumed by her father. She spread some dripping on the bread and shared it with Norman. They had just finished eating when their brother, Barney, arrived. They were overjoyed to see him, and he hugged them both tightly.

"What are you doing here, Barney? I didn't think you'd be home today; do you have the day off? I hope you've not had the sack?"

"No, Dad, nothing like that, but Mr Morris went out on his horse yesterday and didn't come home, so his neighbour has got together a search party to find him. We can't understand why he didn't come home, but if he spent the night outside, I don't give much for his chances. I reckon he'll have frozen to death. I don't think I've ever known it so cold; even the river is frozen over, and I've never seen that before. I wondered if you two would like to come out with me to search for him?"

The two children nodded happily, pleased to think they could spend some time with their brother.

"Yes, that would be good; Dad mended our shoes yesterday because they were falling to pieces and he did a good job, look."

Barney looked at the rough repair to the shoes. "Well, I've got something here that might help too. Mr Morris's mother is getting to know me now and she's kinder than I first thought. Her bark is worse than her bite. She's knitted me two pairs of socks, look. They're thick and warm, and they come up to my knees. I know you two haven't got any socks, so I thought you could have these old ones of mine. There's a pair each. Mum let me have them when I left home. They might be a bit big, but they'll keep your feet warm."

The children excitedly pulled on the grey socks. "Oh, Barney that will make such a difference; thank you ever so much."

"That's all right," Barney mumbled gruffly, embarrassed at Betsey's delight over an old pair of socks, "'tis bitter cold out, mind. Put on something warm."

"Well, we haven't got much more than what we're wearing, but I turned out a cupboard yesterday and found a couple of Mum's shawls; I think we'll wrap those around us. Are you going to come, Dad?"

Adam was not keen to spend his one day of rest out in the cold, and he told them he would join them a little later. As they left the cottage, the children were delighted to see Mal, Ned, and Silas, also leaving the inn to join the hunt. Mal noticed the pale, thin faces of Betsey and Norman and their strange outfits.

"How are you getting on, Betsey?"

"Oh fine, thank you, Uncle Mal. Dad mended our shoes yesterday, and Barney brought us some socks, so our feet shouldn't get quite so cold today."

Ned fell into step beside Betsey. He hadn't seen much of her lately apart from at school, and he missed her company.

"How are you really, Betsey? Is your dad looking after you?"

"Yes, we're all right thanks, Ned; we're managing."

When Adam joined the hunt for the miller later in the day, he was not best pleased to see his three children in the company of Mal Carter. However, he decided not to make a fuss in front of all the villagers. The search party covered several miles around the village, and as the day wore on, and no sign of the man was found, Mal told Ned and Silas to go home to get something to eat and get warm. Adam, listening, realised his children should probably do the same, and so the five youngsters walked back together. Betsey was relieved to be going home, for she had been dreading the body being found, and didn't want to see it again.

"Betsey, your dad won't be home for a while, so do you want to come into our house and have something to eat?"

Betsey glanced at Barney. "What do you think, Barney?"

"No, you'd better not; you know what Dad's like if he's disobeyed, and you don't want a hiding. I'll tell you what, though, Ned, I have three pennies here, that I've saved from my wages. Mr Morris knows what Dad's like, and he always lets me have a few pence instead of giving all my wages to him. Do you think your mum would let us have some bread or even a pasty to share between us?"

"Yes, I'm sure she will."

A few minutes later, Ned appeared with three hot pasties. He refused the money, telling Barney to use it for something else. The three children sat in front of the fire, and warmed their cold hands and feet, as they ate the delicious pasties. It was the happiest Betsey had been since her mother died.

It was, in fact, their father who found Jasper Morris. The search eventually took the villagers in the direction of Shebworthy Pond and the woodlands surrounding it. Adam found the miller's body lying at an awkward angle, and he called to his fellow searchers.

"It looks to me like he was thrown from his horse and knocked out," said Mal, "I expect the cold did the rest. We'd better search for his horse. Can someone give the doctor a shout so he can examine the body?"

They found the beast a few hundred yards away, and the horse allowed Adam to approach him and take the reins.

"It looks like he's had enough of being out in the cold."

Doctor Abernethy came panting up the hill. He had been helping with the search and was not surprised to learn the missing man was dead. He knew it was highly unlikely anyone could have survived the freezing temperatures overnight. He bent over the body and carried out a quick examination.

"Yes, I should think he was thrown from his horse and knocked out. There's a deep wound to the back of his head, which most probably would have been fatal, even if he had been found sooner. I'll ride his horse back to the mill and tell his parents."

The men surrounding the body nodded their agreement. No one envied him the job of breaking the sad news to the family.

CHAPTER 19

Jasper's parents, John and Morag, were distraught when the doctor broke the news to them about their eldest son. A couple of days later, John instructed Barney to ride the ten miles or so to tell their other son, Seth, about his brother. Barney had become accustomed to riding the horse since he had worked at the mill, but this was the farthest he had ever travelled in his life, and he was excited to have such an adventure. He found Seth Morris's cottage easily enough, and luckily, found the man at home having his dinner. Barney explained what had happened to Jasper, and told Seth his parents were hoping he would come home and run the mill, for they couldn't manage on their own.

Seth lived in a tied cottage with his wife, Emily, and four children, and was employed as a farm labourer. Realising the situation was urgent, he went straight to the farm manager and explained what had happened. Under the circumstances, his employer agreed to let him go immediately, knowing there were plenty of others who would be delighted to take his place. Although upset about the death of his brother, Seth was excited to have the chance to run the mill. Before his marriage, he had lived at the mill all his life, and he loved the place, though he understood that Jasper, as the eldest, would rightly inherit the property. His wife, Emily, was less pleased; the thought of living with her in-laws filled her with dread, despite Seth assuring her she would be able to run the house as she saw fit. Something she doubted. However, within the week, Seth and Emily had loaded their few belongings onto an old cart and travelled with the children to the mill. Barney wondered how he would get on working for this new man.

The roof of The Red Lion Inn had now been replaced, and for several days, Mal and Kezia kept going outside just to admire the smart new yellow thatch. The buckets collecting rainwater had been removed from the attic, and the old tin trunk replaced, still containing the Spanish pieces of eight, the leather bible, and the old documents written in Latin, that no one could read. Mal hoped that someday, either he or one of his descendants would profit from the hidden treasure. The loan was proving every bit as difficult to repay each month as they had feared, and Mal and Kezia worked long hours trying to earn as much money as they could.

Since their argument with Adam Lovering, they had not seen a hide nor a hair of him, apart from when he and Mal helped to find Jasper Morris. He now drank at The Three Pigeons, the other inn in the village. Kezia wondered how Betsey and Norman were faring, but Mal had forbidden her to interfere, telling her it was none of her business, and that they had enough to cope with. However, she quizzed Ned and Silas when they came home from school, and it was clear the children were being neglected. Ned was often upset when he came home, saying Betsey and Norman were poorly, or they had nits again, or a bruise here or there.

Kezia had been frantically busy all week with guests staying overnight en route to Exeter or London to spend Christmas with their loved ones. There were even one or two who were staying over the festive period. Mal was delighted they were so busy, and when they finally sat down at the end of a long day, he reminded Kezia that things would be even worse if they had no business and couldn't meet the loan repayments. He knew that a debtors' prison would await him if the worst came to the worst.

On Christmas Eve, Adam arrived home at midday, much to the surprise of his children, especially when he greeted them with a wide smile.

"Now, I have a little present here for both of you because it's Christmas Day tomorrow. When you see Mrs Chown at the butcher's shop next time, you must thank her because she's knitted you a new jacket each. See, there's a green one for you, Betsey, and a blue one for you, Norman; they'll keep you warm, won't they? You're so lucky to have some smart new clothes. Do you like them?"

"Oh Dad, they're lovely; we'll thank Mrs Chown next time we see her. Shouldn't you have given them to us tomorrow, though?"

"Ah, now that's the other thing I need to tell you, Betsey. I won't be here tomorrow, or for another day or two, as I have to go away for a little while. I'll chop up lots of firewood for you, though, and I've brought home a loaf of bread, and some eggs, butter and dripping so there will be enough food to keep you going until I get back. There are three new candles too, so don't waste them, and be careful to put them out before you go to sleep."

"Aw, Dad, do you have to go away? We don't like it here on our own."

"Now, Norman, you must be a big brave boy. Yes, I do have to go away, so you'll be the man of the house while I'm gone. Do you think you can look after your sister?"

The little boy nodded slowly. "Yes, I suppose so, but I'd rather you stayed home with us."

"Well, I'm going to see if I can get a different job with more money, and then I'll be able to feed and clothe you better. It would be best if you stayed in the house until I get back; we don't want any nosy neighbours poking their noses into our business. Now, let's see what I can do to make you more comfortable while I'm gone."

Adam dragged the palliasse that Betsey and Norman slept on down the stairs, and put it close to the fire so that it would be a bit warmer for them. He also fetched the two blankets off his bed and added them to theirs. Later, having chopped plenty of firewood, and again instructed the children to stay in the house, Adam gave them both a hug, before saying goodbye, and closing the door firmly behind him.

Betsey did her best to care for her little brother for the next few days. Christmas Day came and went, but was no different from any other day. She kept the fire going with the logs her father had chopped, but apart from going to the woodshed, she did not venture out. The children were now wearing their new jackets and were glad of the extra layer of warmth. They continued to sleep on their palliasse near the kitchen range, and barely left the room, for the rest of the house was freezing. Within a couple of days, their food had almost run out, and Betsey had no idea when her father would return. Norman begged her to go next door, and ask Aunty Kezzie for some food.

"I'd better not, Norman. Dad will be angry if he comes home and finds I've done that. You know he'll give us a hiding if we don't do as we're told. Anyway, we have a little bread and dripping left; so let's eat some of that and cheer ourselves up. Dad said he'd only be gone a couple of days, and it's been more than that already, so he should be home soon. After we've eaten, I'll sing to you if you like."

With Christmas over, it was time for the children to return to school, and when Ned and Silas set off on the first morning, they were surprised not to see Betsey and Norman. They waited for several minutes, but then their mother shouted at them to get moving or they would be late. At school, Mr Billery asked Ned where Betsey and Norman were.

"I don't know, sir. They usually walk to school with us, but we haven't seen them since before Christmas. Their father fell out with my mother, you see, and she's not allowed to go to their house anymore. I'm a bit worried about them."

After school that day Mr Billery walked the short distance from the school to the Loverings' cottage. It was a cold day with a couple of inches of snow underfoot, and he rubbed his hands together briskly and then shoved them deep into his pockets. Upon reaching the cottage, he let himself in through the front gate and knocked loudly on the front door. Inside, Betsey and Norman cowered quietly in the kitchen and made no move to answer the door.

"Betsey, why don't we answer the door? It may be someone who will give us some food."

"Shh, be quiet, Norman. No, Dad told us not to, so we'd better stay quiet. I'll peep out of the bedroom window in a minute and see who leaves."

A minute or two after the knocking stopped, Betsey inched her way up the stairs and then peered cautiously out of the front bedroom window. She was just in time to see Mr Billery retreat down the lane. She sighed, wishing she could have spoken to him, for she was sure he would have given them some food. No doubt, he was wondering why they were not at school. That evening, as she sang Norman to sleep once more, Betsey wondered what could have happened to her father. He had been gone for five days, and she was puzzled why he had not returned to work at the butcher's shop. For the last two days, the children had not eaten, and the firewood that Adam had chopped would only last one more day. Norman was listless and miserable and continually begged Betsey to go out and get some food.

It was another two days before Mr Billery visited the butcher's shop to collect some sausages for his tea, and there he found several of the customers gossiping. He noticed that Mrs Chown, the shop owner, was looking most uncomfortable, and his curiosity got the better of him, and he asked what was going on. Mrs Chown seemed reluctant to answer, but Nellie Rudd, the wife of the village blacksmith, was delighted to oblige.

"Seems 'er daughter, Becky, 'as run off wi' that good for nothing rake, Adam Lovering. We all know 'e was carrying on wi' 'er long afore his poor wife died. They should be ashamed of themselves, running off, and not wed, with not a word to anyone; not even her own mother."

Mr Billery was shocked but then asked. "Did they take his children? Has anyone seen Betsey and Norman? They haven't been to school since before Christmas."

The crowd around him shuffled uncomfortably, and Nellie Rudd piped up again. "No, I ain't seen nothin' of 'em, poor little mites. 'Tis common knowledge he hasn't looked after them properly since poor Ellen died. Turnin' in 'er grave that poor woman must be."

Abandoning his shopping, Mr Billery turned on his heel and hurried from the shop. When he once again received no answer after knocking on the cottage door, he went into The Red Lion, where Kezia and Mal were standing behind the bar. He explained the reason for his visit, and Kezia was shocked.

"No, I've seen nothing of them since before Christmas. Nor Adam, but then he's been drinking in The Three Pigeons, so I haven't missed him. Come on, we must check because I doubt he took them with him. We'll go in the back way; the door's never locked. Leaving Mal to continue serving the customers, she led the schoolmaster around to the back door. She knocked and called out, but getting no response, she pushed up the latch and opened the door. It was just as cold inside the cottage as it was outside, for the fire had burned out the day before. She called out.

"Betsey, Norman; where are you? It's Aunty Kezzie; where are you?"

She stepped from the outhouse through to the kitchen and saw the two children huddled on their palliasse close to the fire. They were so still, she feared they had passed away, and she glanced anxiously at the man who was close on her heels.

Mr Billery bent over the children and tried to rouse them. Betsey stirred and wearily opened her eyes, but Norman barely moved.

"Oh my God; I wonder how long they've been like this?"

"Mrs Carter, if I carry Betsey, can you manage Norman? We must take them somewhere warm."

"Yes, of course; we'll take them to the inn."

Wrapping each child up in a thin blanket, they carried them to The Red Lion.

"I think we'd better put them in our bed for now, and I'll fill a warming pan with hot water to try to warm them up. Do you think they'll be all right?"

"I don't know. I'll help you to get them settled, and then I'll fetch the doctor; he'll know best what to do."

Kezia was anxious, knowing the doctor would need to be paid. Mr Billery noticed her reluctance and patted her hand.

"Don't you worry, Mrs Carter, I expect the doctor will come for nothing, but if not, I'll pay him."

Doctor Abernethy was shocked when he saw the state of the children. They were covered in flea bites, and their hair was crawling with lice. Worse still, they were so thin, that every bone could be seen, and he was concerned about their rapid breathing.

"Our first job is to get them warm, but not too quickly. I think that could be dangerous. When they regain consciousness, we could feed them with a little warm broth. Can you provide that, Mrs Carter?"

"Aye, of course. Oh, I could swing for that father of theirs. What was he thinking of leaving them alone for so long, and why on earth didn't Betsey come for help?" She turned away in tears.

CHAPTER 20

Leaving the doctor and Kezia to attend to the children, Mr Billery went straight to Mr Wilson, the constable, to report the incident. He was so angry that all thoughts of the sausages for his tea had long since vanished. Mr Wilson promised to make enquiries, and talk to the children as soon as they could be questioned.

Kezia hastily made up a spare bed for Mal and herself, not wanting to disturb the two children. The period since Christmas had been less busy, and she was glad the inn was not full of visitors. This was both a godsend and a worry, for whilst it gave them a little respite from the long hours of work, it also brought less profit. She had been fearful of her husband's reaction when she broke the news to him that she had put the children in their bed, for she knew they were financially in dire straits. However, as Mal gazed at the two little ones he had known since birth, the tears ran down his cheeks, and he brushed them away angrily, swearing the next time he saw Adam Lovering, he would beat him black and blue.

Within a few hours of her body warming through, Betsey opened her eyes and looked around in puzzlement. "Where am I?" Her voice was weak but loud enough to wake Kezia from her uncomfortable vigil in the chair beside the bed.

"It's all right, Betsey; you're at The Red Lion, and I'm looking after you."

The child sat bolt upright in consternation. "Oh no, Dad will be ever so cross; we must go home."

Gently, Kezia pushed her back against the pillow. "You're going nowhere, young lady; and if your dad ever shows his face around here again, there's a queue of customers downstairs just longing to have a word with him. Do you know where he's gone?"

Betsey shook her head. "No, he didn't say. He said he'd be away for a couple of days looking for a job with more money, so he could look after us better, but then he didn't come back, and I didn't know what to do. He told us not to leave the house, and not to answer the door."

"Right, well don't worry about any of that now. Do you think you could eat a little broth if I feed you?"

"Oh yes, please, Aunty Kezzie; we're so hungry. The food Dad left us ran out days ago. What about Norman; is he all right?"

"I'm not sure, Betsey; he hasn't woken up yet, but let's get you fed, and then we'll see if we can wake him."

Kezia returned with a bowl of broth, which she spooned slowly into the little girl's mouth. A little colour returned to Betsey's cheeks, and when she had finished, Kezia tucked her in again and told her to go back to sleep. The woman was pleased Betsey had taken some nourishment and more hopeful she would make a full recovery. She was less sure about her brother. Norman remained unconscious, and she was unable to rouse him. His breathing was rapid, his brow hot to the touch, and his skin clammy. She was glad the doctor planned to visit again in the morning.

The next day, Dr Abernethy frowned after examining the little boy, but then smiled reassuringly at Betsey and told her she was on the mend.

"You need a few more days in bed, Betsey. You must keep warm and eat as much as you can."

"But what about Norman, sir? Will he be all right?"

"I'm not going to lie to you, Betsey; your brother is seriously ill, and I think he has something called pneumonia, but I'm doing my best to make him better."

Stepping outside the room, he spoke quietly to Kezia.

"Is it possible to move Betsey to another room, Mrs Carter? I need to bleed the boy, and she may find that distressing, but I think it's his only hope. To be honest, I don't give much for his chances. His breathing is laboured, and he's so thin, he's got little strength to fight the illness."

"Yes, sir, I've put another single bed in with my two sons; their room is quite big enough. I don't have any other spare rooms, as we can't afford to turn away paying guests. Could I bathe her, now she's a bit better? I want to get rid of those nits before we all have lice."

"Yes, I think a bath would be beneficial, and it might be best to shave her head. I know it's a bit drastic, but I don't think I've ever seen so many nits on one child, and her hair will soon grow again."

Betsey was dismayed when Kezia suggested shaving her head, but the constant itching was driving her mad, and so reluctantly, she agreed and cheered up a little when Kezia found a pretty bonnet for her to wear.

"There, you look lovely now, Betsey. Don't worry, it will soon grow."

As Kezia put the child into her new bed, Betsey looked up at her worriedly.

"Aunty Kezzie, what's going to happen to me and Norman, if Dad doesn't come back? Will we have to go begging on the streets?"

This question had been keeping Kezia awake ever since the children had been discovered. She had not yet discussed it with Mal, as for some time it had seemed unlikely either child would survive. However, she knew she would have to broach the subject with him.

"Now, don't you go worrying about that, Betsey. I'm sure we'll sort something out. Look, here come Ned and Silas, ready for bed. You'll be sharing their room for now."

Ned and Silas crossed the room to Betsey, and Ned sat on the bed beside her. "Oh, Betsey, I'm glad you're all right. I was so worried. Do you feel better?"

"Not too bad, thanks, Ned, though I wish your mum hadn't had to cut off my hair."

"Well, you look pretty in that bonnet, doesn't she, Silas?"

Silas didn't look too sure, but he nodded and then lost interest. Their mother urged the boys into bed and walked thoughtfully down the stairs. She found her husband stoking the fire in the kitchen, and she put her hand on his arm.

"Mal, we need to talk."

"I know what you're going to say, Kezia, and yes, I agree, we'll have to take Betsey and Norman in, that's if they both recover, but I don't think it's looking too promising for the little lad."

"Do you think Adam will come back?"

"I don't think he ever had any intention of coming back. I think he told the children to stay in the house, and not go out so that it would be a long time before anyone missed him. Becky Chown told her mother she was going to stay with her friend in the next village over Christmas, but she never turned up there. It's obvious they've run away together, and he's left all his responsibilities behind."

Kezia put her arms around her husband's neck and kissed him fondly. "I love you, Mal Carter; it's been worrying me for days."

"I know, and it's not going to make life any easier for us, but I can't turn them out when there's nowhere else for them to go. Since Ellen's mother died, I don't know of any other living relatives, apart from young Barney."

The next morning, Mr Wilson arrived and asked Kezia if he might talk to the children. Explaining that Norman had still not regained consciousness, she took him to Betsey, where he gently asked her about her father. She remained loyal to her father, and told how he had brought them a new jacket each from Mrs Chown, mended their shoes, chopped wood, and left them with what he seemed to think would be enough food to last them until he returned.

"Did your father tell you where he was going, Betsey?"

"No, sir, he just told us to stay inside in the warm, until he got back. I wonder if something has happened to him because he said he'd be back in a couple of days. Perhaps he's poorly, too."

"Yes, he might be, Betsey. Now, I understand from Mrs Carter that she and Mr Carter are going to offer you a home here until your father returns. Would you like that?"

Relief flooded Betsey's face. "Oh, yes, sir, that would be wonderful. I've been worrying about how I could look after Norman."

"Well, you needn't concern yourself anymore, Betsey. I'm glad you'd like to stay here because I'm not sure there is anywhere else for you to go. You must remember how lucky you are, and always behave nicely for your benefactors. Can you promise me, you'll do that?"

The child nodded emphatically. "Yes, I promise, I'll be good, sir."

"Excellent, now, I'm going to ride to the mill, and tell your elder brother what's happened, and see if he has any idea where your father might have gone. I expect he'll come and see you, as soon as he has a day off."

For the last week or two, Barney had been trying to adjust to working with Seth Morris, who was now running the mill. He sometimes got the impression that all was not well between the two women in the kitchen when he went in for his meals but decided to mind his own business, and just hope the food kept coming. Seth was a fair man and pleased when he saw how hard Barney worked, so the lad was hopeful that his position was safe. Mr Wilson found him loading sacks of flour onto a cart.

"Hello, Barney, I'm sorry to tell you that your father appears to have run off, and your little brother is seriously ill. I'm afraid the doctor is concerned Norman may not survive. He's still unconscious and gets thinner by the day. I've had a word with Mr Morris, and he says you can ride back to the village with me if you like. I think it would do Betsey good to see you, and she's going to need you if her little brother dies. She did everything she could for him, and it will be a terrible shock for her if we lose him."

Tears sprang to the young boy's eyes, and he dashed them away, angrily.

"Thank you, Mr Wilson, yes, I'll come with you now."

However, by the time they arrived at The Red Lion Inn, the little boy had lost his fight for life, and Betsey was sobbing bitterly. Barney took her in his arms and told her he would always be there for her. As he gently wiped her tears, he swore to himself, that one day, his father was going to pay dearly for his actions.

CHAPTER 21

A few days later the little boy was laid to rest in Hartford churchyard in the same grave as his mother and several of his siblings. A carpenter made the tiny coffin free of charge, and most of the village attended. After the service, there was a collection for Betsey, and folk were incredibly generous considering their own struggles to survive. Many could only afford a farthing or a ha'penny, but they gave it willingly for the sad child. People were delighted to hear that Mal and Kezia were to offer Betsey a home, despite their financial difficulties, and hoped their small contributions would help.

Betsey was now well on the mend. Plentiful food, and a loving household, were more than the child had known since her mother passed away, and she could not believe how lucky she was. However, she was quiet and subdued, and Kezia knew the little girl felt guilty that she had lived, and her brother had died, and she told her repeatedly that no one could have done more than she did.

There was still no sign of Adam Lovering, and most folk never expected to see either him or Becky Chown again. It was hard on Mrs Chown, for it was her daughter after all, but even she could not condone their behaviour. She knew if her daughter did return home, she would be in for a difficult time.

Betsey was not yet attending school, and each day when Ned returned home at dinner time, he would ask his mother where she was.

"I'm not sure, Ned, but I suspect you'll find her in the graveyard."

Every morning, Betsey asked permission to go for a walk, and Kezia thought it would be beneficial for her to get a little fresh air, though warning her not to go too far. The church was only just across the lane from the inn, so it was no distance for the weakened child to walk.

"I'll just make sure she's all right, then."

Ned strolled across to the lychgate, and let himself into the churchyard. In the distance, he could see Betsey, kneeling on the cold ground beside her mother's and Norman's grave. There was no headstone, nor ever likely to be, but as long as Betsey lived, their resting place would never be forgotten. Not wanting to startle her, Ned called out.

"Hey, Betsey; can I sit with you for a while?"

The child turned, and Ned was distraught to see her face was wet with tears, just as it was every time she came.

"Oh, Betsey, I wish you wouldn't keep coming here; you know how it upsets you."

This time prepared, Ned reached into his pocket for a clean piece of rag.

"Here, dry your tears; I'm sure Norman and your mother wouldn't want you to keep upsetting yourself."

He sat down beside her and put his arm around her. Despite being only a few years older than Betsey, Ned had always been fond of her, and it broke his heart to see her so unhappy. They sat quietly for some minutes, the silence broken only by the occasional sob, or sniff, from Betsey.

"Mr Billery asked me this morning when you might come back to school. I said I'd ask you. He'd like you to come tomorrow if you feel up to it; what do you think? Would you like to come back?"

Betsey sat quietly for several more minutes, and then seemed to come to a decision.

"Yes, I would like to come back, and I feel all right now, but I like coming here to talk to Mum and Norman every day. It's all I can do for them now, and it's too dark after school."

"Well, I could walk home with you at dinnertime, and we could come then. I know Mr Billery used to give you some lunch, but he doesn't need to, now you live with us. The dinner break doesn't give us much time, but the school's so near it's easy to do."

"Yes, all right then, I'd like that; thank you, Ned, but sometimes I just like to be here on my own because I talk to them you see. Do you think that's silly?"

"No, of course not, if you find it helps. I can always wait by the gate." The boy was curious. "What do you say to them?"

Betsey was embarrassed. "Well, I say sorry to Norman for letting him die, and then I say sorry to Mum, for not looking after him well enough."

"Oh, Betsey, none of this was your fault; you looked after Norman and yourself so well. You're only a little girl, and everyone is saying how brave and clever you are."

"Are they? I thought everyone was talking about me, and saying I should have done better."

"No, really, they aren't saying that at all; they all think you're amazing. I must get back to school now, though, so I'll see you later. Why don't you tell your mum and Norman that you're going to school tomorrow, and so you'll come and see them on Saturday, and tell them all about it? I'm sure they'd rather you sat and ate your dinner in the warm than come here and kneel on the frozen ground, and your mum always wanted you to go to school, didn't she? We don't want you to be ill again, do we?"

Betsey nodded her head. "Yes, Mum always insisted I didn't miss a day at school. All right then, tell Mr Billery I'll be there tomorrow, and tell Aunty Kezzie I'll be home soon." She held on to his arm. "Thanks, Ned, you're a good friend."

Once she was strong enough, Betsey visited the gypsy camp again, and both Gypsy Freda and Jane were delighted to see her. They had heard the story of how her father had abandoned her and her brother, and how Norman had subsequently died. The old woman hoped the curse she had laid on the evil man would ensure he never prospered.

"Well, Betsey, I'm pleased to see you looking so healthy. That's such a pretty bonnet you're wearing and are those new shoes that I see?"

Betsey grinned at the old woman showing a gap where she had lost her two front teeth.

"Yes, and I have warm socks and clothes. The villagers collected for me after Norman died, and Aunty Kezzie bought me some new clothes and shoes; I've never been so warm. Look, I even have a coat, and my hair's growing."

Betsey removed her bonnet revealing hair an inch long.

"I'm so pleased for you, my dear. Now, shall we get back to our important business of making medicines?"

Betsey nodded happily, and so she resumed her lessons with the old gypsy and enjoyed concocting all sorts of potions to cure common ailments. Gypsy Freda loved the child as if she was her own, and was delighted to pass on her knowledge to a child so interested. As she was about to leave the camp, Jane followed her, wanting to speak to her alone.

"Betsey, I just want you to know that Thomas and I are so grateful to you for your help with Jasper Morris. No one has questioned that he fell from his horse, and his death doesn't seem to have aroused any suspicions. Thank you so much for your help, and for keeping it a secret."

"That's all right, Jane; you've always looked after me, and fed me when I was starving, so I was glad to help. Are you still seeing Mr Fellwood?"

"Yes, I am, and that's why I wanted to speak to you. We have another secret we want to trust you with, Betsey. Tomorrow, in the early hours of the morning, Thomas and I are going to run away together. You see, we love each other, and there's no way he could live with the gypsies, or me with him at Hartford Manor. Somehow his father has found out we've been seeing each other, and Thomas has been told he must never see me again. We're sad to be leaving our families, but there's no other way we can ever be together. I'm only telling you, Betsey, because I know it will break my granny's heart when I go, and I want you to tell her I'm all right, and where I've gone. I can't write to her because neither of us can read or write, so would you tell her, that one day I'll come back to see her? Tell her Thomas and I love each other, and I know he'll always take care of me. She won't worry so much about me then. Would you do that for me? There's no one I trust more than you."

"Oh Jane, I don't want you to go, either. Where will you go?"

"Thomas is paying one of the local smugglers to take us to France. He has enough money for us to get by for a while, and if we leave the country, no one will find us. Will you tell my granny for me?"

"Yes, of course, I will, Jane; but it will make her sad."

"I know, but if you carry on visiting her that will help. You mustn't breathe a word to anyone else, though. Do you promise me?"

"Aye, of course, I do; you needn't worry. My mum always told me I must keep my promises, and I would never let her down."

"Thank you so much, Betsey. Now, I have a gift here for you from Thomas." She held out a small leather bag.

"No, thank you. Please tell Mr Fellwood I'm grateful, but I don't want his money. I was pleased he hit Mr Morris when he was attacking you, and I was glad to help get rid of him to save you both from getting into trouble. You didn't deserve to, because neither of you meant for him to die; he was just unlucky his head hit a stone. Anyway, I don't need the money now, because Aunty Kezzie and Uncle Mal have said I can live with them, and they're so kind."

"Yes, but Betsey, one day you might want to marry, and then the money would be useful to you; just hide it somewhere, and forget about it for a few years."

"No, thank you; but I don't want it. If it was ever found, people might think I had stolen it, and I wouldn't be able to explain how I got it without betraying you. No, you use it to make a home in France, and I hope you'll both be happy."

Jane was dismayed but could see the sense of what the child was saying.

"Oh Betsey, how did you get to be so wise?" She hugged the child. "There is just one other thing, Betsey, Thomas has lost his grandfather's gold watch, and he's worried in case it came off in the fight with Mr Morris. When the villagers were searching for him, did you hear if anyone found it?"

"No, I've not heard anything about it, but then I expect most folk would just pocket it and try to sell it."

Jane sighed. "Yes, I guess so. Well, not to worry; it won't matter once we're in France, and in any case, it would be where they fought, not where the body was found. Thomas is upset about it, though, because it was his grandad's watch."

"I'll search for it, and if I find it, I'll keep it, just in case you both come back."

PART TWO 1834

CHAPTER 22

Ephraim Fellwood was sitting at his desk; a pile of documents spread out before him. However, he was making little headway with his paperwork, as he admired the magnificent view from the window. He could see way down the valley to a small hump-backed bridge, where a horse and cart were making their way along the lane. The trees were clothed in the vivid green of early spring, and the banks were covered in primroses, bluebells, and red campion. It was late April; his favourite time of year, and, in his opinion, this was one of the best views from the house, though the property afforded a picturesque vista in every direction. Ephraim knew he was a lucky man to have inherited the Fellwood Estate. He had never wanted for anything in his life and yet would trade it all, to have his wife and son back with him.

Since the death of his wife, Helena, in 1820, he had shown no interest in other women, though plenty had vied for his attention. Sadly, Helena had never been strong, and several miscarriages and stillbirths had taken their toll on her weakened heart. He remembered how distraught she had been each time a child died. The one thing he was thankful for, was that she never knew of their second son, Thomas's disappearance. Despite paying a small fortune to private investigators to find him, no trace of the boy had ever been found, and now, some fourteen years later, he was no nearer to finding him.

Just before his disappearance, Ephraim had become aware of his son's interest in a young gypsy girl and had forbidden him to see her again. However, when Thomas went missing the very next day, he found it hard to believe that his young son could have run off, and left everything behind so quickly. It surely must have been planned. The gypsies had moved on within days, and although pursued and questioned, they had remained stubbornly silent, and never confirmed if the girl too, was missing.

Year after year, Ephraim paid for the fruitless search to continue, but he had recently concluded, that if Thomas was still alive, then he did not want to be found. His solicitors had urged him to change his will, but that was something he was not willing to do. The estate would be inherited by Joshua, his first-born son, as had always been the plan, but Thomas would be left a small fortune, just in case he ever returned. He could not, and would not, turn his back on his son.

He was dragged back from his thoughts by a knock on the study door, and his daughter, Lady Margery, poked her head around the door.

"Hello, Papa, I've just come to say goodbye before I leave for London. Are you sure I can't persuade you to come too? I'm sure a change of scenery would do you good. Anyway, I'm glad Joshua has agreed to accompany me, as I intend to do a spot of matchmaking. It's ten years since Marianne died giving birth to Charles, and it's high time he sought another wife, but he's just like you, and so obstinate in his ways."

Ephraim smiled at his daughter. She had recently turned twenty-one and was off to London to enjoy her season. With her looks, breeding, and wealth, he knew she would be a popular debutante with many suitors at her feet, and he hoped she would choose wisely. It was now, that she would have benefitted from the care and attention of her mother, but sadly that was not to be. Fortunately, his sister, Genevieve, was more than capable of presenting her niece to the royal court.

"No, London never was my scene, thank you, Margery, but I hope you have a wonderful time, and you should do with the amount of money I've spent on your wardrobe. I'm glad Joshua will be there to escort you but don't pressure him to find a wife, my dear. He'll seek another, if and when, he's ready. We all have to deal with grief in our own way, and there's no time limit."

"Oh, Papa, I know, and thank you so much for your generosity. I love all my new clothes, and I can't wait to wear them. It's so exciting; I'm longing to be presented to the royal court."

"Just remember everything your aunt tells you, and make sure you behave yourself. Do not display any of your tomboy tendencies when you're in society, or I'm sure you'll have your aunt to reckon with. Come on then, I'll wave you off. Charles is going to miss you, and his father, I'm afraid, and me too."

He escorted Margery to the front door, where Joshua was waiting with his son, Charles, and his friend, Johnny. Ephraim's third son, George, had been unwell for several years and had sadly died two years earlier. With his disabilities, he had never been expected to reach adulthood, but his death had still come as a shock. Being childlike, despite being in his twenties, he had been a good companion for Charles, and the boy missed him. Johnny, a neighbour's son, was now a regular visitor to Hartford Manor, and a valuable playmate for the boy.

Joshua hugged his son, and shook his father's hand, before helping his sister into the carriage and then boarding himself. As the carriage made its way down the long curving driveway, the siblings waved until the house and their family were out of sight.

Margery sat back and heaved a sigh of relief. "Oh, I'm so glad we're finally on our way, Joshua. I've been longing to visit London, but there was so much preparation. I can't believe I'll ever wear all the clothes that have been made for me, but I'm assured I will. I suspect after a few weeks, I'll be glad to get back to the peace and quiet of Hartford, and go riding across the moors in my old clothes."

"Well, I know I will be, but we have to find you a suitable husband first."

Lady Margery's maid, Rosemary, and Joshua's valet, Michael, were travelling in a second carriage along with masses of luggage. They too were excited to be included in a trip to London, for neither had ever ventured from North Devon before, but they knew they would be kept busy.

Back at Hartford Manor, Ephraim ushered Charles and Johnny inside and then left them to their own devices. Charles took Johnny's arm.

"Come on, Johnny, let's go to the kitchen, and see if we can get something to eat."

His friend nodded. "Yes, an excellent idea, Charles. I'm so glad you didn't go to London with your dad."

"Me too; it takes days to get there. It would be so boring sitting in the carriage for all that time. I'd quite like to go one day, though."

They entered the kitchen where Violet Clark, the cook, was busy making some sort of pudding, and a young girl called Ethel was chopping carrots and onions. The tears flowed down her cheeks at the pungent smell, but she smiled when she saw the boys, and the cook glanced up from her labours.

"Now, what have we here? Two hungry boys, I'll be bound. Am I right?"

"You know us too well, Mrs Clark. Yes, we're hungry and it's hours until our evening meal. Could we have something to eat, please?"

"Aye, I know growing lads are always hungry. Ethel, take a break, and get the young gentlemen a piece of cake, and a drink of milk; you've worked hard this morning, so you can have a piece too if you like."

The young girl did not need to be told twice. At eight years old, she had recently joined the Hartford Manor staff as a skivvy, where she worked long hours. However, she loved it, for she had come from the workhouse, having never known her parents, and although the work was hard, the food was plentiful.

The boys sat at the table and were soon munching their way through a large piece of carrot cake, while they discussed what to do with the rest of their afternoon.

When Ephraim returned to his desk, he endeavoured to get on with his accounts, but he felt restless and couldn't concentrate. Eventually, exasperated with himself, he gave up and decided to ride into Barnstaple and visit the investigator who was still searching for Thomas. For some reason, his missing son had been in his thoughts a lot recently. It was a bit late in the day for such a long ride, but it was a fine day, and he knew he could always stay in the town overnight if he so wished. He went to the stables where he had a chat with young Arthur Potts, a lad who worked with Isaac Hammett. The boy saddled his horse and Lord Fellwood set off, enjoying the countryside views, and he realised he had made the right decision in putting off his paperwork for another day. In the town, he stabled his horse and paid an unexpected call on Mr James, the man who had for so many years, been searching for Thomas.

Mr James was surprised, and not a little concerned, when he saw his wealthy client, for in truth he had made little progress for some time, though not for lack of effort. He rose to his feet, as his assistant announced Lord Fellwood.

"Why, Lord Fellwood, what a pleasant surprise. May I offer you some refreshments? A glass of port maybe?"

"Yes, thank you, that would be most pleasant after so long a ride. I'm sure you know why I'm here, Mr James; do you have any news?"

"No, sir, I'm afraid not. It's as if your son vanished off the face of the earth. I heard that he and the gypsy girl had fled to France, and I've even visited that country twice seeking news, but to no avail. I travelled through much of the countryside in the north, but although I found many gypsy camps, none had seen or heard of him, or at least, if they had, were not willing to tell me. I'm afraid I've come to the conclusion, that if your son is still alive, then he simply does not want to be found. He was so young when he left; has he never contacted you for money?"

"No, I've heard nothing from him. He had a substantial amount of money left to him by his grandmother, as well as her gold locket. When he disappeared, he took all the money from his bank account, and the locket has never been seen since, so presumably, he took that with him as well. It was a tidy sum, and if he was careful, it would have kept him for some time, particularly if he invested it in a business, to provide him with an income. He was an intelligent lad, and always excelled at languages. He spoke French fluently, so he would have been able to blend in without too much difficulty. He knew France well too, having lived there for six months with some relatives the year before to practise his use of the language. They, of course, have seen nothing of him, either. The thing is, my family and friends have been urging me for some time to stop the search, and save my money. What say you? I know you're a trustworthy man, Mr James, who would not take my money if you thought there was no chance of finding him. Tell me, do you think it's worth continuing the search after all these years?"

The investigator scratched his head and looked his client in the eye. "Well, to be honest, sir, no; it seems unlikely I'll find him after all this time. It may be best if we call off the search; after all, as you rightly point out, it's been several years now, and I have no new leads."

"Very well then, let's call it a day. If you can send me my final bill, we'll leave it at that. I'm reluctant to give up but I can see you have nowhere else to look."

"Indeed, sir; however, I have my feelers out, and if there is ever any news, I promise I'll contact you immediately."

The old man left the office, sadly resigned to the fact that he would probably never see his son again. He decided to call on his bank manager, whilst he was in town and discuss his finances. He had recently undertaken a daring project to build a canal in Hartford, a bold venture which would cost a small fortune. For many years, packhorses had carried sand and crushed shells inland from the local beaches to improve the quality of the acidic soil for farming. Limestone too, from local quarries, was transported to the many limekilns in the county, to be burnt and crushed for the same purpose. However, most of the North Devon roads were just rough tracks, unsuitable for transporting such heavy goods, and this made the journeys slow and arduous.

The previous year, on a visit to London, Lord Fellwood had made the acquaintance of an engineer called James Griffiths and was infected by the young man's enthusiasm for canal building. Originally born in Birmingham, Griffiths was the son of an engineering family and had learnt much from his father. Intrigued by the promise of transporting goods quickly and efficiently, and at a fraction of the usual cost, Lord Fellwood invited Griffiths to dine at his club. He was astounded to learn that his guest had lived in Devon for the last ten years. Deciding it must be fate, the wealthy aristocrat decided there and then, that he wanted his own canal, and furthermore, he wanted Griffiths to build it. Now, many months later, and with the finances in place, work on the canal was underway.

The plan was for the canal to be seven miles long, with a towpath alongside for the donkeys or mules to pull small tub boats containing the cargo. The boats would have wheels on the underside to enable them to be hauled from the canal up an inclined plane. Lord Fellwood had visited South Wales and clinched a deal to import both limestone and coal to feed his inland kilns. This would produce a ready supply of lime fertiliser which would greatly increase the fertility of the acidic Devon soil, increase productivity, and thus the value of his agricultural land. The rich landowner was also in discussions about exporting Marland clay via the seaport of Bideford, a regional port at the estuary of the River Torridge. Many local businessmen were sceptical of these ambitious plans and wondered if Lord Fellwood would end up bankrupting himself. However, none could deny that should his plans come to fruition, then they would greatly benefit the area.

A couple of hours later, having been reassured at the bank that his finances were in good shape, Lord Fellwood decided to spend the night in the town, rather than travel home in the gathering dusk.

CHAPTER 23

Betsey Lovering was red in the face as she kneaded the dough on the large wooden table. There was a smudge of flour across her upturned, freckled nose, and her unruly curly brown hair had escaped from its ponytail. The weather was unusually hot for early May, and in the kitchen, with the range pouring out heat, it was stifling. She wiped the back of her hand across her sweaty brow.

"Phew, I don't know about you, Josie, but I think I'm melting. Shall we go outside for five minutes to cool off?"

"That sounds like an excellent idea, Betsey; we could have a glass of lemonade. I'll just give Ma a shout and see if she'd like to join us."

Betsey put the dough into a large bowl, covered it with a damp cloth, and left it close to the range.

"There, I have to wait for that to prove anyway, so it's a good time for a break."

Josie was originally from Somerset, where her family had a smallholding, on the county border with Devon. She had married Silas Carter the previous year, and they lived in the small cottage previously occupied by Adam and Ellen Lovering. The cottage was owned by The Red Lion Inn and rented out, though Mal had seldom seen any money from Adam. Josie went to the bar in search of her mother-in-law and found Kezia serving a tankard of ale to her brother, Jonathan Chugg, who lived at Hollyford Farm.

"Hello, Mr Chugg; are you here for a dose of your usual medicine?"

"Aye, maid, I enjoy the occasional tipple; it keeps me going. You're looking well, too, if I may say so; blooming in fact. How long is it now until you present me with a new niece or nephew?"

Josie blushed and glanced down at her swollen stomach. "Just a few weeks to go; Silas and I can't wait for our baby to be born."

"I hope it all goes well, for you, my dear. Do you want a boy or a girl?"

"Thank you, Mr Chugg; I don't mind what it is, as long as it's healthy, though I think Silas would favour a son. Ma, Betsey and I are going to sit outside for five minutes to cool off; it's that hot in the kitchen, and we wondered if you would like to join us for some lemonade?"

"That sounds like a splendid idea, Josie; Mal, can you manage for a little while?"

"Yes, of course, my love; take your time. You've been on your feet all morning, and it'll soon be time for the dinnertime rush."

"I'll leave you to chat to Mal, then Jonathan, and I'll see you soon."

The three women left the kitchen, each carrying a glass of freshly-made lemonade, and sought the shade under the old apple tree. They sat down on the cool grass; Josie, with some difficulty.

"Ah, that's better, though I'm not sure I'll ever get back up again. I don't know how old this tree is, but it's a cool place to sit on a hot day. There's plenty of blossom too; it'll be a bumper crop this year, as long as we don't get a late frost. We should be able to make lots of cider."

Kezia gazed up into the tree, which was laden with frothy pink and white blossom. "Yes, if we can just get past the Franklin nights, then the tree should be safe from frost."

"What are the Franklin nights? I've never heard of them?"

"Have you not, Josie? I would have thought coming from Somerset, where they grow so many apples, you would have; but then I think it's an old Devon tale."

Betsey joined in the conversation. "Go on, then, Aunty Kezzie, tell us the story of the Franklin nights."

"Well, it's probably just an old wives' tale, but the story goes that Franklin was a brewer of ale, who lived on Dartmoor. He was worried because folk were beginning to enjoy cider more than ale, and his sales were suffering, so he sold his soul to the devil in return for three late frosts to come and destroy the apple blossom each year."

"What are the dates?"

"The Franklin nights fall on the nineteenth, twentieth, and twenty-first of May, and although the story is probably a load of old rubbish, it's surprising how often we get a late frost on those nights. All the gardeners are careful to keep their fruit and vegetables protected until after those dates anyway."

Betsey had lived at the inn with the Carters for more than fourteen years. Her life before that was something she preferred to forget. After deserting his two children, her father, Adam Lovering, had never returned to the village, though his lady friend, Becky Chown, had come back some six months later with her tail between her legs. It had not taken her long to discover Adam was not the catch, she thought. After miscarrying her first child, and receiving no sympathy from the father, who still drank like a fish, and gambled all his money away, she had seen the light and came running home to her mother. She received a frosty welcome, and even now, so many years later, many folk in Hartford refused to speak to her. She still lived at home with her mother, working in the butcher's shop, an old maid, and content to stay that way.

When her path first crossed that of Adam's daughter, Betsey, she had the grace to look embarrassed and mutter some kind of apology. The child had simply glared at the woman who had stolen her father away, and left her to fend for herself and her little brother, who had subsequently died. To this day, Betsey had never acknowledged Becky and still crossed the street if she saw her approaching. Kezia, knowing how Betsey felt, never sent her to the butcher's shop for meat, but always went herself, if no one else was available.

The Red Lion Inn was prospering, and as busy as ever, with travellers often staying en route to London or Exeter, or at the very least, changing their horses before resuming their journey. The customers usually wanted something to eat, and so the women were busy all the time, baking pasties and bread, and making stews. Mal had invested in two cows and six pigs, and so they now had their own supply of butter, milk and cheese. The livestock was Silas's responsibility, though any member of the household would turn their hand to do the milking, and caring for the animals if necessary.

The bank loan that Mal had agonised over so many years before, had proved every bit as difficult to repay as he feared, and even now they still struggled to make ends meet. However, with just eleven years of repayments left, Mal thought he was beginning to see the light at the end of the tunnel. His son, Ned, was now twenty-three, and although he had courted one or two of the local girls, he never seemed that keen on marrying, always ending the relationship before it became too serious. His mother urged him to settle down, for one day the inn would be his, but her pleas fell on deaf ears, as he steadfastly ignored her advice. Ned worked in the bar with Mal most of the time, leaving Kezia free to attend to the visitors. He also oversaw the ostler, who was responsible for changing the horses of the stagecoaches stopping at the inn. There were three stable boys, and Ned made sure everyone pulled their weight.

With their short break over, Kezia and Betsey helped Josie to her feet, and the three women returned to the kitchen, where Kezia busied herself preparing the food which would soon be in demand. The stagecoach to Exeter passed through Hartford around noon, and most of the passengers would require a meal, whilst their horses were changed. She carved ham, glistening moist and pink, ready to serve up for the ploughman's lunches that were proving so popular. She put a couple of slices onto each of the six plates and added a chunk of her homemade cheese, two hard-boiled eggs, three pickled onions, and a large slice of bread, spread thickly with golden butter. Putting the platters in the cool larder, out of the way of the flies, she stirred the rabbit stew, which was simmering on the old range. Dipping a large ladle into the bubbling liquid, she lifted some out and blew on it, then put it to her lips to check the taste.

"Mm, that and better will do any day, as my old Mum used to say; just a little bit more salt, I think. How are those pasties coming along, Josie?"

"Yes, they should be ready; I was just going to take them out of the oven."

The young woman grabbed a thick cloth and opened the hot oven door, wafting the steam away from her face as she peered inside. She reached in, and withdrew a heavy tray of twenty pasties, all golden brown and smelling delicious.

"Yes, they're done. Betsey, do you want the oven now to cook your loaves of bread?"

"Yes, please; good timing, thanks. They're ready to go in."

The three women were well-practised at getting the best results from the limited equipment available to them. The cooking of the hams, pasties, stew and bread was timed to perfection, to ensure the oven was never empty, and the top of the range was fully employed. Josie stood and surveyed their handiwork, and eased her aching back.

"There, I think we're ready for the first stagecoach. How many are we expecting today?"

"One any time now, and then another around two o'clock, so by four o'clock we might be able to take another breather. Ah, Ned, there you are. Are the horses ready for the stagecoach? It will be here soon."

"Yes, they're all fed, and fresh for the journey, so I thought I'd come in now for a bite to eat before it gets too busy. Can I grab one of those pasties? They smell so good."

"Yes, of course, Ned, sit yourself down and I'll get you one; they're scalding hot, mind. I've only just taken them out of the oven."

"That's just how I like them. I timed it right, again."

The young man sat down at the large kitchen table and cut his pasty in half so that it would cool more quickly. He had coppery-red hair and many freckles; both characteristics of the Carter family, for many generations.

"What have you been making today, Betsey?"

"I've made a batch of scones, some cakes, and six loaves of bread this morning, and they're in the oven now. We take it in turns to cook something different, and then we all get a bit of practice at everything."

"That's a clever idea; do you like baking?"

"Aye, I do, but more than that; it's such a pleasure to have the ingredients to cook with. When my mum was alive she tried to show me how to cook, but there was so little food she couldn't teach me much, though she wanted to. She worked at Hartford Manor before she married my dad, and she helped with the cooking there, so she knew how to make lots of wonderful things. I think she missed being able to do that. Mind you, Aunty Kezzie has taught me such a lot."

Ned remembered Betsey's sad past, and he looked at her fondly as she washed her hands. She looked back over her shoulder.

"Aunty Kezzie, is it tomorrow there are no stagecoaches?"

"Aye, that's right, Betsey. There are none on a Wednesday; not at the moment, anyway but it's getting so busy with folk travelling around, that it wouldn't surprise me if they started running every day. Why do you ask?"

"Well, if it's quiet tomorrow, and if you can manage without me for a few hours, I wondered if I might go for a stroll in the afternoon?"

"Yes, of course, you know you can have time off whenever you want; you work so hard, I don't know what we would do without you. It was a lucky day for us when you came to live here, Betsey Lovering. Now, just a minute though; would you be needing time off to meet a certain young man?"

The girl blushed. "Yes, Daniel Abernethy has asked me to go for a walk with him. I've been seeing a bit of him recently."

"Well, he'd be quite a catch, being the doctor's grandson and all. Is it right, he's training to be a doctor?"

"Yes, he's come here to get some experience working with his grandfather before he sets up his own practice. Ned, are you going so soon? Wouldn't you like one of these scones, I made earlier?"

Ned's face had darkened at the mention of Betsey's young man, and he rose swiftly from the table.

"No thanks, I need to get on; I have a lot to do."

As he abruptly left the kitchen, his mother gazed after him thoughtfully.

CHAPTER 24

Daniel Abernethy called for Betsey after lunch the next day. He was a good-looking young man of twenty-six, his hair so dark, it was nearly black, and his eyes a vivid blue. He was from a rich family, in which many were doctors, including his father and grandfather, and he had completed his medical training in Edinburgh. His parents were currently taking a long holiday in the South of France where they had recently purchased a property, and his father thought it would be a good experience for him to work with his grandfather for a year.

His grandfather, Hamish, had introduced him to Betsey and told him of the hardships she had endured as a child. Daniel was besotted as soon as he set eyes on her, for although she was unaware of it, Betsey had grown into a beautiful young woman. Her thick, wavy, soft brown hair was one of her most attractive features; her delicate skin was unblemished, and her grey eyes were clear. When not working, she often wore her hair loose, and it cascaded down to her waist, the auburn tints shining in the sunshine. Having been so neglected and lice-ridden as a child, she kept herself scrupulously clean.

Unfortunately, Ned was in the kitchen when Daniel called for her, and Kezia sighed to herself, knowing he resented the young man's interest in the girl. Betsey opened the door, her eyes shining warmly.

"Hello, Daniel, come in for a moment, whilst I fetch my coat; Ned tells me there's a cold wind, today."

"Hello, Betsey, yes, there is. Hello, Mrs Carter, hello Ned; I hope you're both well?"

Ned merely grunted and pushed rudely past the visitor, but Kezia assured him that everyone was in good health.

Once outside, Daniel pulled Betsey towards him. He kissed her firmly on the lips, but she pulled away.

"Not here, Daniel, someone might see."

"Well, it doesn't matter, does it? You're my girlfriend, so surely I can kiss you?"

"Not in public, it's not seemly."

"Let's go somewhere a bit more private then; I've been counting the hours until I could kiss you, Betsey Lovering."

Hand in hand, they walked through the woods, which were carpeted with bluebells and white wood anemones. They came to the clearing in the woods where the gypsies used to camp, and Betsey was lost in thought, wondering what had happened to Gypsy Freda, Jane, and Thomas. She missed them all and longed to know if they were all right, though she supposed the old woman must have passed away by now. She hoped Jane had returned to England before that happened. She remembered the day when, as a little girl, she had carried the message from Jane to Gypsy Freda, telling her she was eloping to France with Thomas Fellwood. The old woman had paled, and sat down shakily, clearly distraught by the news. That had been the last time Betsey had seen her, for, within a few days, the gypsies moved on, and never returned.

"A penny for them, Betsey. What are you thinking about? I've been chatting away to you, and I swear you haven't heard a word I've said."

"What, oh, I'm sorry, Daniel; I was miles away. I was just thinking about a tribe of gypsies, who lived here when I was a little girl. I was often cold and hungry back then, and an old lady called Freda, and her granddaughter, Jane, were kind to me. I wonder where they are now? They always used to turn up every year without fail, but for some reason, when they left in the year I was about six, they never came back."

"Oh well, they probably found a better campsite somewhere else; does it matter?"

"Well, I was fond of them so I was just thinking about them." Betsey suspected the reason the gypsies had never returned was that they did not want the disappearance of Thomas Fellwood, to be linked to that of Gypsy Jane. Only she knew the true story. She thought about explaining it to Daniel, but then remembered her promise to Jane, that she would never tell another living soul, and knew she must abide by that vow.

The young couple wandered on a bit farther and came to the copse where Jasper Morris had tried to force his attention on Jane. It was also where he met his untimely death, after a tussle with Thomas Fellwood. Betsey decided these woods were full of memories, and not all of them pleasant. A day or two after the young couple had absconded, and the gypsies had moved on, Betsey searched for Thomas's gold watch. After a while, she found it in the middle of a gorse bush and was scratched as she retrieved it. Fortunately, although bitterly cold when the watch was lost, there had also been a dry spell, and when she opened the watch, she could see that the moisture had not penetrated its tightly fitting cover. She smuggled it back to the inn and then wondered what to do with it. She had promised to keep it safe in case Thomas ever returned, but knew she could never explain how she came by it.

One of the few possessions she had retrieved from her childhood home when she left, was the colourful little tin where her mother kept her housekeeping money. The little tin, so prettily painted with the bright blue forget-me-nots, red poppies, and yellow buttercups, now resided on her bedroom windowsill. The tin was in full sight of everyone, and yet she knew no one would open it, as they knew it contained her precious memories; a red ribbon, bought for her so many years before by Aunty Kezzie, a lock of her little brother, Norman's hair, so thoughtfully saved by her Aunty Kezzie, a cheap paste brooch that had belonged to her mother, and, of course, the shiny gold watch, which lay buried right at the bottom.

She had shared a bedroom with Ned and Silas for several years until it was felt she needed her own room. Not wanting to sacrifice a bedroom that could be let out to paying guests, Mal had built a partition wall down the centre of the large bedroom. As it was previously a dual-aspect room, this conveniently left a window in each room. Betsey's room was tiny, but she didn't mind at all; in truth, she would have been content sleeping in the barn, if it meant she could stay at the inn. Ned still occupied the room next to Betsey, but Silas, of course, now lived next door with Josie. Betsey never visited them, for the house held too many unpleasant memories for her.

Daniel spread his jacket on the damp ground. "Come and sit down, Betsey; you're so thoughtful, today."

"Yes, sorry, Daniel. It's just that I used to visit this area a lot as a child, and I can't help thinking about things that happened back then."

He sat down and patted the ground next to him. Betsey joined him, and he put his arm around her and kissed her tenderly. Gently, he pushed her back and, leaning over her, kissed her again more passionately.

"You're so pretty, Betsey; I'm lucky to have you as my girlfriend, and I think Ned's jealous."

"Don't be silly; I was brought up with Ned and Silas, and they're like brothers to me. No, he just worries about me. He's always been protective of me, ever since I was tiny, but that's all it is."

"Well, if you say so, but I think he fancies you something rotten. It's a good job I got your attention first, isn't it?"

He carried on kissing her, his hand softly caressing her breast through her blouse, but when he slowly started to undo her buttons. She pushed him away.

"Stop it, Daniel. We can't go any further."

He sighed. "You know you want to; I can tell by the way you're kissing me. Come on, Betsey, let me have a little peek at your lovely titties. There's no one to see, and I want to kiss them; I'm sure you'll like it."

Reluctantly, but curiously, Betsey allowed him to undo her buttons and gasped as he put his mouth to her breast and kissed it gently. She became aware of his hand reaching down over her legs and pulling up her skirt. He caressed the inside of her thigh.

"Betsey, we've been seeing each other for months now; let me make love to you. I love you so much. I promise I'll be gentle, and I won't hurt you." He gazed into her eyes. "You're so beautiful."

His hand was now fumbling with her pantaloons, and she was sorely tempted to allow him to continue, but suddenly she pushed him away firmly and sat up.

"No, stop it, Daniel! I'm not that sort of girl. It's not right, and I can't risk getting in the family way. I would never disgrace Aunty Kezzie and Uncle Mal, after all they've done for me."

"Oh, Betsey; it would be all right to do it just once. I'm a doctor and I've studied these matters. Virgins never get pregnant the first time they do it. It'll be all right; trust me, I know what I'm talking about."

"No, I'm sorry, but I can't risk it."

He leapt to his feet. "Fine, if that's how you feel; we might as well go home, then."

"Well, we can still enjoy each other's company, can't we? I thought we were going to Shebworthy Pond?"

"No, not today. I need to get back; I have work to do."

Betsey knew he was lying, as he had told her he had the rest of the day off, but she said nothing. She was disappointed in him, knowing he was in a foul mood and cutting the afternoon short because she had refused him. They walked back to the inn together, no longer holding hands and barely speaking, and giving her a peck of a kiss on her cheek, he bid her good day.

Ned was grooming one of the horses when he saw Betsey pass through the yard with Daniel. He was surprised and pleased to see them back so soon. He would never have admitted to his feelings for Betsey, as he knew she saw him as a brother, and with her looks, she could have any man in the village, and probably farther afield. He knew that and accepted it, but for some reason, he had taken against Daniel Abernethy. He couldn't quite explain why, but he didn't trust the man, and he hoped Betsey would see through him before it was too late.

He was delighted when Betsey saw him busy at work and went to join him.

"Hello, Betsey; you're soon back. I thought you'd be out longer with Daniel; is everything all right?"

"Yes, of course, but he had to get back to catch up on some work. Shall I get another brush, and groom this side?"

"Aye, that would be grand, Betsey, thanks, you can help me do the other two if you like."

"Yes, why not? I like grooming horses; it's restful and soothing."

"It is that, and I'll enjoy it all the more with your company."

The two of them spent a pleasant hour together, grooming the next two horses before they returned to the kitchen in time for their tea.

CHAPTER 25

Friday mornings were always frantically busy at The Red Lion, as it was market day in Barnstaple. Mal and Kezia were usually up at half past five, gathering everything together, and getting ready to go. In addition to running the inn, taking in travellers, and providing a change of horses for the stagecoaches, Mal had branched out, using every inch of the ground he owned, to make more money to repay the loan for the new roof.

Two of the pigs he had reared were now fully grown, and he had recently slaughtered them, ready for the market. He charged slightly less than the butchers' shops in the town, and by so doing, knew he was likely to sell all the meat with no problem. He kept back a few joints, which Kezia salted down for use in the inn. They would keep nicely for up to a month. He found rearing pigs a profitable business, for they would eat virtually anything, and the saying that everything on a pig could be used except for the squeal, was indeed true, for nothing was wasted.

The two cows they kept, produced far more milk than they needed, and so it was turned into butter, cream, and cheese. One cow, Daisy, was a black and white Friesian, and she gave an incredibly high yield of milk. A docile animal, she was a pleasure to milk. Her companion was Buttercup, a little Jersey cow, and she gave far less milk, but it was rich and creamy. Although considerably smaller than Daisy, Buttercup was a feisty animal, and handy at striking out with her hooves or horns, if she had the chance. Together, their milk provided a good mix. The milk was carried to the market in churns, and Mal would pour it by the pint, or half pint, into the jugs that folk carried with them for the purpose. The rich milk made thick clotted cream, a well-known Devon delicacy. Kezia would slowly warm the milk on the top of the range in a wide enamel bowl, to allow the water in the milk to evaporate. When the liquid had reduced by half, she would skim the cream off into a bowl, and leave it to cool in the larder.

The most recent venture of Mal and Kezia was the purchase of twenty new chickens, which were now laying well. Kezia's first job on a Friday morning was to collect the eggs, wash them, and add them to the others she had put ready earlier in the week. Later in the year, there would also be green vegetables from the allotment at the back of the inn, but at the moment, there were only swedes, carrots, parsnips, and potatoes, from the previous year's harvest to sell.

Sometimes Ned or Silas would take the cart to market, but it was a task that Mal enjoyed, and so on a sunny Friday morning in mid-May, Kezia, Betsey, Ned and Silas, helped him to load the cart with the produce, and waved him off, hoping he would return with an empty cart, and his pockets full of money. It was a chilly morning with a nip of frost in the air, but he could see that it was going to be a fine day, and he was looking forward to meeting up with some of the other farmers, who also sold their goods in the market. His pitch was situated right outside The Three Tuns Inn, an area coveted by many. However, his family had used the same plot for many years, and it was an unwritten rule that it belonged to the Carter family. At lunchtime, he would ask another stall holder to keep an eye on his produce and nip into the inn for a pasty and a pint of ale or the landlord would bring it out to him.

As the old horse plodded slowly along the lane, Mal whistled to himself, thinking he should make a tidy profit today. It took a while to get to Barnstaple, for it was a fair distance, and he had to go slowly along the rutted tracks to avoid the risk of anything falling off the cart. On the way, there was a steep hill with a nasty bend at the bottom, where the road crossed over a stream, via a narrow bridge. He took it slowly down the hill, knowing from experience, it would be difficult to stop quickly if he was travelling at a fast pace. The bend at the bottom was so sharp, it was impossible to see around it, and often, if two carts met, one would have to reverse to allow the other to pass.

As his horse rounded the corner, he was horrified to see a large black bull galloping straight toward him. The animal was wide-eyed and frightened, and in the distance, he could see a couple of men in hot pursuit. It was impossible for the huge beast to pass the cart, and the horse reared as the bull careered into it. Mal was thrown from his seat, and the cart overturned, the eggs smashing onto the ground, and the churns of milk spilling as they fell.

The farmer and his two labourers arrived, wheezing, as they tried to catch their breath, and were distraught to see what had happened. With the cart now lying on its side, the bull had managed to squeeze through the narrow gap and was nowhere to be seen. The horse was still attached to the upturned cart and could go nowhere, but it was whinnying and rearing in fright, as the farmer caught hold of its bridle, and tried to calm the animal.

"Jake, where's the driver? Can you see him? I think it's Mal Carter from The Red Lion; I recognise the horse."

Tom Jones, the farmer, was panicking as to what had happened to the driver, and when they rounded the cart they could see that Mal was unconscious, and pinned down by the cart.

"Oh no, look, it is Mal; we must see if we can lift the cart and free him. Jake, you and Billy lift it, and I'll try to pull him out."

They had to clear away some of the fallen produce first, but eventually, after a few attempts, the two men managed to lift the cart high enough for Tom to pull his friend out. Mal was still unconscious, a large gash on his forehead bleeding heavily, but the farmer was relieved to see his friend's chest rising and falling, and know that he was alive.

"Jake, can you hurry to the village and fetch the doctor; Billy, you'd better run after the bull, and see if you can find him and secure him somewhere. Bloody animal! He's caused enough mayhem already this morning. Just find any empty field to put him in for now. We'll worry about getting him back later; I'm worried about him causing more damage while he's on the run. I'll come and help you, as soon as I can."

After ten minutes or so, Mal began to groan, and Tom mopped the wound on his head with a cloth he had dipped in the stream. "It's all right, Mal. It's me, Tom; are you all right?"

Mal opened his eyes and stared in bewilderment at the anxious man leaning over him.

"What happened? Where am I?

"I'm afraid my bull bolted, Mal, and it collided with your horse and cart. I'm so sorry. I only bought the beast a month or so ago, and he's a vicious bugger. No wonder he was a bit cheaper than usual; he has an evil temper. We were moving him to a new field, and something must have scared him because he took off like a bat out of hell. I've been putting the job off for days because I knew it would be difficult. How are you feeling? Can you get up?"

Mal held on to the farmer, and tried to get up, then looked anxiously at him.

"I can't feel my legs. Am I trapped? Is something holding me down?"

Tom was astounded. "No, Mal, the cart was pinning you down, but the lads lifted it, and I pulled you out. Your head's bleeding, but I don't think you're injured other than that. Are you sure, you can't get up?"

The wounded man tried again without success, and a look of panic came into his eyes.

"Oh no, Tom, what am I going to do, if I can't walk?"

"Now, don't worry, Mal; I'm sure it will be all right. It's probably just shock, or bruising, or something. I've sent Jake to fetch the doctor, so he should be here soon, and I'm sure he'll know what to do."

It was another half an hour before Doctor Abernethy, and his grandson, Daniel, arrived on their pony and trap. The young man helped his elderly grandfather to alight, and they approached the patient. Hamish Abernethy knelt on the ground next to the ashen-faced man.

"Now then, Mal; what have you been up to?"

"Oh, doctor, I can't move my legs. In fact, I can't even feel them. What's wrong with them?"

The doctor first examined the wide cut on Mal's head and asked Daniel to bandage it. Then, he asked Mal to close his eyes, and felt down each of his arms, asking him if he could feel what he was doing, to which the innkeeper nodded. The doctor lifted Mal's jacket and undid his trousers. He carefully felt down over the stomach and the hip bones, and then gently pricked the area with a pin.

"Can you feel that Mal?"

"Yes, I can feel it on my belly."

"What about on your hip bones?"

"Just slightly, but not much."

The doctor took off his patient's boots and socks and pricked each of his toes, and then up his legs, but Mal could feel nothing at all.

"Now, Mal, I don't want you to worry too much. It may be that you're severely bruised, and that's what's causing the paralysis. The feeling may come back at any time. You could also be in shock, and you were knocked unconscious too, so that won't have helped. I think we need to get you home and into bed, and see how you go on for the next few days. Once you're in bed, I can examine your back properly."

His soothing words were lost on Mal, who was already wondering how the others would cope with running the inn without him.

The doctor turned his attention to the farmer. "Now, Tom, can you fetch your horse and cart, and put a thick layer of clean straw on it; we need something soft for Mal to lie on, whilst we transport him home. He mustn't be jolted about too much. I'll stay here with Mal until you return. Daniel, you take the pony and trap to The Red Lion, and tell them what's happened. Someone will need to come and attend to the horse and get the cart back on its wheels. There's a fine mess here too, of milk and smashed eggs; but hopefully, some of it can be salvaged."

Kezia and the rest of the family were distraught to hear what had happened. Beside herself with worry about her husband, Kezia made up a fresh bed for Mal, and sent Ned, Silas, and Betsey, to sort out the cart. Josie was unable to help them because of her advanced pregnancy, so she stayed in the kitchen to keep an eye on the baking. Ned harnessed the inn's other carthorse, and Betsey rode up in front of him. Silas travelled back to the bridge with Daniel on the pony and trap. They were shocked when they saw the scene of the accident. By this time, Tom had arrived with his cart, and carefully, under Dr Abernethy's watchful eye, they lifted Mal gently onto the bed of straw. Daniel once more drove the pony and trap back to The Red Lion, ensuring the road was clear, and Tom followed with the horse and cart with the doctor riding beside Mal. Once there, they summoned more help from the inn, to carry the man to his bed.

Back at the bridge, Ned unbuckled the horse from the cart, and Betsey tethered the distressed beast to a gatepost. The poor animal was shaking with fear, and she spent some time stroking its nose and talking to it to calm it down. Jake returned with more help from the farm, and another horse. He tied two ropes to the cart and attached them to the saddles of the two horses. The other men went to the side of the cart and heaved, whilst Jake led the horses away to take up the strain. The plan worked, and in no time at all, the cart was back on its wheels, again; fortunately, not seriously damaged. However, the men were dismayed at the state of the produce which was thrown all over the ground. Two churns of milk had spilt when the lids flew off, but another two were undamaged. Most of the eggs, of course, were broken, but they managed to salvage the remainder of the load.

Ned scratched his head thoughtfully. "One of us will have to take this lot to the market, or it will all go rotten. It's going to be pretty late by the time we get there now, but if we reduce the prices, hopefully, most of it will sell. I'm happy to go, Silas unless you want to?"

"No, that's all right, Ned, you go, and I'll get back to the inn and help Josie. She'll be rushed off her feet by now, with the first stagecoach due any time, and it's not advisable for her to do too much in her condition. I'd rather be there to keep an eye on her. Betsey, why don't you go with Ned, and tidy up the produce while he drives the cart?"

"Yes, all right, Silas, if you think you can manage at the inn. It does all look a bit battered and dusty, doesn't it? The butter's a bit bashed about, but it will be all right, and, luckily, the lid didn't come off the cream; it fits quite tightly."

They travelled as fast as they dared, and by the time they arrived in the town, Betsey had tidied everything up. They hastily set everything out on their trestle table and explained to their friends what had happened. They reduced their prices, and when folk heard of Mal's accident, they made a point of buying as much as they could, for he was a popular man.

It was long after three o'clock before they could even think of getting a bite to eat, and leaving Betsey in charge, Ned vanished into The Three Tuns and returned with a hot pasty and a tankard of ale for each of them. As they sat chatting on their bench, munching the pasties, and drinking their ale, Ned felt ashamed, for he had thoroughly enjoyed having Betsey all to himself for the day, and he felt guilty it had come about because of his father's accident.

CHAPTER 26

Lady Margery found the journey to London, tedious. She was not a young woman who enjoyed sitting still for any length of time and found the long hours in the coach passed slowly. When she was tired of looking out of the window, she read her book but found it difficult to concentrate. The travellers were, in fact, extremely fortunate to be in the family carriage, for the journey would have been far more uncomfortable, had they been in a public stagecoach, where the occupants were often crammed in tightly, and some of them none too sweet-smelling. Joshua and Margery were also able to decide when and where they wished to break their journey.

"Have you been to Aunt Genevieve's new house before, Joshua?"

"Yes, when I last visited London, a couple of years ago. It's an impressive mansion, I must say. Aunt Genevieve was one of the first people to move into the new houses in Belgravia when the area was developed back in the twenties. I think it became popular when the king moved into Buckingham House, and now it attempts to rival Mayfair."

"I wonder why they called it Belgravia? Is it another country? It sounds like it."

"I'm not sure, but I think Aunt Genevieve said it was named after a village in Cheshire. A lot of the land here is owned by the Grosvenor family, and that's where they have their country seat. Mind you, I did read somewhere, that back in the Middle Ages, Belgravia was called the Five Fields, and it was used for grazing sheep and cattle; it's hard to believe that, now it's so built up. I think it was a popular area for duelling in the past."

"Is it far now, do you think? I can't wait for this awful journey to end."

"No, I think we're almost there now. In fact, yes, I'm sure of it. There's the Bloody Bridge which crosses the River Westbourne, and Aunt Genevieve's house is not far from here."

"Goodness, why is it called the Bloody Bridge?"

"Well, the story goes, that this area used to be frequented by robbers and highwaymen, and it was dangerous to cross the fields at night. About a hundred years ago, a man's body was found near the bridge, with half his face and five fingers removed. I don't know if it's true, but that's how it got its name."

Margery studied the bridge in fascination, her vivid imagination working overtime. Within ten minutes, the carriage stopped beside two large, black, wrought iron gates. On either side were huge stone pillars, and on top of them, were two lions, painted in gold. The gateman noticed their arrival and opened the gates to allow the carriage to pass through and make its way down the long drive to the house.

Margery gasped, as she took in the splendour of the impressive building, and she was overawed at the wonderful gardens that surrounded it.

"My goodness, it is grand, isn't it? It makes Hartford Manor look shabby."

They were shown into a lavishly furnished drawing room, where Lady Fitzherbert awaited them. She hugged her nephew and niece. A widow now, Ephraim's sister had married well. Her husband, the wealthy peer, Johnathan Fitzherbert, had died two years earlier, after a marriage that had lasted nearly fifty years. It had been a happy relationship, blighted only by a lack of children, and the lady had only recently discarded her widow's weeds. She missed her spouse and knew this would not change until her dying day.

"My dears, how delightful to see you; I'm so glad you've come to stay with me for a while. How exciting it will be to present you at court, as one of the debutantes this year, Margery. We simply must visit the Modiste, Madame Eva; she will make you look exquisite, with your lovely, slender young figure."

"That's kind of you, Aunt Genevieve, though Papa has provided quite a lot of clothes for me, already."

"Well, we'll see, but a young lady can never have too many clothes during her season. And you, Joshua, may we possibly find you a bride?"

The young man frowned at his aunt. "Now, please don't start going on about that, Aunt Genevieve; I'm all right as I am. It's this young lady, we need to find a beau for."

"Well, we'll see. You never know, you might find an attractive young lady who will steal your heart. In my experience, love often appears, when least expected. How is young Master Charles, anyway?"

"He's well, thank you, though he misses his Uncle George; they thought the world of each other."

"Yes, I was sorry to hear that George had been taken from us; he was such a pleasant young man, and it was a shame he was born with disabilities. He managed them well, though, and I think he had a happy life."

"Yes, he did, and he always made the best of everything."

"Do you have any plans whilst you are in London?"

"Yes, one or two. I have a friend who lives in Pall Mall, and I'd like to spend some time with him."

"Oh, who is it? I might know him."

"He's called Timothy Vulliamy. His family was originally from Switzerland, and he's a distant relative of

Benjamin Vulliamy, who I think is quite famous for making clocks. I believe he even provided one for Windsor Castle."

"Oh yes, I have heard the name, though I'm not acquainted with the family, and I believe I'm right in saying that the clock in the dining room is a Vulliamy. How do you know the young man?"

"Well, he also has family connections in Exeter, and I met him there one day in an art gallery. We share a love of art, and he wants me to accompany him to the Royal Academy, and the National Gallery."

Lady Margery joined in the conversation. "What a strange name for a place, Pall Mall is. I wonder who dreamed that up. Where is it, in London?"

"Yes, it is a strange name, isn't it? It's situated in Westminster, and Timothy tells me that the name comes from pall-mall, a ball game similar to croquet. It's said King James I was a fan of the game, and it became popular in that area. I understand there are also a lot of gentleman's clubs there, and Timothy has invited me to dine with him at the Travellers Club, where he's a member."

"Oh, you'll enjoy that, Joshua, your Uncle Johnathan was a member, and loved going there. I'm glad you have a friend to spend time with whilst you are here. Margery, did I ever tell you of the time that I attended the first ball for debutantes?"

Her niece shook her head, and her aunt continued. "Well, it was arranged for Queen Charlotte's birthday in 1780, when I was just twenty. She was the wife of the old king, of course, George III. It was such a pity he lost his mind, for I believe they had a happy marriage and many children. Anyway, the ball was a grand affair, and I remember the queen, standing next to a huge birthday cake, and all the debutantes curtseyed to her. I think that's how the custom of being presented to court began. At twenty-one, you're a little older than most debutantes, my dear. Quite a few of them are only seventeen or eighteen, but I know you've been reluctant to come until now, and of course, George's death delayed matters."

"Yes, I'm more the outdoor type, and I admit I've been putting this off. I've never liked all the dressing up and fuss associated with society, but I don't find it quite as tedious as I once did, and Papa so wanted me to come. I must confess, now I'm here; I'm looking forward to it all immensely."

"I'm so pleased you're here because it will give me something new to focus on. I've been so miserable since I lost Johnathan; I've had no interest in anything, and of course, not having had any children, I don't have a daughter of my own to present to the Queen. We'll have great fun together, Margery. I've met Queen Adelaide once or twice at various functions, though not for the last couple of years, as I've not ventured out much, whilst I was in mourning for your uncle."

"I'm feeling quite nervous about it all; I just hope I don't trip when I'm walking towards her, and make a fool of myself."

"Of course, you won't; everyone worries about that. We must practise your curtseying, though. It's essential that's done correctly. There are other things you need to know too. For example, if you drop your handkerchief or your fan, in front of a gentleman it means you want to be friends. However, if you drop your parasol, you're telling him you love him, so great care needs to be taken."

"Oh, my goodness, I'll never remember. I think I'll just be careful not to drop anything."

"You'll soon get the hang of it, and it can be great fun, especially watching what your rival debutantes do. If your mother, God bless her soul, had lived longer, she would have educated you in these niceties."

"Is there anything else, I should know?"

"Well, if you want to deter an admirer, tapping your chin with your glove tells him you love another, but if you put a finger of your left hand on your chin while sitting in the window it means you would like to get to know the young man better."

"Oh, please, don't tell me anymore, Aunt Genevieve, I'll never remember it all. I think you've made me even more nervous now; I shall almost be afraid to move."

"You'll be fine, and I'll be there to instruct you. Now, tomorrow morning, I thought we would promenade around the park. It's the done thing and the best place to make new acquaintances. I particularly want you to meet Lord Clarence Montgomery and Sir Edwin Ponsonby, for either one would be a suitable match, and they seem to be personable young men. You needn't worry, my dear, I don't intend to pair you off with an old man, however rich, or titled, he may be. I want you to marry well, of course, but I also want you to be happy. Hopefully, with a little care, we can achieve both."

CHAPTER 27

Kezia tossed and turned in the bed beside Mal. She had been awake for hours and was trying to keep still, and not disturb her husband. However, he reached down and took her hand.

"What's the matter, love, are you poorly?"

"No, there's nothing wrong with me, Mal. I just can't get off to sleep, since I got out to have a wee."

Her husband sighed. "You have too much on your mind, that's the trouble, and it's all down to me. I'm so sorry, I'm no help to you, anymore."

"Don't be daft; it's not your fault you had an accident, and you still help a lot. I'm glad you can do all the paperwork, and you've become a dab hand at preparing veg."

"Yes, that's something I never thought I'd be doing, but if it helps, I'm glad. I don't know what we're going to do though, Kezzie. It was hard enough to make ends meet and repay that blasted loan when I was working all the hours God sends, but now you and the others can't cope. It's too much work, and Josie's baby will be here before we know it. She shouldn't be doing so much at a time like this. I'm looking forward to being a grandad, though, how about you? Will you mind being a granny?" He chuckled in the dark.

"No, I'll love it, and when you see how many folk die young, you have to be glad we've lived long enough to be grandparents. Do you think we could afford to take on an extra pair of hands?"

"No, I don't think it's advisable at the moment. I mean, it's not as if another worker, would bring in more money is it? No, I'm afraid you'll have to struggle on a bit longer, my love. I keep trying to move my legs, but it's no good; I can't feel a thing. Anyway, come here and cuddle me, and let's see if we can nod off together, or you'll be even more tired tomorrow." He raised his arm, and she snuggled up to his warm body.

Betsey had been giving their financial problems a lot of thought, and the next morning at breakfast she told the rest of the family she had a plan. It was the one time of day when they were all together, and she felt it was an ideal opportunity to run her ideas past them.

Ned grinned at her enthusiastic face. "Go on, then; tell us how you're going to make us rich."

"Well, since Lord Fellwood started building his canal, there have been far more people in and around the village, and folk are saying the work is likely to go on for at least another couple of years. Sometimes, the workmen come to the inn, but there's no room for them inside, because we're so busy with the stagecoach travellers, and often we don't have any food left to sell them. I think we're missing an opportunity to sell more."

"So, what do you suggest, Betsey?" Kezia waited for her answer with interest.

"I think we need to find somewhere to serve more food. The stables are in use for the horses, which are swapped for the stagecoaches, but there's the big shippen, where we keep the cows. I suppose in years gone by, the inn probably had more cows, but there's enough room in the little linhay for our two. It would work well because we store the hay in the tallet above the linhay, so that's ideal for feeding them in winter. If we clear out the shippen and tidy it up, we could serve food from there. On a dry day, we could put a trestle table outside, and if it rains, we could bring it into the shippen. We could even have a few seats if there's enough room."

"It's an interesting suggestion, Betsey, but we struggle to cook all the food we serve now in the one oven, and we make full use of it; it's never empty, whilst it's hot."

"No, I know. That's why we need to ask the bank to lend us enough money to install a new oven and a sink into the shippen and turn it into a kitchen, then we could cook loads of food. If I do the baking the night before, ready for the next day, I think we can manage on our own, until we see if it will pay for another pair of hands."

"Betsey, you can't work night and day; you're already busy all day helping in the inn, and you can't possibly do another shift when you finish there."

"Yes, I can. I'm young and fit, and I want to do it. I'm sure I can make it pay. I think we need to serve cheap grub like rabbit stew with a chunk of bread, pies and pasties, of course, but also pastry squares; they're filling if you've nothing else, especially if we sprinkle some with sugar or raisins. We have loads of milk left over every day, so we have plenty of cheese and butter, and lots of men just like bread and cheese, with a pickled onion for their dinner. If we can make the food cheap, I'm pretty sure a lot of the canal workers will come and buy some, and no doubt, whilst they're here, they'd enjoy a tankard of ale to wet their whistle, and wash it all down."

"Well, there's no doubt you're an excellent cook, Betsey. I was amazed at how much your mother had taught you, even by the time you were six. I mean, it's not many children of that age who can fry eggs, and make porridge. You coped brilliantly at that difficult time."

A sad expression crossed Betsey's face, and Kezia was sorry she had mentioned the past. She hastened to move on. "Anyway, I think it sounds like a great idea, and we can but give it a try. Of course, it all depends on what the bank says. They might not be willing to lend us any more money. What do you think, Mal?"

"Well, we've never missed a payment yet, so that will go a long way. Unfortunately, I can't travel to Barnstaple to see the bank manager, though. I don't know if he's heard about my accident, but that might put a dampener on things. Ned, could you go tomorrow? I think you should go with him, Betsey; after all, it's your idea, and your enthusiasm might rub off on him. I can help in the new kitchen, and even serve people. The bar's too high for me to see over, so it's difficult to serve people with ale, and I can't carry food, but the trestle table would be lower, so I could hand out food over that. I'd like to feel useful again, and make more of a contribution."

Josie joined in. "Yes, I feel the same way, but now I've only a couple of weeks to go, I'm limited in what I can do. I'm happy to do what I can, though, it might be more difficult once the baby's here. What do you think, Silas?"

Her husband nodded. "Yes, it's a bold plan, but I like it. I think it's a risk, but we have to do something different because there isn't enough money coming in at the moment. If we can manage the extra work ourselves for a couple of months, we might be able to take on another pair of hands, if it starts to make a profit. We need to get a move on with it all, though."

The next morning, Betsey was up even earlier than usual, and had baked a batch of pasties, and put some loaves of bread proving, before any of the others even came down for their breakfast. Ned walked into the kitchen at dawn and raised his nose to the delicious smell that was coming from the oven.

"Good Lord, Betsey, what time did you get up? It must have been the middle of the night. You won't be able to keep that up for long; you'll wear yourself out."

"I'm all right, Ned; I've never needed much sleep, and I'm so excited about this I couldn't sleep anyway. I wanted to do all I could this morning because Aunty Kezzie and Josie are going to have a busy day without me. Silas, too, without you. Now, I've made the porridge, so if we eat that, perhaps we can get going early, and be back in time to help out later."

Ned was thoroughly looking forward to spending another day with Betsey. "You have it all worked out, don't you, Betsey? I just hope the bank manager says yes, because, without another oven, none of it can happen."

"No, I know, but I'm sure I can persuade him. I think this is my chance to repay your family for all they've done for me over the years. I'm pretty sure I wouldn't even be here if it wasn't for Aunty Kezzie and Uncle Mal."

"Maybe not, but I do know they've never regretted it, not for one moment, and I certainly haven't." Ned looked at her fondly.

She smiled at him warmly, and then ruined his day, as she remarked. "You and Silas, are like brothers to me, Ned. I lost Norman, and I hardly ever see Barney, since he married and moved to Wales. I'm an aunty now, and I haven't even seen my two nephews yet."

Within half an hour, they set off in the pony and trap, as that could travel faster than the horse and cart. Their destination was the Barnstaple Old Bank, which was housed in an old merchant's house, built in the early 17th century.

"Have you ever been to the bank before, Betsey?"

"No, I've only been to the town a handful of times, Ned. Why, have you?"

"Yes, I went one day with Dad, when he had to see the manager. The building's impressive. Just remember to look up at the ceiling; it's amazing. I had to wait for Dad on the day we came, and I got chatting to one of the young men who worked there, and he was telling me that the ceiling bears the completion date of 1620. Just think, that's over two hundred years ago; I'm surprised they could do such fine work, so long ago."

"What's it like?"

"The plasterwork depicts four Bible scenes and the coat of arms of the company of Spanish merchants who had it built. They must have been rich. Anyway, you'll see for yourself soon. I love looking at things like that. It must have taken such skill and patience."

They tethered the pony to a rail outside the bank and went in nervously. The manager agreed to see them in an hour, and so to pass the time, they strolled along by the river and admired the large ships moored at the quay. They arrived back at the bank in plenty of time, and as they were shown to the manager's room, Betsey remembered to glance up at the magnificent ceiling, and had to agree with Ned that it was impressive. The manager was sorry to hear of Mal's accident and listened intently to Betsey's plan. He sat with his two hands steepled together as if he were praying, whilst he considered their request, and eventually, he smiled at the young pair.

"Well, I've given this careful thought, and the answer is yes, the bank will lend the money. I can see you have to make some changes to improve the situation you find yourselves in. I'll lend your father enough money to cover the cost of a new oven and sink, but there will be none to spare, and I think you'll need to work extremely hard to make this venture pay. However, Mr Carter has been one of our most reliable customers over the years, and disabled or not, I know he'll do his utmost to meet his obligations. As you've brought a letter expressing his wishes, I'll put the money into his account today, so that you can start the work immediately. I think, in this case, time is of the essence. The loan will be added to that already outstanding, with the same interest arrangements, and you will have an additional five years to clear the debt. Is that agreeable to you?"

Ned nodded eagerly, for this was better than Mal had anticipated. "Yes, thank you so much, sir; we are much obliged."

"Please convey my best wishes to your father for a speedy and complete recovery, and tell him I'll put all this in writing, and have the documents delivered to him for signature within the week. Now, good day to you, and good luck."

Once outside, Betsey and Ned grinned at each other gleefully, and Ned picked her up and swung her into the air, in the same way, that he had when she was a little girl. Betsey laughed, and held on to him, hugging him, and kissing him on the cheek. The nearness of her, made his heart ache just that little bit more, as he realised she would always see him as a brother, despite the fact his feelings for her, were nothing like those of a sibling.

CHAPTER 28

Betsey excitedly pulled Ned by the hand. "Come on, let's buy an oven and a new sink, while we're in the town."

"My goodness, you don't let the grass grow under your feet, do you, but yes, you're right, we should do that, and get it installed as quickly as possible."

An hour later, they had ordered a new range and a sink, from a supplier in the town. Luckily, the man had one of each available and was persuaded to deliver and install both a few days later. Betsey was delighted with their morning's work, and couldn't wait to get back to the inn to tell Mal and Kezia their wonderful news. However, Ned insisted they must have something to eat first, and took Betsey to the Three Tuns Inn, where he bought her a bowl of lamb stew. After they had eaten, they walked down the High Street and looked in one or two shops. Betsey had brought a little money with her to buy a present for Josie and Silas's new baby, and she chose a knitted outfit in white, which she planned to hide away until after the birth. Whilst they were in the shop, she idly fingered some brightly coloured ribbons, and Ned asked her what she was thinking about.

"Your mum once bought me a bright red ribbon for my hair after my mum had died. She bought a toffee apple each for Norman and me, and also the ribbon. She said I deserved a present for looking after Norman," her eyes filled with tears, "I didn't though, did I? I didn't care for him properly, because the poor little mite died."

"Now, Betsey, you know that wasn't your fault, don't you? We talked about this at the time, and there was nothing more you could have done. It was your father's fault, not yours; surely you can see that now you're older? My goodness, you were only six, and you nearly died yourself."

"I know, but I still feel guilty that I lived, and he died. Poor little lad."

Ned took her hand in his. "Please stop blaming yourself, Betsey; it doesn't do any good. Now, which colour ribbon would you pick if you were buying one today?"

"Well, I think I'd pick red again; it's such a cheerful colour, and I like how it looks in my brown hair, but I have no money to waste on such fripperies. We need every penny we can lay our hands on to help your dad pay the bills."

"Well, it just so happens I have a few pennies to spare, and I would like to buy a ribbon for your hair; will you let me?"

"Go on then, thank you. That's so kind of you, Ned."

He handed her the ribbon, and she caught up her long brown curls and tied them up. The bright colour suited her, and Ned thought he would like to buy her so much more if only she would realise how much he loved her.

It was late afternoon by the time they arrived home, and Kezia, Silas, and Josie were rushed off their feet. Mal was taking a rest because he tired so easily these days. Ned and Betsey asked the others to take a five-minute break to hear their news, and they all joined Mal in the sitting room.

With a big grin on his face, Ned told them their news.

Mal was elated. "Oh, well done, both of you. That's amazing, and you say the range and sink will be coming at the end of the week?"

"Yes, we'll have to get busy tomorrow, clearing out the shippen. There's an awful lot to do, but I thought it was sensible to order what we needed whilst we were in the town, and luckily we got just what we wanted."

"I'll just have a cup of tea, and then I'll start baking some of the food for tomorrow. I can spend the day helping Ned clear out the shippen, then."

"Oh, Betsey, surely you're too tired to do more baking now? You've had a long day already, travelling to Barnstaple, and you were up so early."

"No, I'm all right, and I can't wait to start clearing the shippen out tomorrow; it'll be fun."

"Daniel called for you earlier on, and he wasn't best pleased to hear you'd gone to town with Ned. I didn't tell him why, for 'tis none of his business, but he's going to call back to see you later."

"Oh, thank you, Aunty Kezzie. That's good; maybe he'll help us, tomorrow."

Betsey was so excited about everything that was going on, that she quite failed to see the dismay on Ned's face.

Later, she was busy again, making another batch of pasties when Daniel arrived, and Josie showed him into the kitchen.

"Hello, Daniel, I'm sorry I missed you earlier; but I'm pleased to see you now."

"Why did you visit Barnstaple with Ned? I would have taken you, but you never said you wanted to go."

"It was arranged at the last minute. You see, we have to find a way of making more money now that Uncle Mal can't do much, and so we're going to expand, and sell more food. We're going to clear out the big shippen, and install a range and a sink so that we can prepare and sell food there."

"I see, will you be taking on more staff then?"

"No, we can't afford to, so to begin with, I'll do the baking in the evenings, then, if we start to make money, we'll take on someone to help."

"Oh, great, I hardly see you now; you'll have no time for me from now on."

"Of course, I will, though I am going to be busy. I have to do this, Daniel. Aunty Kezzie and Uncle Mal saved my life when they took me in, and now they need my help. It's the least I can do, and I'm looking forward to it. I'm sure I can make a success of this. Will you give us a hand to clear out the shippen, tomorrow? We can spend the day together then and it'll be fun."

Reluctantly, Daniel agreed, but Betsey could see his heart wasn't in it. She put the pasties in the oven and then embraced him.

"Thanks for saying you'll come tomorrow, Daniel. I'm sure you'll enjoy yourself."

"I doubt it, but yes, all right. Can we go for a walk later on tomorrow, then?"

Betsey frowned. "There's an awful lot to do, but yes, I'm sure we can."

The next morning, Betsey raced through as many chores as she could, to make life a bit easier for Kezia and Josie, and Ned cleaned out the stables with Silas. Then, after a hearty breakfast, which Kezia insisted they ate, Betsey and Ned made a start clearing out the shippen. The two cows had been milked, and turned out to graze in the orchard, so whilst they were out of the way, Betsey cleared the little linhay and made it ready for the evening milking. She was just putting down fresh straw when Ned came to see how she was getting on.

"There, I think they should be comfortable in here, Ned. Mind you, I expect there will be fun and games later when we let them back in. They're so used to going to the shippen, they won't like going somewhere new."

"No, they won't, but they'll soon get used to it, and there's plenty of room in here, for the two of them."

"Yes, I'm sure they'll soon settle down. I'll come and help you in the shippen, now."

First, she cleaned up the mess left by the two cows, loading the dung into a wheelbarrow, and taking it to the dung heap in the corner of the yard. The other end of the building was full of implements and junk, which had accumulated over the years.

"What shall we do with all this rubbish, Ned? I'm making a pile, but we need to do something with it."

"There's so much of it, I think we'll load it all onto the cart, and take it to one of the fields and have a bonfire. I dread to think when this place was last emptied; some of the wooden stuff just disintegrates, when I touch it, and some tools are so ancient I don't even know what they're for. I'd better check with Dad, before we throw them away, in case he wants to keep any of them."

Around mid-morning, Daniel turned up, and Betsey greeted him with a sunny smile, unaware of a wide smudge of dirt across one cheek. Her hands were filthy, and her hair was tousled and dusty.

"Hello Daniel, I'm so glad you came. We're busy, as you can see."

Ned nodded to the young man, but carried on with his work, without stopping.

"Goodness Betsey, you are in a mess. You shouldn't be doing dirty work like this. Can't you leave it to Ned?"

She was dismayed and glancing down at her grubby hands and dirty dress, she attempted to tidy her hair.

"Oh dear, yes, I must look a sight. You must forgive me, Daniel, but we're so busy, and there's no way to do all this without getting dirty. Nothing that soap and water won't put right later, though, and no, I can't leave it all to Ned; there's far too much to do because the new range and sink are being installed at the end of the week, so time is against us, and after all, this was all my idea."

Her young man sighed. "What would you like me to do, then?"

"Ned's just brought the horse and cart here, so we can load up all the rubbish and take it to the meadow and have a bonfire. If we continue to bring stuff out from the shippen, could you load the cart?"

For the next hour, all three worked hard, and eventually, they could see into the corners of the old building. The cart was piled high by this time, and though there was still more junk to move, Ned decided he had better take one load to the meadow.

Betsey took Daniel's hand. "Come on, Daniel let's follow the cart, and help Ned to unload it. We can have a bonfire then, and bring the cart back for another load."

"I've got a better idea actually, Betsey."

Putting his arm around her, the young man drew her into a corner of the shippen and embraced her. He pushed a wisp of hair back from her red, sweaty face, and put his lips to hers.

"Do you know, Betsey Lovering, even in such a dishevelled state, you are still irresistible, and I can't wait to make you mine."

For a few minutes, Betsey relaxed in his arms and enjoyed his kisses. However, when his hands started to wander, she pulled back from him.

"Daniel, we must help Ned. This isn't the time or place for this."

"Ned, Ned, Ned, that's all I ever hear from you, these days. Do you love me, or not?"

"Yes, of course, I do, but surely you can see how busy we are at the moment. We have to make a success of this venture, or Uncle Mal will end up bankrupt, and be sent to prison. This was all my idea, so I have to do my best to make it work; besides I'm enjoying myself, aren't you?"

"No, not at all. I'm a gentleman, training to be a doctor. Why would I want to get filthy, turning out an old shippen? This is hardly a date, is it? Now, are you going to spend some time with me properly, or not?"

"No, I'm afraid not. I want to spend time with you, Daniel, and get to know you better, but I have to see this through. Come on, let's help with the bonfire; that will be exciting."

"No, I've had enough graft for one day; I have better things to do."

To Betsey's dismay, he turned tail and walked off, and she called after him.

"When shall I see you again, Daniel?"

However, he ignored her and quickened his pace.

Kezia was standing at the sink in front of the kitchen window, and she had witnessed the young couple enter the shippen alone. She was a bit concerned but knew Betsey wouldn't let her down. When she saw Daniel leave, obviously in a temper, she snorted with amusement, and Mal, who was sitting at the table chopping onions, asked what was so funny.

"Well, young Master Abernethy has just stormed out of the shippen in a bit of a temper, I think. I guess Betsey did not welcome his advances."

"And why is that so amusing? It's not like you to thrive on trouble, my dear."

"No, and I wouldn't normally, but I don't like him. I think he's only interested in one thing, and if Betsey allows him to take advantage of her, I don't think he'll stand by her. He's certainly nothing like his grandfather; he's a real gentleman."

"Have you had a word with Betsey about it?"

"No, she's old enough to make up her own mind, and I'm sure she'll be sensible. If only she would show as much interest in our Ned; they're made for each other, but unfortunately, she's not seeing what's right under her nose."

CHAPTER 29

Betsey and Ned stood back and proudly surveyed the results of their hard work. The shippen, now empty, looked far bigger than expected. Ned had repaired the plaster on the walls, and Betsey had spent hours brooming the floor, removing the dirt of many decades. After waiting overnight for the dust to settle, she had scrubbed the rough flagstones on her hands and knees, and was barely able to stand when she had finished; so fatigued was she. The following day, they limewashed the walls together and agreed this made such a difference. They finished with just hours to spare before the new range and sink were installed. Now, with all the work completed, they were thrilled with the result.

"Do you know, I think we could put a couple of tables, and some stools, in that corner by the window so people could eat in here if they want to; what do you think?"

"Yes, there's room, isn't there? With the double doors, they wouldn't get in the way of folk queueing up for food."

"You're expecting a queue, then?"

"Well, yes, I hope so. After all this hard work, I expect people to be queueing across the road to the church and beyond; you know how delicious our food is."

"I certainly do, and I hope you're right. If we're going to open in a couple of days, there isn't time to make tables and stools though, so we'll have to improvise. If you remember, there were a couple of old doors that I stacked behind the barn, in case we should ever need them. If we rest them on something, they could be used as tables, to begin with, and I'll go to the sawmills, and buy a few wide planks, that can be used for seats. It'll be a bit rough and ready, but I'm sure folk won't mind if it's raining, and they just want somewhere dry, to sit and eat their dinner.

"We'd better get moving then because there's still a lot do to. I want to clean the windows, and I'm going to pick a few flowers to put in jars on the windowsills."

"You don't seriously think the workmen are going to appreciate jars of flowers, do you? They'll only be interested in the grub; how nice it tastes, how much they get, and how much it costs."

"Maybe, but you never know, a few of their wives might come to see what we've been up to, and in any case, it will be wildflowers, so they won't cost us anything, and I want it to be perfect."

"I'm sure it will be, and it's all thanks to you, Betsey. You've worked so hard." Ned tentatively put his arm around her shoulders, and gave her what he hoped, was a brotherly hug.

She responded by slipping her arm around his waist and giving him an affectionate squeeze. "Well, so have you, Ned, and I don't know about you, but I've enjoyed every minute of it. It was such hard work, but I think it looks amazing now."

It was unfortunate, that as they stood with their arms loosely around each other, Daniel Abernethy rounded the corner, and scowled at the sight before him. Betsey and Ned immediately let their arms fall to their sides, and Betsey ran towards him.

"Oh Daniel, I'm so pleased you've come. What do you think of our new kitchen?"

Begrudgingly, the young man looked around him. "Yes, it looks good, I must admit. You've both worked hard, and I hope it's a success. When do you open?"

"On Monday, the day after tomorrow. We're just making the finishing touches today, and then tomorrow we have a busy day preparing the food. We want to make sure we have plenty."

"Good, does that mean I can steal you away for a few hours then? I've barely seen you, lately, and I thought we could walk to the beach, and sit looking out at the waves."

"That does sound nice. Ned, could you manage without me for a couple of hours?"

"Yes, of course, you go and enjoy yourself. You deserve to relax for a while; you've worked so hard."

Daniel beamed and took Betsey by the hand. However, they had only gone a few paces, when Kezia burst out of the back door, looking worried. Seeing Betsey holding Daniel's hand, she paused, as if she had changed her mind about something.

"Is everything all right, Mum?" Ned could see his mother was agitated.

"Yes, it's just that Josie's baby's on the way and she's had to take to her bed. I'm pretty sure she started having pains early this morning, but she soldiered on. The trouble is, the oven's full of food, with more to go in, and the first stagecoach is due any minute. I don't know which way to turn."

"Don't worry, Aunty Kezzie, I'll take over in the kitchen. Most of the work's finished here now, and the rest can wait until later." Betsey looked at Daniel apologetically. "I'm so sorry, Daniel, but you can see how we're fixed. Why don't you come to the kitchen, and have a cup of tea, whilst I carry on with the baking? We can have a chat then, and you can tell me how your studies are going."

Looking annoyed, the young man dropped her hand. "No, you clearly have more important things to do, than go for a walk with me; I'll leave you to it." He turned on his heel and walked off abruptly. Betsey began to run after him, but Kezia grabbed her arm.

"Betsey, let him go; you're worth much more than him."

Ned turned away, hoping to hide the smug smile that had spread across his face. However, Betsey was dismayed. "Oh dear, he's angry again, now, and he has a point. I've barely seen him for weeks; we've been so busy. He thinks I'm messing him around."

"If he can't see how hard you've worked, and make allowances then it's a bad job. If he thinks anything of you, he'll come around, and if not, you're better off without him. Go after him if you must, and we'll manage somehow, but I must take the bread out of the oven, or it will be ruined."

Kezia hurried to the kitchen, and Betsey followed her thoughtfully. However, once she saw the amount of work that needed doing, she soon forgot about Daniel, as she hastily removed the loaves of bread from the oven and replaced them with the next batch. They heard hooves outside on the cobbles, and Kezia sighed.

"Ah, there's the stagecoach now. I'll leave you to carry on here, then, Betsey, and I'll see what the travellers want to eat, while Silas gets the fresh horses ready. He's already fetched Nellie Rudd to attend to Josie, so she's in capable hands. We'll see how she's getting on when this rush is over."

It was tea time before Betsey had a minute to herself, and then she went outside to see how Ned was getting on. He had laid the two heavy doors onto some old water butts and purchased four wide planks of wood from the sawmills. These rested on smaller brandy kegs, providing rough seating. He had made a sign to put outside, listing the food that would be available, and how much each item would cost. He stood scratching his head, as he tried to remember his letters.

"Oh, Ned, it looks so good, doesn't it?"

"Aye, it does. If this doesn't work it won't be for lack of trying, and that's for sure. Now, you're better at your letters, than me; so, can you write this for me?"

"Yes, of course. Right, let's see."

BRING YOUR OWN DISH
Pies and Pasties, 2d each
Rabbit Stew, 3d a ladleful
Roast potatoes, a farthing each
Bread and Cheese 2d
Pastry Squares, Cakes and Buns, a ha'penny each

"Do you think I'm charging enough?"

"Is that what we normally charge in the inn?"

"No, it's slightly cheaper, but this is mainly to take away, isn't it? Do you think I should lower the prices a bit more?"

"No, let's see how it goes. If the stuff isn't selling, we'll reduce the prices as the day goes on, but we need to make a decent profit. What are we going to do, if people don't bring a plate?"

"They can just eat it in their hands unless it's stew. We have plenty of tin dishes, but I'm going to charge another farthing if they use ours. People will soon get used to it, and if they use their own, we don't have to wash them, or worry about getting them back."

"How's Josie?"

"I went up to see her about half an hour ago, and she was starting to push, so Nellie didn't think it would be much longer. Poor Silas wants to see her too, but Nellie soon gave him his marching orders. Your Mum's with her now because Mary's arrived to help in the bar. Right, I'd better help Uncle Mal peel the vegetables for tomorrow because I have a lot of cooking to do if we're going to open on Monday. I want to make sure we have plenty of food available for our first day.

By ten o'clock that night, Josie had delivered a healthy baby girl. She was a decent size, and cried lustily, bringing Silas running to the bedroom door. A little later, Nellie Rudd, at last relented, and let the new father in to see his daughter. He went straight to his tired wife and hugged her tightly.

"Are you all right, Josie?"

"Aye, but my goodness, I've never worked so hard. I feel like I could sleep for a week. Take a look at our little daughter."

Silas went to the old wooden cradle and stared at the tiny baby. She was fast asleep, and he grinned widely. "Oh, she's beautiful; I think she looks like you, Josie."

"Well, she's certainly got your red hair; it may be curly too, by the look of it."

"Yes, I'm afraid a lot of the Carter family are born with red hair, and usually a temper to match. I was hoping to have a cuddle, but I won't disturb her now. You get some sleep, while she's quiet, and I'll see you again later when she wakes up."

"Have Ned and Betsey managed to get everything finished in the new kitchen?"

"Yes, it's been one hell of a day, but everything's ready now, and they're busy chopping meat and vegetables for a big baking session tomorrow." He kissed the top of her head and left his exhausted wife to rest.

Sunday passed in a blur for Betsey, as she baked batch after batch of bread, pasties, pies, and cakes. Mal chopped so many vegetables, he thought he would be doing it in his sleep, and Kezia concentrated on making a huge cauldron of rabbit stew. This was all in addition to their normal day's work, but they were pleased to discover that the new range cooked so much more quickly than the old one.

The next morning, Betsey was up before daybreak and walked briskly around the meadow and orchard. She collected pink cock-robin flowers, white stitchwort, purple foxgloves, and a few pieces of greenery. She was determined to make the place as welcoming as possible. That done, she opened up the double doors of the shippen and started to put all the food onto the long trestle table that Ned had built. They had decided to open the yard gates at eleven o'clock but had put the sign outside, two days earlier, so the villagers knew to bring their own dishes, and decide what they wanted.

At eleven o'clock, Mal was seated behind the trestle table on a chair, ready to collect the money and give change if necessary. Ned opened the gates and was dismayed to see only one or two people waiting. He turned back to his father and gave a slight shrug.

"Don't worry, lad; it's early days, and it's not even dinner time yet." Mal smiled reassuringly at his son.

Betsey continued baking all morning, knowing the food could be used in the inn the following day if it didn't sell outside. Just after noon, Mal gave a shout.

"This looks like business to me."

The lime burners had left work for their dinner break, and a dozen or more of them were making their way to the inn. They queued up outside the new kitchen and held out their tin plates. Betsey gave each a broad smile, and a kind word, as she ladled the delicious-smelling rabbit stew onto their dishes, and handed them a chunk of fresh bread. They moved along and deposited their pennies into Mal's open hand. Within minutes, they were joined by a long line of canal workers, and by two o'clock, Betsey was beginning to worry she would run out of food. A few beggar children also joined the queue; several with no money and seeing their thin limbs and ragged clothes, Betsey gave them each a pastry square, much to their delight.

They shut the gates at three o'clock and grinned broadly at each other.

"Wow, that was amazing; just see how much money we've taken."

Mal was delighted, and he hugged Betsey and shook Ned warmly by the hand. "Well done, you two; if every day's as busy as this, we'll soon be making a profit. I'm so pleased."

"What an excellent idea this was, Betsey; you're so clever."

"Yes, that went well, didn't it? And I loved every minute. Now, we must start baking for tomorrow." The two men groaned loudly but had wide smiles on their faces.

CHAPTER 30

Joshua and Margery had been in London for a couple of weeks, and to their surprise, they were both enjoying themselves. Joshua, in particular, had been dreading his visit to the capital. However, he had taken pity on his father, as someone had to accompany his sister, and his father now found travelling tiring. Joshua loved spending time with his friend, Timothy Vulliami, and he particularly enjoyed their visits to The Royal Academy, and The National Gallery, where they were both in awe of the amazing artwork they saw there. Timothy had arranged membership to The Travellers Club for Joshua, and they frequented the establishment regularly. Founded in 1819 by Lord Castlereagh, the club was for gentlemen who had travelled outside the British Isles to a distance of at least five hundred miles from London. Having toured Europe in his younger days, Joshua was easily able to meet this requirement. The Club was situated in Pall Mall, and the building and the gardens were impressive, and according to Timothy, inspired by Raphael's Palazzo Pandolfini in Florence.

Although Joshua greatly enjoyed Timothy's company, he was careful not to neglect his younger sister. Margery was enjoying her season, but occasionally she needed to escape the company of their Aunt Genevieve, whose exuberance and enthusiasm could be a little wearing. With this in mind, he organised sightseeing trips, and they visited the Tower of London, St Paul's Cathedral, and Westminster Abbey. One morning at breakfast they discussed their next excursion.

"Good morning, Joshua, good morning, Margery." Aunt Genevieve swept into the room. Despite the early hour, she was immaculately attired in the latest fashion. "What are you two dears going to do, today? I know you're having a day out together."

Joshua patted his mouth with his napkin. "We were just discussing that very matter, aunt, and I think we have a plan. This morning we're going to the Canopy Room, at the Queen's Bazaar in Oxford Street, to see this amazing Royal Clarence Vase that everyone is talking about, and then, after some lunch, we might go to see the giant whale skeleton in St Martin's Lane."

"Goodness me; why on earth would you want to see a whale skeleton? I would imagine it will be smelly and obnoxious."

"Oh, I'm just curious, aunt. I heard a couple of the maids talking about it the other day. It only costs a shilling to go into the pavilion, and it's not every day you get the chance to see a whale skeleton, is it? Would you like to accompany us?"

Joshua glanced anxiously at Margery, and they both held their breath, waiting for the old lady's reply. However, Lady Genevieve was well aware that her niece was only being polite, and she quite understood that the young people needed some time to themselves, so with a beaming smile, she replied.

"Oh no, thank you so much for asking, my dear, but I'm afraid such things are not my cup of tea at all. No, you two go off and enjoy yourselves for the day, and then I'll not feel guilty about spending my time with a couple of my oldest friends. I haven't seen them for quite a while, and I simply must catch up with all the latest gossip. It's imperative to know who is courting whom when one has a niece enjoying her season. You may rest assured, that by the end of the day, I will know exactly what's going on in the ton."

Joshua and Margery quietly sighed with relief, and a few minutes later, they excused themselves and set off together to enjoy their day out. Their carriage took them to Oxford Street and stopped outside the Queen's Bazaar.

"What do you know about this vase, then, Joshua?"

"According to Timothy, who is ridiculously knowledgeable about everything in London, it was made for King George IV, and took three years to complete."

"Goodness, what's it for?"

"Well, just to impress people, I suppose. It's said to be huge. Come on, look, there's a bit of a queue, but we're early, so that's good."

They joined a short line of people at the door and having parted with the entrance fee of a shilling each, Joshua led his sister inside. The room was brightly illuminated with fifteen lamps, and they had to admit the vase was a spectacular sight. Made of the finest cut glass, it was magnificently ornamented with gold and enamelled tints, and the effect was dazzling.

Lady Margery gasped in awe. "Oh Joshua, it's gorgeous. I never imagined it would be so big. It's massive."

"No, I didn't either. I knew it was large, but this is colossal. Look, it says here, that it weighs eight tons, and it's fourteen feet high, and twelve feet across. Apparently, it will hold five thousand and four hundred bottles of wine."

His sister giggled. "How can they possibly know that? Do you think they filled it, to find out? That's some party."

"I don't know, but I wish I'd been invited. I bet it cost a small fortune, too."

"Yes, it is impressive, and I'm so glad we came to see it, but I can't help thinking the money could have been spent on a more useful cause. When you see all the beggars in the streets, surely it would have been better to do something for them."

"I don't disagree with you, but I guess that's a bottomless pit. I mean, where would you stop? I suspect this was made to impress all the king's rich friends from around the world. Anyway, have you seen enough? Shall we go back to the carriage?"

She nodded, and Joshua duly gave the driver instructions to take them to St Martin's Lane.

"Is it far to St Martin's?"

"No, I don't think so, and anyway, it's still only eleven o'clock. When we've seen the whale skeleton, I thought we'd get some lunch, and then make our way to the zoo this afternoon. Is that all right with you?"

His sister nodded. "Yes, I was looking forward to seeing the whale, and the zoo, more than the vase, but I must admit it was impressive and so pretty. How do you find out about all these things to take me to?"

"Timothy suggested seeing the vase and going to the zoo. He's lived in London all his life, so he knows all the best places to go."

The carriage stopped outside the pavilion, where the whale skeleton was housed. This time there was a long queue, as people were fascinated to see the huge creature. They waited for some fifteen minutes until they reached the entrance, where once again, Joshua parted with a shilling each to enter. They walked around the massive skeleton, which, according to an information board, was ninety-five feet long, and had been found by fishermen in Belgium in 1827. Presumably, it was now on tour and making lots of money. As they reached the middle part of the beast, there was another sign, informing them, that for an additional shilling, they could sit inside the belly of the whale.

"I suppose you want to do this?"

"Well, how often do you get the chance to sit inside the belly of a whale? I mean, what a story to tell our grandchildren."

"You think we'll have grandchildren, then?"

"Yes, of course. I'd like to have a family, not for a while, but eventually, and I'm sure Charles will provide Hartford with an heir at some point. You'll be able to impress your grandchildren by telling them you've sat in the belly of a whale. Anyway, you might go on to have more children yourself yet, Joshua. I haven't given up on my intention to find you a bride, whilst we are in the capital."

"Come on, then, but leave my love life to me, if you please. I'm fine as I am, thank you."

It didn't take long to see all there was to see inside the skeleton, and they were soon back in their carriage, which took them to an inn. They decided to eat their lunch in the delightful garden, and before too long, they were feasting on game pie, followed by some delicious cake, washed down with a tankard of ale. It was a warm June day, and with their stomachs full, they felt lethargic. However, before long, Joshua stood up and stretched.

"Come on, then, shall we visit the zoo, or have you had enough for one day?"

"I do feel a bit lazy now, but no, I want to see the zoo. What was it called again?"

"It's the Surrey Zoological Gardens, and it's only been open for a few years. I'm told there's another zoo planned at Regent's Park, but I don't think that one's open to the public yet. The Surrey Zoo is situated on the grounds of the Manor House at Walworth, near Kennington Park."

"It means nothing to me because I don't know my way around London. How big is the zoo?"

"I'm told it covers fifteen acres, and there's a huge glass conservatory, full of exotic plants and wild beasts."

"Ooh, how exciting; come on, I can't wait."

This time, the carriage ride took longer, and it gave them time to rest and digest their dinner. When they arrived, Joshua groaned as he observed a long line of people waiting to enter the grounds. Margery took his arm, smiling widely.

"Come on, the people are moving quite quickly, I don't think we'll have to queue for long, and at least it's not raining."

She was right, and within twenty minutes, they were meandering along a well-laid path leading to a large lake. In the distance, they could see the conservatory, and on the way there, they stopped to admire a field containing a herd of zebras.

"Oh, aren't they cute? Just like ponies, but with stripes. Come on, let's see what's in the glasshouse."

They spent a pleasant afternoon observing the impressive tropical flowers and plants, as well as the pelicans, and monkeys, but the star of the show was a recently imported rhinoceros. Tired from their day's sightseeing, they both fell asleep in the carriage on the way home. At their evening meal, they regaled their aunt with tales of all they had seen that day.

"Well, I too, have had an educational day, my dears. I have learned that Alexander Chichester has proposed to Lady Wellingborough, so he is one we can cross off our list. I had hoped he might be a suitable beau for you, Margery, but no matter, there are plenty of others to choose from. However, the little titbit of gossip that I'm most delighted with today, is that Lord Clarence Montgomery has been making enquiries about you, and apparently cannot wait to be introduced. Now, isn't that pleasing news?"

CHAPTER 31

It was a sunny morning in late June, and the carriage was waiting to take Joshua, Margery, and Aunt Genevieve to Hyde Park for their morning promenade. This had become their habit, in all but the most inclement of weather; for it was important for Margery, the young debutante, to be seen out and about, as much as possible. Lady Genevieve had accompanied her niece to the modiste on several occasions, and the young lady's wardrobe was now extensive. Margery enjoyed all the attention at first, but having to stand still for fitting after fitting, had soon become tedious, and she welcomed the days of freedom, exploring London with her brother.

On this particular morning, she was attired in a striking pale green dress. The bodice was plain with a wrapped front and a full skirt. The popular gigot sleeves ended with a puff at the elbow and were then pleated to the wrist. Her blond hair was parted in the middle; the curls at the back adorned with ribbons, and achieving the perfect ringlets at each side of her head, had almost driven her maid to distraction. Joshua grinned at her, knowing she would prefer to be wearing a comfortable old day dress, her hair cascading freely around her shoulders, with not a ribbon, or a pin in sight. However, his compliments were sincere, for she looked amazing. Lady Genevieve surveyed her niece with satisfaction.

"Well, my dear, you will turn many heads this morning, I have no doubt. Let's hope we chance to meet Lord Montgomery on our little excursion. Although she had not told Margery, she was confident this would be the case, for she was reliably informed that the young gentleman would also be in Hyde Park, and hoped to see young Lady Fellwood.

After a short ride, they alighted from the carriage, and Joshua instructed the driver to wait for them, the same as every other morning. Taking his aunt's arm on one side, and his sister's on the other, they walked down the path together, enjoying the birdsong, and the warm sunshine. They had not gone far, when they saw Lord Montgomery in the distance, accompanied by his elder brother, and his wife. The peer raised his hat politely, wished Lady Genevieve a good morning, and begged to be introduced to her nephew and niece. After a little conversation with the entire group, the young man offered Lady Margery his arm and asked if he might escort her around the park.

"I've been so looking forward to meeting you, my dear. Would you mind, if I called you, Margery?"

She smiled at him, revealing a set of perfect white teeth, and blushed becomingly.

"No, of course not, but tell me, what is your name? I only know you as Lord Montgomery."

"Well, you can't keep calling me that, for it's quite a mouthful; my name is Clarence. How long are you expecting to stay in London, Margery?"

"I think Joshua is planning for us to go home sometime in August. He doesn't want to be away for too long, as he misses his young son."

"I see, and how old is the young man?"

"Charles is ten, and an only child. Unfortunately, his Mama died in childbirth."

"Oh dear, that is sad; it can be a hazardous business. And how about you; do you have any other siblings?"

"Well, yes and no. My elder brother, George, was born with disabilities, and he died not so long ago. My nephew, Charles, misses him dreadfully for the two were inseparable. I do have another brother, Thomas, but sadly he went missing many years ago, and we do not know of his whereabouts, or even if he is still alive. I suspect he is not, for we were close, and I'm sure he would have returned to see me before now if he was able."

"That is a sad tale; still at least you have your brother, Joshua, to take care of you."

"Yes, indeed. How about you, Clarence? Do you have a large family?"

"No, just Sebastian. He and Julia have two children, so, fortunately, that takes the pressure off me to provide the family with an heir. Tell me, Margery, do you have a companion to attend Queen Adelaide's ball, where I presume you will be presented to the queen?"

"My Aunt Genevieve will attend, and Joshua will present me to the queen. I must confess I become more nervous with every day that passes, and though I'm greatly looking forward to the event, I'm terrified I'll trip, and end up on my hands and knees before the gracious lady."

Lord Montgomery laughed out loud. "I believe you're not alone in that fear, my dear. I've heard other young ladies express the same concern, but I'm sure you'll manage the event, superbly. Naturally, you must be presented to the queen by your brother, but I wonder, would it be presumptuous of me to ask if I might accompany you into dinner? I would be delighted to see you, again."

"I'd like that, Clarence, thank you. There's not long to wait now, with it being only a week or two away."

"Thank you, I shall look forward to the evening, immensely. Now, here we are at the Serpentine; shall we amble on a little, and survey the ducks and swans? They always fascinate me."

An hour or so later, Margery took her leave of the handsome young man, and beaming widely, boarded the carriage with her brother and her aunt.

"Well, how did it go? You were both engrossed in conversation." Lady Genevieve looked like the cat who had licked up the cream, and her wrinkled face was wreathed in smiles.

"Yes, it went well. Clarence has asked if he can escort me into dinner at Queen Adelaide's ball."

Her aunt clasped her hands together, a rapturous expression on her face. "Oh, that's such marvellous news, Margery; he's obviously taken with you. How about you? Do you like him?"

"Yes, he's charming, and I'm looking forward to his company at the ball. In the meantime, he's asked me to Montgomery House tomorrow, to play croquet. He says you're welcome to come, Joshua. Please say you will; I don't want to go on my own."

"Yes, of course; I'd like to. I quite enjoy a game of croquet now and then, and I need to check out this young man, who's so interested in you. He may be rich and titled, but I want to make sure he'll take care of you, and make you happy."

"Goodness, Joshua, he hasn't asked for my hand in marriage; only a game of croquet."

"I think we can all see where his intentions lie, and he would be a favourable match for you, Margery, and you him, so I have no objections. I'd just like to get to know him a little."

"You never know, Joshua, there might be some attractive young ladies present, who will also be of interest to you."

"Perhaps, but please don't try to rush me, Margery. I loved Marianne deeply, and I still miss her so much every day. I'm in no hurry to remarry, and anyway, I have Charles to think about; I wouldn't want him to be unhappy, with a new stepmother in his life. If love finds me, all well and good, but I'm not actively seeking a new wife."

They spent an enjoyable day spent playing croquet at Montgomery House, where Joshua won several games, and Margery became even more enamoured with Clarence. They arranged to meet every morning in Hyde Park, and by the time of the ball, were firm friends. The young man had dropped several hints that he would like their relationship to develop more fully, and Margery was hopeful that it would.

The ball itself passed in a whirlwind of introductions and dances, and Lady Margery enjoyed every moment. She was dressed in a richly brocaded white silk dress, as was customary for debutantes. It had short sleeves and a low neckline, and she wore long white gloves. Her hair was adorned with white feathers, and around her neck, she wore a sparkling string of pearls; a present from Aunt Genevieve. She looked beautiful, and Joshua was proud to accompany her. The presentation to the queen went smoothly and relieved the ordeal was over, Margery gladly took Clarence's arm to walk into dinner. During the evening, several young women vied for Lord Montgomery's attention, but he only had eyes for the young woman on his arm. After dinner, he suggested they go outside onto the terrace, and enjoy some fresh air. It was stifling in the ballroom, and Margery was glad to take him up on the offer. He led her to the end of the terrace to a secluded area, surrounded by sweetly smelling pink roses. Dropping self-consciously to one knee, he reached into his pocket and took her hand in his.

"Margery, will you marry me? Please say yes, or you will break my heart."

Margery was taken aback at such a sudden proposal, for she had only known the young man for a couple of weeks.

"Oh, my goodness, Clarence. This is so sudden; we've known each other for such a short time."

"Yes, I know; but when you find the right person, you know, and I'm convinced we could find happiness together. I've fallen in love with you, Margery. I think I loved you, from the moment I first saw you. Do you think you could come to love me, too?"

She gazed into his warm brown eyes. "Yes, I believe I could."

"Is that a yes, then? Do say it is."

Slowly she nodded. "Yes, all right then, yes, Clarence, I would love to marry you."

The young man was overjoyed as he slipped a gold ring onto her slim finger. The sole diamond was the largest Margery had ever seen, and she held it up to the lamp, where it sparkled.

"Oh, Clarence; it's so beautiful. Where did you get it?"

"It's a family heirloom, and about two hundred years old, I believe. It looks so elegant on your finger. It was left to me by my grandmother. Shall we go in and announce our engagement?"

"Yes, let's do that. My aunt is going to be so pleased; she's taken to you."

"She's a wonderful lady, and the feeling is mutual. Come on, then."

Taking her hand, he led her back into the ballroom, where he made the announcement.

With stars in her eyes, Margery accepted the many congratulations bestowed upon her and happily showed off her new engagement ring. Lady Genevieve was almost happier than the young couple themselves. Joshua shook Clarence by the hand and admitted to being rather surprised by the speedy proposal.

"I'm not one to procrastinate, Joshua. When I see something I like, I go after it, and although I've only known your sister for a short time, I know that I love her. I believe she has similar feelings for me, that will, no doubt, grow in time. By the way, I'm so sorry I've not behaved as I should. In your father's absence, I should have asked your permission, before I proposed. Please accept my sincere apologies; I'm an impetuous fool, and I'm afraid I got rather carried away."

"Well, no harm done, and my sister is ecstatic, so you'll get no complaints from me."

"That's gracious of you, Joshua. Now, as you must know, my family is one of the wealthiest in the country, and you'll find I'm a generous man. I've heard that the Hartford estate would benefit from an injection of cash, and I'd like to tell you, that on our wedding day, I'll provide a substantial sum to your father."

"Well, that's exceedingly generous of you, Clarence, but I assure you our finances are sound, and it is us, who should be providing a dowry for my sister."

"There's no need to worry about that, Joshua, and my intention was not to offend. It's just that I've heard of your father's plans to build a canal, and that it's going to cost a colossal amount of money. I'm simply telling you, that I would like to become an investor, should your father be agreeable to the idea. However, that's a discussion for another time, so if you'll excuse me, I simply must have one more dance with my bride-to-be, before the evening draws to a close."

CHAPTER 32

The hot July sun beat down upon two men deep in conversation, as they watched the workers on the Hartford canal. Now, some four months into the project, the course of the canal had been decided, and the work was progressing, albeit slowly. The engineer, James Griffiths, took a handkerchief from his pocket and mopped his brow. He smiled reassuringly, at his employer.

"The work at the beginning of a project such as this, is always slow, Lord Fellwood. It takes time to plot the exact course of a canal, for one has to consider how many tracks it will bisect, and, therefore, how many bridges will need to be built to cross it. In this case, there will need to be at least five bridges over the seven-mile stretch of the canal."

"I appreciate that, James. It's more the aqueduct, that concerns me. How long did you say it will need to be?"

"I estimate it will need to be nearly three hundred feet long to cross the valley, and twenty-two feet wide."

"That's a mammoth undertaking, James. Just consider the amount of stone you'll need, never mind the manpower."

"Yes, I know, and it's the aqueduct which will be the most expensive part of the canal. However, it's unavoidable, and there's no shortage of workers. As you know, this area is full of hills and valleys, and I've been unable to plot a route to avoid them all. I've ordered the stone from the local quarry, and the workers there, are already busy producing it. That will take some time naturally, and in the meantime, we can progress with other, more straightforward areas. Now that the route of the canal has been identified, one group of workers is concentrating on removing all the trees that are in the way, and that too is time-consuming work. A few of the trees are massive, having been growing there for probably a couple of hundred years, in some cases. Looking on the bright side, the villagers of Hartford are not going to be short of firewood, or employment, this winter."

"No, that is one benefit, but I presume the majority of the wood will be sent to the sawmills?"

"Oh, yes, of course. We'll offset the costs in whatever ways we can, but as far as the aqueduct is concerned, it is essential, I'm afraid. It will avoid a long loop in the river, where the steep sides of the valley would make construction extremely difficult, and probably just as expensive. Anyway, let's stroll along a little, and you can see the progress we've made."

The two men walked along, what would become the towpath, next to the canal. It was wide enough to accommodate a horse or mule, to pull the tub boats along. At their side, men were working, digging out the actual canal.

"How deep will the canal be?"

"Between two and four feet is what I usually aim for. Look, the first bridge is underway."

Men were selecting stones from a huge pile in the nearby field, and working on them with a hammer and chisel to carve them into the right shape. The two gentlemen paused for a few minutes, watching a stonemason at work.

"What's he doing now?"

"Oh, he's carving his mark onto the stone. Most of these labourers are unable to read or write, and so they carve their mark onto the stones they've produced. Then, at the end of the day, the foreman will come along and count up how many stones each man has made, and they're paid accordingly. It ensures they're paid fairly, and encourages them to work hard if they want to make a decent living."

"The work is impressive, though I must confess, I'm becoming a little concerned about the final cost of this venture. I was looking at the accounts only this morning, and we seem to have spent a huge amount already and there's so far yet to go."

"That's always the case, my Lord. Most of the investment is used up quite quickly, as the work is so intensive at the beginning of a project. I'm confident I can keep the costs within the parameters I suggested, and remember, you'll reap the benefit of this venture, for many years to come. Cargoes transported by ship around the coast of Devon, are notoriously prone to shipwreck in stormy weather, and that can be costly. Also, I don't know if you're aware, but at a steady walking pace, a horse or donkey can move approximately forty times as much weight in a barge, as it can on a cart. You see, on the water, the load moves with little friction. Once this canal is in operation, your goods will be transported quickly and efficiently, and it is then you'll reap the benefits of this venture."

"Well, I hope you're right, James. Thank you for showing me around this morning; it's interesting to see the canal beginning to take shape. However, it's so hot I think I'll bid you farewell, and return home where it will be cooler. I'm expecting my son, Joshua, and daughter, Margery, to return from London later, and I want to be there to greet them."

"Of course, my Lord. It's been a pleasure meeting with you this morning. Please, come again, soon. I assure you the project is making excellent progress."

The old man instructed the driver to take him home. As he entered the spacious hallway of the Manor House he heaved a sigh of relief at the cooler temperature. His valet removed his boots, and he went to his study, intending to glance once more over the accounts for the canal project. Having rung the bell for some refreshment, he gazed out of the window at the view, that so often distracted him from his work. Far down the valley, he could see the Fellwood carriage making its way slowly up the hill, and he smiled to himself, thinking his paperwork would have to wait, whilst he welcomed his family back home.

Some ten minutes later, Lord Fellwood was waiting outside as the carriage arrived, and its occupants alighted. With a wide smile on his face, he shook his son by the hand, hugged his daughter, and then realised there was another occupant in the coach.

"Genevieve, I had no idea you were coming to visit; I'm so pleased to see you."

His sister embraced him. "I hope you don't mind me arriving uninvited, brother, but Margery and Joshua convinced me you wouldn't mind."

"Mind, of course, I don't mind; I'm delighted to see you, my dear, and you know Hartford Manor will always be your home. Now, come inside all of you. Travelling in this heat must have been exhausting. Did you have a reasonable journey?"

Joshua nodded. "Yes, thank you, Papa. It was uncomfortably hot in the carriage, but we made good time and did not experience any problems. How are you? And where is Charles?"

"I'm fine, my boy, thank you. We didn't expect you until later in the day, or even tomorrow, so I advised Charles to go ahead and visit his friend, Johnny. The boy has been excellent company for him, whilst you've both been away. He'll be back this evening, but come inside, where it's cooler, and tell me all about your trip."

When the group was comfortably seated in the cool drawing room and had been served lemonade, tea, and cakes, Ephraim questioned his daughter.

"So, come on then, Margery, how did it go? Did you enjoy being presented to Queen Adelaide?"

"Oh, I did, Papa, but I was so nervous. She was so kind, and she smiled at me, and said I looked beautiful."

"Well, that was nice of her. I'm not sure she speaks to all of the debutantes. And have you enjoyed your visit to London? Is there any news, I should be aware of?"

"I loved London, Papa, but I'm so glad to be home, and yes, I do have some news to tell you." Her eyes shone, as she held out her left hand, where the enormous diamond ring sparkled. "Lord Clarence Montgomery asked me to marry him, and I accepted."

"Oh, my goodness, that's wonderful news, my dear. I met him some years ago, and I know his parents. He's an extremely wealthy young man, though I believe he's the second son in the family, so he'll not inherit the estate. That doesn't matter, though; the main thing is, do you love him?"

"Yes, I do, Papa, and I'm sure he loves me. Whenever we're together, he's the perfect gentleman, and so attentive. Nothing is too much trouble for him to make me happy. I've met his family, and they are all delighted at our engagement. Had you been present, he would have asked your permission to propose to me, but I believe he could not wait."

Lady Genevieve took up the story. "I think it's an excellent match, Ephraim, and I believe the young man sought permission from Joshua?" She raised her eyebrows at her nephew, questioningly.

Joshua nodded, deciding not to share the fact that his permission had been obtained after the event. "I've invited Clarence and his parents to visit us in a couple of weeks, Papa. I thought we might hold an engagement party here. We celebrated with them in London, but it was always the intention to hold another party when we returned home. The other news is that Clarence is aware of your canal project, and he's interested in investing in it, should you so wish. His family is so rich, he doesn't even seem interested in Margery's dowry."

"Oh, well, the money has long been set aside for Margery's dowry, and we are not yet so poor, we can't pay our way; I shall insist he receives it. However, the canal project is proving extremely expensive and has caused me more than a few sleepless nights already, so I might take him up on his offer of investment. I'm surprised he knew of it."

"He seemed well-informed about the whole thing, and more than a little impressed. How's the work going?"

"It's going well. I'll take you to meet James Griffiths tomorrow, and you can see for yourself. He seems to know his stuff, but it's a far greater undertaking than I'd envisaged. Just clearing the land of trees and shrubs is so labour intensive, and then there are five bridges to be built, where the canal will cross the roads, not to mention the aqueduct, which I'm told will be around three hundred feet long."

"My goodness, that's a lot of work, Ephraim. It must be costing a small fortune?"

"Yes, Genevieve, it is expensive, but I think it will pay off in the long run. Goods can be transported so much more efficiently and cheaply, by the canal, than by road. It will take a few years for us to reap the benefit of the investment, but I think I'm doing the right thing." He smiled ruefully. "I hope so, anyway, or I might leave you with a heap of money problems, one day, Joshua."

"No, I think it will be all right in the long run, Papa, and I agreed with you to go ahead with the project at the outset, so if it doesn't work out, it will be as much my fault as yours."

Genevieve intervened. "Now, enough of business; we have a party to plan. I don't want to interfere, Ephraim, but I'm conceited enough, to believe you might like me to organise the engagement party for Clarence and Margery. Do say I may. It will be such fun."

Her brother took her hand. "My dear, you would be doing me the biggest favour. You know I have no idea about this sort of thing. It's such a shame, my darling, Helena, is not here to see Margery wed, but I know she would approve.

Thomas, too, would be delighted for you, Margery; you do know, he adored you?" He smiled wistfully, remembering with fondness, the wife, and son, he still mourned.

CHAPTER 33

The church clock struck five o'clock and Kezia groaned inwardly, thinking how she would love to stay in bed for just a little longer. However, it was already light, and she turned over onto her back and lay still for a few minutes, thinking about the tasks she needed to complete before the day was over. The list was endless. She became aware that Mal was also awake, and noticed he had a wide grin on his face.

"You look happy this morning, my love."

"I am. I'm a very happy man."

"I'm pleased to hear it. Now, I'll bring you a cup of tea as soon as the kettle's boiled, and you can enjoy that before I help you to wash and dress."

He put his hand on her arm. "No, just stay there for a minute; I've got something to show you. Can you pull the covers off me, please?"

"I need to get on, Mal. I have a million and one things to do, today."

However, she pushed the covers back, and he put his arm around her and cuddled her.

"What do you think of this?" He nodded towards his feet.

She gasped, as slowly he wiggled the big toe on his left foot.

"Oh, Mal! That's amazing. Can you move the other one?"

"No, not yet, but I'm getting pins and needles in my right foot, and that's how this one started a week ago."

"Why didn't you tell me?"

"I didn't want to get your hopes up until I was sure, but I do believe the feeling is beginning to come back. Isn't that wonderful?" His voice broke, as he impatiently brushed away a tear. "Oh, my goodness, now I'm weeping like a child."

"Oh, I'm so pleased for you, Mal; the doctor did say you might get the use back in your legs, didn't he? Perhaps it was just severe bruising to your spine after all. Oh, this will make such a difference, especially for you. I know how hard it's been for you."

"Aye, but it's not been easy for you, either; still, let's not get too carried away. It's only my big toe so far, but I think there might be some feeling coming back a bit higher up on my leg. Can you scratch my shin?"

He closed his eyes as his wife reached down and complied. "Yes, it's only faint, but I can feel something. When I touched it myself, I wasn't sure if I was imagining it, because I could see what I was doing. You know what this means, don't you?"

Well, yes, as I say, it will be marvellous if we can get you up and about again."

"True, but I was thinking that I may be able to be a real husband to you again."

"Oh, trust you to think of that, first."

"Are you against the idea?"

"No, not at all. Fingers crossed. Now, I must get up. You keep working on that toe. Shall we tell the others?"

"Yes, I think so. I mean, it is what it is, and it might not improve beyond this, but I think it will."

When Mal had drunk his cup of tea, and Kezia had helped him wash and dress, Silas and Ned carried him into the kitchen and put him in his chair. Since his accident, the couple had been sleeping in the sitting room to avoid using the stairs. When the two men had settled him into his favourite chair near the kitchen table, Kezia called to Betsey and Josie to stop what they were doing and come into the kitchen. Josie arrived, carrying her baby daughter, whom they had named Amy. The child was now a few weeks old, a placid little soul, full of smiles and chuckles. Her grandfather was devoted to her, and spent hours cuddling and talking to her; one job he excelled at, and was more than willing and able to do. He took the little girl and kissed her soft downy cheek.

"Mal has something to show you; go on, Mal."

"She makes it sound as if I'm going to carry out some sort of trick. It's just this, look."

His feet were resting on a stool with a cushion on it, and Kezia removed his sock and shoe. He proudly wiggled his big toe, much to the excitement of all present.

"Oh, Dad; I'm so pleased for you. Does this mean you'll be able to walk again?"

"I don't know, lad, but it's an encouraging sign, don't you think? I have a little sensation in my lower leg too, and pins and needles in the other foot, so I'm certainly hopeful. Now, let's have some breakfast because I want to hear how 'Betsey's Kitchen' is doing."

They had taken to calling the new venture in the old shippen, 'Betsey's Kitchen', and the name had stuck with the locals.

"It's doing well, Uncle Mal. I can barely keep pace with the amount of food we need to prepare each day. I think we opened it at just the right time."

Ned joined in. "Yes, Dad, Betsey's right. Lord Fellwood seems to employ ever more men to work on the canal, and they all like our food because it's cheap and readily available. They can just come and grab a pasty, or a chunk of bread and cheese, and be on their way. Mind you, most of them want a tankard of ale, while they're here, especially in this hot weather. They've just started work on the aqueduct, and that's going to take some time. I've seen the foundations, and it looks as if it will be huge. I hope it works out all right for his lordship, but it must be costing him a pretty penny."

"Ah well, he can afford it. The Fellwoods are rolling in money. What about the other workers? Do many of the farm labourers, and the lime burners, come to buy food? We'll have to rely on them, once the canal is finished."

"Yes, not as many as the canal workers, but more and more each week. I've purposely kept the prices as low as possible, to encourage people to buy the food, and I think it's paying off. We don't make much profit on each item, but we're selling so much, that makes up for it. Maybe when folk have got used to buying our food, we can put the prices up a little, but I think it's too soon at the moment. Quite a few of the villagers are buying the food too, because now, through the summer, it saves them lighting their ranges. I just wish we could cook more food."

"At least I can help in the kitchen again, now that I've got over having Amy, and you've been such a help looking after her, Mal. If only she would learn to sleep at night."

"Aye, and it's a real pleasure. I won't deny it's been hard, not being able to get around, but having this young lady to entertain me has made such a difference. As for sleeping at night, well, if I remember rightly, her dad wasn't very good at that, either. Now, I've been looking at the finances, and we're doing well. We've managed to meet the loan repayment again this month, and there's a little left over at the end of each week, but you're all looking exhausted. I think it's time to employ another maid to help in the kitchen. Ned and Silas, what do you think?"

Silas nodded. "Yes, I think it's an excellent idea. Ned and I are busy, but the three women are working morning, noon, and night, cooking and cleaning, and they can't keep it up forever. Not only that, but most days we run out of food when we could sell more. I think an extra pair of hands would make all the difference, and if we sell more, the profits should cover the wages. Do you have anyone in mind?"

"I do," said Kezia, "I think I know just the girl; young Matilda Yeo. You know, her family live in that little cottage next to the smithy. I think she's about fifteen. She's been in service to a wealthy gentleman at the far end of the village for a couple of years. Mr Wills, I believe he was called. Anyway, he was a widower, and he died a couple of weeks ago. I spoke to her mother, only the other day, and she was telling me Matilda needed to find another job. Shall I see if she's still available?"

"I'll go, Aunty Kezzie. I know Tilly, and I like her; I think she'd work hard too, and living so near, she wouldn't need to live in."

"Yes, all right, then, thank you, Betsey. If she'd like the job, see if she can start as soon as possible."

Wasting no time, Betsey finished her breakfast and hurried along to the cottage, occupied by the Yeo family. Tilly was outside in the front garden leaning on the wall, and talking to Benjamin Rudd, as he hammered a horseshoe into place.

"Morning, Betsey; what a lovely day it is. How are you?"

"It is, Tilly, and yes, I'm fine, thanks. Have you found a job yet?"

"No, not yet. I've been looking, but there's not much around at the moment. Why, do you know of one?"

"Yes, I do. We need a maid at the inn, to help with the cooking and cleaning, and we wondered if you'd be interested?"

"Would I have to live in?"

"No, not unless you want to. You live so near, you could easily walk to work; we'd need you bright and early though, at least by half past six. Could you manage that?"

"Yes, of course."

"Can you cook?"

"Yes, I did all the cooking for Mr Wills, as well as everything else. It was only him to attend to, so I lived in as his housekeeper and did all the cooking and cleaning. He was a kind and generous man, and I'm going to miss him. I cleaned his cottage yesterday because he's left it to his nephew and his wife, and they'll be moving in soon. I believe they've recently married, and are living with his parents, so they're pleased to get a place of their own."

"Do they live locally?"

"They live in South Molton, at the moment, and I understand Peter Webber's got a job as a lime burner on the Hartford estate. I believe Mr Wills said his wife's called Mary Jane. I remember Mr Wills going to their wedding, a few months ago."

"Well, it would be a big help, if you can cook, Tilly. Would you like the job?"

"Oh yes, please, Betsey, I'd love it. Mum will be so pleased, and I'd rather not live in if it's all the same to you."

She grinned at Ben, who had been listening to the conversation with interest. Betsey saw the glance that passed between them and smiled.

"When could you start, Tilly?"

"If I just tell Mum where I'm going, I can come now, if you like?"

"Oh, yes, please; we have so much to do, but don't rush; I'll go on back, and you come when you're ready. See you later."

CHAPTER 34

Since the return of Margery and Joshua from London, and the announcement of her engagement to Lord Clarence Montgomery, the staff at Hartford Manor had worked hard. Aunt Genevieve had taken charge, and she was not an easy lady to please. She summoned Mary Brown, the housekeeper, and advised her there was to be a grand engagement ball, which would be attended by the noble and the rich. The entire house must be cleaned from top to bottom, and the staff warned they would need to work long hours, to ensure every need of the guests was catered for.

The next two weeks were a frenzy of activity, and something of a nightmare for every single member of staff, who worked at the Manor. All time off was cancelled, and the servants were fitted with new uniforms, which they were instructed not to wear, until the day the guests arrived. Then began a major cleaning operation. There were to be over a hundred guests at the ball, and many of them would be staying at the Manor. Therefore, every nook and cranny must be cleaned to the high standards expected by Lady Genevieve. Many of the rooms had not been used for decades, and the furniture was covered in dust sheets. Cobwebs were removed, the floors scrubbed, and the windows cleaned. The furniture was highly polished, and the family silver was restored to its full shining glory.

Lady Genevieve and Lady Margery met with Violet Clark, the cook, and Mary Brown, the housekeeper, and together the four women planned a feast fit for a king. No expense was to be spared. Not only, would the meal for the ball need to be perfect, but many of the guests would be staying for several days and would need to be catered for. By the time their meeting was over, Violet was almost wringing her hands in despair, for she knew that just obtaining the ingredients for many of the dishes requested, would be a challenge in itself.

The engagement ball was scheduled to take place on Saturday, the eighth of August, and Clarence and his guests arrived a few days earlier. Ephraim and his family went outside to meet the two stylish Montgomery carriages, containing Clarence and his parents, and his brother, Sebastian, and his family. Two additional carriages contained their servants and luggage.

Clarence alighted from the carriage first and went straight to Margery. Smiling widely, he kissed her hand, and then that of Aunt Genevieve. He shook Joshua's hand warmly and was introduced to Ephraim and Charles. His parents, Lord and Lady Montgomery, and his brother, Sebastian, and family followed. Most of the household staff were also lined up outside to welcome their noble guests, and each one bowed or curtseyed, as was expected. When the formalities were over, Ephraim led the party inside to the drawing room, where they were served some refreshments.

Sebastian, and his wife, Julia, had two small boys, Arnold, aged four, and Seymour, aged two. The children were fractious, having been cooped up in the carriage for so long, and Julia went with their nanny to see them settled into the nursery. Taking their leave of the rest of the party, Clarence asked Margery, if she might like to show him the beautiful rose garden, he had noticed, as they arrived. Margery glanced at her aunt, for permission to walk with Clarence alone, and Genevieve smiled.

"The rose gardens are just outside the drawing room, Margery, and I do not think you will need a chaperone on this occasion. You will be in sight of us all, and it will be nice for you and Clarence to have a little time to yourselves."

Margery gratefully took Clarence's arm, and together they strolled down the dozen or so steps, leading to the garden. The roses were magnificent, and Clarence remarked on their heady fragrance. Each bed contained roses of a different colour and was bordered by lavender bushes, which also smelt divine, and were covered with swarms of bees. It was a sultry afternoon, and the gardener had been forecasting a thunderstorm for several days.

"Did you have a pleasant journey, Clarence?"

"Yes, not bad at all. It was long and tedious, as such journeys always are, but we had no mishaps. I was glad I was travelling with Mama and Papa, and not with Sebastian and Julia, for I think the boys were something of a trial."

"Well, it's a long way from London, and I expect they were bored. They're lovely children, though; I hope to get to know them better, over the next few days."

"We've not discussed our honeymoon yet, my dear. Do you have anywhere in particular, that you'd like to visit, or are you content to leave it to me?"

"I haven't given it much thought, Clarence, but I've always wanted to see Venice. I've seen pictures in books, and it looks so romantic. It's amazing to see so many canals and bridges. Have you ever been there?"

"Yes, I have. I went on a grand tour of Europe with my tutor, some ten years ago, and it's a fascinating city, if somewhat smelly. I was going to suggest we travel through Europe, so we can easily visit Venice, whilst we're in Italy. We need to choose a date for the wedding, and then I can start making all the arrangements. I thought maybe we could get married in October if that suits you. It's rather a nuisance to have to wait so long, but Mama insists it will take at least two months for all the arrangements to be put in place. We have so much to talk about, Margery; where the marriage will take place, where we'll live; so many things."

"It's exciting, isn't it?"

He nodded, and gently pushed a stray curl back from her face. "I love you, Margery, and I promise I'll be a faithful husband."

"Yes, I'm sure you will, Clarence. I love you, too, and I can't wait for us to be married. I think October sounds perfect, and it's not long to wait at all. I'm sure your Mama is correct about the time needed to prepare, and I think Aunt Genevieve will say the same. At least if we marry in October, it will not be too hot in Europe."

"Good, when we return indoors, we'll announce the date to everyone, then. Now, my next question is, where do you want to get married?"

"Here, in Hartford Church, please. I know there are much grander establishments in London, but it's where I've always wanted to marry since I was a little girl, and it will please Papa to walk me up the aisle of our local church. Is that all right with you?"

"Yes, of course, my dear. I'm rather hoping you'll be willing to live in London, though. It's where I carry out most of my business."

"Yes, of course, I thought we would probably live in London. Do you have your own house?"

"I do, indeed, and not far from your aunt's house in Belgravia. I've never lived there, but it's just one of many houses, my father owns in the area, and he's always promised it to me when I marry. I don't think you'll be disappointed. It's a grand house, with gardens every bit as impressive as these."

"How convenient, that it's not far from Aunt Genevieve's house; I'll be able to visit her. I'd like to return to Hartford regularly, though. I love Devon with its rolling hills and moorlands, and the coastline is picturesque. I'll enjoy showing it all to you when we're married."

"And I'll enjoy exploring it with you. With regards to our honeymoon then, I suggest we travel to Dover and cross the English Channel to France. We'll visit Paris, and then on to Switzerland and Italy. I can escort you around Turin and Florence before we make our way to Venice and Rome. You'll love Rome; there's so much to see. We could travel back through Austria and Germany. I've visited many of these places already, and I know exactly the best sights to take you to see."

"It sounds fabulous, Clarence, but how long will we be away?"

"As long as it takes, but certainly a few months; is that a problem?"

"No, not at all. I'm looking forward to it already, but it's a lot to plan; do you want me to do anything?"

"No, my dear, you can leave it all to me, or rather to my clerk. He's skilled at this sort of thing, and I bought a helpful book myself, a few months ago. It's written by a woman called Mariana Starke, and it's full of the most useful information, for travellers to the continent. Just getting all the passports sorted out is a challenge in itself, as you need one for every county you visit, and not everyone knows that. Miss Starke also advises what to take on your travels, as regards clothing, medicines, etcetera. I'll let you borrow it, and you can see for yourself."

"Thank you, Clarence, that's kind of you. Now, I think maybe we should return to our families, or they will be sending out a search party."

A couple of days later, Ephraim and Joshua took Lord Montgomery, Clarence, and Sebastian, on a tour of the Hartford Estate. Their visitors were impressed by the splendid scenery, that the county had to offer; for the moorlands were swathed in purple heather and yellow gorse, and the sea was a vivid blue in the hot sunshine. Lord Montgomery mopped his brow, as they sat on a hill, overlooking the Valley of the Rocks at Lynton, and admired the amazing view.

"Well, you certainly live in a wonderful place, Ephraim. What a view. My goodness, it's hot today, though. Do you think we could get some refreshments somewhere? My throat is in need of lubrication."

"Yes, of course. I thought we'd call into a tavern I know in Lynton, for a bite to eat, and a tankard of ale, and then we can ride back to Hartford. I'd like to show you how my canal is coming along if you're interested?"

"Yes, indeed. Clarence mentioned it to me the other day; it sounds like a bold venture, and I'd love to see how it's progressing. Having travelled on your local roads, I can understand why it would be better to transport the goods by boat, for they are truly appalling. I believe you're interested in the canal too, Clarence?"

"Yes, yes, I am. In fact, I might invest some money in it, if you're welcoming shareholders. I need a new project to interest me, and what better, than a family business."

"You'd be most welcome. I must admit, it's costing far more than I anticipated, and I cannot deny that an injection of capital would be helpful. I'm convinced it will soon pay for itself, once it's up and running, but that's still a year or two away, I'm afraid."

After a satisfying lunch at The Rising Sun, an ancient thatched inn, the men galloped back to Hartford, where Ephraim introduced them to James Griffiths. Clarence shook the engineer warmly by the hand.

"I'm pleased to meet you, Mr Griffiths; how's the work going?"

"Very well, thank you, sir. There's a lot to do, but we're making progress. We're working on the aqueduct at the moment. This is a major part of the project and will be the most time-consuming and expensive. You can see the foundations here, look. We've been lucky with the weather, so far. Over a month of dry weather, we've had, though the farmers keep forecasting thunderstorms. I'm hoping the rain doesn't come for a few more days, as the last thing we need is for any flash flooding around these footings before they're solid."

The Montgomery family was impressed with the canal, and with the engineer's knowledge and confidence, and to Ephraim's delight, Clarence promised a sizeable investment, which they shook hands on, before returning to Hartford Manor.

Lady Margery awoke early on the eighth of August and smiled when she realised it was the day of her engagement party. She enjoyed a few minutes alone with her thoughts, and then reached for the bell, and rang for her maid, knowing the day would be filled with preparations for the evening.

Thankfully, despite the sleepless nights endured by Violet Clark, the cook, and Mary Brown, the housekeeper, the preparations for the grand party had gone according to plan, and as far as they could tell, everything was ready. Hartford Manor was looking spick and span. The large hall, which was to be used for the ball, was decorated with brightly coloured, exotic blooms from the hothouses; the renovated chandeliers, and the silver tableware gleamed, and the servants were neatly attired in their new uniforms. Lord Fellwood, or perhaps more correctly, Lady Genevieve, had spared no effort, or expense, in the attempt to impress the wealthy Montgomery family.

At seven o'clock, precisely, Lady Margery walked gracefully down the staircase on the arm of her father. She looked simply beautiful in a pale blue dress, which matched her eyes, and the ribbons in her hair, to perfection. She wore an intricate gold necklace, that had belonged to her late mother, and her father had tears in his eyes, as he noted how much his daughter resembled his much-missed wife. At the foot of the stairs, Clarence was waiting, and taking his bride-to-be's arm, led her into dinner.

Violet Clark had done herself proud, having produced no less than seven courses for the diners to enjoy. This being the case, the guests lingered over and enjoyed the sumptuous food and the delicious wines that accompanied each course. It was after half-past ten, before the minstrels struck the first notes for the dancing to begin, and approaching three in the morning before they were permitted to put their instruments away and seek their beds.

Everyone who attended the ball agreed it had been a night to remember, and Lord Fellwood, and his sister, Lady Genevieve, went to bed, elated at a job well done.

CHAPTER 35

The hot and humid weather continued for another day or two, and the villagers of Hartford struggled to work in the searing heat. In the kitchens of Hartford Manor, the temperature was unbearable, and tempers became frayed. The stream that ran through the village, where Betsey and her friends had enjoyed paddling in their childhood, was now barely a trickle, and there were fears that some of the wells might run dry. The heatwave was the main topic of conversation, and the old folk insisted they had never known anything like it.

Then, late one afternoon, the skies darkened, as brooding storm clouds gathered. Large raindrops began to fall, slowly at first, but then with an intensity, which sent folk scurrying for shelter. In no time at all, the lanes and paths were a sea of mud, and the rain found its way through many a leaky roof. James Griffiths allowed the canal workers to head off for home early, as it was impossible to work, during such a deluge. The farm labourers hurried in from the fields and sought work undercover, and Ethel, the young skivvy at Hartford Manor, was scolded by the cook, for running outside to stand in the rain and cool off.

At The Red Lion Inn, Kezia heaved a sigh of relief, as the last stagecoach trundled away down the lane. She did not envy the passengers, for the torrential rain would quickly turn the roads into a quagmire, and she knew they might become stranded, before reaching their next stop. Betsey and Ned were pleased, for they had closed Betsey's Kitchen for the day, just before the rain started, and had all but sold out of food once again. Mal had been serving customers all day from his chair. He was now able to move his left foot, and wriggle the toes on his right, and the doctor was more than hopeful, he would one day, walk again. In the meantime, he still had to be carried everywhere, so Silas and Ned picked him up, and carried him, chair and all, back to the kitchen, where Kezia provided them all with a welcome cup of tea. Mal watched the heavy rain through the window, and felt relieved, knowing his roof would not leak.

"Here you are, look. Grab a couple of scones to have with your tea to keep you going until supper time. I'm roasting a brace of pheasants, but they won't be ready for a while. Oh, my goodness, did you hear that clap of thunder? It always frightened me as a child, and my mother used to tell me it was just God moving his furniture about. It didn't make me feel any better, though, and I still don't like it."

Ned pushed back his chair and reached for his hat and coat. "Right, I'd better get on with the milking. I can see Buttercup and Daisy, waiting by the meadow gate. They don't like this stormy weather, and who can blame them."

He ran across the yard and opened the gate to the meadow, to allow the two cows to make their way to the linhay. The animals were used to their new home now, and walked, a little faster than usual, across the yard. Suddenly, a bolt of lightning struck Ned, and the cow in front of him, and both were thrown to the ground! Betsey, who happened to be looking out of the kitchen window, screamed in horror and ran outside, where she found Ned unconscious, the linhay on fire, and the cow not moving. She was shocked to see that Ned was practically naked, his clothes smouldering, and his flesh charred black. The wooden milking stool he had been carrying, lay broken at the far side of the yard, its legs knocked out.

Kezia and Silas were quickly by her side, and for several seconds, they just stood there, stunned, not knowing what to do. Kezia was the first to regain her senses, and she shouted above the thunder and the rain.

"Silas, we must get him inside. Lift him under his arms. Betsey, you take one leg and I'll take the other."

Quickly, they carried the unconscious man inside and laid him on the floor. Kezia instructed Betsey to run for Doctor Abernethy, whilst she sat beside her son and smoothed his hair away from his rain-soaked face. She spoke to him quietly. "Ned, Ned, it's Mum. Can you hear me, Ned?" Tears ran down her cheeks, mingling with the rainwater, dripping from her hair.

Silas hurried back outside to douse the fire in the linhay, for it adjoined the shippen, where Betsey's Kitchen was situated, but to his horror, the roof of the newly refurbished building was already alight. Several neighbours, having seen the smoke, arrived to help, and they formed a line, passing buckets of water to throw over the blaze. However, although their efforts helped, it was more due to the torrential rain, that the fire was eventually extinguished. Silas then turned his attention to poor Daisy, the cow, but could see no signs of her breathing, and with the extensive burns to her body, he was thankful she was dead. Buttercup had bolted back into the meadow and stood trembling under a large oak tree. Silas debated whether to fetch her, but decided to let her calm down for a while, as he was sure she would just run off if he approached her. It was more important to find out how his brother was; the cow could be milked later.

Doctor Abernethy arrived with Daniel and Betsey some twenty minutes later, to find Ned still unconscious. The doctor examined his patient, finding the man's undamaged skin to be cold and clammy, and his breathing ragged. He quickly took charge.

"Right, we must bathe all of his clothes off immediately, with cool water, and it's probably better done, whilst he's still unconscious. Is there a bed downstairs, we can use for him?"

"Yes, put him in our bed. I can sleep on the floor, if necessary." Mal was shocked at the sight of his son, and tears ran down his cheeks. "Dear God, as if we haven't had enough trouble lately, and now this. Poor lad. Do you think he'll live, doctor?"

"I must be honest with you, Mal. I think it's unlikely he'll survive. His burns are extensive, and they cover more than half of his body. Patients with that number of burns to their skin, often perish. However, we shall do everything possible to help the young man, and aid his recovery."

They carried the unconscious man to the bedroom, and the doctor, assisted by Daniel and Kezia, gently bathed his entire body with cool water and removed the charred shreds of his clothing. Once he was naked, they could better see the extent of his burns. His left arm was blackened, and charred from the shoulder to the elbow, and it was possible to see the muscles of his biceps. The burns extended all over his back, from the nape of his neck to his buttocks, and down the left leg to the ankle. The front of his chest was also burned, as was his abdomen. Thankfully, his head, right arm, and leg had escaped injury. Betsey spoke nervously to the doctor.

"Doctor Abernethy, I've no wish to interfere with your treatment, but I know of a remedy for burns, that was given to me by an old gypsy woman when I was a child. It's a salve that I've used in the past with excellent results, though never for burns as extensive as this. I could gather the herbs, roots, and berries that I need if you think we should use them?"

Betsey was well-known in the village for her remedies and cures, and she still spent hours each week, preparing them. Folk who came to Betsey's Kitchen, often bought medicine as well as food. She had paid attention to Gypsy Freda as a child, and many of the villagers sought her help with their aches and pains, and many swore by them. The doctor was aware of this.

"Well, Betsey, your cure is likely to be as effective as anything I have to offer. I do know it's important to bathe the wounds at least three times a day and change the dressings. If any of these burns become infected, that will be the end of him. What exactly do you put into your remedy?"

Betsey was embarrassed. "I'm afraid I can't tell you that, sir. I promised the old lady I would never divulge her cures to another living soul until I was old and grey myself. What I can tell you, is nothing in my salve would harm Ned. Uncle Mal, and Aunty Kezzie; do you want me to mix up the salve, to use on Ned's wounds?"

Knowing how effective Betsey's medicines usually were, they both nodded. "Yes, do what you can, Betsey; we know you'll do your best for Ned."

Heedless of the heavy rain, Betsey ran from the house, a sharp knife in her hand. She stripped the bark from a pine tree, and then collected a bowlful of rosehips, thanking her lucky stars, this was the time of year they were plentiful. She continued into the woods, where she knew hemlock plants grew. She carefully dug up the root of the deadly plant, handling it with great care, knowing how dangerous it could be. Nevertheless, Gypsy Freda had taught her not to be afraid of the plant, for, in minute doses, the crushed root could ease pain, and treat skin infections. She returned to the inn, where she put the bark soaking in a bucket of boiling water. She crushed the rosehips in the mortar and pestle, she had saved for many months to purchase and then added the tiniest amount of hemlock root. When the water containing the pine bark had cooled, she strained it into a bowl and added a few other ingredients. Last, but not least, she added a jar of honey, stirred the mixture, and took it to the bedroom, where Ned was still being attended to by Daniel and his grandfather.

"Here we are. This is a lotion to bathe his wounds with, every time we change his dressings. It will soothe the burns, and hopefully, prevent infection. Has he shown any signs of waking up?"

"No, I'm afraid not, Betsey, but it's early days. I'll stay with him for the next few hours. If the rest of you want to get on with your tasks, I'll tell you straight away if there's any change. Someone will need to sit with him through the night, and I think the dressings should be changed every six hours for the first few days, day and night. I'm afraid it's going to be hard work, nursing him for many weeks, or months, to come. Daniel, can you return home, and collect the medicines you'll need to complete my rounds, and attend to my other patients, please?"

His grandson nodded. "Yes, of course, Grandad. Betsey, would you like to see me out?"

Betsey followed her young man outside, and they sheltered under the porch from the persistent rain.

"Oh, Daniel, Ned's so badly burnt; do you think he'll recover?"

"I don't know, Betsey, but Grandad will do everything he can. I must go now, but I'll see you, tomorrow."

He pulled her to him and kissed her passionately, his hand straying down over her buttocks. She returned his kiss, but then pulled away.

"Oh, Daniel, you shouldn't kiss me like that, right on our doorstep; anyone might come along, and how would it look at such a time."

"Well, I'm sure folk would understand. Good heavens, I've barely seen you recently; you've been so busy. I hope you aren't intending to nurse Ned, as well; you can surely leave that to his mother and Josie?"

"I shall take my turn, Daniel, because I'm fond of Ned. It's going to be difficult for us to manage without his help, let alone have to nurse him too, and just look at the damage to the shippen roof. The Kitchen was so successful, but there will be a lot of work to do before we can open that again. Just as things were improving, with Uncle Mal getting the feeling back in his legs, now this had to happen. It'll still be some time before he can get about on his own, and without Ned to help Silas carry him, it's going to be so difficult. It's such rotten luck."

"Well, I'd better go now, and visit the other patients. I'll call for you tomorrow evening, and we can go for our walk as usual."

"Yes, please come, Daniel; but I don't know if I'll be able to get away. You can see how we're fixed with so much to do. I'd like to see you, though, and perhaps Ned will be conscious by then, and we might know a bit more."

The young man hurried off down the road through the heavy rain and was soaked to the skin, long before he reached the doctor's house. At the bottom of the hill, he had to wade through a foot of water, as the river had burst its banks, and was rising fast. As he passed the site of Lord Fellwood's canal, he frowned, for the foundations of the new aqueduct, were almost underwater, and surrounded by a sea of mud.

CHAPTER 36

It was a fine day in late September, and Betsey was enjoying a rare break in the garden at the rear of the inn. She closed her eyes, and lifted her face to the sun for a few moments, enjoying its warmth. There was a loud buzzing in the air; for close to where she sat was a patch of Michaelmas daisies, their delicate lilac blooms attracting numerous bees and butterflies. Sighing deeply, she rose from the upturned wooden crate she had been sitting on, picked up the basket of clothes she had removed from the washing line, and returned inside, remembering how she once helped her mother peg out the washing each day. It seemed a million years ago now.

It was some four weeks since the bolt of lightning had killed Daisy, the cow, and burned Ned Carter, severely. The young man had remained unconscious for hours following the accident and had hovered between life and death, for several days. Betsey and Kezia had taken turns sitting with him for nights on end, each of them getting only a few hours of rest, before having to work another long day. Josie, although willing, had the baby to attend to, and being the only able-bodied man left working at the inn, Silas had to get his rest.

Doctor Abernethy had been a godsend, spending long hours at Ned's bedside, supervising the bathing of his wounds, and the changing of his dressings, until Kezia and Betsey were as skilled at the task as he was. The doctor had not taken a penny in payment, for he knew how hard the folk at the inn were finding it to make ends meet.

Betsey had seen little of Daniel over the last few weeks, and she was worried she was losing him. At first, he called regularly and tried to persuade her to spend more time with him, but his visits gradually became less frequent. She tried to explain how much pressure she was under, and how exhausted she was feeling, but he had no patience with her excuses.

"Why on earth don't you seek another position, where you can have some time to call your own? It's ridiculous, the number of hours you're working; it's no wonder you're always so tired. You're no fun anymore, and I bet you don't get paid for all the work you're doing."

"Oh, Daniel, I couldn't leave the Carters now, in their hour of need. They rescued me when I was destitute, and but for them, I doubt I'd even be here; you know that. I don't get paid at all, and I don't want to. As long as they put a roof over my head, and feed me, that's all I ask."

"Can't you see you're just an unpaid skivvy? You'd work fewer hours, and be better paid if you went into service."

"Well, I doubt you'd see much more of me, then. I believe most of the kitchen maids at Hartford Manor, only get a half-day off a sennight. At least I can come and go as I please, at the inn. Maybe things will be better when you're qualified as a doctor and have your own practice."

This was the closest hint Betsey had ever made regarding marriage. She had been walking out with Daniel Abernethy for over a year and had hopes he might, one day, propose. However, he had made no mention of it, though he regularly tried to persuade her to lie with him. At their last meeting, a few days earlier, she had relented and had gone for a short stroll in the woods with him. He had made a big fuss of her, and she enjoyed his kisses. However, it ended, as it usually did, with him wanting to take rather more liberties than she was willing to permit, and with him storming off.

With the thatched roof damaged, it had been necessary to close Betsey's Kitchen, and the facility was sadly missed in the village. Even with the help of Tilly, their new servant, the women struggled to get all the jobs done, and some of the stagecoaches began to call at other establishments, where the service and food, were more reliable. Silas was run off his feet, caring for the horses, milking Buttercup, their one remaining cow, and generally doing the work of three men. Mal continued to make steady progress and was slowly trying to teach himself to walk again. The doctor was pleased but warned him not to overdo things. However, seeing how his family was struggling, the man was impatient and pushed himself, as hard as possible.

For the first time since Mal had taken out the bank loan for the new roof, the inn had been unable to meet the last repayment, and Kezia and Mal were dreading the arrival of a letter from the bank. Though she protested, she could not afford the time away from the inn, Mal persuaded Kezia to go to Barnstaple, and explain to the manager, the difficulties they were facing.

"But Mal, if I go to town, who will do all the baking, and everything else?"

"I know it's difficult, but Mr Barlow is a reasonable man, and if you explain to him what's happened, I'm hoping he'll give us a bit of time to get straight. I think it will be worse if we don't keep him informed. Instead of offering stews and pasties, we'll just have to offer bread and cheese to the travellers for a day or two. It can't be helped."

Taking his advice, Kezia drove herself to Barnstaple, rather than take Silas away from his duties. It was something she had never done before, but the journey was uneventful, and the bank manager was sympathetic. He agreed to allow the Carters a brief respite from making their monthly payments.

"You've already missed one repayment, Mrs Carter, but I appreciate you coming to explain matters to me, and you and your husband, have been excellent customers of this bank for many years. Indeed, I've checked our records, and this is the first time you have ever missed a payment. Such reliable customers deserve to be well-treated, and so I will agree to a further three months, when you may withhold payments. That will take us into the new year. Will that help?"

"Oh, yes, sir, thank you, it will help a great deal. My husband is beginning to get the feeling back in his legs, and once he's able to do a day's work again, it will make such a difference. I'm becoming hopeful, that my son, Ned, may now survive, though it will be some time before he's fit for work. Unfortunately, we've had to close our other food outlet, which we named Betsey's Kitchen, as the roof was damaged in the fire. It's not beyond repair, but at the moment, we have no one fit to do the work, and can't afford to employ anyone. However, we've covered everything inside with tarpaulins, and I hope one day, we'll be able to re-open. It was doing so well, too. Betsey worked incredibly hard to make it a success."

"Yes, I remember Betsey, from when she came to see me with your son. I was struck by her enthusiasm and energy, and I wish her well. I'm sure if anyone can make a success of the venture, it will be her. Please pass on my regards to her, and wish your son a full, and speedy, recovery."

Delighted with the reprieve from their money worries, Kezia was in a better mood when she returned home. Having explained to Mal and Silas, what the manager had said, she went into the bedroom to see Ned.

"I have excellent news, Ned. The bank manager was kind and understanding, and I'm so glad I went to see him. He says we can miss the repayments for another three months, so that will take us into the new year. Your father's getting better every day, so maybe, by then, he'll be able to work again. How are you feeling today, anyway?"

"Yes, I'm all right, thank you. I wish it would all heal a bit quicker, though."

Ned was still swathed in bandages, and his left arm was a cause for concern. However, the doctor was pleased he could move his fingers and hopeful, the young man would eventually, make a full recovery. They had reduced changing the dressings to twice a day, something Ned was delighted about, as it was an intensely painful business. The ugly scars, he would carry for the rest of his life.

"You're a bit flushed. Are you sure you feel all right?"

"Yes, I'm fine. I have a bit of a headache, but nothing to worry about. I just feel guilty lying here, when you're all so busy. How badly is the shippen damaged? The others tell me it's not too serious, but I'm not sure I believe them."

"Well, one side of the roof is damaged, but luckily, the heavy rain put the fire out, before it took hold. There isn't much damage inside, apart from what the water did, and we've moved everything to the far end, where it's dry, and covered it with tarpaulins. The main thing is, the stove wasn't damaged. Once we get you, and your dad, up and about again, I suspect you might be able to do the repairs with Silas's help. It doesn't matter at the moment anyway, because we don't have enough hours in the day, to bake enough food for the inn and the Kitchen. We have to help Silas with his jobs because there's too much for one man to cope with. Don't worry, Ned, I'm sure it will all come right, again. I'm just glad you're still with us." Suddenly overcome with emotion, Kezia paused. "Oh, Ned, I thought I was going to lose you."

He took her hand. "Hey, I can't remember ever seeing you cry, Mum. I'm all right. I'm on the mend. I just wish it was a bit faster."

Impatiently brushing a tear from her eye, Kezia patted his hand.

"Patience, lad, patience. You're getting there. Now, I must remind Betsey to collect the ingredients for her salve; I do believe that concoction is working miracles. She's a clever girl, is that one."

After tea that day, Betsey went to the woods to collect what she needed for the salve. It was a sunny evening, and she enjoyed walking in the dappled shade. She had worked hard in the stuffy kitchen all day, and it was a treat to be out in the fresh air. She paused as a red squirrel ran up a tree, and she smiled at its antics, as it leapt gracefully from one branch to another. Suddenly, she thought she heard low voices, but looking around, could see no one. She strolled on; her footsteps silent on the mossy floor. As she walked into a secluded glade, she gasped in dismay, at the spectacle before her.

A young woman lay on her back, her bare legs wrapped around her young man, as, oblivious of an audience, they passionately made love. Recognising the young man's shirt, Betsey took a step back in horror, and a twig snapped under her foot. The young man glanced behind him, and Betsey's worse fears were confirmed, as she stared into the eyes of Daniel Abernethy.

CHAPTER 37

Distraught and white-faced, Betsey returned to the inn with the ingredients for her salve. She said nothing to anyone about what she had seen, but it was obvious to all around her, that she was not her usual self, and Kezia took her to one side.

"What's the matter, Betsey? You were fine, earlier on. What's happened to make you so miserable? It's not like you. Do you feel poorly?"

"No, no, I'm fine, Aunty Kezzie. It's nothing."

"Well, something's upset you; I can see by your face, and you're not far from tears." The kindly woman put her arm around the girl. "Come on, tell me what's wrong, and I might be able to help."

The warmth of the embrace was Betsey's undoing, and tears flowed down her cheeks.

"Oh, Betsey, who's upset you like this? They'll have me to reckon with."

Between sobs, Betsey stammered. "It's, it's Daniel; I went to the woods to pick the herbs, and he was lying with a girl."

Kezia's face was like thunder. "What! Well, I've thought for a long time, he was a good-for-nothing scoundrel, and this just confirms it. I've not liked the way he's treated you for some time. My goodness, you've been walking out with him for over a year, and I presume he hasn't proposed in all that time?" She raised her eyes in question.

"No, he's never even hinted at it. He's been angry with me lately because I've had so little time for him, but he knows how difficult it is with Uncle Mal and Ned, both injured."

"Not that it matters, but did you see who the girl was?"

"No, I couldn't see, and I ran away."

"Did they see you?"

"Yes, Daniel did; I stepped on a twig, and he heard it snap. He looked around and saw me, and I ran off."

"He's not worth worrying over, Betsey. If he's unfaithful now, there's no doubt he would be, if you married him, and the way he treats you, why, don't you even give him a second thought. I shall tell his grandfather of his behaviour when he comes to see Ned, later."

"Oh no, please don't tell Doctor Abernethy. It doesn't matter. I'm glad I found out because I've been uncomfortable with our relationship for some time. Nothing I do seems to be right. He's been pestering me to lie with him for months, and every time I say no, he gets angry and storms off. He insists a girl can't get in the family way the first time," Betsey continued hastily, "not that I'd let him love me before we were wed, anyway."

"Oh, my dear, I can certainly put you right on that score. You can definitely get pregnant the first time you lie with a man, and I know of plenty of girls who have."

"He says he's a doctor, and that it's impossible."

"Well, he's not going to make much of a doctor, then. Now, dry your tears, and get on with that ointment, because we need to change Ned's dressings."

An hour or so later, the two women entered the bedroom, to attend to their patient. Ned was fast asleep, which was unusual at four o'clock in the afternoon. They had got into the habit of changing his dressings at five o'clock in the morning, before starting their chores for the day, and then again, late in the afternoon. Betsey leaned over the young man, and gently brushed his hair back from his face.

"Ned, Ned, I'm sorry, but can you wake up? We need to change your dressings."

She glanced at his mother in concern, for his brow was hot, and he was sweating profusely. He opened his eyes but seemed confused.

"Ned, are you all right? Do you feel ill?"

His voice came out as a croak. "No, I don't feel too good. I have such a headache, and I ache all over."

"I'm sorry, Ned, but we must change your dressings; can you bear it?"

"Aye, get on with it. Have a look at my belly, will you? It feels more tender than usual."

Gently, they bathed away the dressings, not wanting to destroy the new skin that was slowly forming. Betsey anointed his wounds with her salve and put on fresh dressings.

"It's all healing nicely, Ned. Even your arm's looking better every day. Now, we just have your belly to do."

Soaking the dressings in tepid water, they carefully peeled them away, then gasped, for the wounds on his abdomen, were looking angry and sore, and in one place, pus was oozing from the wound. Ned groaned as the tender area was touched, and he became aware of the silence surrounding him.

"What is it? Is something wrong?" He glanced down, and was distraught to see how angry and inflamed the wounds were. "Oh no, they weren't like that earlier, were they?"

"No, they weren't, lad. I thought this morning these wounds were a little angry but not as bad as this. Not to worry, we'll get Doctor Abernethy to examine them. I'm sure he'll have the answer."

Quickly, they reapplied the dressings, and Betsey fetched Ned a drink of cool water. She sat on the bed beside him, put her arm around his sound shoulder, and helped him to drink. She eased him back onto his pillows, then bathed his feverish brow with a cool cloth.

"Don't worry, Ned; I'm sure it's just a temporary setback. I'll see you, later."

Once outside the bedroom, Betsey looked anxiously at Kezia. "Do you think he'll be all right?"

"I don't know. He's taken a turn for the worse, and that wound looks infected to me. I've sent Tilly to fetch the doctor, so let's see what he has to say.

At the doctor's house, the maid admitted Tilly, and Mrs Abernethy advised her that the doctor and his grandson were attending a birth, and she told Tilly where to find them.

Knowing the situation was urgent, Tilly ran to the other end of the village, where she found the two medics. Unfortunately, it was a complicated birth, and Doctor Abernethy felt unable to leave the young woman. However, he instructed his grandson to accompany the maid, and examine Ned Carter. Daniel, knowing the welcome that most likely awaited him at the inn, was reluctant, but his grandfather insisted.

Together, Tilly and Daniel hurried to The Red Lion Inn. When Kezia saw them approaching, she met them at the door.

"No, you're not welcome here. Where's your grandfather?"

"He can't come. He's delivering a baby, and the woman is in trouble. I assure you, I'm more than capable of examining your son, and deciding on the best course of action."

"That you might be, but you certainly don't know how to treat a woman. Luckily for you, I haven't told Mal and Silas yet, how you've treated Betsey, but I will, and then you'd better keep out of their way. How dare you string her along for over a year, and then behave as you've done?"

The man surveyed the angry woman in front of him, coldly. "Do you want me to examine your son, or not? Whom I see, and what I do, is no business of yours, but whilst we are on the subject, maybe if you didn't make the girl work every hour of the day, she'd have had some time to spend with me."

"Yes, maybe, but I don't make Betsey do anything. She has values, and is loyal and reliable, which is something that cannot be said of you. I'll be telling your grandfather of your behaviour; you mark my words."

The angry young man turned on his heel and made to walk away, but suddenly, he found his path blocked, by the formidable figure of Silas.

"I don't know what's going on here, but you have a duty to do, mister, and I'll see you do it. You'll help my brother, to the best of your ability, or I'll give you a beating, you'll never forget. Silas grabbed the man by the scruff of the neck and dragged him into the inn.

Betsey was sitting beside Ned, bathing his forehead with a damp cloth, and she was horrified when the door opened, and Silas all but threw the doctor inside. She rose from her chair, and silently left the room, leaving Kezia to take her place. Outside, in the corridor, Silas put his arm around her.

"I don't know what's been going on, Betsey, and you don't have to tell me, for I think I heard enough to guess. For what it's worth, though, I'm pretty sure you're better off without that young man. He has no morals and is the talk of the village. He may be wealthy, and good-looking, but you can do far better. You do know, you could have your pick of all the young men in the village, don't you?"

"Don't be silly, Silas; there's no one else interested in me."

"Have you looked in the mirror, lately, Betsey? You may not realise it, but you're beautiful, and not only that, but everyone loves you. You know what an awful life your mother had with your father. All I'm saying, love, is be sure the man you marry, will treat you right. Mind you, if he didn't, he'd have me to reckon with."

In the bedroom, Daniel examined Ned and confirmed the wound on his abdomen was infected. As the man was running a fever, the young doctor bled his patient and instructed Kezia to keep the room as cool as possible. Unfortunately, none of this reassured Kezia.

"Please ask your grandfather to call as soon as he's free. He's older than you, and might have other ideas."

The young man nodded, and hastily left the room, hoping not to bump into Betsey.

However, she was waiting for him outside the back door. She was furious, and he sneered at her.

"Look, I don't know why you're angry with me. It's not like you would lie with me, is it? Surely, you knew I'd look elsewhere? I'm only human, and a man has his needs."

"I thought you loved me, Daniel? At least, you said you did, but you have no respect for me. You know it's wrong to lie together, before marriage."

"Oh, I see; you were holding out for a ring on your finger! Are you serious? Did you really believe I'd ever marry you?"

Betsey paled, and her gaze dropped to her feet, as her eyes filled with tears.

"You did; didn't you? You truly thought I'd marry a skivvy like you? Me! A wealthy doctor, with ambitions to practice in Harley Street, in London. You thought I would marry the likes of you." He was still laughing loudly as he sauntered off down the road.

CHAPTER 38

The thunderstorm, a few weeks earlier, had caused a great deal of damage to the foundations of the new aqueduct and was likely to delay the canal project significantly. In some places, the new footings had washed away completely; such was the ferocity of the torrent, that had swept down the hillside. James Griffiths, the canal engineer, had broken the bad news to Lord Fellwood, that it would be necessary to dig out some of the foundations and start all over again. The young man was honest with his employer.

"Unfortunately, sir, the weather caught us out, and the footings were not secure enough to withstand so severe a flood. The weather was unprecedented. I, for one, have never seen anything like it, and doubt I ever will again."

It was a bitter blow, for the project was already costing far more money than anticipated, and any delay would only exacerbate the problem.

The heavy rain had also caused severe flooding in the village, and a few of the cottages were damaged. Most dwellings were made of cob, a mixture of mud, straw, and sand; a hardy building material, which would last for many years, but it was not good for it to get too wet. Lord Fellwood walked around the village with his estate manager and surveyed the damage. Sighing deeply, he instructed the man to oversee the repairs as soon as possible. As tied cottages, the buildings were his responsibility, and he was not one to shirk his duties.

Now, some six weeks later, he was visiting the site of the canal again and was pleased to see that progress had been made. He shook the young engineer's hand.

"How's it going then, James? Have you made up for the time we lost?"

"No, not quite, sir, but we're getting on well. See, the new foundations are in place, and God-willing, I hope to complete them without further interruption from the weather. Fortunately, we've had a dry spell for the last few weeks, and that's helped us no end. There's no doubt the incident will add considerably to the overall costs, but it could have been far worse, had the wet weather continued."

Thankful that the project was once again making progress, Ephraim left the man to get on with his work and climbed aboard the pony and trap. He clicked his tongue to encourage the animal on its way and drove back to Hartford Manor.

The marriage of Lady Margery and Lord Clarence Montgomery was due to take place in a few days, and the bridegroom, and his family, were expected at any time. The bride-to-be was excited beyond words, and could not wait for the event to take place. As Lord Fellwood approached the Manor House, he was immediately aware that the visitors had arrived, for the cobbled area outside the grand house, was surrounded by carriages of all descriptions, and there was a flurry of people coming and going, carrying copious amounts of luggage into the house.

Lady Margery met him in the hallway and took his arm excitedly.

"Papa, Clarence, and his family have just arrived; do come into the drawing room, and join us for some tea."

Ephraim smiled at his radiant daughter, thinking how happy she looked, and with no small effort, he put his financial worries to one side and joined the party. He was not looking forward, to the difficult conversation to be had later, concerning his future son-in-law's promised investment in the canal project. Smiling widely, he entered the room and welcomed his guests.

The Hartford Manor cook, Mrs Clarke, was known for her impressive culinary skills. Now widowed, and with no living children, her job was her life, and she enjoyed trying out new recipes, repeating every one, until satisfied they were perfect. However, for the meal that evening, she had decided to keep it simple, for there were a number of distinguished guests, and she did not want to risk any mishaps. A large silver and glass centrepiece sparkled in the light of two huge crystal chandeliers, and the snowy white tablecloth enhanced the well-polished cutlery and glassware.

To start the meal, Mrs Clarke had made a leek and potato soup; a dish she was renowned for. She made sure the portions were small, as it was a substantial meal in itself, and there were several other courses to tempt the guests. Served with freshly-made warm bread rolls, and golden farm butter, the soup went down a treat, for the visitors were hungry, and it was followed by a light dish of salmon mousse. Leaving the party to digest their first two courses for a while, Mrs Clarke busied herself, putting the final touches to a dish of rare roast beef, and all the trimmings. By the time they had finished the delicious main course, most guests were declaring they could not possibly manage another mouthful. However, their willpower soon deserted them, when they spied the treats available for dessert. A choice of lemon posset, rhubarb fool, or chocolate pudding, served with thick Devonshire clotted cream, proved the undoing of most.

The meal over, the women left the men to their port and cigars, as was the custom. Aunt Genevieve and Margery, led their guests to a pleasant side room, where a fire was burning brightly in the large fireplace, for it was a chilly night, in such a large and draughty house. Lord Fellwood waited until the men had been served with their chosen drink, for most, port or brandy, and then took Clarence to one side.

"Would you accompany me to the library, Clarence? There's a matter I must discuss with you in private, please."

Begging the pardon of their guests, to excuse them for a few minutes, he led the young man into the old library, believed to be one of the oldest rooms in the house. The solid old furniture gleamed, and there was a faint, but pleasant smell of beeswax, a testament to many hours of polishing. The room was lined, from floor to ceiling, with books of every description, and above the fireplace hung a portrait of a much-loved horse.

"Clarence, I'm afraid I have disturbing news concerning the canal. I don't know if you've heard, but we had a torrential storm here recently, and the river burst its banks. Several cottages were damaged, and one poor man in the village was struck by lightning. I understand his life still hangs in the balance, and the cow he was about to milk, was killed outright. However, the reason I'm telling you all this is because the foundations of the new aqueduct were practically washed away, and need to be rebuilt. This will set the project back by some weeks and will increase the expenditure even further, and the budget was already overspent. Now, you kindly offered to invest in the project, and your money would have been most welcome, but I must be frank with you, Clarence, and tell you, that it may not be a wise investment. James Griffiths assures me that once built, the aqueduct will be of solid construction; the timing of the cloudburst was unfortunate, to say the least."

"Lord Fellwood, Ephraim, may I call you, Ephraim?" The older man nodded.

"Ephraim, I confess, I am aware of this, as I overheard a conversation between two of your servants, earlier." He waved his hand, dismissively. "No, they weren't gossiping; they were expressing their concern for the injured man, and had no idea I was listening. Now, as I understand it, this canal project is costing a lot of money, but once it's up and running, then you, and all the other shareholders, will reap the benefits for many years to come. Am I right?"

"Well, yes, that's what we all hope, of course, but there are no guarantees, and in all conscience, I cannot allow you to risk your money."

"That's for me to decide, and I'm happy to proceed. I know there are risks, but I always have my people carry out extensive investigations on any project I put my money into, and the word is, your canal will pay handsome dividends in the future."

Lord Fellwood heaved an audible sigh of relief.

"Well, if you're sure, Clarence, I must confess it will be a load off my mind. I believe our legal people drew up the necessary paperwork in preparation for your visit, so maybe we can deal with that, in the morning. Now, shall we return to our guests? I have a special vintage port, that I want you to try; I've been saving it for tonight, and now we have something else to celebrate, as well as your marriage to my daughter."

Three days later, an over-excited and nervous, Lady Margery, held onto her father's arm as he proudly walked her up the aisle of Hartford Church. It had rained heavily earlier in the day, but thankfully, the weather had cleared up, and a weak sun was trying to shine. Many villagers lined the street outside the ancient church, hoping to catch a glimpse of the young bride, who wore a simple white dress of Honiton lace. Lady Margery had ignored the current fashion for red or yellow wedding dresses, preferring a dress similar to the one she had worn when presented to Queen Adelaide. Her father had tears in his eyes, as he helped her out of the carriage.

She was attended by three young bridesmaids, all children of various friends of the family, and they were also dressed in white silk gowns. The bride and the bridesmaids carried pretty posies of pink rosebuds, and baby's breath;

the flowers having been carefully nurtured in the hothouses of the Manor House.

It was indeed a stylish wedding, as befitted the only daughter of the Lord of Hartford Manor. Following the service in the church, the guests were transported back to the Manor House, where an impressive feast awaited them. The celebrations continued long into the night, and there were more than a few sore heads, the next morning.

The guests, family, and servants lined up outside to wave goodbye to the newlyweds, who were setting off on their lavish honeymoon across Europe.

CHAPTER 39

Doctor Abernethy's face was grim, as he left the bedroom with Kezia and Betsey. He had visited Ned every day for the last three days and was concerned he might lose his patient. He had purposely, not asked Daniel to take a turn in caring for the sick man, for Kezia had not held back, in telling him exactly what she thought of his grandson. Sadly, he believed every word she told him, for it had not escaped his notice that the behaviour of the young man in question, left a lot to be desired. He turned to the two anxious women; his face filled with concern.

"I'm afraid Ned is very poorly, and I must be honest, and tell you I fear for him. His wound is infected, and he's running a high fever. I hope it will break soon, but sadly I have no other remedies, or medicines, to offer."

Each night, Betsey and Kezia had taken turns to sit with Ned, constantly applying a cool compress to his fevered brow, and reassuring him in the rare moments, he regained consciousness.

"If there's nothing more you can do, doctor; do you think it's worth me trying one or two of Gypsy Freda's cures?"

"Yes, by all means, Betsey; if you think you can help Ned, then I think you should. I fear he's losing the battle for life."

Tears coursed down Kezia's cheeks, as Betsey took her hand. "Aunty Kezzie, all those years ago, when I spent time with Gypsy Freda, she showed me how to make a poultice to draw the poison from a wound, but I've never used it, so I don't know if it would help. I remember how to make it, and we could apply it to Ned's wounds. I also know how to make a potion to break a fever, but again, it's not something I've used for a long time. I only provide salves for people these days; I don't have time to do more. Do you want me to try these cures on Ned?"

"Yes, please do, Betsey. I know you'd never harm Ned, and it might work. That old woman was so clever; I wish she was here now, but I guess she must have been laid to rest years ago. At least she passed her knowledge on to you. Go, go, and collect what you need, and hurry, for I fear Ned is not long for this world."

Betsey hastily grabbed a basket from the kitchen, and wrapped a shawl over her head, for it was raining heavily. Before she left, she told Kezia to boil some onions and garlic, until they were soft. She hurried to the woods and went straight to where she knew she would find the bark of a willow tree and some berries. Sourcing meadowsweet, took much longer, for it was a summer-time flower, but eventually, she found a few blooms in a sheltered glade. She continued with her foraging, until she had all she needed, and then returned home as fast as she could.

Kezia had the onions and garlic ready, and Betsey quickly soaked some bread in warm water and mixed it into a paste with the onions and garlic. Stirring the mixture, she quickly added the other ingredients needed to make the poultice, to draw the poison from Ned's wounds. Together, she and Kezia passed some strips of material under his body and lifting his nightshirt, spread the warm mixture across the angry wounds, and bound the poultice in place. Ned groaned loudly, as the heated mass made his wounds smart even more, and Betsey smoothed his brow and persuaded him not to touch the bandaged area.

"There, we must leave that in place overnight, to allow it to do its work. I think one of us will have to sit with him all the time, to make sure he doesn't pull it off. It's bound to hurt, as his belly's so inflamed. I'm going to make a potion for his fever now, and we'll spoon some into his mouth; I just hope he can swallow."

Using her mortar and pestle, she pounded the ingredients she had collected, until they were smooth. She mixed them with cool water, then carried her precious potion to the bedroom, where she spooned some of the liquid into Ned's mouth. Kezia helped her, and by the time they had finished, it was tea time.

"I'll sit with him, tonight, Aunty Kezzie. You must get some rest; I can see you're gone in."

"Yes, I am tired, but I can't bear to leave him. Perhaps we'll both sit here."

"No, I think we must take it in turns, or we'll never manage. You catch up with some jobs, and then get a few hours of sleep. I promise I'll fetch you if there's any change."

"Very well then. I must see how Josie and Tilly are getting on. I've had to leave everything to them, today, and I expect they're almost asleep on their feet. Mal, too, I've neglected him, these last few days."

In the kitchen, Kezia found Mal, Silas, Josie, and Tilly taking a short break. Silas was holding his daughter, and as soon as she saw her granny, the child held out her arms. Kezia took Amy from her father and kissed her warm, plump cheek.

"Hello, my lovely. How's my favourite granddaughter?" She tickled the little girl, and she giggled.

"Is there any change?" Mal was anxious.

"No, not really. He's delirious and seldom conscious. Betsey's put a poultice on his wounds, and we've spooned some of her medicine into his mouth, but he struggled to swallow it; I think we got some down him, though. We just have to wait and see if the fever breaks now. Betsey seems to think this is the most crucial time, so we must see what the morning brings." She studied her husband, anxiously. "And how about you, Mal? I've barely paid you any attention for days. Are you, all right?"

"Yes, of course, I am. Tough as old boots me, but you look as if you need cheering up. So, what do you think about this, then?"

Smiling widely, he raised first his right foot from the ground, and then the left. See, my knees are working again. Silas helped me to stand earlier, and I tried to take a few steps, but that wasn't too successful. Luckily, he caught me before I hit the ground. I showed Doctor Abernethy what I could do this morning, and he's sure I'll walk again, eventually, but says I mustn't rush it. It's all right for him to say, isn't it? I think he's right, though, and even being able to stand will help."

"Oh, Mal; that's marvellous news, but I'm so worried about Ned."

As tears began to flow down her cheeks, Josie reached across and took the little girl. Silas rose, and put his arms around his mother, trying to soothe her.

"Come on, now, Mum. You know our Ned's a fighter. If anyone can see off this fever, it'll be him. I've never known him to give up on anything, and I've every confidence in Betsey's skills. Her lotions and potions always seem to work, and at least, they never harm."

Blowing her nose in a piece of rag, Kezia impatiently brushed away her tears and stood up.

"Yes, I know, and I must get a few jobs done before I start cooking the tea. How did you get on with the stagecoach visitors, today?"

"Well, a few moaned, that there were only pasties, and bread and cheese, but we simply didn't have time to make a batch of stew. Young Tilly, here, is a blessing. She's worked hard all day, with no complaints. Why don't you get off home, now, Tilly; you must be tired."

"Yes, I am, but then so are all of you. I'm just going to finish this cup of tea, and then I'll make a batch of stew for tomorrow's customers. I bought three rabbits from an old poacher earlier, and I've already skinned and gutted them. I'll put them simmering, while I prepare the vegetables. It will be one job less for tomorrow."

"You're such a big help, Tilly. Thank goodness, we took you on when we did. Now, if you pass me the carrots and onions, I can do them, while you peel the potatoes." Mal smiled at his wife. "It will all come right, again, Kezzie. Once Ned's over the worst, and I'm back on my feet, we can start to rebuild the business."

Betsey struggled to stay awake during the long night. Kezia, and the others, had instructed her to wake them in a couple of hours, to let her get some sleep, but she had no intention of doing so. They were all older than she was, and the strain of the unrelenting hard work was showing plainly in their faces. Young Amy was teething, and so Silas and Josie often had disturbed nights, anyway. Betsey fully expected Kezia to appear during the night, for she was frantic with worry about her son, and she smiled to herself, as she realised that the light sedative, she had added to her aunt's hot milky drink before bedtime, had worked. Throughout the night, she held the cold compress to Ned's fevered brow, and once or twice sponged his body to cool him down. In the early hours, she reheated the remainder of the poultice mixture and applied a fresh dressing. She wasn't sure if it was her imagination, but in the weak candlelight, she thought the wounds appeared to be a little less angry.

Eventually, just before dawn, she lost her fight against sleep, and her head slumped forward, resting on the side of the bed. She awoke to the sensation of someone stroking her hair gently and she was annoyed to think she had fallen asleep. Lifting her head, she found herself looking into the lucid eyes of Ned. He smiled, and she gasped, as she realised the fever had left him.

"Oh, Ned, you're all right!"

"Aye, of course, I am, especially with you beside me."

"Oh, Ned, I've been so worried about you; I thought we were going to lose you."

Without thinking about what she was doing, Betsey flung her arms around the young man and kissed him firmly on the lips. He winced, as she leaned on his wounds, and then she realised what she had done, and was horrified.

"I'm so sorry, Ned; I don't know what I was thinking of."

"Don't be sorry, on my account. If that's my reward, for being struck by lightning, then I wish it had happened sooner."

"But Ned, we're like brother and sister; it's not right. I should never have kissed you like that."

"But we're not, though, are we? We're not even related, and let me assure you, my feelings for you are not at all brotherly. But don't worry about it, I know you love, Daniel, and he's got far better prospects, than me."

She frowned. "Not anymore, I don't."

"What do you mean?"

"Oh, well, I haven't bothered you with it all, because you've been so ill, but I caught Daniel lying with another woman. When I tackled him about it, he said it was my fault because I refused to."

"What! As soon as I'm better, I'll give him the hiding he deserves. How dare he insult you."

"No, he's not worth it; I realise that now. I told him I'm not that sort of girl, and I wouldn't lie with anyone until I'm married."

"Quite right too, and if you had, he'd have lost respect for you. He can't have it all ways."

"Oh, that's just it. He never wanted to marry me, at all. Over twelve months I've been walking out with him, and he said he never had any intention of marrying a skivvy, like me."

Ned was furious. "He'd better keep out of my way, then because as soon as I'm stronger, he's got it coming."

"No, don't bother. I'm more interested in what you said about your feelings." She looked into his blue eyes. "Do you have feelings for me, Ned?"

"Oh, Betsey, I worship the ground you walk on; surely, you know that?"

"I think I've been blind, Ned. No, I never realised you thought of me, as anything other than a sister, and I've certainly only ever thought of you, as a brother."

His eyes dropped. "Well, there you are, then. It can't be helped. You can't make yourself love someone; the heart rules the head, in these matters."

She took his sound hand in hers, put her other fingers under his chin, and raised it until he was looking at her once more.

"No, you're not listening, Ned. As I said, I've been blind, but that kiss has opened my eyes. I realise now, that the man I love, has been under my nose all the time. I think I'd better just make sure, though."

Leaning over, she took his face in her hands and kissed him firmly on the mouth.

Suddenly, Kezia burst through the door and was amazed to see Betsey, kissing her son fully on the lips, and then relieved, as she realised he was no longer at death's door.

"What's going on here, then? It's lucky I came in when I did."

Ned and Betsey laughed.

"Oh, Aunt Kezzie; Ned is so much better. The fever has broken, and his wounds are less angry than they were."

"Well, thank goodness, but just what did you put in that medicine, Betsey? Was it a love potion, because you both looked very much like two people in love when I opened the door?"

"No, it was just something to relieve Ned's fever, but I've come to realise, that the man I love, has been right here all the time. I've been so stupid, wasting time on that silly doctor."

"And another thing, I can't remember the last time I slept as soundly as I did last night, and I didn't intend to. I was coming to take over from you because I was so worried about Ned. Did you slip something into my hot milk?"

"Oh dear, I think I've been rumbled. Yes, I did add a little something to help you to sleep, because I was worried about you. I would have fetched you, though, if Ned had taken a turn for the worse."

"Well, thank you, Betsey. I feel almost human this morning, and it's a real tonic to see you sitting up, and looking so much better, Ned." His mother hugged him, tightly.

"Right, if you two women have finished fussing, I feel like I could eat a horse. Any chance of some breakfast?"

CHAPTER 40

It was a couple of months, since Ned had turned the corner, and started down the road to recovery. The burns on his abdomen, which had been such a cause of concern, were now healing, as were his other injuries. He would carry the scars of his terrible accident, for the rest of his life, but no one was concerned about that. Everyone who knew him was just glad he was going to survive. He was still not fit enough to do any heavy work, but little by little, he was regaining his strength and had started doing a few light jobs in the kitchen to help out.

His father, on the other hand, was almost back to normal. Once the feeling had started to come back in his legs, there had been no stopping Mal, despite the doctor telling him, not to rush things. Every day, he pushed himself just that little bit farther, repeatedly practising getting up and down, out of a chair, and then taking one or two steps around the kitchen, holding on to the table, or whatever piece of furniture was nearest to hand. Gradually, to his delight, and immense relief, his wasted muscles began to respond, and grow stronger.

Unfortunately, the run of bad luck experienced by the Carter family, over the last few months had taken its toll, and the inn was not making enough money to meet the loan repayments. Although Mal, and to a lesser extent, Ned, were now able to help with some of the work, quite a few of their regular stagecoaches, now called at The Three Pigeons; for there, the passengers could choose from a wider range of food, and the horses were better cared for.

The shippen which housed Betsey's Kitchen had not been repaired, and was unlikely to be, any time soon. The new oven and sink were covered up, to save them from the elements. Thankfully, the bank had not yet been chasing them for money, as the manager had agreed to a reprieve from the repayments, for three months. However, that agreement would end in the new year, and Mal and Kezia were resigned to the fact, that they would probably have to sell the inn, or face the debtors' prison.

If it hadn't been for their worries about the future, Betsey and Ned would have been completely happy. Betsey had continued to nurse Ned, changing his dressings, helping him wash, and encouraging him to get up and about, as his strength returned. Ned had loved Betsey all his life, and couldn't quite believe, that she now returned his feelings.

Christmas Day had been a quiet affair, made special for Betsey, when her brother, Barney, came to stay at the inn for a few days. She had not seen her brother for several years, as he now lived in Wales, with his wife, Bronwen, and their two children, a boy and a girl. He had left the mill in Hartford, some years earlier, deciding to travel and seek his fortune. However, after taking the boat from Ilfracombe across to South Wales, he had fallen in love with Bronwen, the daughter of a Welsh farmer, and his intention to see the world, was abandoned. He now lived happily on the family farm, working alongside his father-in-law. Ned knew a man who worked on the ferry and he sent word to Barney, inviting him, and his family, to come and stay over Christmas. He had consulted Mal and Kezia, before issuing the invitation, as it would be more mouths to feed. However, they agreed it would be a wonderful surprise for Betsey, to see her only living relative, and something she more than deserved, for all the years of hard work, she had put in at the inn. They were rewarded for their trouble, by the sheer delight on her face, when Barney appeared at the door and gathered his little sister into his arms.

Betsey enjoyed Christmas that year, knowing she was surrounded by people who loved her. None of them could afford to spend much on presents, but Barney gave Betsey a warm blue shawl, which she was thrilled with. She was sad that she had bought nothing for her brother and his family, especially the children, but, as Barney reminded her, she had not known they were coming. To make up for it, she baked a batch of gingerbread men, decorating their faces with currants, and blobs of icing, and the two youngsters loved them. The time sped by, and Barney and his family went home on the first of January. As he left, he hugged his sister, and thrust half a crown into her hand, promising not to leave it so long before he saw her again. He also told her, there would always be a home for her in Wales, should she ever need it.

That evening, the inn was deserted, folk having spent what little money they had on New Year's Eve, and Mal decided to close early. Betsey shot the bolts across the heavy old oak door and smiled at Ned.

"There, we can have a bit of peace now. I love seeing the customers and hearing all their news, but it will be nice to have a bit of time to ourselves, this evening."

Ned nodded. "Yes, shall we sit in the front room, by the fire? I thought we could roast a few chestnuts."

She linked her arm through his. "Yes, that would be lovely, and perhaps we could have a game of cards? I can't remember the last time I played; it's always too busy these days, or I'm too tired. Do you know, that was one thing about my dad, he occasionally played cards with us. Not often, I'll grant you, but it was one nice thing he did, now and then."

Ned scowled. "Well, there weren't many nice things he did, were there? I wonder if he's dead?"

Betsey sighed. "I've no idea. I expect he is, the way he drank. Either that or in jail for stealing to pay for his ale. It's quiet here without everyone else, isn't it? I like it, though; we never have any time to ourselves."

"I know, I can't believe our luck. I'm so pleased the vicar invited everyone to his house for supper, and it was a brainwave of yours to offer to babysit, Amy. I'm surprised Mum was all right with us being here on our own, though, completely unchaperoned."

"Well, it's not like we're gentry is it, and they know they can trust us." She laughed. "After all, I even used to sleep in the same bedroom as you, and to be honest, there isn't much of you, I haven't seen already, what with changing your dressings, and washing you all over."

"Hey, are you trying to embarrass me? A nursemaid should not speak of such things."

"Sorry, I didn't want to do that."

"Come and sit beside me, because I have something to ask you."

"Do you? What's that, then?"

With some difficulty, Ned dropped to one knee, taking his weight on his sound leg. He reached into his coat pocket and withdrew a ring. Gazing into her deep brown eyes, he took her hand. "Betsey Lovering; will you marry me?"

"Oh, Ned, you know I will; I love you. I can't believe I was so stupid, not to realise it long ago. But where did you get such a fine ring? I know we have no money."

"I told Dad I wanted to propose to you, and he was delighted, and said he could help with the ring. When he and Mum got engaged, she wanted her mother's ring, as she had passed away some years before. This one's been handed down through the Carter family, and it once belonged to my Great Grandmother, Katel Trethewey. She was from a well-to-do family in Cornwall, and it's something of a family heirloom. As the eldest son, Dad wanted me to have it when the time came. I believe it's quite valuable, and it's got a secret, look."

Slowly, Ned fiddled with the golden ring, until it fell into two halves.

"Oh, Ned; have you broken it?" Betsey was distraught, but he shook his head.

"No, it's called a gimmel ring, and it can be taken apart to make two rings. The idea is, that when we become betrothed, you wear one ring, and I wear the other. Then, when we marry, I give my ring back to you, and it becomes one again."

"Oh, how clever, and what a lovely idea." Betsey's eyes were shining, as he slipped the delicate gold ring onto her finger. It was engraved with a pretty pattern, and she gazed at it in delight. "Will the other one fit you? It's quite small."

"I can just about get it on my little finger, so I'll wear it there. There is one thing, though, Betsey. I've wondered for a long time, whether I should ask you to marry me when I know the family is facing ruin. I don't know what will happen in a week or two when the bank wants us to start repaying the loan again. Dad might have to sell up, to prevent him from going to jail. You might be better advised, not to accept my proposal, but to find a wealthier man. I decided I had to ask you, though."

"Don't be so silly, Ned Carter, I don't want to marry a wealthy man. You can't buy love, and whatever happens, we'll face it, together. I've just had an idea, though. Much as I love these rings, I think they're gold, so why don't we sell them, to save the inn?"

Ned was shocked. "No, we can't do that! They've been in the family since the 1600s, maybe even longer. Grandma Katel would turn in her grave, and haunt us!"

Betsey giggled. "Don't be silly; she'd probably approve. Just think about it. I don't need a fancy ring to be betrothed to you. I can easily wear one made out of iron, or even straw, and it may solve the money problem."

"I'm not sure the rings would fetch enough money to do that, and Dad would be horrified if I suggested selling them, but I wish we could find the money to repair Betsey's

Kitchen, and get it up and running. It was making a profit before, and once Dad and I can do a full day's work, I'm sure it would again. We'd soon win the trade back from The Three Pigeons; their food has never been as popular as ours. I wonder if we visited the bank manager again, whether he'd lend us a little more money to get back on our feet?" Ned sighed. "Anyway, more importantly, come here, and kiss me. I think I'm entitled to kiss my future bride."

Ned gently pushed Betsey's long curly brown hair, away from her face, and nuzzled her neck. "Oh, Betsey, I love you so much; I'd give you the world if I could."

"Too much talking, Ned Carter; you're wasting time." Betsey passionately returned his kiss.

When the family returned from their supper at the vicarage, they were delighted to hear the young couple's news. Mal had kept Ned's secret, even from his wife, and Kezia eyed him sternly when she saw the ring and realised he must have been in on Ned's proposal.

"It's lovely, Betsey. You have such tiny, slender hands; it's just right for you."

"Thank you, Aunt Kezzie. It's beautiful, but I've been trying to persuade Ned, that we should sell it. I'm sure it's made of real gold, and it would help to keep the inn afloat until we can pay our way, again."

"No, Betsey, certainly not. That ring belonged to my grandmother, and it has to stay in the family. I'm hoping to visit the bank manager in a day or two, and explain that if he can just give us another couple of months, we should be able to pay our way, again."

Kezia grimaced. "I hope that goes well, Mal. Mr Barlow was kind when I saw him, but I think I was lucky to get the three-month reprieve, that I did. I'm just wondering if there's anywhere else, we could borrow some money from for a few months. Anyway, more importantly, when are you two getting wed? There's no point in delaying it, is there? I mean, you'll have to continue living here with us, at least for the time being, because you can't afford to pay rent, and Silas and Josie are in our cottage next door."

At this point, Josie stared at Silas, and he shuffled uncomfortably.

"There's something we need to tell you all. We've been putting it off for months, as things have been so difficult here, but Josie would like us to move to her family's smallholding."

Josie joined in. "We don't have to go straight away, it's just that my parents are getting on a bit now, and Dad's struggling to cope with all the work. He'd like Silas and me to go there to live and help out. As you know, I'm an only child, and they had me late in life, so there's no one else, and the farm's been in the family for generations. It's only a few acres, but Dad wants it to come to us when the time comes."

Kezia and Mal were shocked, and Kezia recovered first. "Of course, you must go; it's only fair, and thank you for staying this long. If we have to sell up here, then it will be a relief to know that you two have a roof over your heads and a livelihood."

Mal joined in. "Yes, that's splendid, Silas. I know you always got on with George when you visited. Maybe you could stay just a few more weeks, to let Ned and I get a bit stronger?"

"Yes, of course, Dad. That's what we intended. At least if we move out, it'll leave the cottage free, for Ned and Betsey," he turned to his brother with a wide smile on his face, "so when are you going to make an honest woman of her, then, Ned?"

"Well, we haven't even thought about it yet, and we certainly can't afford much of a do, but how about Saturday, the twenty-fourth of January? I believe that's a special day, anyway?"

Betsey nodded. "Yes, that will be my twenty-first birthday. That would be perfect, but would there be time to call the banns, before then?"

Kezia counted the days on her fingers. "Just about, I think. It only needs three weeks, but you'll need to see the vicar as soon as possible."

CHAPTER 41

It had not been a white Christmas, but on the second of January, the snow began to fall heavily. It was bitterly cold, and folk went about their business, wearing as many clothes as they could lay their hands on. There was a strong easterly wind, which caused the snow to drift, and for several days, no stagecoaches called at The Red Lion Inn. There were few customers at all, other than one or two hardy locals, who braved the icy temperatures, in search of a pint of ale.

Rather than allow Ned to go outside in the freezing temperatures, Betsey visited the vicar on her own and asked if he would call the banns. The Reverend Thomas Patterson was a kindly man, who had known Betsey all her life, and he was delighted when he heard she was to marry Ned.

"Oh Betsey, I'm so pleased for you and Ned. What a shame, your dear mother, will not be here to witness the happy event. Ellen was a fine woman, and it was wrong, she died in the way, that she did. I presume your father will not be here to give you away?"

"Of course, I'd forgotten you knew my mother. Yes, it would be perfect, if she and Norman could be here for my wedding, and no, I've no idea, where my father is, or indeed if he's still alive."

"No, well, it's not often I say this about another man, but in this case, I think you're better off without him, my dear. I think he had his difficulties, but he treated your mother disgracefully, and in my mind, there's no excuse for such behaviour. Anyway, yes, of course, I can marry you and Ned and will do so gladly. We'll have to get the banns published, as soon as possible, to allow you to marry on the twenty-fourth of the month. Is there any particular reason, why it must be that Saturday?"

"Well, it doesn't matter, if it's not possible, but that's my twenty-first birthday, and we thought we could celebrate both occasions at once. We certainly can't afford to have two parties, so it makes sense to combine the two."

"What a splendid idea, and yes, I'm sure we can manage that if I call the banns for the first time, tomorrow. Will you, and Ned, be able to come to church, in the morning?"

"Yes, I expect so, providing the weather's no worse. I'll be there, but Ned's still weak from his accident, and I don't like him going out in this bitter cold. The last thing he needs is to catch a chill."

"Of course; in that case, you tell him to stay at home in the warm. If the weather improves, perhaps he can come on one of the following Sundays. Let's hope the weather is fine for your wedding day. Speaking of which, in the absence of your father, who will give you away, my dear?"

"I would have liked it to be my brother, Barney, but unfortunately he's returned to Wales now. I hadn't seen him, or his family, for years, but they came and stayed with us at Christmas, which was wonderful, and he only went home a couple of days ago. Of course, at the time, I had no idea I was to marry, as he left before Ned proposed to me. Anyway, no matter, Uncle Mal will give me away, and Silas will be Ned's best man."

"Perfect, now I appreciate you will not want Ned venturing out in this cold weather, but a little nearer to the time, I'll call on you both at the inn, to finalise all the arrangements."

A few days later, Kezia and Betsey were enjoying a well-earned cup of tea with Tilly and Josie. It was mid-morning, and the four women were seated around the kitchen table. Inevitably, the main topic of conversation was Betsey's forthcoming marriage.

"Do you want any bridesmaids, Betsey?"

"Well, I'd love to have Amy as a bridesmaid, if she was a bit older, but she's far too young, so no, I don't think so. No one has a lot of money in these hard times, and I certainly can't afford to buy bridesmaids' dresses, or even a new dress, for myself."

"No, it is difficult; what are you going to wear, then?"

"It will have to be my Sunday dress; I don't have anything else."

"Well, that dress is lovely, and if we can find a few snowdrops for you to carry, you'll look beautiful. I wish we could afford to buy you a new dress, Betsey, or even the material to make you one, but unfortunately, we can't."

"It doesn't matter, Aunty Kezzie, I know Ned has a little money saved, and he's going to give that to you, to put on a bit of a spread for the guests, though there won't be many. You can have the half-crown, Barney gave me as well."

"No, you keep that for a rainy day; you might be glad of it, in the weeks to come."

"Well, if you're sure, thank you. I'd like to buy Ned a little something for a wedding present, though I don't know what, and no doubt, he'll tell me I shouldn't have wasted my money."

"Why don't you bake him a cockle bread, Betsey?"

"I don't know what that is?"

Kezia and Josie had all but choked on their tea and were laughing.

"Tilly Yeo, behave yourself. What would your mother, say?"

"Do you not know what cockle bread is, Betsey?"

"No, I don't, but it's amusing all of you, so come on, tell me."

"Well, if a girl wants to give her young man a love token, and has no money, then she bakes him a loaf of cockle bread."

Betsey still looked puzzled.

"The only thing different about cockle bread is that when you have kneaded the dough, you press it against your lady parts between your legs, to mould it, before you bake it!"

Kezia and Josie shrieked with laughter, and Betsey was shocked.

"No! Do people really do that?"

"Yes, I think some do."

"Well, no, I'm not going to bake Ned some cockle bread. I'll just have to think of something else."

The next morning, Betsey was surprised when Mal came into the kitchen from the bar and said she had a visitor. She was up to her elbows in flour, making the pastry for the next batch of pies, so, rubbing her hands together briskly, to remove the dough, she quickly washed her hands, pulled down her sleeves, and followed him into the bar. Sitting on a chair in the corner, was Doctor Abernethy.

"Hello Betsey; I hear congratulations are in order. I'm so pleased for you and Ned; you'll make the perfect couple."

Betsey felt a bit embarrassed, considering she had walked out with his grandson for over a year.

"Thank you, Doctor; it's strange, but I never saw Ned as anything other than a brother, but then I looked after him for weeks and weeks when he was so ill, and then …"

She broke off and looked awkwardly at the older man.

"And then you discovered that your young man was not true to you. It's all right, Betsey, I'm aware of my grandson's shortcomings, and I'm not proud of him. I can assure you I've made my feelings known, and if he wants to continue to live here with me, and his grandmother, then he'll have to improve his behaviour and morals. Anyway, enough about him. I know your family has faced many difficulties over the last few months, and I'm ashamed of the way, Daniel has treated you."

He held up his hand, as Betsey was about to speak. "Just hear me out, please. Now, my wife is a terrible hoarder, and she has a wardrobe full of clothes, from her younger days. She was from a well-to-do family, and I'm afraid I haven't been able to keep her in the style to which she was accustomed, though she never complains. Now, we don't wish to offend you, but she wondered if you would like to come to our house, and see if any of her old dresses, would be to your liking, for your wedding day. She's put on a bit of weight over the years, as we all do, as we get older, and she's kept some of her favourite clothes, in case she could ever wear them again." His blue eyes twinkled. "Between you and me, I think that's unlikely, and to be honest, I think she looks better carrying a few more pounds. What do you say? She won't be offended if you say no."

"Oh, Doctor; that's so kind of her, and yes, of course, I'd love to see her dresses. There's no way we can afford to buy new clothes at the moment, with the inn in so much debt, but I'd love to have a new dress, to surprise Ned with on our wedding day."

"Well, in that case, why don't you come tomorrow morning, and inspect what there is? My wife will enjoy it, and it will make up a little for my grandson's despicable behaviour. Don't worry, I'll make sure he's not around when you come; I plan to send him to visit a patient on one of the outlying farms. We never had a daughter, but if we had, I would have liked her to be just like you, Betsey. You've had such a hard life, and yet I've never heard you complain, even when you were little."

At the doctor's kind words, Betsey impatiently brushed away a tear and agreed to visit Mrs Abernethy in the morning.

Betsey raised the shiny brass door knocker on the front door of the Abernethy residence, and let it fall gently a couple of times. She was excited at the thought of a new dress, but she barely knew the doctor's wife, and now that she was here, she felt nervous. Within a few minutes, a maid opened the door and greeted Betsey.

"Good morning, ma'am; I guess you must be Betsey Lovering?"

Betsey nodded her head. "Yes, that's right; I've come to see Mrs Abernethy."

"Well, if you'd like to follow me, she's waiting to receive you in the drawing room."

Betsey followed the maid through the old house. It was pleasantly furnished and had a homely, comfortable feel, and there was an aroma of lavender. The old lady was sitting on the sofa, and she smiled at the young girl.

"Good morning, Betsey; I haven't seen you for such a long time. What a pretty girl you've grown into. My grandson must need his head examined, to let you get away."

Betsey was a little uncomfortable, but the old woman patted the seat next to her.

"Come and sit down, my dear, and we'll have some tea and cakes before we examine the dresses. My maid has laid out all the ones, that I think may be suitable, in one of the spare bedrooms, and I'm hoping that one of them will be to your liking."

Half an hour or so, later, the doctor's wife led Betsey upstairs and opened the door to a large bedroom. Betsey gasped, for laid on the bed, were eight dresses of different styles and hues.

"Oh, my goodness, they're all so lovely; are you sure you can bear to part with any of them?"

"Yes, of course, and anyway, I can't get into any of them. Some of them I've had for donkey's years, and one or two belong to my niece, but she's married now, with three children, and I'm afraid her waistline, has also expanded somewhat with motherhood. Would you indulge me, and try them all on? I think it would be fun, and some will look better on than off, and in any case, we have to make sure the dress you choose, fits you properly. If it needs any adjustment, I have a woman in the village, who does all my alterations, so that won't be a problem."

The dresses seemed to span several years and were of differing styles, most being frilly, with flowing skirts, and much padding. They came in a variety of colours, with some made of linen, cotton, or muslin, and one or two, of silk. Betsey enjoyed trying them on, and the old lady sat in a chair and watched, as the maid assisted her. Most of the dresses fitted, though one or two, were a little on the large side. In the end, Betsey chose a dress of a simple style. Made of a dusky pale pink silk, with a delicate, understated floral design, it had short sleeves, and a low round neckline, and fell in shimmering glory, from the empire line beneath her breasts. As soon as she put the dress on, Betsey knew this was the one. She smoothed the soft silk beneath her fingers and looked down at the exquisite dress, which reached the ground and was exactly the right length. When she raised her eyes to her two female companions, she could see they agreed.

"Oh, my dear, you look simply beautiful. I wanted you to choose the lavender sprigged muslin, as it looked so wonderful on you, but this one is even better. What do you think, Polly?"

The maid was pleased to be asked for an opinion, and she replied readily. "Oh, yes, ma'am, they all look wonderful on Betsey, but I think that's the best one by far, and it fits so perfectly, it could have been made for her."

"I don't know how to thank you, ma'am. It's such a fine dress; I've never worn anything so lovely, nor ever expected to, but you could have it back after the wedding, for I doubt there will ever be another occasion, for me to wear it."

"No, I don't want it back, Betsey. You keep it and enjoy it, and wear it as often as you can. I'm glad to have been of help, and I think we have all enjoyed our morning."

CHAPTER 42

During the second week of January, Mal decided to visit the bank manager. Business at the inn was still slow, and the inclement weather of the last couple of weeks had not helped. Although his fitness was improving daily, he was not as nimble, or as strong, as before his accident, and he was often frustrated when he simply had to rest. Ned, too, was on the mend, and it would not be long before he could return to work, and pull his weight. However, with Silas and Josie leaving in a matter of weeks, Mal knew that the rest of them would continue to be overstretched, and unlikely to be able to win the trade back from The Three Pigeons.

As he lay in bed one Thursday night, cuddling his wife, he told her he planned to take the horse and cart to the market the next day for the Friday market in Barnstaple.

"Oh, Mal, are you sure you're up to it? Remember what happened, last time."

He chuckled. "Well, yes, I know, but surely not even I can be so unfortunate as to meet another rampaging bull. My goodness, that was one angry animal. I don't know how they ever managed to get him back to the right field again. Do you want to come to town with me?"

"I'd love to come, but if you're out all day, I'd better stay at home and help with the chores; there's always so much to do." She sighed. "I hope the bank manager is sympathetic, but when Silas and Josie go, we'll need to take on extra help or offer less food. They work for their keep like the rest of us, but obviously, an employee would need to be paid. No, you go on your own and enjoy a day out. There's not a great deal of produce to take to the market at this time of year, but there are still potatoes, turnips and swede, and, of course, eggs, butter, and milk. I think there are still a few jars of jam and pickle, too. I'm sure someone will keep an eye on the stall while you visit the bank."

It was cold the next morning when Mal and Silas loaded the produce onto the old cart, but at least the snow had melted, and the lanes, though thick with mud in places, were once more passable. There was a light frost, and Mal could see his breath hanging in the air, as he encouraged the horse to a steady pace. As he traversed the bridge where the bull had careered into him, he grimaced, remembering all the months of pain and anguish he had suffered. That incident had been bad enough, but then with Ned being struck by lightning, he could not believe how unlucky they had been for two freak accidents to occur simultaneously. Surely, the bank manager would see that none of it was their fault?

This time, however, there were no delays on the journey, and he got to the market in record time. As he busied himself setting out his produce, he enjoyed a bit of banter with his fellow stallholders, who were pleased to see him back. They shook his hand, slapped him on the back, and were delighted he had made a full recovery. At ten o'clock, he left his stall in the care of his neighbour and set off reluctantly for the bank. The manager was pleased to see him up and about, and having shown him into his office, begged him to take a seat. He looked at Mal expectantly, hoping to hear good news.

"First of all, I want to thank you, Mr Barlow, for being so understanding when my wife came to see you and explained our predicament. I appreciate your help in allowing us a three-month reprieve from the loan repayments."

"I was pleased to be of assistance, Mr Carter, for you have always honoured your debts, and it was most unfortunate, you had such a nasty accident. I'm pleased to see you have fully recovered, and I hope the inn is prospering now you're back on your feet?"

Mal gazed down at his worn-out shoes, and turned his cap round and round in his hands; then he raised his head and looked the manager in the eye. "No, sir, I'm afraid it's going to take a while to get the business back to what it was. You see, I don't know if you're aware, but my eldest son, Ned, was hit by lightning in the August storms and was severely burnt. For a long time, we thought we were going to lose him, and our cow was killed outright. As you know, we borrowed the additional money from the bank, to set up what came to be known as Betsey's Kitchen, where we sold food to workers in the village. It was doing so well, but the lightning struck the roof of the building and it was badly damaged. With all our financial troubles, we've not been able to repair it yet, and so we've lost all of that trade, and some of our regular stagecoaches have started going to the other inn in the village. With both myself and Ned out of action for months, the business has suffered, despite my wife, and the rest of the family, working so hard."

The bank manager was dismayed. "Oh dear, I'm sorry to hear you've had such a run of ill luck, Mr Carter. I must ask, will you be able to make your loan repayment, this month?"

"No, sir, I'm afraid not. You see, the weather has been so atrocious over the last month or so, that several of the stagecoaches were cancelled as the roads were impassable, and even the local trade, has been far less than usual. I'm confident, that given time, we can build the business up again, for none of us is afraid of hard work, but we now have another problem. My youngest son, Silas, is married with one child, and in a week or two, he's moving to

Somerset. He feels guilty about leaving us, but his wife's father is ailing and he needs help to run his smallholding. So, you see, even though Ned and I are back working, we are going to lose Silas and Josie, and I think the only way to resolve the situation, is to take on another couple of workers. The problem is paying them, until we begin to see a profit, again," Mal, once more raised his head to look the manager in the eye, "so, I'm here to ask; can the bank support us, for a little while longer?"

"Oh, Mr Carter, oh, that I could say yes, and help with your predicament. What has happened to you, and your family, is most unfortunate, but I'm afraid my hands are tied. You see, it's not just up to me; there are other shareholders to consider, and at our last meeting, they made their position clear. They were adamant your loan repayments must recommence by the end of this month. If that's not possible, I'm afraid you'll have to put the inn up for sale to clear your debts. I'm so sorry."

Mal sighed deeply. "It's all right. I'm not surprised. It's what I was expecting, though I was hoping you might be able to give me just a little more time. Ah well, it will be the end of an era. The Carter family has owned that inn for generations, certainly over two hundred years, I believe. Maybe, ever since it was built. What a disgrace, that I'm the one responsible for its loss."

"I wish I could do more to help, Mr Carter; I feel for you, I do, and I did plead your case at the last meeting in case you needed more assistance, but to no avail, I'm afraid. Is the inn well maintained?"

"Aye, the main building is, and at least it has a new roof." Mal smiled ruefully. "That's when all this trouble started, with the loan to pay for the new roof; not that I had any choice, for it leaked like a sieve. Anyway, thank you for your time, sir. I'll put the word out that the inn is up for sale, and hopefully, it will bring us enough money to clear our debts and leave us a little to live on. I won't sell the cottage, that's situated next to the inn, for we'll have to move in there. I bid you, good day."

Mal was in low spirits for the rest of the day, though business was brisk throughout the rest of the morning, and he sold nearly all his produce. When he drove the horse and cart into the yard, Kezia came out to meet him and looked at him, anxiously.

"Well, what did he say?"

"Tis no good, I'm afraid, my dear. The manager was not able to give us any more time, though I think he wanted to. He has to keep the other shareholders happy, and they had already decided enough, was enough. They discussed our loan last week and instructed him to call it in. I've put the word around the town that The Red Lion Inn is up for sale, and I think there are one or two interested already."

"Oh no! Oh, Mal; it's been in your family for so long. Is there nothing, we can do?"

"No, I'm afraid not, my love; nothing I can think of, anyway. We'll move into the little cottage with Ned and Betsey when they're married. It'll be a bit of a squash, but at least there are three bedrooms, although they're small. I'm glad Silas and Josie have somewhere else to go, though I'm going to miss Amy."

"But how will we earn a living, Mal? This is all we know."

"Aye, but I'm hoping we'll make enough money on the sale of the inn, to live on for a while, and you never know, the new owners might want to keep us on as servants. After all, we know the trade better than anyone, and if they mend the roof on the old shippen, and get Betsey's Kitchen up and running again, they'll need help. The canal is coming along nicely since they repaired the flood damage, but the project will still take a year or two to complete. There are a lot of workers around who would like to buy their dinner again. It's such a shame because if we could borrow enough money to get it all going again, I'm sure it would be a success. Still, there it is."

Tea in the Carter kitchen was a gloomy affair that day. Mal did not want to burden his family with the worrying news, but could not avoid their questions. Silas felt guilty to be leaving them in such dire circumstances, but his father insisted it was all for the best, and that he must go sooner, rather than later.

When Betsey retired to her small room, later that evening, she reached for the little tin, which had belonged to her mother. It was the only link to her childhood, and still contained her few treasures; the lock of Norman's hair, her mother's brooch, the red ribbon, bought for her by Aunt Kezzie at a time of such despair, and, of course, Thomas Fellwood's gold watch. No one else knew of its existence, for she had never told another soul, not wanting to divulge how she came by it, and betray the confidence of Thomas and Gypsy Jane. She took it out and turned it over, and over, in her hands. It was such a beautiful object, and she wished she had been able to give it back to its rightful owner, for he had been exceptionally kind to her. The porcelain face of the watch bore roman numerals, and when she gently opened it, to gaze in wonder at the intricate workings, there were some small jewels, and the name T Tompion, London, whom she assumed was the maker. She knew she probably held a small fortune in her hands, maybe more than enough to save the inn, but how could she sell it? Without divulging the story, of how she came by the timepiece, the chances were, she would be accused of stealing it, and even if she told the truth, would anyone believe her?

Sighing deeply, she returned the watch to its hiding place and crept into bed. However, although bone-tired, she spent a restless night, tossing and turning, wondering if, and how, she could sell the watch. By morning, she had decided it was impossible, and that in any case, she could never part with it, just in case Thomas and Jane ever returned.

CHAPTER 43

Word soon spread around Hartford, that the old inn was up for sale. Folk were saddened to hear of the Carter family's financial difficulties, and sorry to see them in such dire straits. A landowner from Barnstaple had already shown an interest, and another from Ilfracombe, though neither had yet put in an offer. An auction was to take place at the inn, on the thirtieth of January, when the contents, and then the building itself, would be sold.

Silas and Josie had been busy packing up their few belongings, storing most of them in the barn, ready for transporting them to Somerset, after the wedding. They had vacated the little cottage, which was now occupied by Ned, and they were using his bedroom at the inn.

A few days before her wedding, Betsey accompanied Josie to the cottage, to give it a thorough spring clean, before filling it with a selection of furniture from the inn. It was the first time Betsey had set foot in the cottage since she had been carried out, barely alive, with her little brother, Norman, all those years ago. She could scarcely believe she would inhabit that unhappy place once more and fervently hoped, that this time, she might find happiness there. She went through the back door, which no longer creaked loudly, as it had in the past, for Silas had repaired it, and oiled the old hinges. The kitchen still looked much the same, but smaller, and she supposed it was because she had grown up. Although the two women had come to clean the cottage, it was already so much cleaner than when Betsey had last lived there. Before they moved in, Silas had given the walls two coats of limewash, and Josie had spent hours on her hands and knees, scrubbing the rough flagstones. Tears ran down Betsey's cheeks, as she remembered how her mother had done the same and kept the cottage sparkling clean, until her untimely death.

"Oh, Betsey, are you all right?"

"Aye, Josie, I'm just being silly. I haven't been in this cottage since I was a child, and it's bringing back a lot of memories; most of them, unhappy ones."

"I know you've never wanted to come here, and I can understand that. Will you be able to face living here?"

"Yes, of course; I've no choice, anyway. Besides, it's just four walls and a roof, isn't it? It's not the building's fault, what happened here. At least, this time, I'll be living with decent folk, who love me. It's just that everywhere I turn, I remember my mum, and Barney, and Norman. I'm trying not to think about Dad."

The two women worked hard all morning until the cottage was spick and span, and even the windows were gleaming in the weak January sunshine. Betsey insisted that her Aunt Kezzie and Uncle Mal should have the largest bedroom, which had been inhabited by her parents. She felt it was only right, and in any case, she could not entertain the thought of sleeping where she had last seen her mother lying, so badly beaten.

Over the next few days, the menfolk worked equally hard, tidying up the old inn, and the outbuildings. They took their pick of the best furniture, and put it into the cottage, ready for when they would all move in. Kezia wanted to allow Betsey and Ned, to have their first few days of married life, alone in the cottage before she and Mal joined them.

There was a light frost on the morning of Betsey and Ned's wedding, which was, of course, also her twenty-first birthday. The water butts were frozen over, and the grass was spiky and white with rime. However, by mid-morning, a weak sun was trying to peek through the clouds. Betsey was longing to wear the beautiful dress, so kindly given to her by Mrs Abernethy. She had not even shown it to her Aunt Kezzie and Josie, for she wanted to surprise them all. On the previous morning, Betsey had gone to the woods, and picked a large bunch of snowdrops, surrounding the delicate white blooms with curly moss, to make an attractive posy, which she would carry into the church.

Aunt Kezzie shooed the menfolk out of the kitchen and filled the old tin bath with hot water from the kettles on the stove. She instructed Betsey to get in first, and she soaped and rinsed her hair. Josie followed, and lastly, Kezia, herself. Ned, Silas, and Mal had bathed the day before. The three women then helped each other with their hair but left it until the last minute to don their best dresses. Whilst they were waiting for their hair to dry, they heard someone knocking on the door, and Kezia opened it. Outside was a young man holding a letter.

"Yes, can I help you?"

"I hope so, ma'am. Does Betsey Lovering, live here?"

"Aye, she does, but who's asking?"

"I'm just a messenger boy, ma'am, but I have a letter for her, from Mr Elias Snell, a solicitor in Barnstaple, and I'm to wait for a reply."

Kezia was astounded. "Well, you'd better come in, then." She led the young man into the front room and asked him to wait, whilst she fetched Betsey. Puzzled, Betsey slipped on an old dress and greeted the messenger.

"Thank you for seeing me, ma'am. If you would like to read this letter, I'm instructed to wait for your reply."

Betsey broke open the letter, which was sealed with red wax. She could not imagine, why anyone would write to her, let alone a solicitor. She spread the letter out on the table and scanned its contents. It didn't say much, only that her presence was requested at the solicitor's office, at two o'clock on the following Monday. The letter asked her to confirm her attendance.

"Do you have a reply, ma'am? I was told not to leave without one."

"Yes, yes, of course, I will attend the appointment, but do you know what this is about? I have no idea, why a solicitor would want to speak to me. Am I in some sort of trouble?"

"I'm afraid I don't know anything about it, ma'am. I was just asked to find out if you would attend, or not."

"Well, yes. Tell Mr Snell, that I'll see him on Monday, with my husband," Betsey smiled at the boy, "it's my wedding day, you see."

"I wish you many years of happiness, then, ma'am, and I'll be on my way." The lad tweaked his cap and left the building.

Betsey was puzzled. "What do you think it's all about? Do you think, I'm in trouble?"

"No, it can't be that, because you haven't done anything wrong. Perhaps it's something to do with your father?"

Betsey grimaced. "I suppose it could be, but he could never afford to pay a solicitor for anything."

"Well, don't worry about it now; you have more important things to do; it's time we put on our dresses."

Whilst she was putting on her lovely pink dress, a horrible thought occurred to Betsey. Perhaps it was something to do with her part in helping Thomas Fellwood and Gypsy Jane when Jasper Morris, had died. Maybe, someone had seen her and reported her to the constable, after all. For a few moments, she felt breathless with fear, but then admonished herself, for being so silly. It was all so long ago, and she was sure she hadn't been seen leading the horse away, with the body draped over it.

With some effort, she pushed all thoughts of Monday, to one side, and tried to concentrate on her wedding. She called to her aunt to help her with the fastenings on the dress, and Kezia was open-mouthed when she saw how lovely Betsey looked. Josie had bought a length of dark pink ribbon for Betsey's brown curls, and it contrasted perfectly with the pale, dusky-pink dress.

"Oh, Betsey, the dress is magnificent, and you look amazing. How kind of Mrs Abernethy, to give you such a lovely dress. Now, give me a moment to go downstairs, and then you come down and show Mal, Silas, and Josie."

With a wide grin on her face, Betsey walked slowly down the ancient staircase, each step creaking slightly under her weight. As she appeared at the bottom, Mal was waiting for her, and when he saw her, he gasped.

"Oh, my goodness, Betsey; you're so beautiful. Isn't she, Silas? You wait until Ned sees you; he won't believe his luck."

Kezia, Silas, and Josie hurried across the road to the church; Josie carrying young Amy in her arms. Kezia, Josie, and the child slipped into the first pew, and Silas took his place as best man, beside his brother. Ned was looking anxious, and Silas grinned.

"There's nothing to worry about, mate; she'll be here in a minute, and you won't be disappointed."

As Mal and Betsey appeared, Mr Billery struck up a tune on the old organ, and the congregation twisted in their seats to gaze at the bride, as she walked proudly up the aisle. Ned could not believe how lovely she looked, and he whispered, "Betsey, you look so elegant; like a real lady."

In no time at all, the ceremony was over, and, as they walked down the church path, they were showered with rice. It was only a short distance to The Red Lion Inn, where Kezia and Josie had laid on the best food they could. All the stagecoaches had been diverted to The Three Pigeons. Mal had decided, that as the inn would be sold in a matter of days, it didn't matter, and he wanted to give Betsey and Ned, a day to remember.

Betsey had invited Doctor and Mrs Abernethy, but not Daniel, and indeed, she had not set eyes on him for weeks. She guessed that his grandfather had instructed him to keep out of her way. Mrs Abernethy clasped Betsey's hand, warmly. "I'm so glad you chose that dress, my dear; you look simply stunning, and I hope you'll have as happy a marriage, as Hamish and myself."

The reception was a jolly affair, with Silas playing tunes on his fiddle, and Tilly leading the singing. She had a fine, clear voice, and enjoyed the opportunity to use it. The festivities continued long into the night, for the occasion had also become an opportunity for a farewell party, for The Red Lion. Folk were sad the Carter family would be leaving the establishment after so many years, and Mal was trying not to think about it. He was distraught, to think the inn had been in his family for so many years, and it was on his watch, it was lost.

Long before the party ended, Ned cradled Betsey's hand in his and whispered in her ear. She nodded, and discreetly, they made their escape to the little cottage. As they approached the door, Ned pulled her to him and put his arms around her, his breath, warm upon her cheek. She smiled at him, seductively, and he crushed her mouth to his. He spoke gruffly, "I think it's time we went inside, Mrs Carter, I'd better carry you over the threshold, as is the custom," he grinned at her in the light of the full moon, "you're as light as a feather, Betsey, and I love you, so much. I can't believe you're my wife."

"Well, you'd better believe it, Ned Carter, because you're stuck with me now; I'm going, nowhere."

Kicking the door shut behind him, he lowered her to the ground, and she curled her arms around his neck and pulled him towards her for another kiss. In seconds, his fingers were busily unbuttoning her gown. Letting it fall to the ground, he ran his fingers through her silky brown hair.

He nuzzled her neck, and his hands roamed over her bare shoulders, as he wondered at the softness of her fragrant skin.

"You looked amazing in that dress today, but so much better without it." He glanced down at her underwear. "May I?"

"Of course, Ned, I'm yours, now."

Her shift fell to the ground, and he pulled her naked body close to him. She could feel the heat and hardness of him through his clothes, and her hands began to tear off his shirt, but he clasped them to him and hesitated.

"Ned, what's wrong?"

He sighed. Nothing, nothing's wrong. I'm so happy, I could burst, but I think I'll leave my clothes on if you don't mind; my body is so ugly."

"No, it isn't, it's beautiful, and I love every inch of it. Don't forget, I've already seen all your scars, and they don't matter to me, one bit."

"Yes, but you've never seen them all at once, or as my wife."

Slowly, she peeled off his shirt, and then his trousers. When he stood before her, naked, she began kissing every one of his ugly scars. He gasped, and closed his eyes, then opened them again, and grinned at her, delighted she wanted him, as much as he wanted her. "Enough! There are so many scars, I can't wait long enough, for you to kiss them all. I have more urgent matters on my mind."

She laughed, as she allowed him to take control of the proceedings.

CHAPTER 44

Betsey told Ned about the letter from the solicitor, and he, too, was puzzled. She wondered whether to tell him of her part in covering up the truth about Jasper Morris's death, but decided not to burden him with it. After all, the solicitor might want to see her about something else, though for the life of her, she could not think what. On Monday morning, they went to The Red Lion to eat breakfast with the rest of the family, as Silas, Josie, and Amy, were to depart for Somerset that day. Kezia was sad to be saying goodbye to her son and his family, but also relieved they would have a roof over their heads. Mal promised her, that one day, he would take her to see Silas in his new home. Privately, he had no idea when that might be, for he would have to find work somewhere and try to earn a living. When the inn was sold, he prayed the new landlord might keep him on, though he knew it would be difficult to work for an employer, where he had once been the owner. Kezia, Betsey, and Ned, too, of course, would soon all be out of work.

Mal had agreed that Silas could take the horse and cart, for there was no other way, they could transport all of their belongings. The journey would take them some time, and Kezia insisted on wrapping blankets around their legs, for though it was a dry day, she knew it would be bitterly cold, travelling on the open cart in January. To the amusement of her family, she also filled a bed warmer with coals from the fire, wrapped it in another blanket, and placed it near their feet, ignoring sarcastic remarks from her husband and sons.

"You may laugh, but I'd put money on it, that before sitting on that cart for too long, you'll be thanking me."

She handed Josie a basket containing pasties, bread rolls, and cheese, to sustain them until they reached their destination. Young Amy happily waved goodbye to her grandparents, little knowing it would be such a long time until she saw them again. As the horse lumbered slowly out of the yard, Mal put his arm around Kezia and led her back indoors, to face yet more packing and cleaning.

Ned went to the stables to harness their other horse for the journey to Barnstaple. He and Betsey had decided to travel on horseback, for it was quicker than taking the pony and trap. With Silas taking one horse, the inn now only owned one other, but Henry Rudd had agreed to lend them his horse for the day. Betsey had dressed warmly, and she clambered up behind Ned, for the short journey to the smithy, where they would collect her steed.

Despite worrying about the visit to the solicitor, Betsey was excited to be out with Ned for the day, and before long, they were cantering along the lanes, and occasionally across open countryside, to cut off a mile or two. They arrived in Barnstaple at a quarter past twelve, and not wanting to spend any money, dawdled along by the river until it was time for Betsey's appointment at the solicitors. They passed the statue of Queen Anne and strolled along the quayside, which was as busy as ever, with the sailors scurrying up and down the gangplanks, loading and unloading, the cargoes. They walked on a little farther, past two inns, and an old lime kiln. They were hoping to find somewhere quiet to eat the lunch Kezia had packed for them. They came to some deserted scrubland, and sat on a fallen tree trunk, for the ground was damp. Betsey unwrapped their food, from the piece of cloth Kezia had wrapped it in.

"Here you are, Ned, your mother's packed us enough for two days, I think." She handed him a cold pasty and nibbled at one, herself. "She's put in some bread and cheese too, but I don't think I'll want that, as well."

"Perhaps we'll eat that later after we've seen the solicitor."

"Yes, maybe; I'll be happier when I know what he wants."

It was too chilly to sit for long, as there was a cold wind, and they were both shivering. They retraced their steps and sought the pump in the centre of the town. Ned slowly pumped the handle, and Betsey held her mouth under the stream of icy cold water, and then he did the same. They wiped their mouths, and Betsey ran her fingers through her hair and tightened the ribbon that was holding it back. It was the dusky pink ribbon from her wedding day, and she hoped it would bring her luck. She smoothed her skirt, and Ned dusted off his trousers. Hoping they were presentable; they approached the solicitor's offices at the bottom of the High Street. It was ten minutes to two o'clock as Ned opened the door to let her go inside. She glanced at him anxiously, and he squeezed her arm reassuringly.

It was a grand building, and they were shown into a large room, panelled in oak. There were a few armchairs and a potted plant on a table. They approached a man sitting at a desk and explained they had an appointment with Mr Snell. He asked them to take a seat for a moment. A few minutes later, he returned and showed them in to see the solicitor.

Mr Elias Snell was a man in his early fifties. Dark-haired, and good-looking with deep brown eyes, he welcomed them both and shook their hands. Begging them to be seated, he introduced his son, Mr Edward Snell, and asked if they would like some refreshments. Puzzled, at being treated so graciously, by such a learned and important man, Betsey and Ned, were hesitant.

"Perhaps a cup of tea, ma'am? I believe you've had quite a ride from Hartford, on such a cold day?"

Betsey nodded. "Yes, that would be most welcome, sir, thank you."

The younger man rose and left the room. When he returned, the two men made light conversation about the weather, and the town, until a young girl entered, carrying a tray of tea and cake. Edward Snell rose, poured them each a cup of tea, and offered a slice of cake to Ned and Betsey. However, although they each took a piece to be polite, they only nibbled at it, as their mouths were too dry to swallow. The two solicitors, however, enjoyed their cake, and Elias wiped the crumbs from his mouth, before speaking.

"Now, I'm sure you're both curious, as to why you have been invited here to see me today, but before I enlighten you, please accept my congratulations on your recent marriage. I have some wonderful news for you, Mrs Carter, some very wonderful news."

Betsey felt relieved that she was not in any trouble. "Well, we could certainly do with some, sir."

"I believe that a few days ago, you reached the age of twenty-one?"

"Yes, that's right, sir." Betsey felt even more puzzled, for how could this man possibly know of her birthday?

"Well, I'm pleased to tell you, that on that day, you became a wealthy young woman," he smiled, enjoying their rapt attention, "I am the solicitor for the Fellwood family, which owns the Hartford estate, and I believe you were a friend of Mr Thomas Fellwood, Lord Fellwood's second son?"

Betsey gasped, and Ned was perplexed.

"Well, I was only a little girl of about six or seven, but yes I met him a few times, in and around the village. He had a younger sister called Margery, and she was about the same age as me. I remember seeing him once when he was out riding with Lady Margery. They stopped and helped me because I had fallen over and skinned my hands and knees.

He was such a kind man, and he bathed them, and gave me a ride on his horse."

Betsey decided to make no mention of the gypsy camp.

"I see, well you must have made quite an impression on him, for he has left you an inheritance, to be given to you on attaining the age of twenty-one."

Betsey's jaw dropped open. "Me? He's left me some money? Is he dead?"

"Ah, that we don't know. I was hoping you might be able to tell us?"

"No, sir, I've not seen him, since I was a little girl. I remember him going missing, of course, and hearing his family were looking for him, but no, I'm afraid I have no news."

The solicitor was disappointed. "Oh, that is a pity. Lord Fellwood still misses his son and was hoping for news. Never mind, but I am curious, why do you think Mr Fellwood would leave money to such a little girl?" He stared at the young woman, and Betsey blushed under his scrutiny.

"I have no idea, sir, and that's the truth. As I said, he was always kind to me, and I enjoyed playing with his little sister. I think he felt sorry for me, as I was not properly cared for as a child. My father drank his wages away, and when my mother died in childbirth, my younger brother, Norman, and I were more or less left to fend for ourselves. I was only six, and Norman, was three, and I tried to care for him, but my father did little to provide for us." Her face crumpled, as she continued. "My little brother died, but luckily for me, Ned's family took me in. They would have taken Norman too, but it was too late for him."

"Oh dear, that is sad; I'm so sorry to have upset you, ma'am."

Ned put his arm around his wife, and Betsey impatiently brushed away her tears. "I remember Mr Fellwood's mother, died on almost the same day as my mother, and he was sympathetic."

"Indeed. He must have been fond of you, for he's left you a considerable sum of money. In fact, he's left you one hundred guineas."

Betsey and Ned were astounded, and he found his voice first. "How much?"

"One hundred guineas and I must inform you, sir, that this money is intended for your wife. Mr Fellwood's instructions are precise, in that, if Miss Lovering was married, then the money was solely for her, and could not pass to a spouse."

Ned was indignant. "Of course not, I wouldn't want to part Betsey from her money."

"No, sir. I'm sure you wouldn't, but as you know, some men would. This young lady's father for one, by the sound of it. So, it just remains for me to congratulate you, ma'am. Are you quite sure you have no idea, why Mr Fellwood left you this small fortune, or any information as to where he went?"

Betsey shook her head. "No, I'm shocked, I really am, but this money has come just in time. The Carter family is in dire straits, and about to sell The Red Lion Inn, to clear their debts. An inn, that has been in their family for generations. I'm hoping this money will do that. Ned, will it be enough, to save the inn?"

"I don't know, Betsey; I should think so, but Mr Snell's right. It's your money, and you don't need to use it to pay off Dad's debts."

"Don't be ridiculous, Ned. If it wasn't for your parents, I wouldn't even be here, and anyway, the inn will come to you and me, one day, so it's an investment. I can use the money as I see fit, can't I, Mr Snell?"

"Yes, my dear, of course, you can, but your husband is right. Are you sure you want to use it for this purpose?"

"Oh, most definitely. Ned, I think we should see the bank manager, straight away." She turned her attention back to the solicitor. "How will I receive the money? I don't want to risk carrying so much money to the bank, in case we get robbed."

"No need to worry, ma'am. I'll give you a letter confirming your inheritance, and you can take that to the bank. You can leave us to sort it out from there."

"I can't believe this; it's like a dream come true. I'm over the moon, that I can save the inn, and take away all the worry for Uncle Mal and Aunty Kezzie." Then she looked thoughtful. "Would you please tell Lord Fellwood, I'm so sorry I have no news of his son; I truly wish I did, but I've never seen or heard from him since I was a child. The only thing I did hear, and it may not be true, is that he sailed to France."

"Thank you, Mrs Carter, we were already aware of that, but thank you for telling me. Now, allow me to pour you both another cup of tea, and maybe you can eat the cake, that you're both still clutching on your lap. In the meantime, I'll prepare a letter for you to take to the bank."

CHAPTER 45

A short while later, Ned and Betsey left the solicitor's office, and she beamed at him.

"Hey, Ned Carter, it's lucky you married me before we knew of my inheritance, or I might have wondered if you were after my money."

"Aw, Betsey, don't joke about it. I feel guilty now, that I married you at all; you could have married someone much grander than me."

She pulled him to her. "Don't you ever think that Ned; there's no other man on this earth, that I would rather be married to."

"Oh, Betsey, I hope you mean that."

"I do, so no more talk of it. Now, let's go and enjoy ourselves in the bank. I can't wait to see the manager's face."

At the bank, they asked to see the manager, and a clerk went to find out if he was free. However, Mr Barlow suspected Ned had come to beg for more time to clear the debt, and the clerk advised them, that, unfortunately, the manager couldn't spare the time to see them that day. Ned was not surprised, but Betsey was having none of it. Smiling sweetly at the young man, she said they would wait, and could he please tell Mr Barlow, they had come to settle the debts of The Red Lion Inn.

It was not many minutes before the manager appeared at the doorway and greeted the young couple effusively. "Hello, Mr Carter and Mrs Carter, may I offer my congratulations on your recent marriage, and how delightful it is, to see you both, again. My clerk tells me you have come to settle the outstanding debt, for The Red Lion Inn; is that correct?"

"It is sir, yes. My wife has a letter here from Snell and Son, Solicitors, advising you of her recent inheritance from the Fellwood family. I understand the Snell's also bank here, and that it will be a simple matter, to transfer the money, from one account to the other?"

The bank manager held out his hand for the letter and surveyed its contents in surprise.

"My word, this is fantastic news. I must congratulate you on your good fortune, Mrs Carter. Please, won't you come into my office, where we can discuss this further?"

Betsey was sorely tempted to comment, on how strange it was, that the bank manager was no longer so busy, but her husband frowned at her, aware of her wicked sense of humour. Having ensured they were comfortably seated; Mr Barlow lifted a ledger down from a shelf and studied the account of Malachi Carter. It transpired that the total of The Red Lion's debts would come to nearly seventy-five pounds. Betsey was delighted to learn there would be thirty pounds left over, for she knew exactly what she wanted to do with it.

"Mrs Carter, I understand from this letter, that the money has been left specifically to you, and that it must not pass to your husband. Therefore, I urge you to think carefully, about whether it is wise, to use it to pay off the inn's debts. After all, the inn is not even owned by you, or your husband."

"Thank you, Mr Barlow, but I'm quite sure. If it were not for Mal and Kezia Carter, I would not be here to receive the money at all, for they saved my life as a child, and now it's my turn to help them. I'm delighted to be able to do just that. As far as the inn is concerned, one day it will pass to my husband, and on down through our family, should we be blessed with children. If not, it would be inherited by his brother, Silas, and his children, so whatever happens, it will stay in the Carter family. What I would like, though, is a letter from you to Mr Carter, telling him that his debt is cleared. I would like to take the letter with me today, please. Is that possible?"

"Yes, of course, ma'am, though you will have to allow me a little time to write it. Now, concerning the remainder of the money; may I suggest we open an account in your name, as is requested in the solicitor's letter? Indeed, it is the one stipulation that the money must be kept in your name, though you are then free to do with it, as you will."

"Yes, thank you, please do that. I think I know why Mr Fellwood added that instruction, for he knew that my father passed barely any of his earnings on to my mother. He drank it away, as fast as he earned it, and sometimes before he earned it. Even after my mother died, he did not use much of it, to care for me, and my brother. I think Mr Fellwood wanted to make sure I did not need to depend on anyone."

"That sounds sensible. I will open an account for you and transfer your inheritance to it, minus the amount used to repay the loan to the inn. Does that sound satisfactory?"

"Yes, sir, that's exactly what I want you to do, thank you."

"May I ask, do you have any plans for the remainder of the money?"

"I do, sir, though I need to discuss those plans with my husband, and in-laws. I would like to repair the building of our other food outlet, known locally as Betsey's Kitchen. We've been unable to afford to do so since the building was hit by lightning some months ago, and my husband was badly injured. Before that, the new venture was doing remarkably well, and I'm sure it would do so, again. It was making a steady profit before all our troubles, for there are a lot of workers in Hartford at the moment. In addition to the many lime-burners, and farm labourers, there are a lot of men working on the Hartford canal, and I believe that project still has a couple of years before it will be finished."

"That sounds like a splendid idea. Now, if you, and your husband, could come back in an hour or so, I will write the letter to Mr Malachi Carter, advising him that his loan has been cleared." The manager grinned at her, his blue eyes twinkling. "Mr Carter is, indeed, a fortunate man, and I am so pleased for him. I don't mind telling you, I would love to see his face when he reads the letter. It is extraordinarily kind of you, ma'am, and I'm sure he will be both relieved, and delighted."

When they finally stepped back into the High Street, Betsey could not stop smiling at Ned. "I think you need to pinch me, Ned, for I keep thinking, I'm dreaming. That's why I wanted a letter to show your parents because I'm sure they won't believe us. What would you like to do now, to kill time?"

"Well, I have a little money on me, which I've been keeping for an emergency, but how about we throw caution to the wind, and go to The Three Tuns, for a celebratory pint of ale?"

With the letter safely in Betsey's pocket, the young couple rode their horses back to Hartford in high spirits. They called at the smithy, and after thanking, Henry Rudd for the use of his horse, Betsey once more climbed up behind her husband, for the short ride to the inn.

They were surprised to find the front door of the inn closed. Worried, there had been some kind of accident, they hastened to the back door, and found Mal and Kezia, sitting in the kitchen, enjoying a cup of tea.

"Is everything all right, Dad? Why is the front door shut? Shouldn't the inn be open?" Ned eyed his father, anxiously.

"Aye, lad, it should, but we've decided to close so that we can get everything ready for the auction. It's difficult to keep trading when everything has to go. We don't want to get in lots of food, and have to throw it away; Lord knows we can't afford to do that."

"Well, you never know what might turn up, Dad. Maybe we'll get a windfall, and be able to stay here, after all."

"Hmm, little chance of that, I'm afraid, but I'm glad you can make light of it. Anyway, what did the solicitor want with you?"

Betsey embraced her uncle. "Uncle Mal, I have the most wonderful news. We don't have to leave the inn. I've cleared your debts. Look, read this letter from the bank. You don't owe them a penny."

Mal stared at her in disbelief. "Betsey, what are you on about? You don't have the sort of money needed to clear my debts, and even if you did, I wouldn't let you."

Betsey handed him the letter. "Just see for yourself, Uncle Mal."

He took the letter from her and recognised the handwriting of Mr Barlow. Slowly, he read the letter, and, handed it to Kezia.

"Where on earth, did you get money like that, Betsey? I can't believe it."

Kezia joined in. "Oh, Betsey, I don't know where you got the money from, but this is such amazing news. Thank you, so much. We'll pay back every penny, won't we Mal? If we can just get back on our feet, we'll pay you all of it, eventually."

"There's no need, Aunty Kezzie, I don't want it. This has been my home for most of my life, and now I've married Ned, it will remain so. There's more good news, too, for I have enough money left over to repair Betsey's Kitchen, and get it going again. When we can find the right people, I think we need to take on three more servants to replace Silas and Josie. Once we're making a profit again, they'll pay for themselves."

Mal and Kezia could hardly believe the tale, the young couple had to tell them, and Mal kept looking at the letter, to reassure himself it was true, and not a dream. Then, of course, came the questions, that Betsey had been dreading.

Ned voiced his thoughts first. "I have to ask, Betsey, why did Thomas Fellwood leave you a fortune?"

Reluctantly, after swearing them to secrecy, Betsey revealed her long-held secret, of how she had helped Thomas Fellwood and Gypsy Jane, hide the truth about the unfortunate accident, that led to Jasper Morris's death.

"But surely if it was an accident, they had nothing to fear?"

"Jane was worried, that if the body was found near the gypsy camp, her people would get the blame, as they inevitably do. Also, it was common knowledge, that Thomas was more than fond of Jane, so it wouldn't have taken long, for folk to put two and two together, and wonder, if he had a hand in the accident. He'd been making excuses to visit the gypsy camp for weeks, and it hadn't gone unnoticed. I saw it all, though, and it was an accident. Jasper fell over backwards, and at first, we thought he was winded. Thomas took the time to get his breath back, for Jasper had been giving him a hard time, but then, when he didn't get up, we realised there was something wrong. He had hit his head on a sharp stone, and there was a lot of blood. I think he was dead, as soon as he hit the ground."

Ned stared at her in wonder. "How old were you, when this happened?"

"I was nearly seven. I remember my feet were frozen, because my shoes leaked, and Thomas had stopped to give me a ride to the gypsy camp on his horse. The horse was so warm beneath me, and Thomas wrapped his cloak around both of us; he was so kind. That was how I came to be there because I was on my way to see the gypsies, to beg for some food. Me, and Norman, were so cold and hungry."

"I don't know how you found the strength to push a grown man off his horse. There was nothing to you in those days. Did someone help you?"

"No, Thomas balanced the body, so that with a slight push, it would fall off. I was more worried, about meeting someone on the way, but luckily, it was such a cold day, no one was around."

"So, do you know what happened to Thomas Fellwood? I remember there was a massive hue and cry when he went missing, and to this day, he's never been found. I've always felt sorry for Lord Fellwood, for he lost his wife, and then, Thomas. Despite all his wealth, that's a lot of grief to deal with."

"No, I don't know where he is now, though I do know he paid some smugglers to take him and Jane to France, where they hoped to live a happy life, together. I hope they did."

"I can't believe you've kept this a secret for so many years, Betsey. What a strong little girl you were, mentally, and physically, and still are, come to that. Do you have any more secrets, I should know about?"

Betsey nodded. "Well, yes, just one, so I might as well get that off my chest, too. I'll be right back."

She returned with the little tin that contained her treasured possessions. She sat at the kitchen table, and, removing the lid, reached inside. First, she removed the red ribbon, and Kezia gasped.

"My goodness, Betsey, is that the ribbon, I bought you so many years ago?"

"Yes, I've always treasured it, for it was the one lovely thing in my sad life. It means so much to me."

She reached into the tin again. "Well, that, and these curls." She had tears in her eyes. "These were Norman's curls, and I'll be forever grateful to you, Aunty Kezzie for thinking of cutting them off for me. Now, this is my other secret, and I've not known what to do about it. This is Thomas Fellwood's watch. It belonged to his grandfather, and I believe it's made of gold. Gypsy Jane told me he had lost it in the fight with Jasper Morris, and I went back to search for it. I found it in the middle of a thick bush, and

I've kept it for him, ever since. I kept wondering if I could sell it, to save the inn, but I was worried folk would think I'd stolen it, for how could I explain, how I came by it? Still, I don't need to sell it now, and you never know, perhaps I'll be able to give it back to him one day. I hope so. I'd love to thank him for his generosity."

"I hope you'll be able to do that, Betsey. Now, I guess we'd better start unpacking, and you and Ned can move back into the inn. I know you don't like that cramped little cottage, which holds so many unhappy memories for you, my dear. I think maybe Kezia and I will move to the cottage, as planned, and let you both return to the inn. It's only right, for it's as good as yours now, and it would have been one day, anyway."

"No, thank you for the offer, but no, Uncle Mal. Your place is here, though Ned and I will continue the Carter tradition when the time comes. No, if you don't mind, Ned, I think I'd like us to live in the cottage. I think it's time those walls witnessed some happiness."

Ned nodded. "Yes, of course, that's fine with me. It'll be nice to have our own little place and a bit of time to ourselves. So, speaking of that, I think we'll go there now, and have an early night." He winked at Betsey, and his parents laughed. "We have a lot of work to do, tomorrow."

"That sounds like an excellent idea, Ned, but I just have something to do, before I join you. I'll only be half an hour or so."

Taking the snowdrops, she had gathered for her wedding, from the jar on the windowsill, she carefully wrapped her precious red ribbon around them, and set off for the graveyard. The flowers were still fresh, for she had picked them in tight buds. Kneeling at the side of the grave, she carefully placed the posy in a jar of water. With tears running down her cheeks, she told her mother, and her brother, Norman, what had happened, and said they must worry about her no more, for she had found happiness at last.

MARCIA CLAYTON

AUTHOR'S NOTE

I hope you enjoyed reading this book as much as I enjoyed writing it. If so, I would really appreciate it if you could leave a short review on Amazon or Goodreads.

An honest review is the highest compliment you can pay to any author and it would mean so much to me.

If you would like to find out more about me and my books, and keep up to date with new releases, please visit https://marciaclayton.co.uk/ and join my mailing list.

Thank you.

Marcia

MARCIA CLAYTON

The Mazzard Tree

Book One in The Hartford Manor Series

Annie Carter is a farm labourer's daughter, and life is a continual struggle for survival. When her father dies of consumption, her mother, Sabina, is left with seven hungry mouths to feed and another child on the way. To save them from the workhouse or starvation, Annie steals vegetables from the Manor House garden, risking jail or transportation. Unknown to her, she is watched by Robert, the wealthy heir to the Hartford Estate, but far from turning her in, he befriends her.

Despite their different social backgrounds, Annie and Robert develop feelings they know can have no future. Harry Rudd, the village blacksmith, has long admired Annie, and when he proposes, her mother urges her to accept. She reminds Annie that as a kitchen maid, she will never be allowed to marry Robert. Harry is a good man, and Annie is fond of him. Her head knows what she should do, but will her heart listen?

Set against the harsh background of the rough, class-divided society of Victorian England, this heart-warming and captivating novel portrays a young woman who uses her determination and willpower to defy the circumstances of her birth in her search for happiness.

The Angel Maker

Book Two in The Hartford Manor Series

When carpenter, Fred Carter, finds a young woman in dire straits by the roadside, he takes her to the local inn where she gives birth to a daughter. Charlotte Mackie is an unmarried mother and has run away from home where she would have no sympathy from her strict parents. A few days later, Fred takes Charlotte to her aunt's house and does not expect to see her again.

When their paths unexpectedly cross, Fred finds Charlotte is distraught as her aunt has arranged an adoption behind her back. Charlotte is desperate to find her baby and Fred promises to help.

However, they are unprepared for the sinister discoveries that lay before them. Set alongside the absorbing detail of country life and budding village romances, dark forces are at work which ultimately test the bravery and resourcefulness of the whole community.

The Angel Maker is the sequel to The Mazzard Tree, and the second novel in a compelling series which follows the lives and loves of the villagers of Hartford. A rare treat for lovers of historical fiction.

MARCIA CLAYTON

The Rabbit's Foot

Book Three in The Hartford Manor Series

Mr Edward Snell was more than a little curious when Robert Fellwood, the heir to Hartford Manor, and his elderly aunt, the Lady Margery, begged an audience on a Saturday morning. However, being such valued clients, the solicitor was happy to oblige. As his clerk showed the visitors in, he was intrigued to see them followed by an old man who, though respectably dressed, had something of a vagrant about him. The crisp suit in which he was attired could not disguise his weather-beaten face or his missing teeth.

Robert introduced his Uncle Sam and explained he had come to claim his inheritance. The solicitor was old enough to remember the extensive search for Thomas Fellwood when his father, Ephraim, died in 1840. However, that was some forty-five years ago and the young man had never been found. Yet, here was Sam, who claimed to be Thomas Fellwood's son and, even more surprising, was the fact that the Fellwood family appeared to have accepted him as such.

The Rabbit's Foot is an intriguing and compelling novel with many unexpected twists and turns. Set in the small village of Hartford, it tells the tale of how an old man, who has spent his life with barely a penny to his name, suddenly finds himself rich beyond his wildest dreams. However, there is only one thing that Sam Fellwood truly wants and that is to be reunited with his son, Marrok, whom he abandoned at the age of five. Will Sam find the happiness that has eluded him for so many lonely years?